ONLY THE LOVELY

THE SINFUL STATE SERIES
BOOK 3

ISABEL JOLIE

ISABEL JOLIE

For those who trade clicks for credibility, and choose truth over tribe.

"It's a pity nobody believes in simple lust anymore."

—Ava Gardner

"Of the seven deadly sins, lust is definitely the pick of the litter."

—Tom Robbins

PLAYLIST

"Earned It" - The Weeknd
"Golden" - Jill Scott
"Diamonds" - Rihanna
"Adorn" - Miguel
"Secret" - The Pierces
"Secrets" - OneRepublic
"Stay" - Rihanna

CHAPTER ONE

ADRIEN

The last thing I expected on a random Tuesday was Alicia Morgan demanding an emergency meeting. I despise being summoned, but when the Scandal Queen clears her schedule, someone's world is about to implode.

The storm system hovering over the city lends a dark haze to the sky, rain pelting the glass. Fitting for a morning hampered by jet lag and a meeting my sister, Margot, insisted I take.

"I vote we order in," Tommy says, ankle crossed over his knee, arm draped across the Chesterfield sofa like he hasn't a care in the world. He wouldn't—Alicia didn't demand *his* presence.

I rub my eyes, debating whether to have more caffeine or an intravenous hydration drip. It's Manhattan—there must be one nearby. Maybe if I hadn't had that third scotch on the plane...

"News says subways are flooding."

"Since when have you taken the subway?"

"Fair. Still, I can't walk into court with soaked trousers."

I press the desk phone. "Can you bring in menus? We'll order lunch."

"Yes, sir. Right away."

Tommy leans back. "So Margot's dictating your schedule. Aside from being a thorn in your side, how's she doing?"

"She's well. Busy."

I hesitate. "She asked about you," I add, though I shouldn't.

There's a rap at the walnut door. "Come in."

A young woman, an administrative temp, enters, beige skirt suit, nervous hands shaking menus.

"You can hand those to the judge," I say.

Tommy barely glances as he takes them.

"Sir, your twelve o'clock is here. Ms. Alicia Morgan. Should I ask if she'd like to join you for lunch?"

"No. We'll be done before the food arrives."

The click of heels announces her before the door opens. To hell with the weather—she's immaculate in ivory Givenchy and Prada heels, hair a dark wave, eyes a sharp blue that take in everything at once.

"Alicia Morgan," I say. She's the founder and CEO of Morgan & Company, a crisis communications firm. From what I've heard, she's the one everyone from celebrities to presidents go to when things go tits up.

"Judge Brennan," she greets Tommy, before adding with smooth authority, "I don't mean to be rude, but I'm short on time. This conversation needs to be private."

"I'm going," he says, and slips out.

I round my desk. Alicia commands the room, something

I'll allow, as from what I've heard, you want her on your side. "Can I get you—"

"No, thank you." The words cut, but the smile that follows is practiced and bright. It softens the edge just enough to remind me she's not all steel.

She opens a pale leather briefcase and passes me a folder. "I need you to confirm whether these photographs were taken inside your club."

The Sanctuary. My chest tightens. Discretion is its foundation—no phones, no cameras. If this trust is breached, everything I've built crumbles.

I flip through black-and-white prints. A man on a sofa. A woman straddling a blurred figure. Too intimate, too familiar. I study the headboard, the chains. Suite 7A.

I close the folder and set it on the table between us. "Where did your client get these?"

"He's being blackmailed."

"Who knows?"

"Right now? Just him. Let's keep it that way."

When she reaches for the folder, my hand comes down over it, stopping her.

"You must know I intend to find the source," I say.

"Unless you're the extortionist."

I flinch. "I don't need money, Ms. Morgan. My reputation —and my business—are inviolable."

"Your sister said you'd never risk this club's reputation. That's the only reason I'm here."

Of course Margot vouched for me. "What did you tell her?"

"That if this isn't handled, your business goes under. Simple as that."

No wonder Margot insisted.

"I need everything you have." *My employees. Everyone is a suspect.*

"My client believes he's not the only victim," she says, sliding the folder out from under my hand and drawing it back toward her. "We're meeting with an investigative team Friday. I want you there."

"That's four days."

"There's no demand yet. This was a preview."

Her client must be political. A divorce. Exposure. Influence at stake.

"I'll work with your team—on one condition. I take the lead on matters concerning the club."

Her eyes narrow. "This folder is one piece of a much bigger case."

"And I'll root out the leak. If the leak isn't the extortionist, the leak will lead you to the source. One team. My lead."

A pause. "I can live with that." She stands. "If I can move the meeting up, I will. Assume your schedule is flexible." The tone is clipped, but when her gaze meets mine, there's a flicker of something else—resolve that feels personal. She's fighting for her client, yes, but also for principle.

"Send me everything—metadata, angles, locations."

"These files aren't moving. You want the digital assets, you come to me. Tomorrow. Eight a.m."

When the door shuts, I stay where I am, staring out at the storm-darkened skyline. Three years I've poured into The Sanctuary—every detail perfected, every indulgence crafted, every weakness anticipated. It was meant to be untouchable, a refuge of discretion. Now someone intends to twist it into leverage, into a weapon. They picked the wrong business to undermine—and definitely the wrong man to cross.

I stand and walk to the windows, forehead nearly

touching the cool glass. To some, the club offered exclusivity and connections. To others, the place offered velvet and shadows, elusive aromas, and silk against skin in darkened corners. I'd always understood what I was building: not just exclusivity, but permission. Permission to want—and act within the protective walls—without consequence.

And someone corrupted it. Turned sanctuary into weapon.

CHAPTER TWO

ADRIEN

Friday morning, Senator Crawford passes through security in the nondescript midtown Manhattan office tower minutes after I do. At the elevator bank, I watch him approach. No one in the lobby gives him a second look. For a man in the middle of a high-profile divorce, I'd have expected greater name recognition. Apparently, he's less familiar to the public than a C-list celebrity.

His gaze flickers with recognition. I scan the suits in the lobby again to confirm no one's paying attention, then extend a hand. "Good to see you," I say, deliberately omitting his title. No reason to draw ears.

There are dozens of businesses in this office tower. Visiting Morgan Publicity doesn't, in itself, mean anything. Still, I know how quickly rumors spread in Manhattan, and I prefer not to be the spark.

"Adrien," he says, shaking my hand with practiced

warmth, holding my eye just long enough to project sincerity.

I wonder—do they all take the same course in charm at whatever academy breeds senators?

The elevator dings. We ride in silence with three others to the sixty-first floor.

David Crawford's problems are legend: an ugly divorce and a chief of staff recently convicted of selling secrets to the highest bidder. Conveniently, the man declared the senator had no knowledge, and the authorities agreed. Still, guilt by association stains. Public perception is rarely merciful.

The photos make sense now—desire as liability. In his world, lust isn't pleasure. It's ammunition.

No wonder he doesn't want illicit photographs surfacing. What I don't yet know is whether the blackmailers want money—or something more strategic.

I've already checked: seven Sanctuary security employees were on duty when the videos were filmed. All seven were hired before my acquisition. Expansion took me abroad, and somewhere in my absence, someone let entrepreneurial instincts run feral. Whoever it is has now put everything at risk.

The elevator empties floor by floor until only the two of us remain.

"You don't travel with security?" I ask.

"Secret Service doesn't cover senators unless there's an active threat."

Meaning: to disclose the threat, he'd have to admit he's being blackmailed. He'd rather not.

A white oak door opens beside the reception desk. A sharp-eyed woman with glasses glances up as Alicia Morgan crosses the lobby to meet us.

"You're right on time," Alicia says. "The others are already in the conference room."

Today she's taupe from head to toe, her dark hair in an elegant chignon, gold catching light at her throat and wrists. Polished, poised—a walking seminar in optics.

"David, before we go in," she says, crisp and measured, "you are the client. If you don't want to answer something, look to me. If you need a sidebar, take it. The KOAN team works for us."

"As a reminder," I say, "they also work for me. I'm paying the bills." David frowns, questions flickering across his face. "This can do as much damage to my business as yours."

"I'm not sure I agree with you there," he replies, southern charm fraying around the edges.

"If you want these investigators inside my club, this is the arrangement. My covering the bills also spares you the headache of explaining line items in your finances."

"No one tracks my personal finances," he bites out.

"Even so," I say evenly, "you're my client. Your privacy has been breached. When we meet this team, I intend to take charge."

Alicia's scowl is quick and sharp.

"Of the investigation into the club," I add. "PR, narrative, countermeasures—that's your arena. But how the breach happened? That's mine."

David inclines his head, satisfied. I look to Alicia. "I've never heard of KOAN. If I don't believe they're capable, I'll bring in someone who is."

"They put my former chief of staff behind bars," David says. "They're capable."

Interesting. The senator approves of the people who gutted his staff.

"You didn't bring anyone from your team?" Alicia asks, leading us down a carpeted hall.

"No. I don't know who I can trust." Margot knows something occurred, because Alicia called her, but she doesn't know specifics. Tommy knows I'm dealing with a leak, because he's Tommy. Again, he doesn't know specifics. Beyond that, silence. A senator's career is at stake, but so is the future of what I've built.

We stop at a pair of white-stained wooden doors. Alicia pauses, hand on the handle. "Are we good?"

Crawford and I nod. She pulls the door open.

David enters first, then Alicia. I follow—and the room rises for the senator. Greetings, handshakes, the shuffle of chairs.

A man in a dark suit with sharp eyes and a trimmed beard introduces himself as Hudson Stone, KOAN's managing director. Beside him stands a tall man with a shaved head. But it's the woman next to them who erases the air from the room.

Blonde hair, sleek and straight, parted and tucked behind one ear. Eyes the blue of the Mediterranean—

The scent hits me first. Jasmine. Not perfume—something lighter, more intimate. Shampoo, maybe, or body oil. The same fragrance that clung to the yacht's sheets; the same fragrance that I searched for in every hotel lobby and high-end boutique for months after. In Monaco casinos. Paris perfumeries. London art galleries. Always chasing a ghost.

Sophie.

Every concern about The Sanctuary vanishes under the weight of memory: Monaco, moonlight, the weekend I thought I stumbled on something authentic in a life built on carefully constructed facades.

The intimacy Crawford hides in shame, I remember as something else entirely—desire that felt unmanufactured, uncorrupted. The difference between appetite and connection.

Three years searching. Six months of investigators scouring Europe for an art consultant who didn't exist. The search turned up nothing. No passport. No employment history. No digital footprint. Vapor.

And yet here she is. In a conference room in Manhattan. Alive. Real.

Her eyes widen—yes, she recognizes me. And I'm unexpected.

She steps forward with professional composure, extending her hand. "Brie Anderson, KOAN Security."

The voice—controlled, cultured, achingly familiar—strikes like a blow. I take her hand, electricity sparking through contact.

For an instant, we're back on that yacht, her laugh carrying over the water, my certainty that I'd found something true in a life built on illusion. Her fingers tighten just slightly before she pulls away, mask intact. But I saw it—the widening of her eyes, the careful step back. She remembers.

"Mr. d'Avricourt," she says, and the sound of my formal name in her voice nearly undoes me.

Heat crawls up my neck. Unprofessional. Unwelcome.

I force my breathing to steady, force my hands to remain still when what they want is to reach for her—to confirm she's real, solid, here. The desire that surges through me feels intrusive, almost violent in its intensity.

I've spent three years learning to separate want from need, performance from authenticity. Built an international firm on understanding the mechanics of desire. And in three seconds, she's reduced me to raw appetite.

I clear my throat. "Ms. Anderson."

But she's not Brie Anderson. She's Sophie Dubois—the woman who disappeared without a trace, leaving me to wonder whether that perfect weekend had been real at all, or only another illusion—beautiful, fleeting, and gone.

CHAPTER THREE

BRIE

Shock hits me with clinical clarity: throat tight, fingers trembling, vision narrowing. Training catalogs the symptoms, but nothing prepared me for this. I never thought I'd see him again, and now time itself feels fractured—slowed—while I stand outside myself, the lone observer.

I study him the way one studies brushstrokes in a painting only ever seen in textbooks. Subtle silver threads his dark hair, his beard trims the angles of a jaw I once knew bare, his suit immaculate. He looks nothing like the carefree man in sun-bleached linen with wind in his hair and salt on his skin. And yet—it's him. Those eyes. Once rimmed in gold, catching every glint of light. Today they're darker, green edged with suspicion, a man accustomed to wariness.

But beneath the wariness, I see heat. No, I feel it, pooling low in my belly, unwelcome and undeniable. I've spent my career learning to compartmentalize emotions, to treat my body as a tool. But some memories are too powerful to lock behind walls without cost. His jagged moans. The scrape of his five o'clock shadow against my inner thigh. The way he'd said my name in his sleep.

"Brie?" My colleague's slight touch on my arm snaps me out of the initial shock of running across Adrien d'Avricourt.

I break free from Adrien's locked stare and lean toward my colleague, seeking comfort in his steady presence while I gather myself.

"You okay?"

I inhale deeply, clearing the fog and quelling the trembles, and force the smile I've practiced in mirrors. "Yes, just…had a moment."

As the others take their seats, I can excuse myself now—retreat, regroup—or I can sit and learn why Adrien d'Avricourt is in the United States, or more importantly, why he's in this meeting.

Hudson provided a list of attendees and Adrien d'Avricourt was most definitely not on it.

But the man hasn't confronted me in front of the others, so stay. Learn.

Adrien has chosen the seat across from me. Alicia Morgan, the woman who contacted us on behalf of the senator, has taken her rightful place at the head of the conference room table, with the senator on her right and Hudson on her left. Noah, my colleague, is between me and Hudson, and there's a noticeable empty chair between the senator and Adrien on the other side of the conference room table.

Flashes of the yacht spark unbidden. His hands in my hair. The way I slipped out at dawn, expecting to never see him again. It's been years since I unwittingly searched for him in crowds. And here he sits across a conference table like Monaco never happened.

In the periphery of my conscience I hear them moving on from introductions and discussing the project overview. Yes, the senator has been blackmailed. Yes, there's video and photographs. We haven't been able to trace the package delivery.

None of this is news to Adrien, either. He's been briefed as well. But why is he here? Did I miss that relevant piece of information?

"He received an additional threat via messenger yesterday," Alicia says, handing us each our own copy of the message. She passes a folder to Hudson Stone, my boss. "The original is inside the envelope, should you wish to have it evaluated for fingerprints, but I expect we're dealing with professionals and don't believe you'll find anything."

"Any more photographs?" Adrien asks after briefly reading the message.

I study the note.

Senator Crawford—

The Perimeter Defense Oversight Amendment will be reviewed Monday, January 19. Vote against it. If you vote for this amendment, we release the attached file to the Washington Post.

In addition, wire $250,000 as our consulting fee. Instructions to follow.

Thank you for your attention to this matter.

"What was attached?" Adrien asks, and I can't help but wonder why he's taking charge. Is it his personality or is he vested?

"A listing of Senator Crawford's expenses, including membership dues, at The Sanctuary over the past eighteen months, plus additional photographs," Alicia answers.

The senator straightens, voice tightening with defiance. "My wife and I had an open marriage. Every encounter was consensual, all well above legal age. If this is the best they have, I could tell them to publish it." He exhales. "But with an election looming, I'd rather avoid spectacle. And if they're targeting me, they're targeting others. This isn't only my problem."

Adrien's glance slices toward me before he addresses the room. "I've reviewed the other photographs and video. All were taken at The Sanctuary. Our policies forbid recording of any kind. Only an employee could have circumvented them. Privacy is paramount. To protect it, I'll cover investigation expenses. You'll have access to the New York property as needed, but for discretion, visits must occur when the club is closed—or under a cover story."

His gaze lingers on me as he says it, deliberate, pointed.

"How many employees are based in New York?" Hudson asks, but what I want to know is what does Adrien d'Avricourt have to do with The Sanctuary? It's a gentleman's club and rumors have always swirled around the activities that go on in private chambers.

"At any given time we have between seventy to eighty employees on payroll. Keep in mind we have an onsite restaurant, three bars, a cleaning crew, and a security team."

He owns the club. Of course he does. The man who showed me real kindness now runs the kind of place where powerful men pay for discretion.

If I recall correctly, the club maintains locations around the world, including Shanghai, London, Paris, and San Francisco. But fashion and fragrance are the domains of the d'Avricourts. I suppose an illicit playground fits the brand image. What's the business tag line I've seen in the occasional ad? Only the Lovely.

When did he acquire it? After we met?

He sounds calm. But I know what lies beneath calm. His clipped answers aren't arrogance—they're distress, reined in.

"Can you get me an employee list? Names, address, and social media accounts," Hudson asks.

"Yes, I will. I hate to think it's an employee, but I've racked my brain and don't see how it could be anyone else."

"You mentioned security? Did you outsource any part of it? Technical aspects? Servers?"

"I bought the club three years ago."

Ah, that's why I was unaware of Adrien's connection to The Sanctuary. It's been nearly three and a half years since the weekend with Adrien.

"The system was already set up." He leans into his right arm, resting on the armrest of the chair, thoughtful. "Let's hope this leak doesn't date that far back." He straightens and adds, "We do maintain video surveillance on site. It's active, nothing is recorded. Or at least, nothing is supposed to be." He casts an apologetic glance at the senator. "The surveillance is aimed at ensuring our guests' safety. Ensuring that nothing gets out of hand, that no one brings someone in of questionable age." Addressing the room, he continues, "We are a true gentleman's club. Consent is required at all times and is only accepted from those legally able to provide consent. I assume you'd like to review our system. We're closed on Monday and Tuesday. There's no staff on site on Monday, so that would be the best day for you to visit. On Tuesday, staff come and go in preparation for the week. In-office staff works Tuesday to Saturday."

"Is your video surveillance online?" Hudson asks. "Could it be hacked?"

"No. It's closed circuit." His lips press together, and a casual observer might read him as angry, but I sense he's distraught. "If you discover it's someone outside of my business, I'll be greatly relieved, but I don't think that's the case." He fingers his copy of the threat that's lying on the table. "And that $250,000. That's paying someone, right? Isn't that how this kind of extortion works?"

"It is," Hudson confirms. "That's why we'll be looking into your employees' finances."

"I do pay them well," he says. "The salary is commensurate with the high expectations we place, with the hope of diminishing the likelihood of anyone accepting a bribe." With an exhale, he looks to the senator, the victim at the table. "Alicia allowed me to examine the materials in her office. There was no sound. Out of curiosity…"

"There's no audio in what I received."

"Interesting," Adrien comments.

"Why?" Alicia prompts.

"Because. I would think the most valuable source of information, this day and age, derived in our club would be audio. First and foremost, especially in our restaurant and in the bars, it's a social club. Deals are brokered. This effort." His finger flicks at the copied threat. "It's amateurish."

"You say that without knowing anything about the Perimeter Defense Oversight Amendment," Senator Crawford says. "Do we have a plan?" He checks his watch. "My chief of staff is waiting outside for me and he'll be full of questions."

"You haven't brought your staff up to date?" Alicia asks.

"No, not yet. I don't know how much I want to involve them," the senator answers.

"Do you trust Marcus?" Alicia asks, referring to Marcus Webb, his newly appointed chief of staff, brought in after the previous one was indicted on charges of treason.

He exhales. "I do. And as I told you Alicia, I plan to read him in, but I haven't had the right moment."

"It will be helpful to have an additional point of contact," she says with enough force that it's clear this isn't the first time the topic has arisen between them.

The senator pushes up from the table. "This weekend. I'll read him in."

As he's backing away, Alicia adds, "And let me know your thoughts on our proposal."

He grimaces, gives her a quick nod, and says to the room, "Thank you. Thank you for your time in addressing this issue. You're doing important work. This is bigger than me."

With that, he exits the room.

"Proposal?" Hudson asks Alicia, voicing the question we all have.

"Simple preparation should these materials wind up published."

"Right," Hudson says.

It's decided that our team will visit The Sanctuary on Monday. We wrap up by discussing the logistics regarding our meeting next week. Adrien asks next to no questions about KOAN, which makes me suspect he was briefed beforehand.

A knock on the door sounds, and the receptionist from earlier peeks in, saying to Alicia, "Your ten o'clock's here. She's in your office waiting."

"Thank you," Alicia says, then to us, "Are we done here?"

"I believe so," Hudson answers. "Until Monday. Once we get the personnel files, we'll dig in."

"Ms. Anderson," Adrien says, addressing me, "Why don't you accompany me back to my office? I'll get you everything you need."

"An electronic file—" Hudson begins.

"Oh, I wouldn't email employee records." Adrien's smile is knife-thin. "Besides, I haven't seen Ms. Anderson in years. Isn't that right?"

Noah hears it too—the jab. I keep my expression neutral. "It has been a while," I say evenly. "I'll go, Hudson. I'll deliver everything to Quinn."

We exit as a group together, filling the space with small talk about weather, weekend plans, anything to mask the silence pressing between us. No mention of the case, no names. We know how to play the game.

At the lobby doors, Hudson gives me a pointed look. "Brie, touch base later."

"Yes, sir." Old habits, drilled into me by my father, snap out in the automatic reply.

Outside, a black Mercedes idles. The driver holds the door open.

"Shall we?" Adrien asks.

Nausea coils low, but I climb in. The sensation low in my belly isn't just dread. And that's a problem. There's no outrunning what I left behind in Monaco. And this time, I'm not the same woman who slipped away before dawn.

CHAPTER
FOUR

ADRIEN

I wait until the divider clicks up, enclosing us in silence, before speaking. Alicia said KOAN employs former Special Forces and intelligence officers. My guess was correct—Sophie, or rather Brie Anderson, is former intelligence. That's why I didn't make a scene in the meeting. And why, after spending tens of thousands searching for her, I'll have my answers in private.

She sits composed, hands folded in her lap. No rings, nails cut short and square—the same as Monaco, when she told me it was for the piano. She played beautifully, and at least that detail wasn't a lie. Her blue eyes flicker, uncertain, and for the first time I see not the woman who vanished, but the operative trained to disappear.

I force myself to look away, but the damage is done. I've cataloged her—a habit from years of studying what people want versus what they'll admit. The way her pulse jumps at her throat. The slight catch in her breathing when I moved closer to close the divider. The tension in her thighs beneath that pristine skirt, muscles coiled as if prepared for fight or flight.

Or something else entirely.

She wants me too. The awareness sears, unwelcome heat in professional cold. I've spent years learning to read desire—it's currency in my world, the foundation of everything people crave. But this isn't performance. This is the same pull I felt in Monaco, that visceral recognition of mutual hunger. Authentic. Rare. Elusive.

"I owe you an explanation."

"We are in agreement."

She lowers her gaze and speaks quietly. "When I met you, I worked for the CIA."

As I suspected. "Was I your target?"

"No." Her eyes spear mine, steady and unflinching. "I can't share details. But when we met, I was compromised. Someone was onto me. You were a man at a bar, nothing more. By engaging with you, I diverted their attention."

"Ah. So I was cover. The Bond woman to your story? A convenient weekend at the edge of a mission."

"I'm not sure that's the Bond girl's function."

Sharp, clever. She always was.

"Your name?" I press. "It's not Sophie."

"No. That was an alias."

"And Brie Anderson?"

"My name."

"No longer using aliases?"

"If the job requires it, I'll use one."

"But not this one?"

"It might before it's over. We don't know, right?" She

cocks her head, those astute eyes studying me, her mind undoubtedly forming questions. "You bought a sex club?"

"It's an elite social club," I correct, clipped. "I acquired the New York location three years ago. Expanded to four cities since. Restaurants, luxury travel, private events."

"That's a unique spin on a sex club."

"Social club," I repeat with pointed emphasis. "We offer private suites that cater to a variety of proclivities. On occasion we host special events that are tasteful," I tilt my head. "And erotic. We plan exclusive, members-only weekend getaways for members. Let me clear up any confusion—we're like another Harvard Club. Not all participate in all of our offerings. Many members have never attended a special event or weekend getaway—they use the club for business connections. For some, privacy is a priceless benefit."

"Did you and your father come to blows?"

The personal question stills me. She remembers. Not just the sex—anyone could remember that. She remembers our conversations. The confession I'd made in the early morning hours, her head on my chest, fingers tracing idle patterns on my skin while I told her things I'd never said aloud. How my father used legacy as chains. How Margot deserved to take the reins more than I did. How I wanted to build something of my own, something that didn't carry the weight of generations. Rare, that I share anything real. Rarer still that someone listens—truly listens—and remembers three years later. The rub is that I was fool enough to believe a stranger in my bed might stay.

"Do you live here now?" she asks, seeming to accept that I won't answer some questions and moving on to less personal ground.

"I do. Almost three years. I travel, but New York is home." I study her in turn. "And you?"

Her lips almost curve—almost. "Eight years."

"Then we were bound to meet again."

"I doubt we frequent the same places." Her finger taps a rhythm on the armrest—always the piano in her. "I appreciate you not making a scene," she says.

"That was chance. I was shocked."

"If I'd known you were there—"

"You wouldn't have come?" My jaw tightens. "Unbelievable."

"Perhaps it's best I don't work this project. KOAN can reassign easily."

"Oh, I want you on the team. I need to trust—" I cut myself short. Trust her? Impossible. But I won't let her vanish again, not without reason. "I want to know how much of Monaco was real."

Her eyes soften—for a breath—before cooling again. Pity flickers there. I don't need her pity.

What I need is to stop noticing the way her lips part when she's about to speak. The elegant line of her neck. The rise and fall of her chest beneath that professional blouse. My body hasn't forgotten Monaco, even if my mind knows better. Desire coils low, persistent, inappropriate. In my business, I routinely exercise control—when to indulge want, when to weaponize it, when to practice denial. She's making me forget every lesson.

"The leak is an employee," I say, hardening, putting the focus where it should be for the moment. "I need the culprit exposed before members flee."

"Assuming it is an employee."

"How could it not be?" It's infuriating. "We treat them well. Raises. Extra leave. Loyalty rewarded."

"Larger enterprises have been hacked."

"Preferable, I suppose." I exhale, releasing some of the tension that's built since she entered the meeting. "At least betrayal wouldn't wear a familiar face."

She shifts. "Where are we going?"

"Lunch."

"It's not even ten."

"Call it brunch."

"Adrien—"

My scowl ends the protest.

"Alright. I can join you."

"We could go to my place. But I thought you'd prefer the club."

Her eyes widen. What has she heard? Rumors, perhaps. Gossip. The photos alone. Let her wonder.

"We should set boundaries," she says, her voice now all business. "This is professional. Whatever happened between us—"

"Was real," I cut in. "For me."

Her tapping stops. For a moment, vulnerability shadows her face. Then the mask settles, immaculate. "We need to focus on the case. Protecting your business, yes?"

"Of course." I lean back, studying her. Lovely doesn't begin to cover it. She's radiant. And I remember every detail of her body, every sound she made. Sex I can buy. What I had with her, I can't replicate.

The sedan's interior feels too small suddenly. Her scent—that damned jasmine—fills the space between us like a third presence. I want to touch her. Not professionally. Not as the man who owns a club built on managed carnality. I want to touch her the way I did before, when we were just two people absconding reality for a weekend, when her laugh was unguarded and my fingers knew the geography of her skin.

The partition feels thin. The driver mere feet away. The leather seat creaks as I shift, trying to create distance that doesn't exist in this enclosed space. Every breath I take tastes like her.

She stares out the window, as if anywhere else would be preferable.

"In your CIA training," I ask, "did they teach you how to forget an unforgettable weekend? One that changed everything?"

The car stops at The Sanctuary. She reaches for the handle.

"They taught me how to compartmentalize," she says.

"And how is that working for you, Brie Anderson?"

She looks back, just once, eyes ocean-deep, the woman who played piano under moonlight breaking through the operative's mask.

"It never fails me."

But her hand trembles on the door handle. Just slightly. Just enough for me to see the lie. The driver opens her door. Cold air rushes in, breaking the spell of memory. She steps out onto the sidewalk with practiced grace, every inch the professional who knows how to disappear. This time, I won't let her.

CHAPTER
FIVE

BRIE

The nondescript entrance in the Meatpacking District isn't what I expect from a seven-figure initiation fee. Black plaque, black brick, black door—understated lure by design. Adrien keys a code; the door glides. The doorman's in black-on-black, the kind of muscle that doesn't advertise.

"And her phone?" he asks.

"She's with me," Adrien says, and the rule evaporates.

Policy overridden in three words.

Inside, marble and gold wash the room in luxury. Windowless, clockless—this place pretends it's always midnight, and everyone looks better by design. Corners hold smoked domes and pin-lens glass. Mostly hidden—just visible enough to remind you that you're seen.

Exits: three. Choke points: two. Blind zones: none apparent.

The motion door sighs open to an intimate bar dressed in velvet and bathed in low light.

"This is the restaurant?"

"This is one of the bars. It offers a casual dining experience or a place to venture for dessert and after-dinner drinks. The New York club has four bars and lounges, one restaurant with a Michelin star chef, a spa, and suites."

"Suites," I repeat when he lists the offerings, hearing the part he doesn't say: curated boundaries and privacy. "How did you get into this business?"

In Monaco, he'd taken me away on his yacht after a vicious fight with his father, who insisted he needed to be the one to take over the family business. Adrien had countered that his sister was more suited, and deserving, and I'd admired his progressive stance. That weekend had been a big fashion event, important for their business, and he absconded on the family's yacht to allow his sister to prove to their father she could handle it all. I'd stumbled on him at the bar after he'd downed a shot, licking his wounds from his father's verbal lashing.

Three weeks later the company announced Margot d'Avricourt would succeed her father as CEO, so I assumed his plan succeeded. The article made no mention of Adrien, but it had been a 150-word announcement buried pages deep in *The London Times* that only those with stock in d'Avricourt Luxe might have registered.

"I studied the fundamentals." His chin lifts, arms to his side, defensive? No, prideful. "Lifestyle made the most sense for an Avricourt Luxe brand extension. We sell clothes, handbags, jewelry, and fragrance in the high-end, luxury market. The high-value segment—clients who spend over fifty thousand a year, have more they could spend, but it's not just about claiming a larger share of their expenditures. It's about understanding this customer in a way we can't from market studies."

Fantasy sells. Reality invoices later. "Aren't these customers your friends and family?"

"A small sample size never provides the insight one needs."

"And a sex club is—"

"Where'd you get the idea that The Sanctuary is a sex club?" Tension threads his response, likely because we've been over this, but I can't shake my perception. "We're an exclusive social community, an unforgettable spa, and a travel experience with private events around the world. Desire is profitable. Intimacy isn't. We offer discreet, safe locations for a variety of activities, all in compliance with regional laws. If you're envisioning strippers and lap dances, that's not us."

"Unless it happens in a private suite? Or event?"

"Precisely."

"So you're telling me that The Sanctuary is market research?"

His lips curve into a composed smile, no, into a conceited smirk. "The businesses complement each other."

I recall the models that attended the event in Monaco, the women outnumbering the men by three to one easily. It had been chance that I'd caught his eye as I moved through the party, uninvited, hoping I evaded the Russian intelligence officer tracking me. "The models—are they paid to attend?"

The thin smile drops with a tsk. "They're contracted for events; consent is explicit and monitored. We don't employ sex workers in jurisdictions where it's illegal, if that's what you're asking."

Explicit consent is good. Power imbalance is better for predators. File under: watch.

"Our members may bring guests, but those guests are not contracted with our organization. And the models, yes, that's an area where the brand extension makes sense. As you know, the world of modeling is highly competitive. Few succeed and even fewer make enough to live off. The number of models who jump at the chance to attend events with wealthy, available individuals is great. What happens at our events is always consensual and we keep a watchful eye to ensure the safety of all attendees."

"I'm certain women are safe in your hands."

"Open your mind, Brie." I raise a pointed eyebrow, and his lips quirk. "Male models attend too. We're equal opportunity in our hedonism."

"Models," I repeat. "Only the lovely," I say, reciting the fragrance ad I once saw in an airport lounge in Paris.

"Words to live by," he says as a back door behind the bar opens, and a young woman dressed in a cleavage revealing black halter top enters with a crate of glasses in her arms. She glances our way but busies herself unloading the crate.

"The bar opens in thirty minutes," Adrien says. "Shall I show you the restaurant? We have quite the business breakfast scene. It's a relief for many to meet without public scrutiny and questions."

"Ah, so not as many models in attendance at breakfast?"

"Would it be out of line to mention that you're making my hand twitch?"

Another door opens from the back right, alleviating the need to answer his question, a small grace, given the implication heated my skin and the memory flash of his palm on my ass with me on my knees sent heat spiraling low in my body.

"There you are." The man addressing Adrien is dressed in the same all-black uniform as the man at the door, so I assume he's an employee. "How'd your meeting go?" He doesn't look at Adrien when he asks; he watches me.

The man is slightly shorter than me, thinning dark hair, with an outmoded thin mustache reminiscent of Clark Gable, but for all I know, the dated style is trending.

"It went well. I believe I'll be satisfied with the renovation." I cut my gaze to Adrien, and he adds for my benefit, "I'm renovating a bathroom in my penthouse. Eddie Thorne, this is an old friend of mine, Brie Anderson. I'm showing her around."

Recalculation clicks behind his eyes. "Ah. If you need membership services Tiffany will arrive—"

"She's with me," Adrien says, cutting him off as if he doesn't want Eddie to finish whatever welcome pitch he might be about to give. "Eddie is the managing director of the New York and Miami locations. He's been with The Sanctuary since its founding and is instrumental in ensuring it runs smoothly and every guest is cared for."

"It's nice to meet you," I say, wondering how unusual it is for Adrien to bring a woman with him to the club. If he does this all the time, then we won't pique any employee's interest. If it's a rare occurrence, or if he typically selects from the latest models, then that could explain Eddie's interest in me.

"Ah, the specials changed on the menu for this weekend. Do you have a minute to review? We also needed to make some adaptations to Saturday's event."

"Certainly," Adrien answers and Eddie hesitates, pointedly looking at me.

"Go ahead. I'll be fine waiting here."

Eddie looks at the bartender who is now taking plastic

wrap off of cherries and fruit slices. "Serene, please give Ms. Anderson anything she wants, anything at all."

Adrien hesitates, and I reassure him. "I'll be fine."

The two men exit through the same dark backdoor Eddie entered from, and I take a seat at the bar.

In a bright, upbeat voice, Serene asks, "What can I get you?"

"Nothing. I'm fine."

She proceeds with her work, her movements quick, while I check my phone.

> NOAH BENNETT
> You good?

I don't type a reply. I don't type anything inside a building I haven't swept. Even if Adrien thinks the system is closed loop, signals bleed. He should be in transit anyway, as we're off this weekend.

Noah's inquisitive, because he's perceptive, and he read my reactions in the meeting earlier today. When I call him, I'll explain. But how will I explain what I'm doing here now? I can't turn on the lights and examine the security system. It won't be believable to any employee that Adrien is giving an unfettered tour of the premises to his lady friend.

I've given him my explanation, and he's given me his, and on Monday I'll work with the team to determine if he has an employee selling secrets or if we're dealing with a clever hacker. He says his security system is closed loop, and perhaps he believes it is, but do I? No, because I guarantee you he's wired to reach emergency services, and if there's a way out, there's a way in.

Unlike the men, Serene's provocative outfit fits like a tasteful glove, highlighting her curves in a satin-like shimmer. The crystal catches the light, refracting rainbows across the bar top, and suddenly I'm back on his yacht, champagne flutes dry as the sun rises over the Mediterranean.

The horizon had started to blush with the faintest hint of dawn, painting the sky in watercolor pastels. We'd talked through the entire night, and I couldn't remember the last time I'd felt this present in a moment.

"The sun's coming up," I murmured, suddenly aware that daylight meant consequences, meant returning to shore, meant the end of this borrowed pause.

"I see it." But he wasn't looking at the sunrise. His gaze remained fixed on my face, studying me like I was art worthy of memorization. "Sophia…"

"Sophie," I corrected automatically, then caught myself. Even my cover name felt like a lie between us and I didn't want it there, but such was life.

"Sophie," he repeated, sounding it like a question. His hand came up to cup my cheek, thumb brushing across my bottom lip with reverent softness. "I don't want this night to end."

Neither did I. That was the precarious truth of it—for the first time in years, I didn't want to return to my real life. I wanted to stay suspended in this moment, on this yacht, with this man who saw past all my careful constructs to something I'd forgotten existed.

"It has to," I whispered, but I didn't pull away from his touch.

"Does it?"

The first rays of sun gilded his skin, and for a moment I couldn't tell if the heat came from the light or from him.

When he leaned forward, I met him halfway.

I should have pulled back, but something about the way he said my name felt real, and I wanted real more than I wanted safe.

His kiss was nothing like the practiced seduction I'd expected from a wealthy playboy. It was tentative at first, questioning, waiting for my permission.

He kissed me like a man testing a theory—and proved it true.

When I gave in—hands fisting in his shirt, pulling him closer—he responded with a hunger that matched my own. He kissed like a man with years of practice, but he treated me like I was a precious gem, perhaps the first he'd ever valued. Heat pooled low in my belly, my body recognizing something my mind wasn't ready to name.

When we finally broke apart, the sun had fully risen, casting diamonds across the water. The spell should have been broken by daylight, but it only felt stronger, more real.

"Stay with me for the weekend," he said, forehead resting against mine. "Come with me to my bedroom. Let's rest. Wake. Have breakfast at sea. If you don't have to go back, let's not."

I should have said no. Every instinct I'd honed directed me to end this now, to say I had to return to shore, that work called. But when I looked into his eyes—those eyes, more green and gold than blue in the daylight, that had listened to my truths without judgment but also shared unexpected common ground—I found myself nodding. The word that would change everything hovered on my lips.

"Yes," *I whispered, and meant it completely.*

He kissed me, and the woman who never broke cover vanished beneath the rising sun.

. . .

"Brie?" Adrien pulls me from the memory. He's carrying a leather portfolio—the only nod to work—while his eyes glint with interest, and I'm the thing catching it. For a disorienting heartbeat, I'm still on that yacht, still tasting sunrise and bad decisions. Then reality snaps back: the bar, the club, the professional distance I should never have let slip in the first place.

"Sorry about that." He slides onto the barstool beside me, while discreetly dropping a USB drive in my bag, which I can only assume contains the employee records we asked for. He's close enough that I catch his cologne—expensive, subtle—undesirably familiar. "Now, where were we?"

"We were finishing up." I stand, needing distance. "This has been educational, but I should head back."

"Educational?" he repeats, amused disbelief softening the edge. "That's the most clinical description of The Sanctuary I've ever heard."

Around us, the club is coming to life. Staff members move in and out of the bar area with practiced efficiency, preparing for the lunch and afternoon crowd, a group I can only imagine includes young, beautiful, pampered souls along with powerful benefactors who belong in this rarefied world of unlimited expense accounts and designer everything.

"The club is exactly what I expected," I lie, because the truth—that it's more elegant, more seductive, more everything than I imagined—isn't something I care to admit.

"Have dinner with me." The invitation is simple, direct. "Not here, somewhere else. Anywhere you want."

The offer is tempting, but dinner would be pointless. Mixing roles blurs lines. Blurred lines get people killed or compromised. I've done both. "I can't. I have plans."

"What plans?"

"Personal ones." I head for the exit, not trusting myself to stay longer. "I'll see you Monday." I'd like to remind him that on Monday we'll be doing the security assessment, just to drive home the reason I'm here, but I refrain from doing so as Serene is within earshot.

"Brie, wait—"

But I'm already walking away, leaving him in his curated midnight—beautiful people, beautiful things, beauty on retainer. It's a world I can infiltrate on assignment, but it isn't a life. Even if I could belong here, surrounded by his world of engineered beauty and careful desire, I'd never want to stay.

CHAPTER
SIX

BRIE

The stench from the street-cleaning unit that passed moments earlier lingers in the early morning air. I check the time, scanning the sidewalks for my team. Noah and Hudson are reliable—punctual to the minute—but if they were ever going to slip, with my luck, it would be today.

A light rain slicks the pavement, pooling along the curb. Noah's train from DC would've arrived hours ago. Hudson's flight from North Carolina—less predictable. If there's a delay, it hasn't hit my phone yet.

A man in a black knit cap and trench coat rounds the corner, stride brisk, certain. At that same moment, a dark gray Mercedes eases to the curb. The rear door opens, and Adrien's on the sidewalk in a flash.

"You're waiting? By yourself?"

The street's quiet, half industrial, half forgotten—back-alley energy. I'm capable of defending myself if a leftover drunk from last night's festivities gets ideas, but I keep that to myself.

Footsteps approach from my left. One glance confirms the skullcap is Noah. A yellow taxi stops behind the Mercedes; even before the door opens, I'd bet it's Hudson.

"Good morning, Mr. d'Avricourt," I say, loud enough for Noah to hear. Adrien's cologne carries on the damp air—something dark and woody with citrus notes. Mediterranean citrus. Monaco citrus. My stomach tightens involuntarily, muscle memory from a weekend I've spent years trying to forget.

Adrien frowns, bends to murmur something to his driver, then shuts the door. Another car door closes and Quinn appears, wrapped in a marled gray scarf that hangs loose against her coat.

"Hudson sent you?"

"We're evaluating tech. Easier if I'm here."

It makes sense. Quinn's the tech nerve center of our team. Still, it's odd that Hudson didn't come himself. Maybe another assignment pulled him, but that's not something you ask in front of a client.

"Wondered if your flight would be canceled," I say instead.

"I did too. Lots of delays." She adjusts the heavy bag slung over her shoulder. "Beat the system that's coming in. Not sure I'll make it out before the heavier rains."

"LaGuardia?"

She nods. "They're temperamental with weather."

"If flights get canceled, crash at my place. Closer than a hotel and my guest room has actual blackout curtains."

A light pressure at my back—Adrien's hand, not quite touching, but unmistakably Adrien—signals his impatience.

"This way," he says.

We follow, our footsteps soft against concrete, the sounds of traffic dull beneath the mist. Adrien unlocks the door; motion sensors trigger a low wash of light across the entryway. He waits until we're all inside before pressing a code on the wall panel. Another click. Overhead lights flare brighter.

"Thank you for meeting early," he says. "Mondays are ideal—no employees scheduled, and discretion matters. Kitchen staff sometimes stop in later to check inventory."

He taps an app on his phone, and the bar area glows fully to life. The glass globes recessed in the ceiling are just as I remembered.

"What about security?" I ask. "No live monitoring today?"

"They're off as well," he says. "Follow me."

We pass through the same door Eddie used Friday night. I glance at the ceiling—smoked glass, perfect cover for cameras.

"Is surveillance shut off when the business is closed?"

"No," Adrien says. "Video runs continuously. After twenty-four hours, footage records over itself. If there's an incident, we pull it before that window closes."

"And no remote access?" Quinn asks. "That app you're using—it's not connected?"

He shakes his head. "We considered integrating the feed but decided against it. Phones can be stolen. Too much risk."

Quinn exchanges a glance with me; she approves of the caution.

"We reviewed your personnel records," I say. "Five employees own properties worth over five million. Is that unexpected?"

"Probably not." He slows as we approach an elevator. "We

pay well. Eddie Thorne, our managing director, earns seven-fifty plus under-the-table tips. Macon Chen, head of security—around seven hundred. The chef's at a million. I stole him from another venue, promised him a partnership once he gets ours running cleanly. Who were the other two?"

"Luz Delgado—VIP liaison. And Christophe Duret, your acquisitions coordinator. Both have verifiable income streams that match their assets."

The elevator doors close, and without a button pressed, we rise. Controlled remotely—linked to his app. Typical of Adrien: convenience disguised as luxury.

The space feels smaller than it should, his height crowding the air. Glass globes overhead form a geometric pattern—too deliberate for design alone. I calculate automatically: three blind spots. One near the panel, one behind the mirrored wall, one where Adrien stands closest to me. His shoulder brushes mine; I shift a fraction.

The elevator stops after two floors. Adrien steps into a quiet hallway lined with labeled doors.

"This level's staff-only—changing rooms, storage, everything an employee might need. And here's the control room."

A green light halos the door frame as he scans in. "Only fifteen people have visual ID access. The system logs entries, but it won't raise alarms. I come in on closed days often enough that no one will question it."

He holds the door for us, and I take care to avoid brushing against him as I step through into the room.

Video screens cover two walls. Adrien moves confidently to the control console, his touch steady and sure. Despite myself, I track his hands—strong, practiced, ringless. The same that once traced the curve of my spine. The screens blink to life, revealing corridors, reception areas, and the main bar.

"No video inside the suites?" I ask.

"No. Only hallways—to verify consent. The suites are private. We have open event spaces with surveillance, and bouncers circulate. Safety first."

His tone is professional, but the tension in his jaw betrays him. He knows how vulnerable his members are.

"If I trusted Chen, he'd be giving you this tour," he adds.

"You don't think you can?" Noah asks.

"That's the point, isn't it?" Adrien's reply is sharper now. "I can't trust anyone. Chen controls surveillance, schedules—everything. If the blackmail originated here, he's in the perfect position to manipulate footage."

"And the surveillance is viewed here?" Quinn asks, lowering her bag onto a chair.

"Yes. Privacy is a close second to safety. That's why I need you to find the source of the breach."

"Alright," she says. "Can I dig in? Will anyone be alerted?"

"No."

"Good." She's already crouched, scanning the console. "We'll need to install our own surveillance in here—discreetly. If anyone notices, we're done. First, I'll map your storage protocols."

I lean against a counter, watching the screens as Quinn murmurs to herself. After she finishes her sweep, I'll ask her about anomalies—any feed not looping back to this room could point to our mole.

"Do you ever have outside contractors?" I ask. "HVAC, pest control, maintenance?"

"Occasionally," Adrien says.

"Can we see service records?"

"Of course. But we don't let technicians in unescorted."

"That's the rule," I say. "Rules bend."

He glances at me—something close to approval flickers in his expression. "You're more thorough than my own security experts."

"It's the situation," I reply, though the warmth in his tone lingers longer than it should.

"Would you care to come to my office?"

"Your office is here?"

"Across the street," he says, a faint smirk curving his mouth. The expression jolts a memory—how he'd looked at me the night we met after a drink and a dare. I keep my face neutral.

"Do you have floor plans?" Quinn asks, still bent under the console. "Electrical schematics?"

"Yes. When I bought the business, I received all physical plans—no electronic copies. They're in my office." He turns to me. "Come with me?"

"You go ahead," Noah says, eyes on the ceiling. "I'll start mapping hidden camera angles."

If Noah were looking at me, I'd shoot him a glare. He still assumes Adrien's presence rattles me because of my CIA cover, an assumption I haven't corrected.

Adrien gestures toward the hall. "Shall we?"

The deep breath I take shouldn't be necessary. I've been alone with arms dealers, double agents, and men far more dangerous than a club owner. But he's not just a businessman. Adrien d'Avricourt is the only one who's ever made me question the choices that built my life.

CHAPTER
SEVEN

ADRIEN

"No photographs."

She says it like an accusation, eyes scanning my office as if she's judging the man through his décor.

"But the room does look like you."

"You mean dark and moody? My sister calls this my 'brooding billionaire lair.'"

"I didn't choose those words," but I take the twitch of her lips to mean she's humored by my comment. "Is that an original Clyfford Still?"

She knows her art. Of course she does.

"I have a few of his pieces." Only one is displayed prominently in the office, a darker abstract that flavored the mood and prevented the deep green walls from slipping into smoking-jacket cliché. "Most people see chaos. What do you see?"

"It's never about what I see—it's about what I feel." Her answer shows she's studied art.

"And what do you feel?" I ask, though what I really want

to know is who she is. How much of that weekend was truth and how much was cover?

"Craven need." Her lips purse, her eyelids lower. "Vulnerability." For an instant, honesty flickers—then defense. Shoulders squared, chin lifted. "Did I pass?"

"There's no test. I only want to get to know you." More than I should. "Do you have an office?" As I ask the question, I attempt to envision her space.

"Not like this." The tips of her fingers drag along the felt lining of the billiard table as she walks, her gaze fixated on the bookshelves lining a back wall.

I'd gutted three offices to make this one—a hybrid of library and study. "Brighter? Airier?"

"It's in my home," she says, "and it doubles as a guest room when needed. And I definitely don't have a Clyfford Still hanging on my walls."

"When you told me you worked at an art gallery…was any of that true?"

"I imagine you already know the answer."

"I went to that gallery. They'd never heard of a Sophie Dubois."

"You visited the one in London?"

I don't answer. My question said enough. I'd spent six months and a small fortune chasing her ghost. My family called it obsession. They weren't wrong.

She wasn't in any database, never passed through customs in any country. But still, I traveled to the places she named, showing photographs, conducting much of the search myself to rely on instinct, hoping to sense fear or reluctance. Blank stares, annoyance at an absorption of time, that's about all I uncovered.

"The Dubois identity was sculpted by my employer. But I

was only supposed to use that alias for one event. I imagine my handler didn't expect it to matter if someone visited a gallery in another country and discovered I hadn't worked there."

"Or called?"

"If you'd called that day, let's hope the person answering the phone would have confirmed my employment. But truly, they weren't expecting anyone to call. The alias was a party girl. If for some reason my employment cover was questioned, I could've played it off as a lie to pretend employment, to weasel my way into the art circles."

"And why were you interested in art?"

"You mean my employers?"

I nod, letting my hands drop into my trouser pockets to fight the urge to step closer and touch her, to pull her to me.

"Money laundering," she says, her tone stripped of apology. "Art was just the vehicle."

For a moment, something like regret shadows her expression before the mask resets. "We were tracking weapons dealers who used gallery sales to move dirty money. And we weren't interested in stopping it; we just wanted the intel."

Disdain echoes in her tone.

"Is that why you're no longer with the CIA?" Her long lashes flutter, her blue eyes zeroing in on me, and I lift a shoulder nonchalantly. "You already told me, it was CIA. There's no surveillance in here."

With that one word, her interest in my surroundings is shut down, and her expression transforms into what one can only describe as business.

"My status as a former CIA officer isn't a secret." She leaves the billiard table behind, and I watch closely as her long legs carry her across the office to my desk. "You have blueprints?"

"I do, but not in a file cabinet."

"If they're electronic I didn't need to come here."

I stride past her to the art hanging behind my desk, push a button behind the credenza, and the framed image raises, revealing a safe.

"You keep the blueprints in a safe?"

"Only because they didn't fit in the filing cabinet, and it seemed like the kind of thing I should save. There are handwritten notes on the edges from the architect and it's easiest to read on the paper."

She steps closer for a better view, but she steps into my space, and I breathe in the subtle hints of saffron and jasmine that I remember from her body wash, a brand I acquired because it stayed with me, long after I'd given up on finding the mysterious golden beauty.

I used to wonder if time would dull the longing. It didn't. It hits me again—the same pull, sharp and inevitable. Stronger, because now I know she's real, not just a perfect memory I chased. The urge to thread my fingers through her hair, to angle her head, to taste her lips...and the way those blue eyes gaze up at me, pupils dilated, her breath catching— she feels it too. Her throat works on a swallow. Not nerves— want. She'd rather die than let me see it, but I do. I could close the distance. I don't.

Because I remember the way she went still when I implied familiarity. Whatever this is between us, she needs to choose it.

The space between us charges with years of wondering, of wanting, of—

A shrill ringtone ricochets through the room. Air I hadn't

realized I'd been refusing fills my lungs and her gaze drops to the ground, then to the safe.

The ringtone continues, a harsh, cut-through-anything ringtone I selected to ensure I'd hear it no matter where I was or what I happened to be doing.

Reluctance and annoyance coil together as I answer, noting Alicia Morgan's name.

"Alicia," I answer.

"Adrien, can you talk?" She doesn't mean do I have time, she means can I talk without being overheard.

"You've got me. Go."

"I have confirmation Senator Crawford isn't the only person who received a threat in the last two weeks. The threat over this second Congressman has nothing to do with The Sanctuary. Given the nature of this second threat, I believe what we're looking at is an individual or group who have a list of senators they aim to influence, and they've hired someone to dig up what they can."

This is marginally better news. The worst situation would have been an employee using security footage as extortion material over any member susceptible to a bribe. "So what you're saying is you believe this person or group struck up a one-off deal with one of my employees, maybe someone caught at a weak moment, unexpected expenses—"

"I didn't go that far."

"But it's unlikely this is an ongoing thing," I say, wanting her to confirm my positive interpretation of this development.

"Maybe. Maybe not."

That's a frustrating response.

Brie steps closer, full of questions.

"Anything else?" I presume Alicia isn't going to share any

details from her other client's case, and she confirms my assumption when she responds with, "Nothing else. Have you made any headway on your end?"

"No. The KOAN team is here today to set up surveillance. If this is an ongoing endeavor, we'll observe something. If it was a one-off..." I let the implication hang. If the employee sold out a member once and never does it again, I'm not sure how we'll catch him.

"Keep me posted," Alicia says, and the line goes dead.

I set the phone on my desk and turn back to Brie, who's watching me with that focused intensity that reminds me she's not just beautiful—she's determined.

"Bad news?" she asks.

"Complicated news. There's at least one other politician being targeted, but not through my club." I retrieve the blueprints from the safe, spreading them across my desk. "Which means we likely have a rogue employee selling secrets, and someone out there is running a broader operation."

She leans over the blueprints, her golden strands falling like a curtain as she studies the layout. I force myself to focus on the documents instead of the elegant line of her neck, or the way her slender fingers trace the club's floor plan with practiced precision.

"Your security is more extensive than most hotels," she observes. "Cameras here, here, and here." She points to locations marked on the blueprint. "But there are blind spots."

"Intentional ones. Members pay for privacy."

"Yet someone exploited them." She straightens, and I catch another hint of her scent—tempting, familiar. "I'll need to see these areas in person. The service corridors, the private rooms, anywhere an employee might access member spaces without being observed."

"I can give you a tour now, if you'd like."

Something shifts in her expression—a flash of what might be anticipation, quickly masked by professional composure. "That would be helpful."

When I look up, she's closer than before, close enough that I can see the faint golden flecks in her blue eyes.

"Adrien," she says, and my name on her lips sends fevered need straight through me. "Before we go downstairs...What happened before—"

"Was the most real thing that's happened to me in years," I finish, unable to stop myself from stepping closer. "A day hasn't gone by since that weekend that you didn't cross my thoughts, that something didn't make me think of you. A scent. A color. Lace. Silk."

Her expression softens, and for a moment, I glimpse the woman from my memories, the one who laughed at my terrible Italian and traced lazy patterns and let loose freely.

"This complicates things," she whispers.

"Everything that matters leaves a mark."

"It's not a good idea."

I'm close enough now to touch her, to cup her face in my hands the way I've dreamed. Her eyes flutter closed, and I lean down, drawn by gravity and desire and the impossible fact that she's here, real, within reach—

Her phone buzzes against the desk where she set it down.

The sound breaks the spell. She steps back quickly, professional demeanor snapping back into place like armor.

"We should start that tour," she says, her voice that of the consummate professional.

I nod, though it's the last thing I want. No, I want to finish what we started. I want her against my desk—close enough to prove to my body this isn't a hallucination. I want to discover if her body remembers what mine can't forget. Instead, I gesture toward the door.

"After you."

As she moves past me, I catch her hand briefly, just long enough to feel the slight tremor in her fingers.

"Brie," I say quietly. "Whatever this is between us…it's still quite present."

She looks back at me, and for just a moment, allows her shield to drop.

"I know," she says. "But that doesn't mean we should give in to it. We have a job to do."

CHAPTER
EIGHT

BRIE

"It?" His eyes light with mischief.

I should've known he'd push. We're still in his office, the blueprints spread before us, his question posed like a dare.

"Sex," I answer, chin-raised.

He's toying with me. Taunting.

The word lands heavy between us, humid as breath against glass. The air changes—thicker, slower—as though the room itself waits for my answer.

"Lust." He steps closer, his height and presence cornering me. "When you say *it*, that's what you're choosing to assign a meaningless pronoun." His fingers lightly tousle my hair and a shiver rolls down my spine. "Am I right?"

Need unfurls down my spine, pooling low, the ache both pleasure and warning. The backs of his fingers skim slowly, oh so slowly, up my arm.

"If it's only lust, what's the harm?"

His question is valid. I've made a point of refusing to be

precious about sex. It's a physical act and in the right circumstances serves as currency, desire the gold standard. Sex being one of the few commodities that's less valuable after the trade. Thinking of it that way hardens my emotions, akin to armor.

His lips brush my temple and my knees go weak.

"If it's only sex, we have options. The desk. This console. The billiard table." My eyes close, lost in his seductive, honeyed, throaty voice and the warmth from his roaming hand along my hip over the curve of my bottom. "A wide selection of rooms with toys."

My eyes snap open. The open safe, the vault drenched in darkness, the stainless metal cold and impenetrable.

"My vote is for—"

"We have work to do." If I let him keep going, that's all I'll think about for the rest of the day.

I step back, breath more shallow and rapid than it should be. The blueprints crinkle when I grab them, the paper thin and malleable.

"But it's not just sex with us, is it?"

I move to step away, careful to keep my back to him, but his strong hand clasps my elbow.

"That's why you ran?"

"You're being ridiculous."

"Am I?" His hold on my elbow loosens and I lower my arm, but still stand there, too close. The thin layer of dust on the blueprints is like grit over silk, and I focus on what's important.

"I left because I had a job."

Never mind that he's touching on truths. I didn't want to go, and I didn't say goodbye because that felt too hard. It shouldn't have been. I could've told him that I needed to get home and I'd call him and then it would've been a closed loop. He would've found the number I gave him to be incorrect and he would've assumed I wasn't interested and it would've effectively closed the door, but I left mysteriously, without a goodbye, and maybe a small part of me hoped he'd search, but I also believed he would move on.

And now?

There's a job to be done and my colleagues are in the building next door.

Hormones are playing with my head and creating an aching need that it's not the time or place to satisfy.

I stride to the billiard table and unroll the plans, spreading them across the smooth surface.

"Can you turn on the light?" A forest green glass light hangs over the table, and I need the light to better see the faded blue lines.

Seconds later, golden light coats the faded paper and I pinpoint the entrance, gaining my bearings, noting the walls, the hallways, elevator shafts, and rooms.

"Perhaps it will work best if I study these while you give me the tour."

He moves to stand beside me, close enough that his sleeve brushes my arm. "Of course." His tone has shifted to something more professional, though the thermal energy between us still radiates like the barrel on a smoking gun. "We'll start with the main floor and work our way down."

I fold the blueprints carefully, creating manageable sections. "Lead the way."

The tour begins methodically. Adrien shows me through the main entertaining areas—the grand salon with its crystal chandeliers and velvet furnishings, the smaller intimate rooms with their own unique themes, the bar area with its gleaming mahogany surfaces. Everything matches the blueprints perfectly. The building's bones are solid, the renovations expertly done.

The hallways are wider than they appear on the blueprints, with recessed lighting that creates pools of warm amber. Cameras are discreetly positioned at regular intervals—for security, Adrien explains, though I wonder what else they might capture.

"Access to the footage? All in the control room?" I ask casually.

"Restricted to myself, management, and the security team. Privacy is paramount. The fourth and fifth floors house the private suites," Adrien explains as we climb the curved staircase. "Each room has been designed for specific...preferences."

The air shifts as we ascend—heavier, headier. That bergamot and cedar scent intensifies, layered now with something warmer. Vanilla. Amber. Even lust, apparently, is branded here.

The silence on these floors is different from the rest of the building. Thicker. More deliberate. Soundproofing, I realize, designed to contain whatever happens behind these doors. But with the club closed, with no members present, the silence feels almost sacred. Like walking through a cathedral built to pleasure rather than prayer.

We pass open doors that hint rather than show—a silk rope coiled neatly on a marble console, a velvet mask resting beside champagne flutes, the ghost of perfume hanging in the air. The building itself feels alive, pulsing with remembered heat even in its emptiness.

"How are the rooms assigned?" I ask, keeping my voice professional.

"Members book in advance. We have a concierge who manages the suites, coordinates preferences, ensures everything is prepared." He pauses at a door with a small brass plate: *Venetian*. "Tiffany, our concierge, would normally handle this kind of tour, but given it's Monday…"

"She's not here," I finish.

"No one is." His gaze holds mine for a beat too long. "Just us."

The implication hangs between us. Alone. In a building designed for intimacy. Surrounded by rooms that exist solely for the exploration of desire.

He scans his access card and the door opens soundlessly.

The room beyond stops me cold.

It's opulent without being gaudy—all jewel tones and rich textures. Deep sapphire velvet curtains frame floor-to-ceiling windows overlooking the city. A four-poster bed dominates the space, its posts carved from dark mahogany, its linens the color of cream and champagne. Candlelight—motion-activated, I suspect—flickers from recessed alcoves, casting amber shadows across walls painted the deep blue-green of Venetian lagoons.

But it's the details that betray the room's true purpose.

Discreet anchor points in the bedposts, so subtle I almost miss them. A chaise longue positioned with deliberate angles to the mirrors—I count three—angled to multiply and fragment. A cabinet against the far wall, lacquered black, its contents hidden but its purpose clear from the ornate lock.

"Soundproofed," Adrien says quietly, watching me take it in. "Temperature controlled. The windows are one-way glass—our members can see out, but no one can see in." He moves deeper into the room. "Everything is designed to create a space completely removed from the outside world."

I follow slowly, hyperaware of his presence, of the door closing behind us with a soft pneumatic hiss. The carpet is thick enough to silence footsteps. Everything is designed to heighten sensation—the lowered lighting, the subtle scent of oud and roses, the way sound seems to pool and thicken.

My tactical mind catalogs automatically: one entrance, no emergency exits visible, two visual blind spots from where I'm standing—near the bathroom door and behind the bed's canopy. But beneath the professional assessment runs something else. A visceral awareness of what this room is designed for. Of pleasure choreographed and surrender invited.

"What happens here?" I ask, though I know the answer.

"Whatever our members desire." He's closer now. I didn't hear him move. "With consent. Always with consent."

I turn to face him, and the mirrors catch us—multiple versions of this moment, fractured and multiplied. Professional Brie in her tailored blazer. Adrien in his perfectly cut suit. But our reflections betray us: the small space between our bodies, the way his gaze tracks down my throat to my collarbone, the tension in my shoulders that has nothing to do with the assignment.

I force myself to move away, toward the cabinet. "May I?"

He produces a small key, crosses to unlock it. The doors open to reveal an array of implements arranged with the precision of surgical instruments. Silk restraints in jewel tones that match the room's palette. Leather cuffs lined with the softest suede. Items I recognize from training—not for use, but for awareness. And some I don't recognize at all.

Everything is high-end, expensive, designed for pleasure and safety in equal measure.

"Our concierge stocks the suites based on member preferences," he explains, his voice carefully neutral. "Everything is sterilized between uses. Medical-grade protocols."

"Your concierge knows what they want?" I ask, reaching out to touch a length of silk rope before pulling my hand back.

"Tiffany makes it her business to know. Anticipation is part of the service." He closes the cabinet, locks it. "The fantasy begins before they arrive."

"One person?"

"By design," he says.

My mind catalogs this professionally—possible breach point, potential blackmail leverage. But my body registers something else entirely. The air in here is thick, charged. My skin feels too tight. Every surface seems designed for touch, for surrender.

I've used my sexuality tactically for years. A tool. A weapon. A means to an end. But standing here, in this room designed for authentic pleasure, I feel the compartmentalization beginning to crack.

"Are all the suites like this?" I ask, my voice steadier than I'd expected.

"Each is themed differently." He moves to stand beside me, not touching, but close enough that I feel his heat. "The Tokyo Suite is minimalist—all clean lines and hidden storage. The Parisian is baroque, almost decadent. The Moroccan has a sunken bath and floor cushions." He pauses. "Members book based on mood. Or fantasy."

"And you designed these?"

"I curated them. Worked with designers who specialize in...experiential spaces." His reflection catches mine in the mirror. "For some, the use of these suites isn't only about privacy. It's about transformation. The ability to become someone else for a few hours. To explore desires they can't acknowledge in daylight."

The words land with uncomfortable precision. Isn't that what I've done my entire career? Become whoever the mission requires? Used desire and attraction as currency while keeping my authentic self locked away?

I should move toward the door. Should maintain professional distance. Instead, I find myself asking, "Do you use them?"

"The suites?" Something shifts in his expression, as if I've hit an old bruise. "You left."

Flustered, I open my mouth in defense.

"I've used them—rarely. I wanted an elusive fantasy—and I quickly discovered these rooms couldn't recreate a weekend aboard a yacht." His voice drops. "A certain someone has made every role I've played since feel hollow."

His throaty admission reveals a rawness that tightens around my throat.

I'm acutely aware that we're alone in a room designed for intimacy, surrounded by mirrors that multiply our proximity, breathing air heavy with intention.

That we're two people who've spent years performing for others, standing in a space built for surrender.

My phone vibrates in my pocket—Quinn, probably, with an update. A lifeline. I step back, breaking whatever spell the room was weaving.

"We should continue the tour," I say, my voice unsteady despite myself. "I need to see the playrooms. The fifth floor."

Adrien holds my gaze a moment longer, and I see the war in his expression—desire versus restraint, want versus wisdom. Finally, he nods.

"Of course. The fifth floor."

But as I move past him toward the door, his hand catches mine briefly. Just fingertips against my wrist, feather-light, barely contact at all.

"Brie." His voice is quiet. "I know this is uncomfortable. The investigation. Being here. Us." A pause. "But I need you to know—what I felt in Monaco wasn't performative. And what I'm feeling now isn't just because you're here in my space."

I should pull away. Should shut this down. Instead, I let my fingers linger against his for one heartbeat longer than professional.

"I know," I whisper. "But that doesn't make it any less complicated. Shall we?"

The fifth floor houses a different aesthetic entirely. Where the suites below were intimate and curated, this floor is theatrical. Dramatic lighting. Strategic sightlines. Areas designed to be seen and areas designed for watching.

The emptiness makes it even more charged. Without members present, I can see the architecture of desire laid bare—the intentionality of every surface, every angle, every piece of equipment.

Through an open doorway, I glimpse a room with a St. Andrew's cross mounted against exposed brick, the leather cuffs hanging empty, waiting. Another features what looks like a performance stage, complete with seating arranged in a semicircle. Everything is high-end, expensive, designed with the same attention to detail as a Broadway set.

"Members sign consent forms before participating," Adrien says, his voice carefully controlled. "No photography, no recordings—at least, none that are authorized." His jaw tightens. "These rooms have surveillance only in public areas, trained on exits and entries. The activity itself is private between participants."

Was private, I think but don't say. Before someone turned it into a surveillance opportunity.

We move through the space in silence. I make mental notes—camera positions, security blind spots, access points. But beneath the professional assessment runs something else. A visceral awareness of what happens in these rooms. Of pleasure choreographed and performed. Of desire stripped of pretense and shame.

I've always maintained distance from my own sexuality—using it tactically, never authentically. A weapon, not a vulnerability. But standing here, in spaces designed for people to be wholly themselves in their desires, I feel something shift.

"How do you separate this?" I ask, surprising myself with the question. "The business from...everything else?"

He's quiet for a long moment. We've stopped in front of floor-to-ceiling windows that overlook the city, the morning light casting long shadows across the polished floor.

"I don't," he finally says. "I used to think I could. That I could curate fantasy for others while remaining untouched by it myself." He turns to face me fully. "But that's a lie we tell ourselves, isn't it? That we can orchestrate intimacy without being changed by it."

The words land too close to truths I don't want to examine. I turn away, pretending to study the view, but I can see our reflections in the glass. Two people surrounded by the architecture of pleasure, both running from our longings.

"We should see the basement," I say, my voice tight. "That's what's remaining."

Adrien doesn't move immediately. I can feel him watching me, reading what I'm trying hard not to show.

"Brie." He says my name like a question. "What are you afraid of?"

The directness catches me off guard. I should deflect. Should hide behind professionalism. Instead, I hear myself say, "That I've spent so long undercover that I don't know how to be real anymore."

I shouldn't have used that word, referenced my work, but it's a truth more intimate than what regularly happens in these rooms.

He moves closer, and I watch our reflections converge in the glass. "You were real in Monaco," he says quietly. "You may have been undercover, but you were more real than anyone I've ever met. That's why I looked for you. That's why I never stopped."

I close my eyes against the reflection, against the truth in his words. "We have work to do."

"I know." But he doesn't step back. "Just...don't disappear again. Not yet."

I nod and exit. We enter the elevator and descend in silence.

"The basement level," he says as the doors open. "Storage, utilities, staff areas."

The basement feels different. Cooler. The air carries a faint electrical hum that wasn't present on the upper floors. I unfold the relevant section of blueprints, comparing what I see to what should be here.

"This corridor," I point to a section on the plans, then look up at the actual hallway stretching before us. "Is it shorter than shown?"

Adrien frowns, moving closer to look at the blueprints. "The plans are from the original construction. Modifications were made during renovation."

We walk the corridor, passing doors marked as storage and mechanical rooms. Everything seems to match until we reach what should be the end of the hall. But there, tucked behind a slight jog in the corridor that doesn't appear on the blueprints, is another door painted to blend with the wall.

I stop. "What's behind here?"

Adrien's expression shifts, confusion replacing confidence. "That's... I'm not sure. Storage, I assume."

The door is unmarked, and if one glanced down the corridor, they might not notice the subtle lines, seeing instead an extension of pewter grey wall. A subtle electronic beep emanates from behind it—rhythmic, like a heartbeat.

"You're unsure?"

"The renovation crew handled many of the basement modifications. I focused on the floors that would serve our members." He's defensive, but his voice lacks the conviction of the blameless.

I try the handle. Locked, but not with the standard keys the other basement doors use. This lock is electronic, a small LED glowing red beside a keypad.

"Adrien." I've no tolerance for lies. "This isn't on the blueprints. This lock is high-end security. What aren't you telling me?"

"I'm telling you everything I know." His jaw flexes and he frowns. "Which apparently isn't as much as I thought."

I study his face in the dim corridor lighting. The confusion appears genuine, but there's something else—a flicker of concern. Perhaps the implications of careless oversight are dawning on him.

"Step back. This might take a moment." I pull the small device from my jacket pocket—a sleek little miracle Quinn insisted I bring "just in case."

"Brie, what are you—"

"My job." The electronic lock picker is a beauty, sleek and efficient. "Funny," I murmur, attaching the device. "Seems I'm often breaking into things."

"You're not the only one," he says quietly.

The lock picker interfaces with the keypad, running through possible combinations at superhuman speed. Within thirty seconds, the LED flickers from red to green.

The door swings open with a soft hydraulic hiss, and cool air washes over us. The electronic humming grows louder.

Inside is a server room.

Rows of black metal towers stretch into the depths of the space; their surfaces dotted with blinking lights. The air conditioning hums steadily, keeping the temperature constant. But it's not just the servers that settle the familiar weight of a serious case on my shoulders—it's the data entry summary of what appears to be catalogued video footage showing on a monitor.

Timestamps. Room numbers. File names that suggest X-rated content. A chair and desk that show someone works from this room.

"Christ," Adrien breathes behind me.

I step deeper into the room, my skin tingling, adrenaline coursing through my veins. The setup is professional-grade, expensive. Someone has invested serious money in this operation. The monitors cycle through what appears to be an organizational system—footage sorted by date, location, participants, and activity.

The servers blink like a thousand watchful eyes. Lust, stripped of consent, mechanized and sold—this is what happens when desire becomes commerce.

"This isn't just storage," I say quietly. "This is a business."

Adrien moves to stand beside me, his face pale in the glow of the monitors. "I had no idea. I swear to you, Brie, I had no idea this existed."

I want to believe him. The shock on his face seems real. But someone in his organization knows about this room. Someone has been operating a side business using his club as cover.

"The question is," I say, watching the monitors cycle through their inventory, "who has access to this room? And how long have they been running this operation?"

The implications are staggering. If someone is harvesting footage from the club's private rooms, cataloguing it, organizing it—they're not doing it for personal entertainment. This is blackmail material. Extortion. The kind of operation that could theoretically destroy lives and topple powerful elected officials, but most likely those threatened pay up, so it's a money-making enterprise.

Adrien stares at the screens, his hands clenched into fists at his sides. "I know you think it's predominantly sex, and I won't deny that's a component, but business is handled here. The backdoor variety. Every member trusts me with their privacy. Their secrets. They say they're paying for the connections, but privacy is understood."

"I hear you. But looking at this room, someone is undoubtedly selling secrets."

The servers continue their quiet humming, processing terabytes of compromising material. Somewhere in those drives could be the private moments of some of the most powerful people in every metropolitan area with a club location. London. Paris. Shanghai. New York. Miami. Politicians, celebrities, business leaders—all of them vulnerable.

I turn to face Adrien fully. "We need to find out who's running this little side business. And we need to do it before they realize they've been discovered. Because you're positive this isn't part of the standard operation?" I mean, if he's hands off, maybe this has a legitimate function and he's unaware.

"Positive. We don't store footage. We don't label it." Any hint of his earlier flirtation is gone. An undercurrent of anger belies his calm exterior, and there's determined conviction in the set of his jaw. "Where do we start?"

I look back at the stacked servers, taking in the array of blinking lights. "We start by figuring out who else knows this room exists. Because whoever built this didn't do it alone. And we find out who's accessing it and using it now."

CHAPTER NINE

ADRIEN

The Sanctuary was supposed to be untouchable. A refuge for the powerful and the weary—a place where secrets stay secret. Instead, it's become a stage for betrayal, and I'm the fool who bought and expanded it.

The Sanctuary promises a place out of the public eye, away from nosy reporters and photographers aiming to make a quick buck off insinuation and lies. A place where friendships can flourish, and a place where business can be discussed without scrutiny. Privacy, the one thing our members crave, is something I've failed to provide.

Brie moves through the space like an appraiser, her gaze cataloguing every imperfection as if she were valuing a piece at Christie's. The low light glints off the brass fixtures—dulled by neglect. The equipment rack hums with a frequency I feel in my teeth—industrial, expensive, maintained. Someone's been caring for this technology while letting the brass fixtures tarnish as camouflage.

As Brie snaps photos of the room and studies every crevice and light, the dizzying effect of the implications comes at me like a vortex with one exit. Every face from every event flashes through my mind—senators, CEOs, celebrities. Trust, bought and paid for. And now broken.

For years, I've sold the fantasy of control—curated pleasure, engineered intimacy. But what happens when the fantasy outgrows its maker? When desire becomes the weapon, not the reward? When intimacy is stripped of consent and sold back as leverage, what do you even call that—lust, or something far uglier wearing its skin?

"I need to shut the club down."

Brie applies pressure to my arm, and I cut my gaze to meet hers. I expect sympathy—or at least a flicker of pity—but she's all business. The same cool precision that once turned me on now slices clean through fresh wounds. I'm probably one of many she never meant to keep—just another weekend folded into an alias.

"Don't be ridiculous. Come on. Let's go. Step out of here and don't touch anything."

"What? Why?"

"Because someone's using this room. I'll show this to the team. When your staff returns tomorrow, by Wednesday at the latest, we'll know who is doing this, then we'll shut it down. How you handle the membership, that's up to you, but you can set safeguards in place to ensure this never happens again."

I exit into the hall, watching as she holds her magical device up to the keypad until it beeps red again, the lock re-engaging.

When was this room added? Was it here three years ago when I bought it? Did I buy my own liability?

As Brie messages someone, I stand in the basement corridor, considering the staff. Eddie Thorne—"Call me Eddie"—has to be involved. I replay the conversation when he showed me the security system, how he casually mentioned the "closed circuit" setup while guiding my attention to the visible cameras, not the infrastructure. The way he always seemed to materialize when I visited unannounced, as if he had advance warning. Jesus. He probably did.

Then there's Macon Chen, head of security. If Eddie's the strategist, Macon is the muscle. Are they working together? If they are, the rot goes deeper—maybe all the way to Miami.

As managing director, Eddie oversees the New York and Miami locations, but Macon only manages security for the New York club.

And then there's Tiffany—that's not even her real name. It's what she chooses for the membership, and I've never questioned it because discretion is currency here. For years I've called her Tiffany, watching her glide through the club in those perfectly tailored shifts, embodying the aesthetic we sell. But her real name is pedestrian... Karen? No. Carol? The irony stings—I don't even know the real name of the woman who knows every member's preferences, every whispered request, every private need.

"Come on. We're going to meet the team in the security room." She stops further down the corridor, her long hair glimmering under the light as she looks over her shoulder. "Adrien, the operation just got a lot simpler. At the moment, this might not seem like it, but this is a best-case scenario."

"Are you out of your mind? There's nothing best case—"

"Come on. You said staff might pop in this afternoon. We have work to do. You need to snap out of it."

She sounds annoyed...with me.

What the hell?

I step forward, following her out of the basement. Maybe she should be annoyed. My stomach feels like it's been hollowed out with ice. I let this happen under my own roof—under my own name. It all happened while I focused on marketing and how to leverage my learnings to grow the family business. What my father called folly I thought had been brilliant brand extension, but that flash of brilliance might cost me my reputation as a businessman to be taken seriously, and well, if the clubs go under, I'd get a fraction of the $1.5 billion I invested.

The irony is rich—I fought to earn my independence from the family business, only to discover I've been played by my own employees. Every conversation with my father about due diligence and hands-on management echoes in my head. Perhaps Papa was right about my naivety after all.

On the first floor, an elevator dings, and Noah exits—broad, steady, lethal calm wrapped in civility. He gives me a curt nod before joining Brie, flipping through her photos like he's building a criminal case.

"And you didn't know about this room?" With his shaved head and dark beard, he reminds me of a bouncer at a high-end nightclub in Rome. Obviously, he's not the same man—based on what I recall from his profile from the initial briefing with KOAN, probably more lethal.

"No. I didn't." A bitter taste lingers on my tongue.

"Alright. We'll need to find the surveillance video of the hallway," he stops, and scans the ceiling. "Actually, we'll see if we can loop the surveillance video for all of today. Whoever's running this operation may check the video regularly for activity. If we're lucky, he hasn't already been alerted of activity, or if he has, he doesn't have remote access. We'll leave the footage of Adrien d'Avricourt and Brie." At this point, he's talking to himself, but he also seems to be talking to a speaker on his phone. "We'll set up our own surveillance. If we don't see anything within the next few days, we'll know they're on to us. But chances are, we're going to figure out quickly who within your organization is behind this."

"It's got to be Eddie. He's been here for eighteen years—since the original Sanctuary opened. There's no way he's not aware of that room. He has master access to everything, schedules all the security rotations, and..." I pause, the implications hitting me. "He's the one who briefed me on the 'closed circuit' surveillance system when I bought the place. He specifically told me nothing was stored." My hand balls into a fist at the realization I've been played this whole damn time. "Then, the question becomes, who's working with him, and I'd say at least some on the security team. As far as other teams, food and beverage, hospitality, marketing, custodial, I'd say they're less likely to be involved but you never know. Thinking it through, I should shut it down. There's too much at stake. I can't risk our members—" I have to stop talking. He gets the point.

"No. You can't stop anything," Noah insists.

Brie says, "Evidence leading to the guilty parties would evaporate overnight. I promise you, we'll figure out who within your company is involved, but the best way to do that is to monitor and catch them in the act. Plus, I'd like to remind you, there are other parties involved. Your organization is one source of information. There's a group out there buying and selling information. That's the group we're really after."

I could argue that point, but it would be pointless.

"Quinn and I are going to plant surveillance. How much time do we have?"

I run my fingers through my hair, thinking through Mondays from the past so I can answer Brie. Given I travel frequently and often work from my home office on Mondays, since the staff isn't here, I'm not a particularly reliable source of information. But I do know that the kitchen staff consists of a lot of night owls, and Eddie himself loves his days off and lives ninety minutes outside of the city on Long Island. He keeps a room here for when he chooses not to go home.

"It's unlikely anyone will stop in before noon. As the day goes on, the chances increase that someone in the neighborhood might swing by to check on something. But Monday is a pretty sacred day off, and Tuesday we don't open until evening service, so, chances are you're safe." Noah's staring at me like he's assessing how much he can trust me, and that's a fair reaction. "There's no guarantee," I say, pissed at myself for this situation. "I have staff with access on days off."

Brie steps closer to Noah, her voice dropping to a professional tone. "We'll need to clone their system architecture before we install our own monitoring. If they're sophisticated enough for this setup, they'll notice new hardware. I'm going to go join Quinn in the security room." She addresses me with a sharp, focused gaze and a crisp directive. "Why don't you go call Alicia to create a plan should this leak to your membership."

She's right. That's what I should do. Right after I console myself with my finest scotch. Jesus, Margot is going to rip me a new one.

"Alicia's your best bet. She knows what's going on, and you can't yet trust your existing marketing team."

Brie didn't need to state the obvious, but I'll grant her she's quite right.

"I'll be in my office," I say, meaning the room where I once thought success could be distilled like good scotch—aged, smooth, and utterly safe. "But don't leave without reconvening."

Yes, it sounds like I'm saying it to the team, but I'm speaking to the blonde beauty who slips easily into the mist.

As I watch her vanish into the elevator, a distasteful realization settles over me. The woman I searched for across Europe is now the one standing between me and professional ruin. Salvation or punishment—I can't yet tell which.

The doors slide closed and she's gone. A familiar ache resumes in my chest—the echo of her absence. Years ago, I thought losing her was the cost of fantasy. Now I'm beginning to understand she may be the price of truth.

CHAPTER
TEN

BRIE

Quinn taps away at the keyboard, her long, thick curls twisted up with a tortoiseshell comb that catches the fluorescent light with each head tilt. The mechanical clicking is rhythmic, almost meditative. She looks every bit like a newly minted assistant professor or grad student, and nothing like a hacker with the ability to break laws at whim.

The discovery of the server room sits foremost in my mind as I watch Quinn work. Someone has been systematically violating the trust of Adrien's members—and whether intentional or not, he's been complicit. The man who showed me genuine tenderness in Monaco has built his expansion on a foundation that's rotting from within. The realization burns —not because of the operation, but because Adrien believed in this place, and he'll feel betrayed when he realizes just how deep the decay runs.

Noah's in the basement, searching for places to install surveillance hardware that won't be noticed, and given the dim lighting, it's conceivable he'll be successful, but what Quinn's doing holds more promise.

"You're sure the loop won't flag?" I replay, reviewing my handiwork, searching for any telltale static where I've taped over the recorded surveillance tape, but given we're looping in still scenes, there's not much to catch us.

"Someone would have to study the files to pick it up. Typically surveillance isn't studied until after an incident, and if they're unaware of the incident, today's footage will probably get trashed. You said there are notations on files?"

Quinn hasn't left the security room since arriving in the building.

"And numerical notations that I assume are part of an organizational system."

"Right. So someone is going through the tapes and juicing it. Discarding the pulp I'd imagine. A bunch of recordings of no one being in the building is a fast discard."

I agree.

I'd imagine that in no more than forty-eight hours we'll have the visual and auditory evidence needed. Adrien can move quickly.

The senator's extortion is a symptom, not the disease. Someone's monetizing the secrets of the rich and powerful. A quiet marketplace hidden behind velvet ropes.

It's hardly surprising an enterprising individual wouldn't attempt to gather and sell information. Every government in the world has intelligence agencies dedicated to doing just that. But, for an employee to do this...whoever set this up didn't care about repercussions.

The bigger question is...how do they find the buyers? Handle the transaction?

Obviously, the senator is our client, and we want to find

the party responsible for his extortion, but Alicia has proof that this is bigger than one senator. My gut's telling me we've stumbled on an operation. The senator is being blackmailed over his vote on pending legislation, but someone with access to the secrets of the rich and powerful owns a goldmine. CEOs discussing mergers. Celebrities arranging NDAs. Foreign diplomats negotiating contracts. Every conversation in The Sanctuary is currency to the right buyer. For all his talk about privacy and pleasure, Adrien built a marketplace of secrets. Now it's consuming itself.

My phone lights up with an incoming text.

> HUDSON
> Status?

"Hudson wants to know our status."

"I'm sure he does," Quinn says.

That's an odd response. But then again, she's the one who works with him day in and day out down in the mountains.

"You two not getting along?"

Her fingers still on the keyboard, the only sign she heard me. I wait. She'll either tell me or she won't, but in my experience, silence is an excellent ally when wanting someone to open up. Her fingers resume tapping, and she says, "He's a lot."

"What does that mean" is on the tip of my tongue, but she's aware enough to know an explanation is needed.

"He's protective. Sometimes overly so." She glances at

me, a flash of something unguarded—fatigue? resentment?—before returning to the screen. "Reminds me why I prefer working alone."

In my experience with him, he's direct and no nonsense, but then again, she sees all his sides. He hadn't wanted her to come here today. Clearly, she needed to be here to effectively do her job, but maybe he finds her to be a lot too.

While I don't have a legion of close friends, mostly thanks to my joining the CIA and purposefully severing past relationships, I'm savvy enough to know that pointing out he might have the same opinion of her won't endear me to Quinn.

"Hudson sent you here because he trusts your skill, not because he wants you in danger," I say, testing the waters.

"Hudson sent me here because I'm the only one who can do this fast enough." She doesn't look up. "The trust part is...complicated."

I file that away. Team fractures are vulnerabilities—ones I'll need to navigate if this job extends beyond Adrien's club.

I glance at my phone: 12:47. We need to be gone before staff might drift in.

"Anything I can do to help?"

She twists in her seat, eyes squinted like I spoke to her in German.

"With what you're doing right now." I point to the basic black-and-white clock on the wall and say, "It's getting late. We want to be out of here by two."

"Oh." Her eyelids close and with a quick shake of her head, she turns back. "Right. I'll be done in just one sec."

I send a message to Hudson telling him we're almost done. As I'm tapping that out, a message from Hudson comes through.

. . .

HUDSON
Noah's going to Alicia Morgan's offices to do a security check. Can you loop back with Adrien? See if there's anything he's not telling us.

Interesting. It was pretty clear Adrien's broadsided by this, but maybe Hudson's worried he's keeping some secrets close to the vest.

ME
Sure

"What's the matter?" Quinn asks.

"Nothing. Why?"

"You sighed." My gaze lifts from my phone screen to the back of Quinn's head. "Noah said you and Adrien had history."

He did, did he?

"From a different life," I say, knowing that's all I need to say for Quinn to understand.

"Well, I suspect Adrien's part of this op will wrap up shortly. Unless you can convince him to let us keep pulling the thread."

She's right. "The problem with letting it run is that every day this continues, more members get compromised. But shut it down too early, and we lose our chance to identify the buyers. Adrien's caught between protecting his business and stopping a larger operation."

"There's no need for him to stress. We won't be able to monitor for long. Someone's going to catch on."

"How long do you think we have?"

"Based on the setup downstairs? This isn't amateur hour. Whoever's running this will notice any disruption quickly. Days, not weeks."

"He was thinking about shutting everything down today, and I talked him out of it."

"Keep talking him out of it." There's one last click of keys and the monitor screen shifts to black. "I'm done here. Let's go."

"How much footage are we talking about?" I ask. "I mean, how much are they gathering and keeping?"

"Based on the server capacity? Years worth. This operation has been running for a long time." Quinn frowns. "And the organizational system suggests multiple buyers. This isn't a one-off—it's a marketplace."

I stand, scanning the space one last time. "It does seem someone with an operation like this would set up their own monitoring system. I mean, when you do something like this, you've got to think to yourself that it's a matter of when, not if, you're going to get caught."

"You would think. But that's the addiction, right? Or maybe not addiction—*arrogance*. People who set up operations like this believe they're smarter than everyone else."

"A smart operator would recruit from the models with club access. Built-in cover, natural access to members."

Quinn pauses, thinking it through. "No. That's risky too. And one of them could tell someone they'd been recruited.

Technology. It's everywhere and so misunderstood. And it doesn't gossip."

She smiles like it's a wicked good thing.

"Maybe," I say, holding the door for her. "But in my experience, sexy delivers."

"Useful for some." Her tone is neutral, but the implication lands: *You're one of those people.*

I could tell her that most of my covers dress me *down*— that the best disguises are forgettable, that beauty is a tool I wield, not who I am. But Quinn's already down the corridor and explaining feels like proving something I don't owe her. The best disguises are forgettable, and when trashed, leave no semblance to the person beneath.

When we reach the bottom floor, taking care to follow the path of the looped surveillance footage, we exit the building. Adrien is waiting with Noah.

We each have our directives, and not much is said before we part ways, with Noah and Quinn heading off to get a cab on the avenue.

After they're out of sight, I turn to Adrien. "Are we going back to your office or…"

A black sedan pulls up to the curb and Adrien opens the back door.

"What's this? Where are we—"

"I'm sending you home. I'm not done for the day. My driver will take you."

"I could've gotten a cab with the others." I'm affronted, but the part of me that's most flustered is the part that will have to report back to my boss that I didn't get more from Adrien.

"Please. Do me this favor." I open my mouth to argue, but

he says, "I'd already asked the driver here and something came up. Take the car."

He sounds like he's managing a subordinate, and it grates. Three years ago, he opened doors because he wanted to, not because he was orchestrating logistics. Now everything between us is transactional.

"And we can meet up...for an early dinner?"

The question lands softer than his tone. There's something tentative in it—a crack in the executive veneer. For an instant, the yacht resurfaces—the gentle sway of the sea, the feel of silk against my skin, his touch. I blink, forcing the image away. Professional. Always professional.

My first instinct is to decline, to keep this clean and compartmentalized. But Hudson wants me to loop back, to probe for what Adrien might be holding close. And if I'm honest, part of me wants to say yes for reasons that have nothing to do with the job.

"Text me the address," I say, keeping my tone neutral. Professional.

As the sedan pulls away, I catch his reflection in the rearview. He's still standing there, watching. I look away first.

CHAPTER ELEVEN

ADRIEN

Instead of going back to my office, I head straight to the judge's chambers, riding in the back of the second car I ordered. The route to Foley Square is a slow grind of yellow lights and brake taps, giving me time to watch the blue dot on my phone slide uptown—north, then west.

Interesting. I would've pegged her for the Upper East Side—classic six, pre-war bones—but the West Side fits better. Less pedigree, more anonymity. I'd bet she runs at dawn when the park is empty and uncomplicated.

Minutes later, a text pings—a photo of Brie entering a building beneath a green canopy, a suited doorman holding the door. *Excellent.*

I'll charm the doorman, have him buzz her, learn her unit. Confirm that her name really is Brie Anderson. Even if I already know it is. Even if what I'm really confirming is that Monaco wasn't a fever dream.

Of course, this shouldn't matter. Not when my first independent venture might implode spectacularly. But obsession, like luxury, rarely answers to reason. We d'Avricourts excel at unreasonable.

Margot's name flashes on my screen. It's after dinner in Paris—she'll be on her second glass of Sancerre, antennae sharpened. She'll hear the strain in my voice within three words, and with Alicia Morgan's name already logged in her mental dossier, she'll extract every detail until I crack. I decline the call. Not today.

When I arrive at the courthouse, I take the concrete steps two by two, weaving through a mix of suits and those who've clearly decided impressing a judge is optional. On the right floor, I'm greeted by Canary, a young Black legal clerk with a bright, white smile.

"He's still in session," she says.

"No problem. I'll wait."

"I'm not sure you can—"

"Consider me the inconvenient husband."

Her brows lift, but she grins, playing along. "I'll look the other way, just this once. You want a soda?"

"A what?"

"I'm getting a Coke. Want anything?"

"I'm fine, thank you."

"If the phone rings, can you answer it?"

"My. I've gone from uninvited guest to trusted secretary."

"A notepad's by the phone. Answer with, 'Judge Brennan's office.'"

"Doesn't he have voicemail?"

"He does, but then I'd have to check it. Easier to read your handwriting."

The second I lower into his office chair, the tan phone rings. Naturally. I let it.

Closing my eyes, I exhale, still reeling from today's discovery.

On some level, I knew there was rot inside my walls. A bug, maybe. A single bad actor. But an entire enterprise? I shake my head. The cleaning crew must have seen something. Or maybe Eddie had help—from every department, every floor.

"Well, shit. Did someone die?"

I look up at Brennan in his robe, tie loosened, the picture of judicial fatigue.

"No. But I need to drink."

He checks his watch. "I have twenty minutes. Tops." He closes the blinds and retrieves two crystal glasses and a bottle of bourbon from a cabinet.

"That's fine," I say, though he pours anyway—one full glass for me, a symbolic taste for himself—and props against the desk.

"What's up? No death, no injury... Betrayal, then?"

I think of Eddie. Didn't know him well but drank with him once or twice. Never thought he'd fuck me over. "Something like that." I stare into the amber liquid. "Ever trust someone completely? Build something on that trust, only to find out they've been bleeding you the entire time?"

Brennan leans back. "Is this about your Monaco obsession? Or the meeting Margot insisted you take?"

"Both, maybe. That meeting Margot insisted I take, with Alicia Morgan? It's confirmed. An employee's stabbing me in the back. Selling member data." Data is the polite word. The real one is leverage.

"Ah. Hence the crisis communications firm called in–the, ah, data as you call it–leaked?"

"Not yet." I admit, swirling my drink. "Extortion."

"Oof. And the woman? Monaco?" I told Tommy she'd surfaced–a decision I might come to regret.

"No progress." Lie by omission. Progress exists… just not the kind I'm confessing yet.

"Well," he says, raising his glass, "at least you can fire one of your problems."

"Hmm. And I will."

He studies me as he takes a slow sip. Brennan always did see too clearly. "Not much rattles you. What is it with this long-lost lover?"

Not lost anymore. I finally know where she lives—or soon will.

"Margot and I both agree she threw you for a loop with that vanishing game."

"She left. Didn't leave a way to reach her. There's no game in that."

"True. More than one girl in college did that to me. Or if I had her number, she didn't answer."

"It's called ghosting."

He smirks. Brennan knows perfectly well, but this is his way of easing the blow. "Why were you talking to Margot?"

"She said you hadn't answered her calls. She's worried."

"Duly noted."

He sniffs his bourbon. "Want to meet up later? You pick the place."

"No. If things go well, I'll already have dinner plans."

"Monaco?"

"If you want to call her that." I drain my glass. "Yes."

When I open his office door, Canary spins in her chair. "I gave you one job."

Brennan laughs. "This is not the man to give a job to, Canary."

He means it as a joke; it still cuts. Maybe that's why Eddie thought he could build a hidden room under my nose—because everyone assumes I only manage surfaces.

Outside, I debate where to go. My thumb opens the Uber app before I've decided. Two minutes later, I'm in the back of a Fisker Ocean, the driver tapping the wheel to a song I don't recognize.

Crosstown traffic crawls, Manhattan's arteries clogged with ambition. Nearly an hour later, I step out across from the green awning.

The doorman appears before I reach the steps. Red beard, thinning hair, polite wariness. "How can I help you, sir?"

"I'm here to see Brie Anderson."

He stiffens. His eyes travel from my face to my Brunello Cucinellis, calculating. Wealthy men show up at buildings like this all the time—some invited, some not.

"Sorry, sir. No one here by that name."

He's lying, of course. The pause before "sorry" gave him away. Whether Brie trained him or he's just protective, I can't tell.

I pull out my phone, showing him the photo—the one taken not thirty minutes ago.

"Do you recognize this woman?"

His lips twitch, like he's in on a private joke. "She doesn't live here, sir."

"Do you—"

"I'll need to ask you to leave."

Right.

I obey, because I plan to play the long game.

I locate an acceptable bistro—exposed brick, floor-to-ceiling windows, authenticity by design—and order an espresso I don't want.

> Decoy address. Nicely done. I'm at Joe Coffee. Join me or I'll assume you're avoiding me.

Perhaps I shouldn't put this in writing. But it's done.

I check my phone with the grim persistence of someone who isn't used to being ignored. Nothing.

Twenty minutes later, I'm debating whether persistence makes me romantic or unhinged when she appears outside the window.

Brie.

She scans the room, finds me. That flicker—annoyance? resignation?—crosses her face, but she comes in anyway. She's traded her work clothes for dark jeans and a cream cashmere sweater—simple, but exquisite. Her hair catches the light like spun gold. Conversations stall; heads turn.

She slides into the chair opposite me, every movement deliberate, fluid, composed. Her knee brushes mine under the table as she settles. Accidental. Still, my body reacts like it's a signal.

"You followed me."

"No. My driver reported your location," I correct. "There's a distinction." Even as I say it, I hear the rationalization.

"Is there?" She gestures to the waitress. "Mint tea, if you have it."

The waitress retreats. Silence hums between us with the unpleasantness of static.

"The doorman was very polite," I say. "Clearly trained to protect your privacy."

"People in my line of work value privacy."

"So do people in mine." I let out a low laugh. "Though I'm learning I'm not particularly good at protecting it."

Her expression softens. "What you discovered today—it's not your fault."

"Isn't it? I own the building. I hired the staff. I trusted the wrong people." I pause. "Trust is the one currency I've always spent too freely—investors, partners, lovers. Each promising permanence; each eventually selling the illusion back to me."

"You've been running a legitimate business," she says gently. "Someone else had a side hustle."

The server returns with tea. Brie wraps her hands around the cup, drawing warmth from it. Her sleeves ride back an inch. A bare strip of wrist. Ridiculous that something that small can feel obscene. Her fingers—long, elegant, ringless—stir memories: her touch, her music, her breath against my skin.

"You could've asked where I lived," she says.

"Would you have told me?"

"Probably not," she admits. "But asking is more civilized."

"Then asking my driver was necessary."

"It was invasive."

"Brie, I need to know—how much of what happened between us was real?"

She sets down her cup with surgical precision, the china clinking against the saucer like punctuation. "Does it matter?"

"It matters to me—more than it should." My voice comes out rough, with more emotion than I care to let on, but that doesn't hinder me. "Because if it wasn't real for you, I've been grieving a woman who never existed. And I need to know if I'm unhinged or just...unlucky."

"You're surrounded by beautiful women who probably fawn over you. You have everything you want in spades."

"Do I?" I gesture to the window. "I searched for a woman who didn't exist. Dated others. Each one felt like a counterfeit."

"That's dramatic. We had a weekend."

"I had hope."

And I didn't know hope could bruise like this.

"You're not that good an actress, Brie. Why vanish? Why stay gone?"

She studies me, long and measured. "What did you see when you looked at me?"

"Freedom," I answer before I can edit myself. "You moved through that world like you belonged but weren't bound by it. Everyone else at those parties—including me—we were performing. You were *playing*. Like you knew the rules but refused to be impressed by them." I lean forward. "And when you played piano, you stopped hiding. That's when I knew—whatever name you gave me, whoever you were pretending to be, whatever you claim—*that* was real."

Her lips purse, faintly. "But I was playing a role."

"Were you? When you listened to me share things I hadn't told anyone? When you fell asleep with your head on my chest? Or when you left without saying goodbye because goodbye might've hurt?"

Color drains from her face.

Bull's-eye, and I hate that it feels like one.

She looks down at her tea, and for three seconds—maybe five—she doesn't move. When she speaks, her voice is quieter. "You don't know what you're talking about."

"Don't I?" I keep my tone gentle, not triumphant. "You left because staying would've meant something. And you couldn't afford for it to mean something."

Her jaw tightens. I've crossed a line, but I'm not backing down.

"I know you feel it too," I say softly. "It didn't die when you disappeared."

She looks out the window. "Feeling something and acting on it are different things."

"Are they? You could've ignored my text. You didn't."

"I came because you're a client."

"Bullshit."

I regret the volume the second it leaves my mouth. Not the truth—just the force.

Heads turn at nearby tables. An older woman in pearls raises an eyebrow. I lean closer, dropping my voice. This isn't a scene I want to make with her. "You came because this isn't finished. And you know it."

Her gaze flicks up—unguarded, vulnerable, real—for just a breath.

"What do you want from me?" she whispers.

"Everything," I say. "Starting with the truth. You. Whatever that looks like now."

"You want a fantasy." She straightens, composure snapping back. "You want the woman who never existed."

"I want the woman sitting in front of me. The one who can pick a lock in thirty seconds and still drink mint tea like it's an art form. I want her not as an escape, as an answer."

Silence stretches, heavy with risky possibility.

Finally, she stands, leaving bills on the table.

"I live six blocks from here," she says quietly. "If you

want to walk me home, that's your choice. But you're not coming in."

The boundary should cool me off. It doesn't. It makes everything sharper. "I'll walk you."

Outside, the October air smells of rain and rusted leaves. A few streetlights blink on early, amber halos cutting through the late-afternoon haze. We fall into step too easily—close enough that I catch her warmth through the wool of her sweater, close enough that one wrong swing of my hand would be contact.

"You really searched for me for six months?" she asks.

"Six months actively. Three years mentally."

"That's…" she exhales. "Romantic."

"Foolish," I counter.

"Foolish," she agrees softly. "But romantic."

"I don't do things halfway."

"I've noticed."

We pass a park where an old man feeds pigeons, the birds trusting his consistency.

"What happened to Sophie Dubois?" I ask.

"She was retired. Exposed."

"But the art knowledge—the piano—that was real."

"The best covers are built on truth."

"And the worst lies," I murmur, "on omission."

Her glance holds reluctant respect. "You're more perceptive than I expected."

"Why? Because I'm wealthy?"

"Because you're a man."

Fair. "Tell me about your real life."

"There's not much to tell. I work. I train. I read. Sometimes I play piano."

"Lonely?"

"Productive."

"You ever miss it?" I ask. "The life you had as Sophie Dubois?"

"Sometimes." She's quiet for half a block. "Not the lying. But the...fluidity. Being able to slip into a room and become whoever was needed. In truth, I still have that from time to time, depending on the assignment."

"That's not so different from what I do," I say. "Every investor meeting, every club opening—I'm performing too."

She glances at me, something like recognition in her eyes. "The difference is you believe your performance. I never do."

"Maybe that's why you're better at it."

We reach her building—prewar brick, elegant in its restraint. No doorman here. Just quiet authenticity.

"This is me," she says simply.

She's one step above me—just enough height that I have to tilt my head to meet her eyes. Just enough distance to keep me civilized. "Thank you. For trusting me with that."

"Don't read too much into it."

But I do.

Every choice she's made today means something.

"Brie," I say, her name tasting different in the city bustle. "Whatever happens with the investigation—finding you again feels like the first good thing in years."

Her expression softens; conflict etched in the glow of the afternoon sun.

"I have to go," she says, not moving.

"Breakfast?"

"Office," she counters. "You're buying time."

"I'm the client."

She exhales, gaze dropping. "This can't happen again."

"Why?"

"Because it can't. Tomorrow, we're back to being professional."

"I can be professional when required."

"You're at my residence—that's not professional."

I nod, though I'm not convinced.

She starts up the steps, then pauses. "For what it's worth," she says softly, "that weekend was real. But that's all it was, and all it can be."

"Why? Are you married?"

She lifts her head, startled. "No. If I were, we wouldn't have happened. I'm not what you want, Adrien. And you're not what I want."

It's astonishing, the precision with which she can unmake me—one sentence, scalpel-sharp.

"We're not good for each other."

Then she's gone, the door closing with a soft, final click.

I stand on the sidewalk longer than is reasonable, scanning windows. Third floor, maybe fourth—I don't even know which apartment is hers. But I watch anyway, like some Victorian suitor waiting for a candle in the window.

The building keeps its secrets. So does she.

But she told me the truth about Monaco. And she let me walk her home. And those two things—small as they are—feel like hope.

When I finally hail a cab, the city glows around me—gold reflected off wet pavement, the last sunlight mirrored in glass. I carry the image of her face in that afternoon light, the one true thing in a world built on shine.

It's not much.

But it's a beginning.

CHAPTER
TWELVE

BRIE

> **QUINN**
> You there?

Quinn's message pulls me away from the romance novel I've been pretending to read for the past hour—some billionaire-meets-spy nonsense that hits uncomfortably close to home. Outside the window, the maple wedged between my building and the street tosses yellowed leaves into the wind.

> **ME**
> Yes. Should I log into the portal?

My socked feet pad across the aged wooden floor to my desk, where I bring my laptop to life. The phone rings, showing Quinn's name, and I answer, setting the phone to speaker.

"You're going to want to see this," Quinn says. "You were right. Didn't take long to solve this mystery."

I'm in the portal, but the video feed hasn't loaded. My fingers hover over the keyboard, waiting.

"Where am I looking?"

A message pops up with a link, and I click it. The window that opens is of a direct feed to the corridor with the server room. The timestamp is from six minutes earlier.

I watch as Edward Thorne—Eddie—taps the glass. His head turns, as if looking down the hall. He's in a dark suit coat and trousers, and a three-button golf shirt. The door slides open, and he steps in. The door seals behind him.

"So he's inside," I say. "What's he doing now?" I check the time: 1:36 p.m., Tuesday. The Sanctuary is closed to members; the kitchen crew should be prepping for dinner service. "Is security on site?"

"No. Security isn't scheduled to arrive until four."

That tracks. The manual says that security arrives an hour before guests to run through standard checks. The first member can arrive as early as five, when the club reopens for the week. On Tuesday evening, the club is partially open, with only one restaurant, one bar, and the spa by appointment only.

A message pops up on screen, and I click the link. The pop-up window shows him at the desk.

"Can you see what files he's accessing?"

"So far he hasn't logged into anything. It's like he's using this room as his office."

"It wasn't soundproof, was it?"

"Cinderblock walls. Probably not technically soundproof, but he likely considers it a safer space to have a conversation than his office."

"His office is in the building across the street, on the same hall as Adrien's, right?"

"Yes, but it's my understanding he doesn't use that office much."

"I suppose it makes sense. Plus, he splits his time between Miami and New York."

"According to flight logs, about a quarter of his time is in Miami, but that's mostly in January and February, with a few short trips the rest of the year."

"Convenient schedule for someone running a side operation," I murmur, scanning the file I've compiled on Thorne. "He's got three kids. One daughter and two sons. Wonder what his wife thinks about his 'travel'. He spends several days at The Sanctuary, too."

"He's probably not up for family man of the year. Think about where he works."

She's not wrong. And that's another reason to support my decision to keep things professional with Adrien. Eddie works at The Sanctuary, but Adrien owns it. He's surrounded by temptation constantly. His life has evolved since we spent a weekend together. As has mine.

Eddie's on his phone, tapping away, not even using the computer.

"We have audio, right?" I ask.

"We do. But he hasn't spoken to anyone."

"Regardless, he's involved."

"If you trust d'Avricourt."

"He's not lying about this. It's eating at him." I study the man on screen. He's got trimmed, dark hair, longer on top with a gelled flip near the brow, and a curved line, a partial tattoo, climbing from beneath his shirt collar up the nape of his neck.

"Long Island. Do you think he's mafia?"

Everything on Eddie's records looks legit. North Shore money or connected? He's had steady employment for eighteen years, but a sex club that doubles as a high-end society club…a mafia connection feels likely. And those guys are some of the original extortionists.

"It's possible. It's a lot more challenging to draw those connections these days."

"Why do you say that?" Quinn asks.

In the CIA, we had files on all the organized crime families the world over. "It's not like they get together every Sunday for family dinner anymore. And crime has advanced. Organized crime isn't limited to drugs or human trafficking these days. Plus, most organized criminal organizations derive a significant percentage of revenue from legitimate, legal business enterprises." I bite the corner of my nail, watching the back of Eddie's head. "I suppose he wouldn't even have to be part of an organized crime family. He could be doing a favor for a cousin or something."

"If he doesn't do anything but sit there and mess with his phone, it's going to take us a while to figure out who he's working with."

"Maybe," I say, clicking my nails against the top of my desk. "We're going to need to tail this guy. See where he goes when he leaves the club." That familiar weight settles in my stomach—the recognition that we're looking at weeks, not days. "If he's selling the intel, we may not see him move until an order comes in. Shit. This could take a while."

"There's no action right now. Nothing for him to record.

Maybe we'll get a better sense of what he's doing when there's activity in the club."

That's true. The only thing we could possibly see him do on an off-day is bookkeeping. "On the bright side, he doesn't seem suspicious that anyone's been in his space."

"No. But if he's been doing this for years, then...we'd have to do something stupid like leave trash in the trash can."

"Was there a trash can in that room?" I think back over the room. I remember it was clean...

"No. I'm just saying figuratively..."

"Yeah. Well, he's not the only employee who knows about that room. One, he's not a tech guy, so he didn't install everything. And two, it's clean."

"Cleaning it doesn't mean you know what it is you're cleaning."

"Do you think he's working alone?"

"No. Probably not."

I'm back to tapping my nails on the table.

"Do you want to brief Adrien or should Hudson?"

"Hudson's in the loop?" It just occurred to me he's not on the line.

"Not yet. He had a meeting with the owners this morning."

"The owner... You mean KOAN's owners?"

"Very ones."

"Do you know when he'll be back?"

"He does not report to me."

"Right, but you can reach out to him."

"If you don't want day-to-day with the client, tell Hudson."

"That's not—" I catch myself. This isn't about avoiding Adrien.

I should shut it down. His words from yesterday come out of nowhere, playing on the audio in my mind.

If he shuts The Sanctuary down, we get nowhere. And something tells me a guy like Eddie isn't going to talk if we let the feds take him in—especially if he's organized crime.

"I'll go visit Adrien. It's better if I tell him in person."

"If I were you, I'd tell him out of the office."

"Why?" But even as I ask, the answer clicks into place. "In case Eddie's listening in on his office. But we swept for bugs yesterday. And Adrien said that security checks…"

A security team that we don't yet know is trustworthy.

Judging by Eddie's behavior at the moment, even if he bugs Adrien's office from time to time, nothing has piqued his suspicion yet that anyone's onto him.

"I'll have Adrien meet me outside of the office."

"Sounds good to me," she says.

"After I meet with Adrien, update him, and confirm he'll let us play this out, I'll reach out to Hudson and create a plan for surveilling this guy. Oh, and text me if you learn anything. You know, if he decides to do something other than play with his phone."

After the call ends with Quinn, I call the number I have for Adrien, using my personal cell, which means he'll now have my number. But, given I allowed him to learn where I live, my unlisted cell number is no biggie. After all, it's easy to change a cell number, but it's annoying to move.

He answers on the third ring.

"This is Adrien d'Avricourt."

"This is Brie."

"I thought so. Otherwise I never answer an unknown. If

you're calling to invite me to dinner, name the date, place, and time."

"I'm actually..." The sigh that escapes is one of frustration, because he's not treating this as a professional interaction, and what I'm about to say is going to make that situation worse. "Would you be up for a walk in the park?"

There's a pause—I can practically hear him recalibrating. Yesterday I let him walk me home; now I'm creating distance again.

"Shall I meet you at your place?"

Of course he'd push. "Columbus Circle. By the fountain."

"When?"

Knowing he's going to insist on taking a car, I estimate the travel time on clogged city streets. "Thirty minutes?"

"Heading out now."

I arrive at the Circle ten minutes early and scout the scene. The usual horse-drawn carriages are lined up down the street across from the park-facing apartment buildings and hotels. An artist sells his work, but judging from his easily moveable stand, I'd guess he's lacking the required permits.

Residents speed by at quick clips, while tourists hold out phones, either to take photos or to check for directions. A police officer on a bicycle passes and turns onto the black asphalt path that leads into the park. Leaves scatter across the ground, and the sweet smell of sugared almonds from the nearby street vendor mixes with the faint scent of exhaust and horse manure.

Waiting for him, a memory ambushes me—not linear, but sensory fragments that refuse to stay buried.

The yacht deck at dawn, cool against my bare back. Salt air mixing with his sandalwood cologne. His voice, rough with desire. "You're fucking gorgeous when you come."

The way he'd watched me afterward—not like a conquest, but like I'd surprised him.

Later, in his cabin, silk sheets that smelled like him. My hands trembling as I reached for his belt—not performance, just want. The shock of that: actually wanting someone while undercover.

"I'm going to do everything I can to ensure you never forget me."

He'd said it like a promise, and I'd let myself believe it for exactly one night.

His fingers in my hair, his voice commanding: "Don't belittle this." The way he'd taken me apart with a precision that felt like devotion. That impossible fullness, his body over mine, his breath hot against my neck.

And afterward—the part that broke me—when he traced patterns on my shoulder and asked, "Tell me something true."

Drowsy and unguarded, I'd whispered, "I've never felt anything like this before—it's unsettling."

His arm had tightened around me. "Good. Then I'm not alone in that."

Even then, I'd known: whatever came next would require me to leave him behind.

The wind knifes through the city, dragging me back to now, cutting through my sweater and sending dried brown leaves scattering across the sidewalk. I step back, aiming to distance myself from the street, and bump into a hard, firm chest. On instinct, my arm bends, elbow poised—then the familiar hint of sandalwood reaches me, and my muscles relax into recognition.

"No coat?" He's shrugging out of his black trench—cashmere-lined, probably costs more than my rent.

"I'm fine." But he's already draping it over my shoulders, his hands lingering just a second too long at my collar.

The lining is still warm, the weight of it unmistakably his. I should shrug it off. Instead, I pull it tighter.

"Better?" His voice is low, intimate despite the public setting.

"We're supposed to be professional."

"And I'm professionally concerned about hypothermia." The corner of his mouth lifts. "Humor me."

The hustle and bustle of the city slips away, and the wind's chill is replaced with a buzzing warmth. I clear my throat, stepping back, and gesture to the path that leads into the park.

"I have news."

He quickly matches my stride, and I wait until we're far past the fountain, and in a section with no one too close to speak. Watching him closely, I say, "Eddie Thorne entered the server room."

His jaw flexes slightly, barely noticeable beneath his trimmed beard, and his thick lashes flicker for the briefest of seconds. "Did you uncover what he's doing? Who he's selling to?"

"The only thing we know for certain is he's sitting in the server room. He hasn't accessed anything."

Adrien's Adam's apple shifts as he swallows. He waits until a jogger approaching passes, and says, "I need to shut it down."

"Please don't."

The words may have come out too quickly, but if he pulls the plug, we lose the thread. From what we've seen, Eddie is a professional, and there won't be any clues or trails to follow once we take the server room out.

We walk for about a block in silence. I steal sideways glances and almost always meet his gaze, but when he's not watching me, I sense he's deep in thought.

"If I let this continue, I could lose everything."

I'm prepared for this. "If you don't have answers, you'll never regain the trust of your membership. There will always be questions."

"You'll stay on the project?"

My assumption had been I would continue, but as he asks the question, there's a part of me that recognizes this is an ideal juncture to step back, to slip away, to move onto the next assignment, and to let the KOAN team follow this lead.

It would be easier to walk away. It always is. But I don't move.

"To be clear, the only way I continue with your team is if you stay on the project."

"Is that wise?" The question doesn't come from a place of professionalism. No, it's me being real with him, and possibly speaking my thoughts out loud.

"Wise or not, it's the only way. Otherwise, I fire Eddie, clear the servers, and never look back."

"If you do that, you'll never know who else is working with him."

"Oh, I'll clean house. Entirely new staff. Send a notice to the membership that there's been an issue. Alicia's connected me with a private consultant to handle the hiring and vetting."

"You've been busy."

"I've been preparing."

"This is bigger than you. We already know of one other

client being blackmailed, and it's not with information from your club."

"These are the kind of projects you work on now? In the private sector?"

"Yes," I answer.

"It's important to you?"

"It's worth pursuing. Look at what the senator's being blackmailed with. Don't you think that's a lead worth following? Learning who out there thinks they can buy legislation? Possibly government contracts?"

He stops. I turn to face him.

"I'll leave the servers," he says. "Two conditions."

"Name them."

"You stay on the team." His eyes hold mine, and there's something raw in them—not manipulation, but genuine need. "And you have dinner with me. Tomorrow night."

"That's—"

"Non-negotiable." He steps closer, voice dropping. "You asked me to keep the servers running. I'm asking you to have dinner with me. Fair trade."

The wind lifts, scattering leaves like paper confetti. I should say no. Keep it professional.

"Deal."

CHAPTER
THIRTEEN

ADRIEN

"Will that be all, Adrien?"

The table is set the way I want the night to feel—close. Low candles, crystal that catches the city's light, the plates near enough that reaching for her hand will never look like a reach. The lamb Maria tucked into the oven perfumes the room with rosemary and promise, ready for me to retrieve. The dining room was too performative. The Sanctuary's restaurant, too public. I want her here.

Not only am I hoping she stays the night, but I'm also hoping that by inviting her to a place I typically don't invite women, she'll open up to me, perhaps be more open to inviting me into her space.

Why?

Because I want to know her. Is sex part of it? Without doubt. But it's not all of it. I have questions I want answered. Doubts I want resolved.

"Adrien?" Maria lowers her coat, and I wave her on her way.

"It's perfect, Maria." I scan the setting one more time. "At least…if a man invited you over and he had this set up… Should I get her flowers?"

Maria's grin spreads far too wide, and as she holds her coat against her chest, the odd sensation strikes that she might reach out and pull me into a hug.

"Whoever this lucky woman is, she's going to love it. And flowers…" She lifts her shoulders and her lips pinch. "She's coming to your place. But if you want, I can go to the florist—"

"Get out of here. I'm good. What time is your train?"

Maria has been working for me for almost two years, but she worked for the prior tenant for almost fifteen. I inherited Maria when I purchased the condo. We've been slowly getting to know each other, and while I haven't yet met her family, I'm aware she commutes through Penn Station. "This time of day, they leave regularly. You're good?" she asks, but she's already stepping back in the direction of the door.

I surprised her when I arrived home this afternoon and asked her to stop cleaning the library and to instead spend her time preparing dinner for a guest.

Could I have ordered in? Yes, but take-away doesn't feel as intimate as home-cooked. Could I have cooked? Yes, but the likelihood that the result wouldn't be palatable is too high. Plus, I'm not sure where Maria keeps the fine china and crystal, but it sets a warmer tone than the black everyday china I use.

My phone vibrates and I pull it out of my trouser pocket, and when I look up from reading my sister's name, it's in time to see Maria waving as she steps through the kitchen into the hallway that leads to the foyer.

I smile and nod, and answer the phone with, "Margot."

"Finally," she says. "Have you been avoiding me?"

"No. I've been busy."

"You're lying."

"Why do you say that?"

"Because Tommy told me you had something going on and you'd tell me when you're ready."

The bastard. "Those things have made me busy."

"Is your sex club about to get bad press?"

Direct and to the point and also making it clear her concern is for the family business and not me. "It's not a sex club."

I love my sister, but damn if she can't be just as infuriating as our parents.

"If there's some exposé coming, it'll hit d'Avricourt Luxe. Your business may not be affiliated, but the distinction will not be clear in the papers. Dad will—"

"Margot. There's no exposé. I had an employee who was... Well, he's a traitor. I'm taking care of it. That's all."

"Oh. Do you have someone in human resources? I can send—"

"I'm good. Alicia Morgan is helping me handle it all, actually."

"Ah. So that's what she wanted with you. But it's all under control now?"

"Yes." I pointedly breathe heavily into the phone, letting my sister know she's fraying my nerves. But, the truth is, while I want her out of my business, she's right to ask. "If anything comes of this, I'll give you a heads up."

"With Alicia on it, you should be fine."

"That's what I hear." Alicia is the older sister of one of Margot's besties, and I swear she's adored her for as long as I can remember. But, even without Margot's connection, I would've heard of Alicia Morgan. She's known as a fixer, and we share clientele.

"How are you doing?" I move into the living area and sink onto the couch, sitting where I will be certain to hear if the doorman buzzes.

"I'm fine."

"And our parents?"

"Have you not spoken with them?"

There's judgment in her tone, but I let my silence serve as answer.

"They're good. In Greece at the moment. Staying with friends."

"Dad's really stepped away then?" I never thought he'd actually retire. He sure as hell didn't show any sign of willingly walking away when he wanted me to take over. Of course, I never wanted to run the family business. But it's annoying that now that he finally allowed Margot at the helm he's truly stepped away.

"His vacations get longer. I'm a little worried about Mom and I think he is too."

"What's wrong with Mom?"

"Some odd symptoms here and there. The doctors say it's stress."

"Hence the regular visits to islands?"

"It's my theory."

"What symptoms—" I'm interrupted by the loud buzz. I set the intercom to the max level so I'd be sure to hear.

"What's that?"

"Someone's here. I need to run. But Mom—"

"She's fine. Don't let it worry you. You go. I need to run too."

"Isn't it late there?"

"Yes, and I'm still in the office. I'm starving. I want to get out before the cafes close."

"Go. I'll call you tomorrow."

"Yeah, I think I've heard that one before."

"Bye, Margot."

The line clicks, and I look at the phone, finding it odd she didn't say goodbye. But then the buzzer sounds once more, and since I'm right in front of it, it's particularly loud.

I press the button. "Yes."

"Mr. d'Avricourt, there's a Ms. Anderson here to see you."

"Please send her up." I lower the volume to its lowest setting on the speaker, then move to open the door and wait, watching the numbers on the display above the elevator.

The doors slide open, and there she is.

Her long blonde hair falls in relaxed waves, and she's in a mid-length champagne skirt and heeled boots with a champagne blouse. The soft slide of her boots over marble carries through the entryway, each step measured but confident.

She's changed since I saw her earlier, and knowing she changed for dinner, refreshed her makeup, even going so far as to apply a floral fragrance, gives me hope for the night. I also wonder…does she remember I told her I love her in skirts? Earlier, she was in a sweater with jeans and sneakers. And she, as always, looked lovely, but this…

She steps past me, through the doorway.

"You look beautiful."

She lifts a bottle of wine and passes it to me. "Thank you for having me for dinner."

The door closes behind me with a click that echoes down the hallway.

"Thank you for coming." She steps to the side, waiting for me to lead the way, because she's never been here before.

"The Sanctuary might have made more sense," she says, those blue eyes glimmering with something…amusement, intrigue? Interest?

"I wanted you here, in my space," I say, being as honest with her as I am with anyone. "Shall we? Would you like a glass of wine?"

"A glass of wine would be lovely."

"You're very formal tonight," I say, meaning it as a tease.

"Well…I agreed to dinner, but it doesn't change the fact one weekend doesn't mean we know each other well, and—"

"Be prepared for questions. I want to change that." She's behind me, following me into the kitchen.

"And you're also a client."

I set the wine she brought on the counter and the glass clinks on the marble. "Come now. Let's not pretend the unofficial group you're working with cares about corporate guidelines."

I open the drawers until I locate the wine opener.

"Nothing more happened since yesterday, by the way. He's not in the server room. He seems to be overseeing the dinner service, but if we were there, we could keep a closer eye on him."

"Perhaps tomorrow night I'll take you to dinner in The Blue Room." Her right eye squints, and I answer before she can ask. "It's the name of one of the restaurants within The Sanctuary."

"The Blue Room," she repeats, accepting the glass of wine

I pour. "Let me guess—blue velvet banquettes and mood lighting?"

"Actually, it's named for the Picasso blue period piece on the wall. The décor is more understated." I gesture toward the kitchen table. "But tonight, I prefer this."

She settles into the chair I hold out for her, and I catch another hint of that floral scent—jasmine, maybe gardenia. Something that reminds me of Monaco nights. Of course, everything about her reminds me of those nights.

"This is lovely," she says, taking in the candles, the view, the careful table arrangement. "You didn't have to go to this trouble."

"It wasn't trouble. Maria did most of the work." I pour wine into my own glass, then move to retrieve dinner from the oven. "Lamb with rosemary, roasted vegetables, and something she called 'proper potatoes'—though I'm not sure what makes them more proper than regular potatoes."

A smile tugs at the corner of her mouth. "Proper potatoes are usually roasted with duck fat and herbs. Very British."

"How do you know that?"

"My mother. She lived in London for two years when she was with the State Department. She came back with strong opinions about proper cooking methods."

"That's interesting. Maria's not British."

"Is she your cook?"

"Yes. House manager. Cooks a couple of meals a week. I eat out mostly."

I serve the plates, pleased when she takes an appreciative bite. "Tell me about your parents. The truth this time."

"Military family. Dad's a retired Marine colonel, Mom was a translator before she became a full-time military wife." She swirls her wine, considering. "We moved every few years. I went to high school in three different countries."

"That explains the adaptability."

"And the language skills." She meets my eyes. "What about you? Besides the obvious luxury empire inheritance."

I lean back slightly. "You mean the notoriety I spent most of my twenties trying to escape."

"Is that why you bought the club?"

"Partly. I wanted to prove I could build something independently." I take a sip of wine, studying her face in the candlelight. "What I didn't expect was to care so much about protecting it."

"Or the people who trust you with their privacy."

"Exactly." The relief she still understands me hits deep. "Most people see The Sanctuary and assume it's all about wealth and excess. But privacy—real privacy—is something money usually can't buy."

"And someone violated that."

"Someone I trusted." The betrayal still stings. "Eddie's been with the club since before I owned it. I thought loyalty came with tenure. Obviously, I was wrong."

"Loyalty has to be earned, not assumed." She sets down her fork. "In the CIA, we learned that people's motivations change. What drives someone one year might be completely different the next."

"What drove you to leave?"

The question hangs between us. She's quiet for a long moment, fingers tracing the stem of her wine glass.

"I got tired of becoming other people," she says finally. "Every assignment required a new identity, a new personality. After a while, I wasn't sure which parts of me were real anymore."

"And now?"

"Now I get to be myself while still doing work that matters." She glances around the kitchen, taking in the details—the appliances, the artwork, the view. "This is very you."

"How can you tell? You barely know me." I'm tossing her words back at her, if anything as a tease, because I don't buy it. The intensity we shared over our weekend together doesn't happen without getting to know the important parts.

"I know more than you think." Her eyes return to mine. "Your art—you prefer modern pieces that make you think. They feed the image you cultivate; traditional works risk conveying age. The kitchen setup—you entertain, but intimately, not for show. The books I glimpsed in your living room—history, philosophy, some fiction. You're more substantive than your reputation suggests."

"What else do you see?"

"You're lonely." The words are soft but direct. "All this success, this enterprise you're building, your bed is likely often filled, but I'm guessing you eat breakfast alone most mornings."

The accuracy of her observation stuns. "And you?" The idea of her bed being filled regularly delivers a surge of undeserved jealousy.

"Lonely? Usually. But it's my choice."

"Is it?"

She considers this, taking another sip of wine. "Absolutely. The CIA practically demands it. I knew what I was getting into. I welcomed the independence. Honing my compartmentalization skills."

"What changed?"

"I met someone who made me remember what connection felt like." Her gaze doesn't waver. "Don't read into that. You've been honest with me, so I'm being honest with you. I spent two years convincing myself the career was worth it."

"But it wasn't."

"A friend suggested there might be a better situation. I became disenchanted with the leadership within the CIA. I still value my independence—highly. I don't need to be with anyone. Lonely implies something's wrong with me, and that's not the case. I'm happy. But I might have taken the compartmentalization to an unhealthy level."

I reach across the table, covering her hand with mine.

"Brie." Her name feels different now, more real than the alias Sophie, a lovely name, but I prefer the honest version. "What happens when this investigation is over?"

"I don't know." Her fingers turn under mine, palm to palm. "I've never mixed personal and professional before."

"And I've never invited a woman into this condo before. In fact, I've never felt like this about another woman."

"Like what?"

"Like I'd risk everything just to get to know you better." The confession surprises me with its intensity—and the truth of it.

"Get to know me?" Her lips curve into a smile, like she's doubting my veracity.

"I won't pretend I've been celibate. But no one was you. The way you taste, the way your breath breaks when—"

"I get the point."

"Do you?"

"I'm the first woman who walked away."

"Don't do that," I say, tightening my grip on her hand while fighting the urge to pull her onto my lap or no, to tug her like a caveman back to my bedroom.

"Don't what?"

"Minimize what I'm saying. Compartmentalizing is another word for constructing walls. Don't do that."

Outside the windows, signs of life abound with golden lights turning on and off, but here in this kitchen, with candles flickering between us and her hand in mine, everything else fades into oblivion. The crystal glasses catch the candlelight the way she once caught me—unexpectedly, irrevocably.

"Stay tonight," I say—not as an invitation but as a plea.

"Adrien—"

"Not for sex. Though I won't pretend I don't want that." I stroke my thumb across her knuckles. "Stay because I want to wake up knowing you're safe. Stay because I've spent years wondering what it would be like to wake with you in my bed, to have breakfast with you again."

She's quiet for a long moment, studying our joined hands.

"One night," she says finally. "Perhaps one night is all it will take for you to see that we're different now, and we can't recreate a holiday from years ago." I narrow my eyes, pointedly doubting her words—another wall. "If I stay, tomorrow we're back to being professional."

"Deal." I lift her hand to my lips, pressing a soft kiss to her palm. "Though I reserve the right to cook you breakfast."

"You can cook?"

"I can make coffee and toast without burning down the kitchen."

Her laugh is the most beautiful sound in what has been a very long day.

"Then I guess I'll stay."

"Excellent. Before we head upstairs, there's something I

want to show you. Something happening at the club tonight that I think you'll appreciate."

"At The Sanctuary?"

She's tentative, but the event tonight is special, and I want her to see it—to understand the club's value.

Within twenty minutes, the waiting driver delivers us to The Sanctuary, and I lead her past our doorman to the event space.

Tonight, for this performance, there's a small round elevated stage, a stool with a warm wash of light over Miley Cyrus. Seventy-five seats are arranged in a semicircle around her. She's been doing these intimate shows for a while now, but this is her first at The Sanctuary. We arrive mid-set, and the room is held in the hush only a voice like hers can command. As she sings about being good and gold, I lean against the painted black wall, gesturing for Brie to lean against me.

"It's a sold-out event, but I thought you'd like to hear some of it."

"She's different than I remember," Brie says.

"She's in a different era." I lift Brie's hair from her shoulders and place a kiss on the slope of her neck. "I prefer this one."

The singer's voice fills the space, soft but threaded with smoke. Each lyric floats like confession, quiet and raw—about slipping away from each other, about how time slides us into new versions of ourselves.

The sound isn't polished or performative—it's intimate, like she's baring something too private for microphones.

While the younger Cyrus is enchanting, what's captivating is observing Brie, watching the songs find her, watching the way her pulse flutters beneath the hollow of her throat as Miley sings about the world cutting and leaving scars.

For a moment, The Sanctuary feels weightless. No secrets. No investigations. Just the echo of a woman's voice and the reminder that beauty, at its truest, is unguarded.

When the last chord fades, Brie exhales, slow and deliberate, as though waking from a dream.

"Come," I say, applause echoing off the walls, a sign that in seconds the lights will flicker on and I'll risk being caught in a vortex of members. "There's another part of the club you should see."

But as we exit the velvet-dark room, Miley announces one last song, and the echo of the song follows through the passage—faint, longing, dangerous as a promise.

"That was amazing. Do you offer shows like that often?"

"When possible. It's a challenge though…our members are all VIPs."

"A sold-out show means some were denied access," she says, understanding.

"Exactly."

With a nod to Tiffany, our concierge, the door to the performance salon opens. Tiffany doesn't approach; she barely acknowledges us. I should possibly ask if she needs something, if she's in the hallway waiting to shuttle a member to a suite, or if there's an issue I should attend to, but she bows her head and presses her hand to her ear, likely receiving a communication, so I trust that if she needs me, she'll find me, and I escort Brie into our most sensual room.

The lighting here is different—amber and shadow, deliberate in its obscurity. Where the performance space demanded focus, this room invites exploration. Low music pulses through hidden speakers, not loud enough to overwhelm conversation but insistent enough to set a rhythm in the blood.

The space is arranged in layers. A central platform showcases a dancer moving with liquid grace, her movements somewhere between ballet and seduction. Around the periphery, curved banquettes in deep burgundy velvet create intimate alcoves, some occupied by couples leaning close, others empty and waiting.

Brie stills beside me.

"This is..." she starts, then stops.

"The part you expected?" I finish.

A couple moves past us toward one of the shadowed corners, the woman's laughter soft and intimate. On the platform, the dancer executes a turn that's both athletic and sensual, her body a study in controlled abandon.

"It's more elegant than I imagined," Brie admits. Her voice has dropped lower, matching the room's energy. "I thought it would be..."

"Tawdry?" I let my hand slide from her back to her hip. "That's the misconception. Everything here is curated."

"But not innocent."

"No," I agree. "Not innocent."

"Are the performers hired?"

"Sometimes. But what they do on stage is their choice. Some members request to perform. Some performers see it as an opportunity to reach a new audience–one willing to pay for private viewings."

"In person? That's–"

"We don't get involved in arrangements, but you're sounding like someone who hasn't spent time online. There are performers who make millions from private showings—I've never done it myself, but I've always perceived it's video sessions."

She's enthralled, and not just by the idea of what's occurring, but what she's witnessing. As are our members.

"You pick the acts?"

I lift her hand and press my lips to her palm. "No. I leave that to Eddie and Tiffany."

A hostess passes with a black-and-gold lanyard that matches the small placard on the wall: HOUSE RULES—Consent. Discretion. Safety. The dancer arcs into a slow backbend and the room exhales as one when she's joined by a muscular, shirtless man in tuxedo trousers and patent dress shoes.

We move deeper into the space. A woman in a black slip dress walks by, her hand trailing along her companion's arm. In one alcove, a couple sits close enough that they could be sharing secrets or kisses—it's impossible to tell in the low light, and that's the point. Somewhere in the shadows, fabric sighs in the dark; on the platform, the dancer's back catches the amber light like poured honey. She's stripped now, donned only in stilettos, and the man lifts her onto the swing dangling from the ceiling.

A pulse flutters at Brie's throat now. I watch it, matching the tempo of the music.

"Adrien," she says, and there's something in her voice that makes my entire body tighten.

"Yes?"

"Why did you bring me here?"

I turn her to face me, my hand still at her hip. "Because I want you to understand what I've built. Not just the performance spaces and the Michelin stars. This too. The freedom to want without judgment. To explore without shame."

Her eyes are dark in the amber light. "That's not the only reason."

"No," I admit. "It's not."

The male performers' back muscles flex, the woman's back arches, their silhouette hypnotic. Around us, the energy of the room builds—subtle but unmistakable. A murmur of conversation from a nearby banquette.

The performers circle, twisting the swing, giving all a view—he's unzipped, and she's toying with him, a condom wrapper between her teeth. In the dim light, it's lurid, more shadow than explicit detail, but the crowd watches, mesmerized, the energy palpable.

Some watch, while some turn to those at their side. The faintest moan, swallowed by the music. The charge of anticipation that fills any space where desire is acknowledged rather than hidden.

Brie's transfixed to the stage, her breaths shallow. With a lick of her lips, her gaze cuts to me. "This isn't keeping things professional."

"My purpose is not professional." I move closer, until there's barely space between us. I coax the curve of her hip, wanting her flat against me. She's seen all she needs to see. "I want to take you somewhere private."

"One of your suites?"

I shake my head. "Too risky. Not until we resolve this situation with Eddie. But back to my home…" I let the words trail off, watching comprehension dawn in her eyes.

She presses against me. My lips find hers. I back her up to a wall, and we become one with the crowd, restrained but only just. Our bodies seemingly meld, hampered more by the constraints of clothes than the presence of others.

On the platform, the performer's routine reaches its climax —noted by a climactic musical finale, a flash of lights, and graceful descent that concludes with a dark stage. Applause ripples through the room, intimate and appreciative. Two men and a woman approach the stage, ready to take the spotlight, and with three, the shadowed crowd's expectations rise.

"I think," Brie says slowly, her palm flattened on my chest, her breath rapid, "we should go."

"To my place?"

"To your place." Her fingers curl into my shirt. "Now."

The urgency in her voice matches what I'm feeling. Whatever the performance downstairs awakened, this room has amplified. The air between us is charged with long-banked wanting, one night of tentative reconnection, and the raw acknowledgment of desire that this space demands.

I take her hand and lead her back toward the elevator. As we pass Tiffany in the hallway, she offers a discreet nod, professional enough not to comment on our obvious haste.

In the elevator, Brie doesn't lean against the opposite wall as she might have earlier. She stays close, her shoulder against mine, her breathing audible in the small space.

"You're quiet," I observe.

"I'm thinking."

"About?"

She turns to look at me, and the heat in her eyes nearly has me pressing the emergency button and taking her right here in the lift. "About how much I want you. About how unwise that is. About how I don't particularly care right now."

The elevator reaches the ground floor. My driver is waiting where I left him, and within moments we're in the back of the car, the privacy screen already raised.

Brie's hand finds mine in the darkness. "I meant what I said earlier. Tomorrow, we're back to professional."

"I know." I lift her hand to my lips. "But tonight isn't tomorrow."

CHAPTER
FOURTEEN

BRIE

We pass the doorman and a group chatting in the lobby, my heels clicking on marble, our hands linked, skin flushed, our steps quick and deliberate.

When the doors close on his private penthouse elevator, he waits just long enough for the hum of cables to rise, for the air between us to grow taut—then he's on me, pressing my back hard into the metal handrail, the jut of his arousal against my hip. Heat seeps down my spine and pools.

He breaks the kiss with a sharp inhale. His dark, glittering stare drops from my eyes to my lips and then lower to the place where my silk shirt opens at the collar, the buttons undone to my décolletage.

The doors chime and it's as if we're on air in a rush, my peripheral vision a blur, my singular focus him. No doorman. No witnesses. Just us and three years of wanting. We don't make it past the living room.

In a flash, his hand is on the back of my neck, fingers

tangled in my hair. His tongue slips between my lips, whispering over my teeth, stealing my breath.

A memory flashes—dawn light through yacht windows, his fingers tracing the pulse point at my wrist. "Your heartbeat gives you away," he'd whispered. I'd told him something true then, something I've never repeated: "I'm tired of pretending." His answer: "Then don't pretend."

I'm not pretending now. Because this time there's no alias to hide behind.

The brush of the stubble on my cheek burns, and the taste of wine and a hint of mint blend, as though at some point he prepared for this very moment.

A slight whimper escapes from my throat. He pulls back a little, pausing—eyes scanning, careful, controlled. The way he reins himself in is almost as intoxicating as the way he grabs me. He's waiting—watching for the smallest sign I want to stop. The restraint in him is a kind of control I can't resist.

"Yes," I say, answering the question I hope he's asking. "Please." I'm tired of waiting, of holding back, of denying myself. I want him, and I want him now. I want him so badly I risk combustion.

He acquiesces. His tongue slips over mine, then over my face, to my neck, pulling my earlobe into his mouth. More of his hands—one in my hair at the back of my head, one moving down to press the small of my back so that my body shifts closer to his. His breathing deepens, quickens, a low groan caught in his throat.

My fingers steal under his shirt. My palm glides along rippling muscle, smooth and toned. His skin is hot and his heady scent and heat envelop me.

His legs press against mine, his chest into my breasts.

"I need to get you upstairs." But I'm feeling what I hear in his strangled words—it's too far.

"Here." I push his suit coat over his shoulders, attacking his buttons with shaking fingers. "Now."

He makes a sound—half-laugh, half-groan—and suddenly I'm pinned against the cushions, his weight divine, his mouth on my neck, my jaw, my collarbone. His hands everywhere.

He has me pinned against the back cushions, and it's enough—but my feet lift off the ground and he carries me across the room, setting me down on the other side. His eyes are dark, focused, and his breathing is no longer steady.

He tugs my skirt up—impatient, urgent—over my thighs, bunching it at my hips. When his fingers trail over the front of my vulva through thin silk, I buck against his hand.

It's been so long since I've been touched there by someone other than me—but that's not it. It's *him*. His hands. His breath hot on my neck. The reality of Adrien d'Avricourt kneeling between my thighs, looking at me like I'm oxygen and he's drowning.

His other hand yanks at my blouse buttons—too slow—so I reach up to help, fingers fumbling. The fabric parts and he doesn't wait, doesn't tease. He yanks the lace cups of my bra down, baring me, and his mouth closes over my nipple.

The sensation shoots straight to my core. I arch into him, fingers diving into his hair, holding him there. He sucks and licks like he's starving, alternating between breasts, and when his teeth graze my nipple I gasp his name.

His legs shift, one knee pressing inside my thigh, opening me, then the other. He settles between my spread legs, and the weight of him, the pressure—I'm practically vibrating.

His fingers hook my panties, yanking them aside roughly,

and then he's touching me where I'm swollen and slick. So wet it's almost embarrassing.

"Fuck, Brie." His voice is gravel. "You're soaked."

The crude words should embarrass me. Instead, they make me wetter.

"Please," I gasp, stretching for his waistband. My fingers find his belt buckle but I'm shaking too hard—from need, from the days of restraint finally breaking—and I can't get it undone. "I just…need…now…*please*."

Adrien understands. He has to be feeling it too—this desperation, this animal need that's nothing like the controlled seduction on the yacht. This is messier. Rawer. Real.

He whips his belt through the loops, fumbles with his trousers. When he frees himself—thick and hard and *right there*—I reach for him without thinking. Hot silk over steel. He hisses, his hips jerking forward, and I wrap my fingers around his length.

"Brie." A warning or a prayer, I can't tell.

He hitches my panties further aside, his fingers brushing where I'm aching, and positions himself at my entrance. I feel his crown pressing against me—not in, just there, the promise of him—and my knees lift involuntarily.

With his mouth close to my ear, voice wrecked: "Next time, everything comes off. All of this. I want to see you properly. Taste every inch. But right now—" He presses forward slightly, just the tip, and we both gasp. "Right now I can't wait."

"Then don't." I'm frantic, nodding against his face, my hair silk between our cheeks. "Don't wait."

"Look at me." Not a command—a plea. Like he needs proof I'm real, that this is happening.

Our eyes lock. His are nearly black, pupils blown wide, and I see myself reflected there—flushed, desperate, completely undone.

He thrusts hard and fast, filling me in one brutal stroke, and we both cry out. The stretch, the sudden fullness—it borders on too much and not nearly enough.

He stills, shuddering, a great rushing gasp escaping. His forehead falls to mine. "Fuck. *Fuck*, you feel good." His voice cracks on the last word.

His biceps strain beside my head, muscle taut, as he holds himself perfectly still. I can feel him throbbing inside me, fighting for control he doesn't want, that neither of us need.

I can't stay still. My feet hook onto his legs, urging him deeper. "Adrien." His name breaks on my lips. "Move. Please move."

He withdraws—not all the way, just enough that I feel the loss—then drives back in. Testing. The angle. The depth. The friction.

"Yes," I whimper, and he does it again. Harder this time. Again. Finding a rhythm that has me making sounds I don't recognize—soft mewling noises, desperate gasps, his name over and over.

His pace builds. Faster. Harder. The couch creaks beneath us. Somewhere in my fractured awareness I know the windows overlook the city, that anyone could see, but I don't care. Can't care.

He reaches between us, fingers finding my clit, and the dual sensation—him inside me, hitting something deep that makes me see stars, his fingers circling with practiced precision—breaks me.

"That's it," he coaxes, voice strained. "Let go. Give it to me."

My body obeys before my mind can catch up. The orgasm slams through me—violent and complete—my back arching off the cushions, legs gripping him in a vice. I'm aware of crying out, of my internal muscles clenching around him in waves.

A jagged moan tears from his throat. He thrusts twice more—deep, desperate—then stills, pulsing inside me. His whole body shudders with release, and I feel it, feel him emptying into me, hot and deep.

We lie tangled together, breathing hard. My skirt is bunched around my waist. His shirt hangs open. My bra is still shoved down beneath my breasts. The sudden oddness of what we've done—half-clothed, frantic, a bed awaiting upstairs in multiple rooms—crashes over me.

Windows overlooking the city glitter with apartment lights, possible voyeurs. From somewhere below—maybe the street, maybe the building's ventilation—I catch a thread of music. That amber-lit room. The dancer's controlled abandon. All those people acknowledging desire without shame.

We just did the same. But worse. Because they had boundaries. Rules. We have none.

My hold on him loosens and he shifts. Wetness seeps between my legs—his and mine, mixed—and the sensation grounds me in awful clarity. He pushes up, and his absence feels like loss and relief in equal measure.

Then it hits me. Really hits me.

He said he rarely brings women here, and suddenly I need that to be true. I need it in a way that terrifies me because it means this *matters*, means I'm not just scratching an itch or breaking professional protocol for meaningless sex.

This is what unnerves me—not the physical act but this: the way my chest constricts when he moves away. The way I want to pull him back. On that yacht, I walked away because it was fantasy, controlled, contained. This is real. And this—this is Manhattan where he's my client, where I'm assigned to protect his interests, and I just—

No condom.

The realization arrives cold and sharp. I should care more than I do. Should be calculating STI risks, pregnancy possibilities—none, thank you IUD, professional consequences. Instead, all I can think is how right it felt. How completely I lost myself. How I'd do it again right now if he touched me.

That's the most frightening part.

No exit strategy. No performance.

Just me, stripped of every defense I've mastered.

He lives in a world of beautiful women on display, many available on request. I'm the one who disappeared. The one who became unattainable. Now that I've surrendered so completely, now that he's had me again—without barriers, without planning, without the mystery—

"Hey." His deep tone saves me from the spiral, and his hand cups my jaw, turning my face toward his. In the dim light from the city, his eyes are dark but potent. Seeing me.

"I can hear you thinking," he says quietly. "Constructing walls between us."

"I don't—"

"You do. You're cataloging why this was a mistake. Why I'll lose interest now that the chase is over, or maybe you're reeling over professionalism." His thumb traces my cheekbone. "Three years, Brie. Do you know how many women I could have had in three years? How many I did have?"

The words sting, but he doesn't let me look away.

"None of them were you. Not because you walked away—because of who you were before you left. The woman who told me she didn't know how to stop pretending." His forehead touches mine. "You're not pretending now. That's what I've been looking for. That's what I want more of."

He stands, reaching down to help me up. "Come with me. I'm going to clean you up, take you to my bed, and then we're taking our time. I'm going to show you just how much I've thought of you these past few years." And the tremor in his voice is what finally undoes me.

CHAPTER
FIFTEEN

ADRIEN

"I can't."

Two words—soft, almost apologetic—yet they split something in me open.

"We should've used a condom." Not caution—distance.

I apologized. She brushed it off, said she was on birth control, that it was fine, *that it was what we should have done.* But the subtext lingered: *you came too close.*

Watching her gather herself, I felt her vanish in increments—the closing of a clasp, the whisper of fabric sliding over skin, the distance forming with every deliberate motion. The woman who'd just come undone beneath me was gone. Not regret—defense. Replaced by the professional—calm, contained, unreachable.

She'd agreed to stay the night. Then she didn't. My fault—too much, too soon. And the way she left... no kiss, no backward glance, her steps soft, quick, final.

My pen taps against the desk, an impatient metronome

keeping time with regret. I've commanded boardrooms, steered acquisitions worth millions, but I can't stop fixating on the sound of her heels fading.

After Monaco, I told myself the connection was fantasy. The perfect weekend, the perfect woman. Gilded memory. Lust painted over with longing. But now she's back—real, tangible, breathing the same New York air as I am.

I know her name now. I know where she lives. I could find her if I wanted. But what would that accomplish?

I used to pride myself on simplicity. No entanglements. No emotional risk. Relationships were convenient arrangements, easily concluded. But with her...simplicity feels like fiction.

I close my eyes. I can still smell her on my skin—amber and something faintly floral, like a memory that refuses to fade. I see flashes of her—blue eyes against the night, the tremor in her breath when I touched her, the way she softened for a heartbeat before she shuttered herself again. She's in my bloodstream. My control—my *discipline*—is unraveling.

A month ago, the idea of anything long-term with an American woman would have made me laugh. Now I can't even define what I want—only that it's her.

Yes, I spend half the year in New York, but my life is flight paths and transatlantic calls. I belong more to the sky than to any city. If I pursue her—if I break through those walls she rebuilds the second they crack—what would that give us? What would it cost her?

There's no denying I lust after her. I swear to God she's *everywhere* and she has been for years. When I see a blonde on the street, I think of her. When I order a croissant, I wonder what she'd choose. I sit here at my desk, supposed to be reviewing financial reports and staff notes, yet my body betrays me—half-hard, restless, remembering the sound of her moan. When I close my eyes, I see her irises—blue and devastating. She's got me completely off balance.

I lean back, exhaling, the leather creaking beneath my shoulders. I should be focused on strategy, not the ache she left behind. But the mind is a weak steward when desire has taken the reins.

Madame Vassante's voice returns, smoke and prophecy in the air of her Paris flat. The Fool. Death. The Tower.

Three cards, drawn in a room scented with mysticism and age. "Major upheaval," she'd said, tapping the Tower. "Everything you think you know will be challenged."

I'd smiled politely, paid, kissed both her cheeks. A bit of Parisian theatre, I'd thought. But the older I get, the more I wonder if she wasn't reading the cards so much as *me*.

The Fool—new beginnings, leaps of faith.

Death—transformation, not loss.

The Tower—destruction that clears the way for truth.

At the time, it was superstition. Now, with the club under threat and Brie back in my orbit, it feels like prophecy.

What if her draw was indeed genuine? Is it a sign that this irrational lust will lead somewhere? Or that my investment is about to implode? That striking out on my own will lead to a blowback on my sister and father?

A knock interrupts the thought. The traitor enters—lazy charm, practiced ease, blissfully unaware that I know what he's done. The gold cross at his neck glints under the recessed light, a saint's token worn by a sinner.

"Good weekend?" he asks. It's Thursday, but in our world of endless work, the question passes for polite.

"Good. You?"

"Bella had a dance competition that took all of Sunday. Should've been called a marathon."

He's complaining in the way he does, about everything and anything. If he didn't complain about the length of his kid's competition, it would be the temperature outside, the idiot broad who effed his breakfast order, or the blooming traffic and the fucking idiots who scheduled road construction during rush hour.

"Did she win?"

"Nah," he shrugs his shoulders. "There's no real winning. Got a ribbon. You know, participation kind of thing. Judges gave feedback. Maybe someone won, but it wasn't her."

Perhaps I should feign interest, mirror small talk, but I can't make myself perform civilly. Eddie and I were never close, so my detachment shouldn't raise suspicion.

"Last night's show was a hit," he says. "Members are already asking for another."

"She's unforgettable," I reply, meaning Brie, not Miley Cyrus. "Everything in order for Saturday's event?"

He gives the expected report. Everything's handled. Always handled. And yet, I can't help staring, wondering how long he's been siphoning secrets beneath my nose. I'd once admired his competence. Now I study him like a contagion that's already spread.

"Do you have any priorities I should address?"

It takes me a beat to process. My mind's already written his obituary. He's a liability I can't excise yet.

My phone rings. It's my personal cell, a number I give out to few, and I glance at the screen and read Alicia Morgan's name.

"I've got to take this," I say to Eddie.

"Will you be at the marketing status this afternoon?"

"Plan to," is what I say, but he knows that I like to pop in to those meetings and not stay for the duration.

"I've got a meeting this afternoon so I might miss it."

He's up and close to the door. He glances back, looking for permission he doesn't need. I don't micromanage, and after three years, he's well aware, but when he glances over his shoulder at me, I sense he's looking for a response.

"If anything's awry, I'll let you know."

I find myself thinking of the Tower card again. Structures built on false foundations always fall—the question is whether you're crushed beneath them or whether you're smart enough to step aside.

I lift the phone to answer, and Eddie gestures at the door. "Open or closed?"

"Closed." *Like you found it* dies on my lips.

I answer the call, but wait until the door clicks closed to say, "Alicia."

"Is this a good time?"

"As good as any."

"KOAN has eyes on your building," she says. "If Eddie leaves, we'll know."

"He's got a meeting this afternoon. Location unknown."

"Good."

I frown. "How is that good?"

"Because if he spent his days and nights inside your buildings, this could take a while. A guy like that's too smart to email from his work email, if he makes any phone calls to clients it'll likely be from an untraceable source—one we can't monitor."

"And if he meets with anyone within the walls of The Sanctuary, it won't look suspicious. He knows everyone. That's his job."

"Exactly."

I stand and pace. "Alicia, I can't let this go on indefinitely. I can give it a couple of days tops. Then I need to kick him out and clean house. I agreed to let—"

"Patience," she says, calm, unflappable.

Madame Vassante's voice echoes again: *The Fool rushes in where angels fear to tread.*

"Alicia, this leak could end everything. If this breaks—"

"Then you want answers first," she cuts in. "Because if this leaks and you don't know who he's working with, you'll be fielding chaos from every member on your roster."

She's right. The Sanctuary's secrets aren't only sexual—they're financial, political, personal. Discretion is our currency. And Eddie's theft is an act of war.

I glance again toward the street below. Cars nose into tight spaces. The city breathes its usual chaos. And somewhere out there, Brie might be watching—surveilling, waiting. The image strikes me like a pulse.

"I refuse to believe he's been selling information for years," I say. "If he had, someone would've come forward. Crawford did, and within a week, you had me in your office."

"Yes, but Crawford's situation was unique," she says. "Most of what Eddie sells isn't intimate footage—it's intel. Meetings, mergers, trades. The kind of information that destroys portfolios, not marriages."

"Insider trading," I murmur. "So that's your other client."

"Give it time, Adrien." Her tone suggests patience is a luxury I've yet to afford.

"Just remember," I tell her, voice low, "if this leaks, I become your highest priority. That was the deal."

"Understood."

If this leaks to the membership, I might as well hand Eddie matches and watch my investment burn.

My gaze drifts back to the window. From up here, every parking space is full. The street below hums with anonymity. Is she down there? Sitting in one of those cars, eyes on my door, waiting for Eddie to move? The idea of her out there—alone, observing through glass—does something to me I can't name.

Lunch?

I send the text before I can stop myself.

If she's nearby, maybe she'll come in. Maybe she'll step out from behind her work and see me instead of the assignment.

Every thought, every breath, every instinct leads back to her. I used to think obsession was weakness. Now I understand—it's the mark she left on me. The space she occupies.

The tower hasn't fallen yet.

But I can already feel the cracks.

CHAPTER
SIXTEEN

BRIE

"He's headed for Wall Street," Noah's voice cracks through the comm.

I glance down at the sensible shoes and thrift-store skirt. "Copy that—but I'm still your seventy-year-old with a cane." My persona blends in a city park, but it'll stick out more downtown. "Who else do we have out there?"

The KOAN driver knows how to tail discreetly—but with his gut grazing the steering wheel, sprinting's off the table. He's a resource Hudson hired for driving, not for tailing someone on foot.

"Jake's two avenues over," Noah says.

"I'm changing into an Oxford. I can cover," a male voice, presumably Jake, comes across the line.

A ripple of unease licks the back of my neck. Instinct—the kind that's kept me breathing—tightens through my gut. I don't like this. If he goes into a building, we'll likely never see who he meets with. Hell, this could just be a meeting with his financial advisor.

"Did you get anything worthwhile on audio?" My question is directed at Quinn, who I know is on the line, probably watching what looks like a series of blue dots cascading down a grid of streets.

The Financial District thrums—a pulse of heels on concrete, a chorus of horns, exhaust that tastes like metal. The city beats against my skin, alive and indifferent. A thousand stories crossing paths, none noticing mine. In theory, it's easy to blend in, but...

"Depending on who his contact is, the safest place to meet would be in an office building," Noah says.

"Witnesses," a male voice that I'm pretty certain is Hudson, says.

I flip open a compact mirror, taking in my applied wrinkles, brown contact lenses, and wig. Then I check the contents of the bag in the seat beside me. "If I pull my hair back into a bun, throw on a sweater coat and ditch the cane, I think I can blend into the office scene. Depending on what building he goes into, I can look like a client."

If I'd brought an executive suit...but the catch is, I can't look too respectable or notable.

Out the window, I read the green street sign and watch the yellow taxi through the windshield.

"He's turning towards South Street Seaport. Do you think he's... The ferry?"

He lives on Long Island. No one commutes to Long Island via the ferry. A familiar rush of adrenaline lights my fingers. This might pan out.

"Does anyone have a ferry schedule?" I ask.

Sure enough, the cab pulls to the curb. Eddie Thorne

emerges in that careless way men do when they believe no one's watching—tie loosened, wind curling his hair. The air smells of brine and diesel, the harbor's exhale. He scans the area, looking up and down the street.

"He's out," I say. "I've got eyes on him."

Shit. If he buys a ticket, there's no way I'll catch up to hear what he bought.

"Quinn. Schedule? I don't know the ferry schedule. What's he most likely buying?"

But as my car pulls up and I hop out, debating if I should ditch the cane, he bypasses the red and blue sign.

"Never mind," I say as Quinn says, "Brooklyn."

"He's going for a stroll," I tell the team.

"Alright. Jake, you head north, exit well above so you can stroll south. Brie, go ahead and exit. Stroll slowly. Goal is to observe. Let's see who he's meeting with. Noah, you come in hot and heavy like a man who missed his ferry. One headed to Jersey left three minutes ago. Run up, make a scene, then you can carry on like you've got an hour to waste."

"Copy," we all three say in unison to Hudson's orders.

The chances of getting audio are slim, but we'll get a face, and then we'll have a name. We'll study the CCTV footage later—derive how his contact arrived, where they came from.

Sure enough, Eddie joins an elegant older woman, steel gray hair, wearing a deep purple silk blouse and loose trousers of a similar eggplant shade. Black framed sunglasses conceal her eyes, but I sense as she hugs him, she's scoping beyond his shoulder.

My cane clicks on the brick, each tap syncing to the thud of my pulse, and the tote I'm carrying slaps into my thigh. My shoulders curve in, stretching my back muscles, reducing my height in a practiced manner.

Where they're meeting, CCTV should cover. But if I can get a photo, that's better.

Too old for a lover, too poised for a relative—this woman was trained. Given her age and gender, she's the perfect runner for a client.

"Stopping on a bench. I'm going to pass by, head to the railing and look over the river," I say to the team, keeping my head low so an onlooker might assume I'm talking on the phone.

"Jake here. I've got eyes on you. Facing the river. I'll stay back on the street."

Eddie and the woman sit on the bench, talking. Pedestrians pass, but most of those hurrying by in this section seem to be aiming for the ferry station.

I shuffle toward the railing, my manufactured favoring of my right leg convincing even to myself after hours of practice. Every movement rehearsed, every limp earned through repetition. Deception, like ballet, demands muscle memory—and god, I'm tired of performing.

The woman's posture is too perfect for her age—military bearing disguised as elegant confidence. Professional, not personal.

"They're exchanging something," I murmur into my comms, angling my phone to capture photos while pretending to take pictures of the harbor. "Small package. She's handing him what looks like a tablet."

Through my camera lens, I catch her profile as she removes her sunglasses to clean them—a calculated move that gives Eddie a clear view of her face. Trust building. She wants him to see her, to feel connected. Or maybe she's gaining a clearer view of him, judging him.

"Maybe payment instructions," I whisper, recognizing the

choreography. "She's establishing personal connection before tackling business."

The woman stands, smoothing her silk blouse with manicured fingers that catch the afternoon light. Her fingers brush his as she passes the device—small contact, deliberate. Connection offered, control established. I know the dance because I've led it.

Eddie pockets the device and pulls out his phone, presumably checking the contents. His shoulders relax and he actually smiles—I read it as genuine. Whatever he sees, he's pleased.

"Moving," I report as she walks north of the ferry terminal. "Jake, she's headed your way. Silver hair, purple ensemble, black Prada bag."

But instead of continuing along the river, she turns sharply left toward the parking garage. Smart. No CCTV in the stairwells, minimal witnesses.

"Shit. We're going to lose her. Jake, can you—"

"On it."

Eddie's now holding the tablet she gave him once more, his expression shifting from satisfaction to interest. I'd bet she just handed him an assignment—or an opportunity.

My own phone buzzes with an encrypted message.

Facial recognition running. Checking CIA, State Department, private contractor databases.

Eddie stands, pockets the device, and heads south, the opposite direction from his contact. Professional trade completed. No lingering, no sentimentality. Minimal interaction.

"He's moving to South Street," I report. "Looks like he's checking his phone. Ordered an Uber or Lyft." Smart. You can't bank on a cab this time of day down here.

Classic misdirection—meeting was the real purpose, ferry station provided cover. Anyone down here is in a hurry.

"Got her," Jake's voice crackles through my earpiece. "Black Mercedes, dealer plates. Should I hot wire a car to follow?"

"Negative," Hudson's voice carries. "Noah, Winston's bringing the car around on South. Hop in. You follow the target as far as you can."

"Copy that."

In my periphery, I catch Noah reach the curb and hop in the back of the car I took to get here.

I start the slow shuffle back toward my pickup point, mind racing through what I've witnessed. The woman's age and bearing suggest she could be classically trained. Ex-government, possibly intelligence. The kind of person who could run a network brokering intel without getting her hands dirty.

"Quinn, any hits yet on the facial recognition?"

"Still processing. But Brie, there's something else. I checked Eddie's credit card charges. He was in Georgetown yesterday. Double-checked it wasn't an online charge or a misdirected merchant charge. Found his license plate on CCTV."

Georgetown. DC. That's where Senator Crawford lives. The Sanctuary doesn't have a location in DC.

What are you up to, Eddie?

My phone vibrates again.

> **ADRIEN**
> Everything okay? I know where you live and work. Ghosting isn't an option.

His name lights the screen, elegant and infuriating. I shouldn't feel the rush in my chest. The sting of longing threads irritation. *Focus, Brie.*

With an eyeroll, I slip my phone into my skirt pocket. As I climb into the back of the car service Hudson arranged, watching Jake's blue dot pursue the Mercedes on Quinn's tracking screen, I realize this isn't going to wrap quickly—we've butted into the sharp edge of an iceberg.

"Hudson," I say into my comm unit. "We need to expand the scope of this investigation. I think we just watched Eddie get his next assignment. Crawford was likely a one-off. This woman's a professional. She's working for someone."

"We lost the Mercedes. Dammit," Jake says.

"Were they onto you?" Hudson asks.

"No, I don't think so. Light changed. Pedestrians flooded the intersection. We couldn't follow."

"Copy that," Hudson says.

Losing the lead is disappointing, but for the first time, it feels like we're finally hunting the hunter instead of just on cleanup duty.

"Eddie's car is headed back to The Sanctuary."

"He's on for evening service," I say.

"Copy that," Hudson says. "Jake, Noah, head back,

resume surveillance. Let's watch him. See if he stays the night."

As my car pulls away from the waterfront, I catch one last glimpse of the park bench facing the river. The trash cans off to the side by a light post.

Watching Eddie, he played his role well. Casual. Unbothered. A meeting—or an exchange. Effortless.

The river glints like liquid glass, catching a smear of sun. Everything looks polished from a distance—like beauty concealing rot, as the car pulls away. Eddie plays his role to perfection. Maybe we all do, until the script slips—and the truth takes the stage.

CHAPTER
SEVENTEEN

ADRIEN

All afternoon I pretended to focus on business—the phone beside me like an unanswered question I didn't dare touch. The marketing meeting dragged—another circular debate about Halloween themes. At The Sanctuary, fantasy sells itself. I should've stayed away; watching people package desire was too on-the-nose today.

Rhonda lobbied for masquerade, Boyton for "fantasy-forward." We host masquerades twice a month—hardly innovation. Common sense should've prevailed without me.

I push open my office door—annoyed that "soon" became an hour—and stop short. Tommy's sprawled across the sofa, coat and briefcase claiming half of it, highball glass in hand, amber light catching the ice.

I make a show of checking my wrist. "Half-day for judges?"

"Case settled early. I'm clear for the day. Just came from The Crescendo—six models at the bar from a catalog shoot."

His mention of models sends my hand to my phone. No missed calls. No text. Just silence dressed in glass and light.

"What am I saying—you're burned out on models. Hudson Yards?"

"I burned out on performance," I say with a defensive edge. "Everyone chasing the same illusion."

He arches a brow, waiting for more, but I leave it there. The Sanctuary attracts people who use beauty as currency. Once, I traded in it freely. Now there's only one woman I want to know beyond the surface.

Beautiful young women and men are desperate for invites to The Sanctuary—all with the hope of landing a relationship that will pay the bills. If the young guests only wished to party, they'd head to a cracking club. No, when they saunter in, knowing full well they can't be photographed, to parties that won't make the papers, they're coming here in the hopes of making a connection—one that ranks as lucrative. A trade of sorts in a circular world where there's no such thing as enough.

"Tired?" He laughs. "You—the curator of scandal?"

I give him a look. When I bought The Sanctuary it thrived on spectacle, not solace, and I've spent years changing that. Sex sells, but power and privacy keep them returning. A true sanctuary offers both—pleasure and silence.

"Something's off," Tommy says, tipping his glass at me. "That woman—she ghost again?"

"You're imagining things."

"I'm a judge, not a fool. It's that woman. Monaco."

My jaw tightens. She's not just *a woman*. But why argue? He might be right. Maybe she wants to ghost me.

Last night was…complicated. If she weren't tied to my

project, I might never see her again. She's not responding to my texts. She hasn't called.

"She's in Manhattan," I remind him—and myself.

I move behind my desk, pulling up the trend report I owe Margot—brands, colors, silhouettes our patrons favor. Macon compiles the footage; I translate it into marketing notes. The wealthiest clientele in the world leave data in the cut of a jacket, the choices for a wrist.

"And you've seen her."

I sink into my chair and let the question hang unanswered.

"But it didn't go well," he presses.

I rub the bridge of my nose. Talking about Brie is out of the question—and I can't tell him the details of what's happening with Eddie—so I deflect. "You've had too much free time since making the bench."

"I don't," he says, rightfully defensive. "But I worry about you—and I've learned to take breaks when I can. Law firm habit."

"Why the sudden concern?"

"Truthfully, it's Margot." His drink sloshes as he gestures. "When she and I talk, I start to understand why she worries."

"Since when are you and my sister confidants?"

My phone lights up, and my gaze falls to the screen lying on my desk. *Fucking finally.*

"I need to take this," I tell him, nodding toward the door.

"Since when…" He pauses mid-sentence, then grins as realization dawns. "Fine, fine. Call me later." He wanders out, drink in hand—headed, no doubt, back to the models at the bar.

"Hi," I answer, gaze focused on the office door, waiting for it to close.

"Hey." Her voice is soft, intimate—threaded with caution. Maybe she's not alone.

The door clicks closed and I lean forward, resting an elbow on the desk, hesitant to set the phone down and set it to speaker.

"Busy day?"

"Yes. Your guy's afternoon meeting paid off. He met with a woman tied to MI5."

"British?"

"Irish. And when I say connections, I mean verified—observed."

"Hmm."

"One of her links traces to someone we'll call a White House insider."

"Interesting. You think she's the one running it?"

"No. She's a well-connected go-between for something lucrative. We're sussing it out, but…"

"It doesn't sound like this has to do with my properties."

"Your man's positioned himself as a source for a very powerful group."

"Meaning?"

"It means you stay quiet. Not a word—until we know who we're dealing with."

"You sound like you've forgotten what's at stake for me."

"I haven't," she says. "But your friend drops by often."

Ah, hell. They're watching. I'd forgotten.

"He knows nothing."

"Good."

"Dinner tonight?"

"Dinner—or cocktails."

My body reacts before my mind can school it. "Name the time and place. I'll make it happen."

"Your club," she says. "I want to see your guy in action."

"Text when you're close. I'll meet you at the door."

Two hours later, I wait outside the nondescript black door of The Sanctuary, scanning the street. A black sedan eases to the curb, and Brie steps out onto the cobblestone—golden hair perfectly coiffed, satin-gray wrap dress catching the city's light, silver heels glinting like dropped stars. Her coat, the same shade, fits like it was made for her. A modern siren stepped out of shadow. Every head inside will turn.

I greet her with a kiss to the cheek, my voice low. "You're stunning."

Her smile is soft but knowing—the kind that unspools restraint, thread by thread. I close the car door as if sealing a spell, and the sedan pulls away from the curb.

We pass security, check-in, and I rest my hand at the small of her back, guiding her toward the bar.

The air is layered with perfume, aged whiskey, and polished leather—the sensory shorthand of temptation. Recessed lights carve pockets of intimacy. Crystal catches the light like scattered diamonds. She takes it all in, and I wonder what she thinks of this haven I've created.

Tommy's here, mid-conversation with two women in dresses short enough to discourage sitting. Surrounded by fleeting company yet he spends his off-hours talking to my sister. Life's strange that way.

The bar hums with understated luxury—amber light glinting off crystal, jewelry chiming softly beneath a seductive beat. I guide Brie to a corner booth where shadows pool like velvet, a vantage point with just enough privacy to watch the room. The faint drift of cigar smoke tells me someone's slipped from the lounge recently.

"Drink?" I ask as the cocktail waitress approaches.

"Something light," Brie says, sliding into the curve of the booth.

Minutes later, cocktails ordered, I'm settled beside her. The leather sighs beneath us; heat from her thigh seeps into mine, grounding me more than any drink could.

"Eventful day?" I ask, voice low.

"Let's not talk here. At least, not about my workday." She looks at me with sultry lashes, and god I want the heat in her gaze to be for me, but I'm sharp enough to pick up that she's playing along in case someone else is listening. Because, after all, her theory is that conversations are being recorded and information sold.

I pause, uncertain what's safe to ask. Work's off-limits, and if she's right about surveillance, even small talk could be ammunition.

Our cocktails arrive, and the scent of citrus and smoked hickory curls between us. When the cocktail waitress leaves us, as if on cue, Eddie materializes beside our table with the practiced stealth of someone who makes a living from being exactly where conversations happen. His smile is warm, professional, but I catch the calculating flicker in his eyes as they assess Brie.

"Eddie," I say, friendly enough to fool a stranger. "You remember Brie." I stop before her surname; no need to hand him a dossier.

"Nice to see you again," he says with easy confidence,

settling into his favorite posture—close enough to listen, casual enough to seem harmless.

Chatting with members is part of his job, and he's good at it. He knows everyone, and he's intrigued because I've appeared with Brie twice and she hasn't entered through any of his channels. She's not someone who came in through our rising stars program—the one that scholarships beautiful twenty-somethings into the club. "Where are you from?"

Brie hesitates. Eddie fills the silence. "France, like this one?" he teases.

"We met abroad," she says smoothly. "But I live here in Manhattan."

"If I'm lucky, you'll see more of her around," I say, meaning it. My gaze stays on Eddie's reaction.

"Didn't think I'd see the day," Eddie says with an affable grin. "You must be something special. He doesn't say things he doesn't mean."

Candlelight gilds her skin, her smile small but real.

"Thank you…I think." Her eyes meet mine, blue and briefly unguarded. The room dissolves into chiaroscuro.

"I'll leave you two to it." Eddie pivots after one step, "Will you dine here or would you like your table in the restaurant?"

"Here's fine," I say. "Thanks, Eddie."

"Friendly," Brie observes, the word edged with irony.

"Good at his job," I say. What neither of us adds: he can't be trusted.

"Should we go to the restaurant? What do you normally do when you bring your dates here?"

I don't bring dates here, if anything I meet dates here, much like Tommy just met his dates.

Across the bar, Tommy lifts his chin in greeting. One

small shake of my head and he understands—don't bring them over. He toasts me anyway, and I turn back to Brie.

"We can order from any menu here," I offer. "Unless you'd prefer a change of scenery."

"What about the rooms upstairs?"

I hesitate. I'd rather be anywhere private with her—but not here. "They're available."

"No event tonight?"

"No. The events are planned in advance."

She looks, for a breath, disappointed, then relaxes into the booth. Golden light pools along her collarbone; her thigh brushes mine—an accidental confession. Her fingers trace lazy spirals on the table, each one a distraction I feel everywhere.

"Are you comfortable here?"

"It's dark," she murmurs, leaning in. Her fingertip grazes the corner of my mouth; I catch it between my teeth, slow enough to taste her restraint. "That's what he gets paid for?" she asks, glancing toward Eddie. "Greeting everyone?"

His job is actually much bigger than a professional greeter, but I tell her, "That's the part of the job he loves."

"Hmm."

I'm not sure what she hoped to see. The Sanctuary is built for discretion; no one overhears by accident. If Eddie's listening, he's planted the means to do it. The booths in the restaurant are designed to allow private discussions, business or otherwise, to go unheard.

"Instead of upstairs," I say, voice lower now, "I'd rather bring you home—or see where you live."

Should I care more about Eddie and what he's doing? Absolutely. And I do. But some battles wait. Tonight, I want something simpler—privacy, not performance. Time with her, real and unscripted.

"Tell me about the people here," she says, voice soft, gaze traveling the room. "Those guys. Barely legal. Are they models?"

I look to the booth she's spotted. Three Asian men—I don't recognize two of them, but based on the one I know, I can speculate. "The guy in the center? Founder of a meme coin creation company. He's only twenty-two, but he's been at it for five or six years. Possibly one of the wealthier individuals in this room."

"And he's a member?"

"Joined this year—after a member invited him as a guest. He won't stay long. If I were to guess, he's here to meet someone interested in launching their own meme token. This is an ideal spot for a speculative discussion—a year from now, there won't be any photographs to document the meeting."

"Why does that matter?"

"It doesn't always but at its essence, it's a pump and dump scheme. The name of the game is to keep it quiet until the announcement, so the price shoots up in the euphoria."

"That's shady."

"Yes. But currently quite legal. I expect those three will have their meeting, maybe dinner, then they'll hit the clubs."

She shoots them one last withering look. "And what about them?"

"A lobbyist. Two senators."

"So again, a meeting they'd just as well remain out of the public eye."

"A meeting. A friendship." I point to the bar where two men are sitting further down from Tommy and the models.

"That guy is a film director. And the man he's speaking to, I can't remember his exact role, but he's an executive at one of the movie studios."

"And they're here?"

"Could be filming. Might be a premiere. There are many reasons one might be in New York. Hell, the director might live here."

"And you don't remember their names?"

"No," I admit with a sigh. "That's why I have Eddie."

"What about that couple?" She points to a candlelit table with an attractive man and a woman.

"They're both actors."

"Oh. Who are they?"

"American actors," I say with a shrug. "The woman's more reality TV. I'm not sure—but I know they're actors. Could be a first or second date. Or maybe they're friends and don't want to attract rumors."

"It's fascinating," she says.

"Is it?" I ask as a group of men with grey-streaked hair in casual business wear enter. Eddie greets them instantly, leading them to a booth. They work nearby in the financial district, and whatever they do, they're high enough on the totem pole, or perhaps behind the scenes, that they don't often wear ties.

Dinner fades into the background hum; the jazz drops an octave, silky, sultry. Around us, conversations blur into white noise—deals being made, secrets being shared, the usual symphony of power and desire that fills The Sanctuary each night. But in this shadowed booth, with Brie's fingers brushing mine, the rest of the world fades.

"Tell me something I don't know," I whisper. What I

mean: something real. Something not for the case, not for the club—just us.

"Hmm. You first," she says, but her gaze flits across the room, ever watching.

"You want me to go first? Fine." I catch her hand, press it flat to my chest.

"Every woman since you has been a pale echo of a weekend I couldn't forget."

For the first time tonight, vulnerability flickers across her face—quick as lightning. "That's…dramatic."

"Maybe not what you want to hear," I murmur, leaning closer, the air between us charged with heat and risk. "But I don't play games. I don't want misunderstandings. I want more." She doesn't pull away—but she doesn't lean in either. And that hesitation tells me everything.

CHAPTER
EIGHTEEN

BRIE

Leave. Just go.

Every trained reflex screams for distance, but my body betrays me—heat where there should be adrenaline, his touch pulsing through my blood.

A million tiny pins prick my skin, my chest constricts, and while my eyes burn I can't seem to break away. It's fear. Clean, bright, humiliating.

Plain and simple. Only cowards succumb to fear. Fear is information. It isn't a verdict. (My father's voice. My training. None of it accounts for the ache.)

What exactly do I fear? Getting close to someone who's willing to risk something—an investment—for me? Someone who looks at me like he's willing to climb over any wall I erect? Or worse—someone who'll wait at the gate until I open it.

He said no one else came close. That every woman after

me had been measured against something I never agreed to become. The logic of longing is cruel—comparison dressed up as devotion.

"Brie? Is something wrong?"

I blink, breaking our locked gaze, as it hits me that I zoned out, pulling away, and forgetting the assignment.

There's no professional need to withdraw. The private group I work for touts work-life balance—unlike the CIA, there's no demand that I sever ties. *Not that I had many to sever this time around. Unlike when I gave up my world for a job.*

He leans closer, concerned...and, if I'm honest, insistent. There's no doubt, if I got up and made my excuses, disappeared—which I'm trained and skilled at doing—he'd find me. Comfort settles over that certainty, blunting the edge.

Watching emotion ripple across his features—unguarded, uncalculated—I feel the ache of my own defenses. I'm tired of living behind reinforced glass, watching life happen on the other side. Tired of giving everything to my goals, or worse, someone else's. That's why I left the CIA. It wasn't just that I questioned the leadership. While that definitely factored into the decision, I want more from life.

"Why don't we go back to my place?" My hand finds his wrist—steadying myself on him as much as choosing him.

He answers with a searing kiss, the kind that eradicates fear, panic, even thought.

After the kiss, his thumb swipes my lips, and he springs to action. His grip is firm, not possessive—urgency wrapped in care. He steers me through corridors washed in amber light, the kind that flatters sin and secrets alike. The golden glow soothes, even as our steps quicken, fully aware others will see us exiting together, but he's not keeping me a secret.

We will be seen. Let them. He isn't hiding me; I'm done hiding from myself.

If Eddie bothers with viewing the footage to learn where Adrien and I got off to, he may raise an eyebrow that he didn't take me upstairs to a room, but he's just as likely to assume Adrien's plan is to take me in the back of his limousine. Chances are Eddie doesn't care what his boss does. After all, he's not suspicious, yet. Let him catalogue exits and angles. He'll misread what matters.

We exit the building on the side, cross the street, hands linked, and as if by magic, a car pulls up to the curb and Adrien opens the back passenger door.

"How'd you do that?"

"I messaged in the restaurant. You were so lost in your head you didn't notice."

"You knew I'd invite you back to my place?" The idea that I'm so transparent to this man... Almost no one reads me correctly. I don't even think I knew I was going to invite him into my home.

"No." He sits in the car beside me, closing the door. "I knew I needed to get you out of there. My place or yours, the location—immaterial." He waits, watching my face, like he'll change course if I ask. I place my hand over his in answer.

His fingers lace with mine; heat coils low when our thighs align.

He presses a button and the divider between us and the driver rises. The quiet that follows is decadent. The low purr of the engine fills the space, and the city's neon staccato paints his face in pulses of blue and gold. For a moment, I let the world blur and listen—to the heartbeat that might be his or mine, synced like a metronome set to something wickedly slow.

"Is this your personal car?"

"One of the clubs. They're on call for members."

"So any member could take a ride in one of these cars?"

"We have membership tiers. Only the highest level has unlimited, on-demand access to private transportation in city centers."

"And there's a divider?"

"Do you honestly care if all of our limousines have dividers?"

His sharp eyes take me in, calling me out for what I am often guilty of, which is staying on task.

The driver turns onto the avenue, and we seem to be in time with intersection lights, our speed fast enough that the storefront lights blur into multi-colored streaks.

"Do you check them? Regularly?" If I were building a honey trap, this is where I'd tuck the wire.

It seems to me that the back of a limousine, especially one with no direct connection to the occupants, would be as good a place as any to have private, discreet conversations, and a valuable resource should someone care to monitor.

His muscles stiffen, and his head shifts an infinitesimal amount, such a small degree of motion I might've overlooked it unless in close proximity.

He sinks back against the cushion, his gaze flicking to the blur of lights, and now it's my turn to watch as awareness washes over him and his thoughts scatter through implications. For a heartbeat the city fades. Only his thumb tracing the back of my hand, the air thick with things we haven't said.

We ride together wordlessly up the avenue until the driver slows in front of my building. Our shoes click against the aged marble, sloped in the center, grooves worn by other lives, other choices. I push the key into the lock, first the deadbolt, then the bottom lock, scanning the perimeter for signs of intrusion, a habit that shall probably never die.

Once we step across the threshold, I proceed with removing my shoes, wincing, as I watch him taking in my space. The configuration is a slightly odd one, probably because this floor used to be one home and someone came along decades ago and split it into three apartments. I suspect someone came along more recently and tore down some of the walls, leaving me with a short entry hall that opens into a much larger living area, with another hall that leads to two bedrooms with a bathroom at the end. The small kitchen is bigger than many in Manhattan, but there's another hallway that leads to a small room. I liked the place for the high ceilings, spacious and plentiful windows, and the fact there's no fire escape leading into the apartment from the outside, leaving only one exit point, if one doesn't count the two-foot-thick walls. (I do. I always count the walls as emergency exit points.)

I pad barefoot, heels dangling from one finger, and join him where he stares at the blank wall in my living area.

"No television?"

"One day I'll put a piece of art there. If I watch television, I usually watch on my laptop."

"I take it you don't possess a media room?"

I bite back an amused smile. "Have you visited many Manhattan apartments?"

"Fair point." He taps the tip of my nose. "So you may not be an art curator but you're an art lover. As such, what would you choose to fill the void?"

It's an interesting word choice. Void. As if he can see the negative space I live around.

"The room is perfectly styled. Comfortable furnishings, a creamy soft rug, muted colors to imbue a soothing environment, and you've left this space open, awaiting something... what do you see?"

He's not wrong. I've envisioned the art hanging in a white oak frame, but the piece I envision would be expansive and likely challenging to move. And my tastes change.

Instead of getting pulled into a discussion of local artists and the pieces I'm considering, knowing we're now in my home, that we can now talk freely, I say, "Moira Kelly." The name tastes metallic on my tongue. "Ring any bells?"

He studies me, thoughtful, but I sense he's more surprised by my change of subject than the name.

"No. Is that who Eddie met in the park?"

"She's a former MI5 operative turned private intelligence broker. It's not who Eddie met with in the park, but we identified the woman he met with and she's widely believed to work for Moira Kelly."

I tap on my phone, accessing the KOAN portal and the file, then the photo. He takes the phone from me, enlarging the photo with his fingers.

"Kelly is widely known to be a broker of information. Corporate competitors, foreign intelligence services, political operatives. Based on this, it would seem Eddie doesn't sell directly to the extortionists, rather he's selling raw intelligence to brokers."

"Plural?"

"Kelly represents one entity. We suspect that if he realizes his commodity is valuable, he shops it. He's got quite the setup."

"Jesus." He rests a thigh against the back of my sofa and hands the phone back to me. "I recognize her."

"You do?" I take the phone from him, looking at the photo of Moira Kelly for the hundredth time. She's in her seventies but stunning in a Helen Mirren way. Time has been kind to her, leaving her silver-streaked shoulder length hair and elegant poise, even when in line at an event. The photo had been taken outside of a London theatrical premiere—a red carpet of convenient associates. With the right AI, threads tie themselves; you simply choose which to pull. This photo and so many others over decades. A connective task that might have taken weeks but with the help of our analysis algorithms, we achieved in hours.

"She attends the seasonal fashion shows. Milan. Paris. I don't believe I've ever been introduced to her, but I recognize her." He's thoughtful. "Following Eddie, tracing this back to a broker, that's not going to help the senator is it? You're no closer to finding the extortionist."

"Oh, we are." *You just don't see the snare yet.*

"What's the plan? To ask Moira Kelly who the buyer is? I can't imagine she could give that information out without committing career suicide."

"You don't get it, do you?" *This isn't a leak; it's a business model.*

He squints, tilting his head, communicating in that debonair way he possesses that he believes he gets it, but he doesn't.

"This is bigger than that one threat. It's about weaponizing information. If you kick Eddie out, they'll send someone else in, and that employee will take steps to avoid getting caught that Eddie didn't take."

"Maybe, but…it's one source. I need to shut it down on my end. I have a responsibility to the membership."

"Give us time. A week."

"And what about you? What are you doing chasing this down? Is this Moira Kelly woman… Are her people dangerous? I have this vision of you going through the streets at night with a gun in hand."

I hold up my shoes, grinning. "And a knife tucked in the heel, or blades on the sole that eject when thrown?"

"Yes, something just like that." He grins—or smirks. Or both. It's sin and sunlight. And it loosens something I didn't know I was clenching.

A laugh erupts and I drop my shoes to the ground.

"You're funny. Do you want something to drink?"

He shakes his head in the negative.

"But if you clamp down on Eddie, it's likely every lead shutters. We need time."

"Hmm. Well, then, I'm going to need something in exchange."

"And what is that?"

"A tour of your home. This…tells me only that you have good taste and that your home is a design work in progress. I want the full tour."

A tax I'm happy to pay. "You want to see each and every room, or one room in particular?" I ask, stepping back with a flirtatious flair. "There's not much to see." I point to the kitchen opening. "Kitchen. Hall."

He follows along behind me and I purposefully add a little extra sway to my hips. Before, I felt a little thrown, but with the open conversation about the investigation, the reminder of my purpose, I'm feeling stronger—and not quite as cautious.

He follows around the corner and into my small, windowless bedroom. Turning, I place my hands on his shoulders, pushing his jacket off, but he covers my hands, slowing me. Not refusal. Reverence.

"I want to know the woman who chooses calm in a city that never sleeps," he murmurs, gaze sweeping over the soft gray folds, taking in my bedroom with the same intensity he brought to studying the Moira Kelly photo. "I want to understand why you have a Steinway baby grand in your living room but no art on your walls."

"The piano was my grandmother's." She gave it to me long ago, when I'd been in elementary school and the last thing I wanted was to take piano lessons. That piano moved with us everywhere. "When my parents retired to Guatemala they insisted I take it." First thing that felt like mine. That had been the first move my parents made that wasn't funded by the government, at least in my lifetime.

He's so close I breathe in his cologne, enticing and familiar.

"Do you play often?"

"Sometimes." When I can't sleep. When the questions won't quiet. When I need to remember myself.

He cups my face, thumb tracing the line of my cheekbone. "Will you play for me again?"

The question is gentle, patient—no demand, just genuine interest. It's so different from the men who've wanted pieces of me, who've seen my appearance as a trophy or commendation. "Maybe," I whisper, leaning into his touch. A fragile word that still feels like yes.

"That's all I ask." His other hand finds my waist, pulling me closer until we're breathing the same air. "For now. Maybes. Possibilities. Time to discover who you are when it's just us." The gentleness guts me more than any demand would.

"What if you don't like what you find? What if I bore you?"

"Impossible." The conviction in his voice tightens around my chest. "I've been searching for you for years, remember? Not the spy. Not the American intelligence operative. You."

This time when he kisses me, there's no urgency, no desperation. Just thorough exploration, like he's memorizing the taste of me. My hands fist in his shirt, and I let myself sink into the feeling—no assignment parameters, no exit strategy, just this moment with this man who somehow climbs the walls I build and smooths my edges.

When we break apart, I'm breathless, my skin literally craving his touch. "Adrien—"

"I know your job isn't the office variety," he says, forehead resting against mine. "I hope it's not too dangerous, but I'm sure safety isn't guaranteed. And I can see how it would be simpler to not have anyone worrying. But I also know what I feel when I look at you. What I felt that weekend, what I haven't been able to forget."

"I didn't forget you either." It shouldn't be a difficult confession, as it's obvious I remember it all, but saying it out loud requires effort. "But you need to understand, I'm not normal. After college, I threw myself into a world where relationships were discouraged, and often impossible to maintain. Yes, I'm in a different situation, but I'm not sure how to spend time with someone without an agenda or an extraction plan. I'm...adjusting."

"Then don't be normal." His smile is soft, devastating. "Be you. The woman designed an apartment around empty wall space because she's still deciding who she wants to be."

He's perceptive.

"I'm deciding," I whisper, liking the sound of those words in my own apartment, in this space that's mine.

"I can help." His smile is soft, devastating. "I know a thing or two about art."

He dips his head, brushing his lips along my temple—tentative, seeking permission. When I tilt my head to give him better access, his kisses trail to the sensitive skin below my ear. Each press of his lips sends heat spiraling through me, pooling low.

This is different from last night. Slower. Intentional. Like we're rewriting what happened on his couch—choosing each other instead of being consumed.

"Will you let me?" His voice is low, hopeful.

Instead of answering with words, I reach for the buttons of his shirt.

We undress slowly this time—no fumbling, no desperation. My fingers work each button deliberately while his hands find the zipper of my dress. The rasp of it lowering sounds loud in my quiet apartment. He peels the fabric from my shoulders, watching it pool at my feet like he's unveiling something precious.

Cool air kisses my skin and my nipples tighten—from temperature or anticipation, I'm not sure. He's still watching me, drinking me in like I'm a masterpiece he's discovered in secret. His touch is reverent when he reaches for my bra clasp, his gaze consuming as he slides the straps down my arms.

I push his shirt off his shoulders, palms gliding over muscle I memorized last night but get to appreciate now. By the time we're both bare and I'm lying across my sheets—the comforter rolled back, my high-thread-count cotton soft beneath me—I'm dizzy with lust and impatient with anticipation.

His exploration of my body is deceptively tender. Not the frantic urgency of last night, but thorough—like he's learning me properly this time. His mouth traces paths I didn't know were sensitive: the inside of my wrist, the hollow of my collarbone, the curve where my hip meets my thigh.

Pleasure unfurls hot and sharp with each pass of his lips, each deliberate touch. He maps my body with his hands and mouth, pulling sounds from me I don't recognize—soft gasps, needy whimpers. Each moan is a confession neither of us dares speak aloud.

His lips close over my nipple and I arch into him. He sucks, teeth grazing lightly, then soothes with his tongue before moving to give equal attention to the other breast. My fingers thread through his hair, holding him there, and when he finally begins his descent—kissing down my ribs, my stomach, the sensitive skin of my lower belly—I'm trembling.

He positions himself between my thighs, spreading them wider, and looks up at me with those golden-green eyes. "You denied me this last night." The reprimand is wicked and worshipful, edged with humor.

My breathing goes fast and shallow, every muscle tight with anticipation.

The first sweep of his tongue sparks fire through my core and my knees rise automatically, thighs spreading wider, opening for him. He groans against my flesh—actually *groans*—like the taste of me is something he's been craving.

Within seconds it's clear he remembers the cartography of me. Pressure points. Rhythms. The exact angle that makes my hips buck off the bed. His tongue circles my clit with practiced precision, then flattens, dragging slowly upward.

When he seals his lips over the sensitive bundle of nerves and sucks, my hands fist in the sheets.

"Adrien—" His name breaks on my lips.

He adds his fingers—one, then two—curling inside to find that spot that shatters reason. The dual sensation of his tongue on my clit and his fingers stroking deep has me making sounds I'd be embarrassed by if I could think straight.

But I can't think. Can only feel. The wet heat of his mouth. The obscene, perfect rhythm. The way he watches me fall apart like it's his favorite view.

My orgasm builds at the base of my spine, coiling tighter with each pass of his tongue. When it breaks, it's toe-curling, back-arching, cry-his-name ecstasy. I ride the waves while he works me through it, gentling but not stopping until I'm shaking and oversensitive.

When I finally open my eyes, it's to greet his satisfied, knowing grin—lips glistening, eyes dark with hunger.

He presses a kiss to my inner thigh, then shifts, moving up my body until his hands are planted on either side of my head. He hovers there—close, contained, waiting.

I pull him down for a deep kiss, tasting myself on his tongue. The intimacy of it should feel strange. Instead, it feels right. Natural.

I push his shoulder, urging him onto his back. "My turn."

Balance is its own kind of power, and after years of wondering what it would feel like to touch him again, to make him lose control, I'm not rushing this.

His powerful heart hammers beneath my palm as I trail kisses down his chest, following his lead. I take my time—nipping at his hip bone, kissing the V of muscle that disappears below his waist, letting my hair brush his skin. By the time I reach him, he's rock hard, his erection straight and thick, lightly veined, crown already glistening.

I wrap my fingers around his base—he's hot, heavy in my hand—and his sharp intake of breath makes me smile. When I flatten my tongue and lick up his shaft, his hips jerk. I catch his hungry gaze, hold it, then swirl my tongue over his crown, tasting salt and him, before taking him in.

The weight of him on my tongue, the heat, the way his thighs tense beneath my free hand—it's intoxicating. I take him deeper, hollowing my cheeks, and the helpless sound he makes is filthy and holy all at once.

He's not the only one who remembers. I haven't forgotten how he responds when I twist my hand at his base while my mouth works the crown. I remember the sound he makes when I take him deep enough to gag slightly. I remember how his fingers tighten in my hair—not forcing, just holding on.

With my hand gripping his base and my mouth working him steadily, it's not long before he swells on my tongue, throbbing, close to the edge. The sensation is crudely erotic—his control fraying, his breath coming in ragged gasps, my name a rough prayer on his lips.

He pulls me off him with a growl, his hand gentle but firm on my jaw. There's a hint of scolding in his expression, but his eyes are dark with need.

"Not like that." His voice is rough, wrecked. "When I come tonight, I'm coming inside you."

It's not a command. It's a claim. My body answers before I do—a clench of need, wetness flooding between my thighs.

I shift, climbing over him, placing a knee on either side of his hips. I'm hyperaware of how exposed I am like this—straddling him, wet and open above him while he watches.

But the hunger in his gaze makes me feel powerful rather than vulnerable.

I position myself, slick and shameless, and rock forward so his crown drags through my folds, circles my clit. The friction is maddening, not enough and too much all at once.

We both groan. His hands find my hips, fingers digging in, but he doesn't guide me, doesn't take control. Just holds on while I tease us both.

"Condom." He growls the word, though his grip tightens like he's fighting the urge to thrust up into me.

"I have an IUD." I still my movements, meeting his eyes. "And I trust you."

Something flickers across his face—surprise, then heat, then something deeper I don't want to name yet. "But last night—you regretted—"

I place my finger over his lips, silencing him. "I didn't regret you."

It's true. Last night we should have handled things differently, should have talked first, been prepared. But we were drunk on lust and restraint finally breaking. Stepping back now, pretending this is casual when we both know it isn't—that feels like the real mistake.

"I trust you," I repeat. And I do. In this, at least. "Do you trust me?"

"Yes." No hesitation. His hands slide up my thighs, over my hips, reverent. "God, yes."

I rise up on my knees, reaching between us to position him. His crown presses against my entrance—hot, insistent—and I hold there for a moment, savoring the anticipation in his eyes, the way his jaw clenches with restraint.

Then I sink down slowly, taking him inch by inch. The stretch is exquisite—a surrender and a claiming all at once.

By the time he's fully seated inside me, we're both breathing hard.

"God, you're beautiful, Brie." He sounds like he's praying. His hands roam—palming my breasts, thumbs circling my nipples, then sliding down to where we're joined.

I rock over him, slow at first, finding the angle that makes my breath catch. The room smells like heat and sex and skin, and the faint sweetness of my perfume clings to him like a secret.

I'm close—muscles tightening, internal walls clenching around him—when he suddenly flips me onto my back with surprising ease. I gasp at the shift, at the loss of control, but then he's covering me with his body, thrusting back inside with a groan that reverberates through my chest.

This angle is deeper, more intense. He braces himself above me, one hand beside my head, the other sliding down to where we're joined. His fingers find my clit—swollen, oversensitive—and circle with relentless precision while he drives into me.

He finds my earlobe with his teeth, nipping, sucking. There's intention in every movement, every shift. Not the desperate fumbling of last night but deliberate, practiced, devastating.

"Come for me," he growls against my ear. "I want to feel you."

His fingers press harder, circles faster, and his thrusts hit that deep spot that makes me see stars. The dual sensation breaks me. Ecstasy tears through me—white-hot and all-consuming—my back arching off the bed, nails digging into his shoulders, his name torn from my throat.

I feel him follow—his thrusts turning erratic, losing rhythm. He groans my name and arches, pulsing deep inside me, filling me with heat. Our releases aren't escape but recognition—two people who stopped running long enough to really *see* each other.

After, he rains soft kisses along my jaw and chest. I cling to him like a woman who finally remembers her own name.

The CIA trained me to compartmentalize. To keep distance. To always have an exit strategy.

This time, I don't reach for distance. I reach for him. This time, I let myself stay.

CHAPTER
NINETEEN

ADRIEN

I wake alone—cool sheets where her warmth should be, her absence beside me an alarm louder than any sound. The room holds no light, yet awareness arrives easily—the kind that lingers when something valuable slips from reach. Wrinkled linen maps the place where she stretched against me, our legs tangled, her breath a soft tide at my throat. Last night taught me what Monaco first revealed: it isn't only the sex with Brie. After, I want the *after*—the talk that opens and opens, the quiet that isn't empty, the nearness that asks nothing but everything.

I pried details from her between silences—fragments, really. She speaks four languages fluently, can hold her own in two more. Krav Maga, she said, came harder. Her brothers went military; she chose a quieter, more shadowed path her parents believed would keep her safer. One still serves, the other now works for the Secret Service. Families like ours worship service—just to different gods. Mine, the market. Hers, the flag.

After brushing my teeth, I pull on my trousers and shirt, leaving the shirt unbuttoned, and step out of the bedroom. Across the hall the door is open and light streams in through the large windows. It's a second bedroom, larger than the one Brie inhabits, only this bedroom is set up more like a den with a desk that's off to one corner and open shelves brimming with clothes. This second bedroom doubles as an office, and I catch glimpses of her life here: a framed photo of what must be her parents, a small stack of novels on the desk, reading glasses she didn't possess in Monaco. Everything precise, organized, but lived-in.

There's no sign of Brie, so listening for sounds, I exit the hallway into the living room. The apartment carries her scent—something clean, faintly floral, as if she refuses to linger anywhere too long.

"Morning." She appears in the kitchen doorway, a loose silk robe floating around her, hair twisted into a careless bun that no stylist could reproduce. Steam curls from the mug in her hand. The moment hangs—quietly domestic, a novelty that feels like déjà vu.

"You made coffee." It sounds more surprised than I intend.

"French press. Figured you'd prefer it to drip." A small smile plays on her lips. "It's almost nine. I wasn't sure if you needed to be somewhere."

That she remembered how I take it—and took the trouble to make it right—feels intimate, like the brush of a thumb at the wrist.

"No, it's fine." I come around, taking the mug from her

and inhaling the coffee aroma before taking a sip. "What time did you get up?"

"I always wake early."

"How? There's no light in that room."

"Circadian rhythm." She moves with purpose now, the woman from last night shifting into her daytime armor—focused, contained.

"Even with no windows?" I gesture toward her bedroom.

"Especially with no windows." She glances at me, and I catch a glimpse of something—maybe vulnerability, maybe just habit. "Training. Habits. Light can compromise sleep schedules on assignment. And I sleep better with one exit point."

The way she says it—flat, unembellished—makes me realize how much of her life has been engineered for control. It's the first real detail she's offered about her work, and I file it away, understanding I'm seeing her world now. One exit point means one entrance point, which means she's always on edge.

I eye her over the mug. I kept her up most of the night. On the yacht, we slept with the light and woke with want, like tide against hull. Here, I wonder—does she ever rest easily?

Her phone buzzes, and the shift is immediate. Spine straightens. Shoulders square. The woman making me coffee becomes the operative—all efficiency and edge.

"Hey," she says, moving toward the den, but her tone has changed. Cooler.

I follow at a distance, fascinated by the transformation.

"Yes, I can talk. I'm at my place."

A beat. "Caroline? Does Hudson know this?"

She nods, twisting slightly so her eyes catch mine. Without mascara, her lashes pale to gold; her skin holds the faint flush of sleep. Silk pajama pants ride low on her hips; the matching tank skims higher, leaving a honeyed strip of midriff I should not be staring at while she discusses classified things.

"Understood. It's smart to monitor Crawford."

With one last glance my way, she heads down the hall to her bedroom. I follow, wanting to hear her side of the conversation, when my phone on the bedside table lights up with Margot's name.

I grab the phone and realize I've got multiple notifications from my mother, father, and Margot. I swipe to answer the incoming call, stepping away from Brie so as not to interfere with her conversation.

"Margot," I answer. "Everything okay?"

"That's what I've been wondering. You've been evading my calls."

"Mother and Father rang separately." That never bodes well.

"And when was the last time you called them?"

I scrub a hand over my face. "Fair. What makes you think I'm evading you?"

"I heard Alicia Morgan is still working with you. Do I need to have PR on standby?"

"No."

"That's what Alicia said."

"You spoke to her?"

"I wanted to confirm you took her meeting."

"I told you I did."

"And I wanted to ensure she's satisfied with—"

"You're checking up on me. What did she tell you?"

"Only that you contracted her services and confidentiality is a part of your agreement."

"Which has made you wildly curious about what I've cocked up."

"Tommy isn't saying."

That's because Tommy doesn't know the specifics.

"You do understand I left the family business?"

"You left the building," she counters. "Not the brand."

"I'm not the brand."

"Yes, brother dearest, you are. And that 'little investment' of yours is global. It will pull more coverage in Italy and France than here. Whatever's happening will come back around."

She's right, and the truth tastes metallic. I could fire Eddie today and shutter the investigation. Crawford won't leak—admitting a threat invites questions about how votes are made. But the longer I let this run, the more likely it is that someone *else* is threatened—someone who won't keep the source under wraps.

"You're going to need to trust me," I say, ending the call. I thumb over to my mother, catching a glimpse in the mirror that stills me: Brie in a wig cap, her golden hair gone.

I move closer, dialing. Mother's call drops to voicemail—the usual: afternoon swim, phone abandoned to a locker or boat bag. "Maman, I missed your call. Papa's, too. Everything's fine. I'll ring you later."

I hang up as Brie juggles with a mousy black wig with a thick braid down the back. When I step closer, I notice her blue eyes are now a murky brown and she's in loose jeans, running shoes, and an unflattering top that loosely hangs below her waist.

"A disguise?"

The transformation is jarring—the same woman, yet removed, like a painting turned to the wall.

"I'll wear a hat and sunglasses too." Practical. Clinical. "From a distance I won't be recognizable."

Up close, of course, she's unmistakable. But then she studs earrings up and down her lobes, and with the small loop in her nose she becomes someone I would overlook in a crowd—some New York student or Jersey kid on an errand.

"What are you up to today?"

"Surveillance. Are you heading into the office?"

"I am." Captivated, I watch her assemble herself—and feel something cold when she reaches for a gun, checks the chamber, tucks it into a backpack.

"Surveillance of what exactly?" The sight of her armed and disguised trips a switch I didn't know I had. Protective isn't a word I've used for myself. It fits now, uncomfortably well.

"It's routine," she says, not meeting my eyes. The distance is professional, and it stings anyway.

"You're not wearing a vest." My voice holds steady; my pulse does not.

"A vest would show under these clothes." She tweaks the fall of the shirt. I want to touch her, to *keep* her. "It's unnecessary. Boring day, most likely. We're rotating shifts." A breath. "Do you think we can have dinner tonight?"

"I'd love that." I take her in again, the vanishing act nearly complete. "This look is…" I let my mouth curve. "Not to my taste, but we could have fun with it."

She snickers, amused but busy. The message is gentle and unmistakable: clear the field.

"Is this all for Eddie?" I ask.

"No. This is for the organization Eddie sells to."

"Who's Caroline?"

She pauses—fraction of a beat—enough to register she clocked my eavesdropping.

"My boss."

I'd thought Hudson wore that crown. "Who called?"

"A colleague. Syd."

"Did I meet her?" I already know the answer.

"No. She's on the West Coast. If we need her, she'll join. For now, remote support."

"And she's a friend?"

"Why the twenty questions?"

Because every detail is earned, and I'm trying not to pry the way I want to. She's doing the work she's built her life around; she won't abandon it because I dislike the idea of her loading a handgun before breakfast.

"Text me. During the day." It's not a request.

She stills, studies my face. The façade thins, and there she is—the softness from last night, the woman in the kitchen making coffee the way I prefer. "Worried about me?"

"Terrified," I admit. "You're carrying a gun and dressed like—" I tip my head, taking her in. "A bike courier or a hungover university student."

She steps closer until her scent finds me beneath the costume. Her palm comes to rest over my heart.

"This is what I do, Adrien. What I'm good at." Gentle, firm. "I'll check in. And we'll set dinner."

"You know your team watches the club's comings and goings on tape," I say, trying for light and failing.

"True. But we're studying interactions. Cameras miss nuance."

"So who are you watching like this?"

"If Eddie leaves during the day. Or his contacts." A small lift of one shoulder. "Assignments shift."

"Then dinner," I say. The word feels like a promise. "As long as you're careful."

As she locks her door, and turns for the stairwell, I catch her wrist gently. "Brie." She pauses, and the disguise falls away for the span of a breath. It's just her—and the truth I can't pretend away. "Be careful," I say quietly. "Some of us don't recover from the same loss twice."

CHAPTER TWENTY

BRIE

"How's that Civic?"

Quinn's on speaker, and I'm crouched down in a velveteen seat that's seen better days. Circular burns dot the worn velveteen seat cushions and the whole thing smells like someone doused it in chemicals to wash away decades of cigarette smoke.

"It works. No noticeable dents on the bodywork. Paint job's faded with age but no identifiable rust patterns." The name of the game is to sit in a car no one looks at twice. Can't be too new or nice, and it can't be too damaged. An early two thousands Honda Civic does the job. "The smell..." I wrinkle my nose, not that she can see.

"Is it bad? If I need a different rental source, say so."

"It's not the best, but it's not supposed to be, right?"

My location on the street is a good one, parked in a row of similar sedans crowded between the limited section of pavement that allows parking, with a view of those getting dropped off to enter the club. Three hours in and every member arrives the same way, via car service or taxi. I snap license plates and send them to Quinn, but given we have been granted interior surveillance access, it's not a necessary step. It's just filling the time and allows us to match plates with members.

"Alright girl. Chain's moving." We've started referring to Eddie as chain because of his ever-present gold chain. "Side door exit."

"No car at the curb."

The side street is one-way and the only access is a right turn from the road I'm sitting on.

"He's out," Quinn says. I hear keys clacking—she's sending it to the team.

One. Two. Three.

There—he appears. I crank the Civic. He's on the sidewalk, scanning south. A small sedan with an Uber light pulls up. I note the plate as I edge into traffic. It's light now, but one wrong turn and the district chokes.

"He's headed north," I announce.

"Noah's up," Quinn says.

"Turning onto Ninth. He might be headed out of the city."

"Noah's on Tenth. If he cuts to the West Side, he'll take point."

I'm about five cars back. From what I can tell, Eddie's head's bent down, not paying attention at all to his surroundings.

"Traffic is light," I say. If it were heavy and he stayed on the avenue, I'd suspect a close destination. Light traffic makes his route inconclusive.

I continue on with the speed of traffic, mostly hitting greens.

It's not a chase as Eddie seems to be completely unaware. It's when we're crossing into the twenties that it hits me. "I bet he's going to Penn Station. He may be heading home."

He turns right onto Thirty-fourth—Penn Station, confirmed. I hunt for parking and radio Quinn. "Drop point: Eighth. Do you have CCTV in Penn?"

"I'm working on it," Quinn says. "It'll be delayed—messy feeds. What's his outfit?"

"No hat. Black sports coat, black crewneck, black trousers."

"Does he always dress like a waiter?"

"Not always, but black seems to be the predominant color of choice for Sanctuary employees." With a smirk, I add, "Gold chain shines."

"So he's not doing anything to avoid being spotted?"

"No. Appears oblivious." Miraculously, there's a spot to my right so I take it. "I nabbed street parking on Thirty-fourth."

As I park, I lose sight of Eddie's car, but I know where he's going. And he'll lose time exiting the car.

Within seconds, I've parked in a way that would make Kristof, my old driving instructor, proud and step out of the Honda, blending into the pedestrian traffic with a walk-run that matches the pace of any rushed New Yorker.

I glimpse a man in black descending into Penn Station's maze of corridors.

Shit.

I tap my earpiece. "Lost him. He disappeared underground."

"Head for the trains," Quinn says. "If he took the subway, you'll never catch him. If he's on a platform, you might."

She's right. He could be anywhere—at a kiosk, grabbing coffee, blending into the crowd.

I cut past Dunkin', Sbarro, the kiosks, scanning collars and hairlines. Plenty of black jackets—none at the right height or with the correct dark trim.

Noah catches my eye across the concourse. He tilts right; I tilt left.

Twenty minutes. Nothing. He's gone.

As I'm headed back to retrieve my car, Quinn's voice flows through my ear. "Did you know the senator had a meeting with Adrien?"

"No." But it shouldn't be surprising that the two would meet. "Could've been unexpected."

It occurs to me that I haven't texted Adrien.

"Happened this morning. It was quick."

"What'd they discuss?"

"We don't have audio in Adrien's office. Only video of the hallway."

Right. "I'll ask."

"You can return the car and head home," Quinn tells me. "Noah's heading back. You've got dinner plans right?"

"Yeah. I'll head back."

I hate losing targets. He wasn't even trying to evade us, which makes it worse. Penn Station and the subways… they're both fucking madhouses. Maybe I played it too conservatively. Perhaps I should've parked closer—never lost sight.

The Civic's a junker. I could've double-parked and let the city tow it. But I know that would've been a poor plan. It would've attracted attention and increased the likelihood he would've turned around.

Back on the West Side, my building in view, my phone buzzes.

> UNKNOWN NUMBER
> STOP

I give the text a second glance, searching for the telltale signs of spam. Some additional message. A link to click. There's nothing.

Holding the phone, I continue ascending the stairs. I have two hours to shower and prep for dinner, which sounds like a lot but with traffic I'm looking at forty-five minutes travel time unless I take the subway.

If Eddie's back down at the club for the evening service, then he may have just had another brief meeting. If he's still gone, then it's conceivable something happened and he needed to head home. Although would someone like Eddie really take the train? Wouldn't he have access to the same fleet of cars that Adrien does? And he chose not to use a car associated with the club. And then he disappeared.

I insert my key into the deadbolt, as my gaze tracks the door frame. It's when I slip the key into the lower bolt that my skin chills and the alertness that only a surge of adrenaline produces hits me. Fresh scratches mark the brass.

Someone jimmied the lock. Then locked it behind them.

I draw my gun. In the Agency we often left them, but habit or not, I've carried for years. This feels necessary now.

I don't know whether they left the lock to trap me or to hide their entrance. Either way, I move like I mean it.

Gun up, I turn the knob.

If anyone's here, they heard the key.

I push the door wide.

The hall is empty. I clear the threshold, shoulder angled to watch the corridor.

I step forward, slow and deliberate.

A draft lifts the edge of my wig.

What? Nobody would jump from a fifth-floor window.

"Hello?" I call.

The room's empty, but black and white glossy photographs scatter across the sofa and floor.

Gun up, I round the kitchen corner.

The windows are open.

The source of the breeze.

Finger on the trigger, I lean and peer down.

Would someone actually hang from the ledge?

I look down—street, ledge—no hands, no rigging.

No plausible exit.

Not without gear.

Broad daylight.

Crowds milling below.

Nobody climbs a façade in broad daylight without being seen.

A rattling sounds.

What was that?

Quiet. Definitely inside.

I leave the window open and step into the living room.

"Hello?"

My gaze falls on one of the photographs. It's of me and Adrien.

STOP.

The message makes sense now.

The blackmailers sent photographs to Senator Crawford too.

My gut says I'm alone in the apartment now.

I can't quite describe how I know, but the place feels empty.

To confirm, I clear the bedrooms, one by one.

Then return down the hall, finger on the trigger for my entire tour.

The front door's closed, whereas I left it cracked.

The window—a distraction.

I close and lock the door—symbolic, maybe—then dial Quinn.

CHAPTER
TWENTY-ONE

ADRIEN

I've never been the man who checks his phone every five minutes. Yet here I am, watching the screen like it keeps my future under glass. What the hell is this woman doing to me?

Any sane man would be concerned. She slipped a loaded handgun into her backpack this morning. "Precautionary," she said. As if the word could blunt the image of cold steel against her palm.

The great irony is I'm the client. I'm the one she's technically working for. She's also the reason I haven't fired Eddie, locked down The Sanctuary, and walked away. Well, that—and I do owe the senator enough to at least give them a chance to trace the blackmailer.

Still, the more I replay what Brie's told me, the clearer it becomes: her organization cares more about exposing whoever trades secrets than the ones buying them. When I discussed this with the senator this morning during his brief visit to my office, he said he believes finding both is of great importance. Although given the threats he's receiving—or more specifically, what action they want him to take—he's narrowed the pool of culprits, at least for his extortion.

It's a mad world, and all I can picture is that gun—weight and chill.

I reach for the phone again—habit, not logic. The day's almost gone and silence hums louder than any ringtone. But I'm not powerless. I click on contacts and press send.

The line rings twice.

"This is Hudson."

"Adrien d'Avricourt." My voice sounds steadier than I feel.

"Hi Adrien, what can I do for you?"

"Calling for a project update." I don't add that I'm really calling to make sure she's breathing. "The senator stopped by this morning. Seems he's narrowed his list of suspects."

"He has ideas, but ideas alone won't win an indictment, or even a search warrant."

"How close are you to catching them?"

Hudson's pause stretches long enough that I wonder if we've lost connection.

"Each threat narrows the field," he says. "But we're not there yet."

"And when can I start cleaning house?" I pointedly avoid saying Eddie's name with the door closed and voices in the hallway.

"We're close," he says. "By the way—do you know where Thorne went this afternoon?"

That gets my attention. "I assume he's here."

"Is it unusual for him to leave during the day?"

I tap my fingers against the desk; aware that I don't actually know, as he's a senior staff member. "I'm not a micromanager. Our hours are non-traditional. Employees don't alert me if they step out for errands or whatnot."

So Eddie's gone. And if he's gone, maybe Brie's following. My stomach knots.

"Why?"

"He was last seen outside Penn Station."

"And?" Surely there's more to that statement.

"The project update. We are making headway. We've found more on Moira Kelly. Intelligence suggests she's part of Magpie, a group that came into existence in the late nineties. A business built around selling secrets. She's a former CIA psychological expert who went private; she might actually be the head of the organization."

"I recognized her. She's a regular during fashion week. Museum showings."

"She presents as a wealthy widow who spends most of her time in Europe," Hudson says.

That matches up with what I recall. Not necessarily the widow part, but she definitely comes across as high net worth and well-connected.

"And I presume she recruits sources?"

"We're still working on how her business functions."

"So you still need me to keep..." I pause, looking to the closed walnut door, and lower my voice, "The subject employed?"

"Actually, no. Proceed as you wish."

"But I was told that would shut down leads."

"It appears she's onto us."

My stomach roils. The absence of communications from Brie... "What happened?"

"There's been a break-in; Brie Anderson's apartment."

I'm on my feet before I register moving, chair slamming

the wall behind me. The office walls blur as I charge to the door, slinging it open and barking to the assistant, "Get me a car. Now. Have it outside by the time I'm downstairs."

"She's fine," he adds, but the words barely penetrate. The palm holding the phone has grown clammy and my throat tightens.

I knew something was wrong. And I sat here—comfortable, detached—a king in glass while she was out there alone.

"This just happened. We're still getting to the bottom of it. But the person who broke in left photographs of both you and Brie. No message but she might have surprised them before they were done. But we're fairly certain it's related to the investigation."

"In what way?"

"They want us to stop."

I sling open the door, squinting into the daylight.

"Which means we're getting close."

A black limousine pulls to the curb and I'm reaching for the handle before the wheels have stopped turning.

I shout Brie's address to the driver and the second he responds with, "Yes sir," I'm pressing the button to raise the divider.

"Say it again," I demand. "She's not hurt."

I know he said she's okay, but I need to see her. I need to touch her and know that she's unharmed. I'm wired, unfocused—scared. There it is, the word I hate admitting even to myself.

Yes, that's the fucking emotion. Fear, clean and corrosive.

"She's fine. There's no damage to her apartment."

That fucking apartment. Her building with its single-entry code suddenly seems impossibly vulnerable. No doorman, no security desk, just a goddamn wood and glass door between her and whoever wants in.

"Why wasn't I told the second it happened?"

"Because it just happened. We're still sorting it out." His tone shifts. "And I didn't realize how personal this is for you."

I glare out the darkened windows. We're on the West Side Highway now, flying north, weaving across the lanes.

"We have history," I say—too clipped to hide anything. It's none of his damn business, and I don't particularly care if he's pissed his employee didn't share. That's her burden to explain, though every instinct in me wants her out of this assignment.

"Understood."

There's a sharpness to his tone but I don't give a damn.

"I'll be at her place momentarily."

"I'll let them know to expect you."

"Them?"

"Brie and a teammate."

"Right."

"We'll be in touch," he says and ends the call.

I lean back, eyes closed, forcing breath into lungs that refuse to expand. Christ, just hearing those words, that someone broke in, when I'd already been worried.

I wipe my palms on my trousers and as I do so, a memory surfaces.

White sheets, sunspots drifting across the ceiling, the scent of eucalyptus and her skin. Monaco. A weekend of light and laughter before she vanished. That weekend in Monaco was the first time I'd felt like I understood what Madame Vassante meant about the Star card—hope, guidance, finding your path. Brie had been my star, and I let her slip away into darkness.

"How lucky am I? Finding you in a bar in Monaco, when you work at an art gallery I pass every day."

"Think of how many times our paths have crossed... All it took for you to see me was for the right aperture."

I lifted her fingers from my chest and nipped at a nail, then pressed my lips to the back of her hand.

"Are you into photography?"

She laughed. The sound light and airy.

Yes, that hadn't been work Brie. She'd been unmoored from the job that weekend. And what did she say?

"Psychology. That's what I'm into. How the human mind works." *She tapped my temple and I caressed her breast.* "What it captures. When and why. If you think about it, we're in the same trade."

"How do you come to that conclusion?"

I hadn't held back on my family connection. On the contrary, I'd used it to lure her away for a night that by morning I wanted to extend infinitely.

"Isn't that what fashion is? Garnering attention? Cultivating want?"

"If my father pitched it to me like that maybe I wouldn't insist my sister take the reins."

"What... You're not?"

"No. That's why I was at the bar last night. Let the old man know I wouldn't be taking the title."

"King?" *Her smile had been so beautiful.*

"CEO."

"Same difference."

I'd kissed her and positioned myself between her thighs. I'd been inside her maybe fifteen minutes prior but I couldn't get close enough.

"Why don't you want it?"

"My sister. It's her passion. It's not mine."

She stiffened below me, ever so slightly. "Does your father not believe a woman can run the ship?"

It was my turn to roll onto my side, propping my head on my elbow, taking in the beauty beside me. "You know, you're the first person who didn't push on why I didn't want it. Who didn't assume that I'm lazy or a no-good oaf, and that's why my father's pissed."

"You want your sister to follow her passion. That's admirable."

She got it. She got me.

The car pulls to a stop and I open my eyes. There are no cops. No crime scene tape.

Hell. They probably didn't even call it in.

I hop out and am crossing the street as the driver calls, "Sir? Should I wait for you?"

I slow on the sidewalk long enough to shout, "Sure. Find nearby parking. I'll text Tally when I need you."

As I climb the marble stairs, I'm reminded of the Madame and her Parisian flat. The smoky room saturated in purple, gold and twinkling lights, and the cards. The Tower. Death.

Suddenly, I'm running.

I take the steps two at a time, and one thought hammers with each footfall: I won't lose her.

Not again. Not ever.

CHAPTER
TWENTY-TWO

BRIE

Three sharp knocks—too loud, too urgent for a neighbor. The sound splits the stillness, vibrating through the floorboards before my pulse can catch up. I recognize the measured, precise pattern before I hear his voice.

"Brie!" Adrien's voice carries desperation I've never heard before. I yank the door open.

"I have neighbors—"

He grips my shoulders before I can finish, eyes wild as they scan my face like he's checking for injuries. His hands are warm, almost shaking, the controlled businessman stripped down to raw instinct.

You'd think he'd shrink back from my annoyed glare but instead his hands tighten, anchoring me as he stares like he's debating if I'm a hallucination. Our eyes lock in silent confrontation, a battle of wills, but then he gives me a slight shake. "You didn't call. Nothing. I heard nothing all day. And then this?" His breath hits my cheek—coffee, rain, something distinctly him—and the contact blurs irritation into ache.

"What did Hudson tell you?"

I shrug out of his grip and reach past him to shut the door.

"Only that someone broke into your place. And left photographs."

I step past him, heading down the hall.

"Why are you wearing gloves?"

Latex bites tight around my wrists, thin cover between me and the mess someone left behind. "Dusting for prints. Though whoever did this was probably smart enough to wear gloves too." I gesture to my supplies spread across the coffee table. "Noah dropped off the kit." I reach into my black duffel and pull out a pair of blue latex gloves for Adrien. "Here, until I'm finished, wear these."

"Where are your colleagues?" He's scanning the space like he expects multitudes of people to exit from the crevices.

"It was only Noah. He went back down."

"Down where?"

"Your office and the club."

"Why?"

"Information." It should be clear.

He reaches for one of the photographs, and I slap at his arm. "Gloves first. Here, look at those." I direct him to the photographs I've already dusted, but with no luck.

The photograph he picks up is one that was taken of the two of us outside my apartment building on the day I let him walk me home.

He studies the image—the two of us caught mid-conversation, my hand briefly touching his arm as we talked. Seeing us on glossy paper feels indecent, like someone photographed a confession neither of us has voiced. The angle suggests someone across the street, probably using a telephoto lens.

"They've been watching us for days," he says grimly.

"At least. And this one—" I point to another photo showing him entering his office building "—could have been taken any morning. They're establishing a pattern, showing us they know our routines."

There are two troubling aspects to these photographs. First, I should've been aware of surveillance. Second, that means someone has been aware of us since the beginning of the assignment.

"Based on these photographs, someone clued in to us investigating as far back as the day when we came to your offices, which means Eddie likely knows we found the server room."

"Are you looking for Eddie's prints?"

"No. Eddie didn't leave these—timing doesn't work. We lost him at Penn Station, and he didn't have a bag large enough for photographs this size without bending them."

Adrien nods slowly. "Hudson gave me the greenlight to fire him. If he's aware we're onto him, this changes things."

"Maybe. But someone is paying him for information. And someone definitely knows about us."

I blow the dust I've layered on the print, scanning for uneven texture.

"Do you think Eddie knows someone broke into your home?"

I consider what he's saying. "I'd expect he's fully aware a team is investigating him. Now, whether he's aware someone texted me to stop and left this little gift, it's conceivable the people who hired him are the ones wanting us to stop."

"The woman Eddie met at the waterfront—could she have done this?"

"That woman works for Moira Kelly. Catriona Murphy. I doubt she'd be sent for this kind of project. She's more of the courier sort."

"Moira Kelly. Magpie?"

"Rumors have abounded about Magpie for as long as I can remember. Magpie trades in secrets the way others trade in stocks."

What we're doing—what we're risking—isn't on that level. It can't be. "It's likely they know very little about us—our group is new. Maybe she's hoping this will scare us, but I'd bet she's more interested in how we react and who we contact."

"Then what has she learned?"

"We didn't call the cops or the FBI. So she's probably assuming we're not the feds."

"Is that a good or bad thing?"

"From Magpie's perspective? I'm not sure."

I move to the last photograph. It's one of me in the back of a car service. It could have been taken any time or anywhere, and I don't hate it as much as the other photos because it'd be next to impossible to notice someone snapping a photo from a building or storefront when speeding past. The grain pattern suggests 400 ISO film—deliberate. Harder to trace. Probably shot from 200 meters with a 600mm lens.

There's also a photograph of Adrien crossing the street into his office from The Sanctuary. I'm not shown in the photo, but again, it's impossible to know the date. The shadows indicate mid-afternoon, between two and four p.m.

based on the building angles. A thought occurs to me. "Did you get a text?"

"From who?"

"An unknown number? Anything threatening? Demanding?"

"No. Nothing like what the senator has been getting."

I pause, looking up from the last photograph. "What'd he get?"

"A second delivery. A threat." He zeroes in on the photos. "Sent to his office, not his home."

"Right. KOAN has security set up at his home."

"What did your threat say?" The timbre of his voice roughens, low and dangerous. At the moment, he's all angry protector with no sign of the aloof businessman.

"Just one word," I say, spreading the dust over the photograph. "Stop. Not exactly threatening, but the timing was suspicious—came right before I found the break-in."

The ninhydrin powder catches nothing—no ridge patterns, no partial prints. Professional work.

He picks up his phone and dials, holding it out, leaving it on speaker.

"Mr. d'Avricourt's office."

"Tally, it's me."

"Oh, hi. I didn't look at the number."

Annoyance flashes across his features, and I bite back an amused smile. "Have you noticed any unknown number texts coming through?"

That's an odd question.

He holds a finger up, gesturing for me to hold my questions.

"Unknown numbers are automatically forwarded to you for review. Have you seen anything odd today?"

"Oh, ah. Let me check. I usually check the spam folder in the morning. I don't see anything... Just the normal phishing."

"Do you see anything with a single word?" I ask, given she probably would look right over a single word text, interpreting it as a half-hearted scam.

"Oh. Yes. There's one. It just says, 'stop.' Do you want me to respond?"

"No," he's quick to say, but then he looks to me. "Do you need her to do anything with it?"

"Is it on your phone?"

"It's on the messaging app in the spam folder, is that right?"

"Yes, sir," Tally answers cheerily.

"I've got it," he says to me. "Thanks. Have you seen Eddie?"

"No, sir. Do you want me to tell him you're looking for him?"

"No. Thanks."

The call ends and Adrien leans against the back of the sofa.

"How should I do this? Fire Eddie? You said you believe someone in security has to be in on it too?"

"Possibly others." With a careful view over the photograph, I drop it and move to the windowsill in the kitchen. Chances are the intruder wore gloves. I'm not going to find anything.

"So what would you have me do?"

"KOAN's still monitoring calls. You can fire him. Block his access. Watch to see who acts. If you want to bring charges—"

"No. I can't involve the police. I'll call him into a meeting tomorrow morning. Have HR present to revoke his credentials, after I confront him."

"We can take care of dismantling the servers. Ensure you have a closed loop environment." I'm standing at the windowsill, when I consider our plans. "Are you sure you want to have the meeting tomorrow and not tonight?"

He doesn't say anything at all, and when I look away from the windowsill, I find him studying me with an unsettling intensity.

"What?"

"The idea of something happening to you."

"Nothing's going to happen to me."

"How can you be so sure?"

I stop myself from answering with the standard *because* response my father used to give me as a child when I worried when he deployed. I suspect that's the same response he gave my mom all those years when she was basically raising my brothers and me as a single mother.

"It's not warfare."

His eyes narrow, and if it's from lack of understanding or if he's trying to call me out, I'm not sure.

"I don't like this."

"This? You mean, the investigation?"

"Someone broke into your home, Brie. And they're clearly trying to show you that they are watching. They have access."

I step up to him, wanting to soothe his worry. It's not needed. "Think about it. Even with the senator, they aren't threatening bodily harm."

"Brie, you don't know what these people will do. They have something to hold over the senator's head. They don't need to threaten his life. Are they going to find something to hold over your head? Because I can tell you, the only thing they'd find to hold over me is either you, my sister, or my parents. Maybe Tommy. People, Brie. That's all they have on me that I could possibly care about given what I do and who I am. What about you? You're not close to your family—anyone observing you or looking into your travel patterns can confirm that—I'd bet your communications, email, and phone confirm that. You're a former intelligence officer. If they don't have a person to hold over your head, what do they do?"

"I'm a spoke in a wheel. Going after me doesn't make sense. By now, they've figured out I'm a part of a team. They aren't going to come for me."

His arms are folded over his chest in classic defensive posture, and I clasp his wrists. "I'm safe. You don't have anything to worry about."

He's quiet for a long moment, jaw working as he processes everything. When he looks up, his expression has shifted from worried to determined. "Get your things. Come to my place—tonight. Until this is settled." It's command layered over fear, and for a heartbeat I glimpse the man who never learned to ask when it comes to protecting someone he loves.

"Adrien."

"No. They've proven they can get into your building. Hudson told me that they may not have finished the message. You may have interrupted them. I live in a secure, doorman building with a private elevator."

"Adrien, you realize that I'm qualified to provide security services, right? I'm skilled and capable."

"I don't doubt your skills." I cock an eyebrow, calling him out on that one. "I don't. You're one of the most intelligent and accomplished women I've ever met. But even skilled individuals need to sleep."

"I don't recall getting a lot of sleep last night."

"Brie, I'm serious. I won't sleep unless you're safe."

That's a more difficult angle to fight, and while I always thought I'd be furious if a man tried to tell me to not take risks, that's not exactly what he's saying. And if I'm honest, it feels good to have someone who cares. The most I've ever gotten from my parents or brothers is the standard Anderson family send-off: "Be smart."

"Alright. Let me shower—"

"I'll pack for you while you finish up fingerprint dusting. Then we'll leave. You can shower at my place."

My instinct is to bristle—to correct him, to prove I can handle this alone.

But his fear isn't about doubting me. It's about needing me alive.

I study him for a minute, debating. It's not the worst idea. Safe houses save lives.

"Okay."

I pat his wrists, and shift, mapping out the remaining areas I should dust, when he pulls me against his chest, arms wrapping around me so tightly I can barely breathe. His body trembles, not with desire this time but with leftover terror. The fine wool of his coat scratches my cheek, grounding me in the reality that I'm alive, that he's here.

Against my chest, his heart hammers like he's been running, and that's when it really hits me—how terrified he was. Not just worried, terrified. For a man built on control, his surrender is devastating.

The way he's holding me feels like proof—of what I mean to him, and what he means to me.

I slide my arms around his waist, holding him just as fiercely. He exhales against my hair, and the sound is half-prayer, half-promise. I don't correct him. I don't pull away. I let it matter.

For the first time tonight, the room feels still.

"I'm okay," I whisper into his neck. "I'm right here."

CHAPTER
TWENTY-THREE

ADRIEN

Brie moves through her apartment with clinical precision, latex gloves ghosting over every surface. Powder blooms, a fine constellation under angled light. I pray she'll find something, though I already know we won't. Watching her work reminds me how easily she could disappear again. Three years I spent chasing the negative space of a woman. Now she's real, in danger, and I'm not letting her out of my sight.

On a high shelf sit two suitcases—one carry-on, one large. I pull down the larger and unzip it on the floor. When I kneel, a row of duffels comes into view—black, brown leather, floral.

Go bags? I've read plenty of thriller spy books, watched plenty of action films. Even if they're packed to go, they're packed with a purpose. Right now, I'm packing her for something else entirely. So I set to work, going through her clothes. Folds clean as scalpel lines. Fabric that doesn't wrinkle, shoes that don't slow you down.

Her closet is immaculate—clothes arranged by color; drawers divided like surgical trays. Even her perfumes are slim travel vials, not the ornamental bottles my mother collects. Everything here speaks of mobility, of a life designed to disappear. The thought unsettles me more than I care to admit.

If this is the life she's chosen, I'm the fool trying to anchor a current. But I'll be that fool. I've already lost her once. Now that I've found her, I'm not going to sit by while she takes unnecessary risks.

What if she'd walked in? Did the intruders have guns? Would they have shot her? Kidnapped her? She's talking about a person or group with enough influence and power to threaten sitting U.S. senators. It's quite possible these people are my customers—either in upscale fashion or at The Sanctuary. As a matter of business, I've studied these people to better understand their proclivities and desires, to better understand how to sell to them. These are people who want to be perceived as attractive—that's the piece I market to, that everything from our advertisements to the experience we provide caters to. And for many, that's as much as there is. But what happens when someone builds themselves up and reaches the top echelon, where every luxury and desire is catered to, if not by me, by others like me? It's a lovely life. I know, I was born into it.

It's so wonderful, in fact, it's not hard to imagine that someone would go to great lengths to never lose this life. Some of the self-made men that I study, who we actually categorize into a different subset when defining our target audiences, what would they do to maintain wealth? And that's what frightens me—because I know how simple corruption begins. A whisper. A favor. A wire. Because in my heart, I know what I'd do. It's far too easy to make a phone call and wire funds.

The wheels roll over the uneven, weathered wood floor. She lingers by the piano, latex fingers brushing the keys without pressing them. One key sighs under the glove and then thinks better of it. The silence hums, filled with everything we haven't said, tuned like a string about to sing. Brie looks up and peels off one of her latex gloves.

"How much did you pack?"

"Enough. There's a car outside. Are you ready?"

She inhales, scanning the room.

"Did you get anything?"

"No." She sounds defeated, but that's the answer I expected.

"Did you expect to?"

"No."

At least she recognizes what we're up against.

She locks her apartment door and we descend. Outside her building, she scans the street thoroughly, as if expecting to spot a camera lens. A delivery truck idles too long. A man pretends to read a menu he never turns. I don't slow, wheeling her bags to the trunk of the waiting sedan. I don't doubt someone is out there. I don't doubt they'll follow. Hell, my driver might already be on someone's payroll.

Let them learn she's with me. My place is a fortress. No one crosses the threshold without my permission. Let them try the handle and taste their own audacity.

I hold the door for her and walk around to the back.

"Do you ever drive?"

"Occasionally. Parking's a nightmare unless there's valet. I keep a car here, two in France. Why—planning an escape?"

She smirks. "No. Just curious."

I glance to the front of the car. There's no divider. The rearview mirror is tilted just enough to be a question. The driver can hear everything we say. She must realize this, as we ride in silence, our hands close to each other on the center seat, but not touching. Static lifts the hairs on my wrist where her skin almost warms mine.

When we exit in front of my building, I thank the driver and lead her into the lobby.

I'm not familiar with the doorman, a thirty-something woman with a stocky build and dark hair pulled back into a tight bun, but I head directly to the counter.

"Hello, I'm Adrien d'Avricourt."

"Oh, yes, Mr. d'Avricourt. I know who you are," she smiles and her spine visibly straightens. "How can I help you?"

She knows who I am. That's the extent of it. I haven't dealt with the front desk in ages—my staff handles everything.

I gesture to Brie and say, "Ms. Anderson will be staying with me indefinitely. Please add her to my authorized access list. Restrict the elevator to my floor until further notice. No visitors without confirmation."

The woman nods, already typing, her eyes darting up once to confirm she heard right.

With that done, I lead Brie to my private elevator.

Once the door closes, Brie's gaze roves the lacquered elevator ceiling with light protruding around the rim, beneath the side panels, and casting down onto the floor. "Is there video surveillance?"

"No," I answer, watching the digital numbers blink past

on the panel. "A lobby camera can view anyone entering the elevator, and there's a security camera in the entryway on my floor, but in no other location."

"So, hypothetically, this elevator is private?"

"Entirely."

She smiles. "Dangerous information."

I fight a smile—half aroused, half exasperated that she can still joke after what happened.

The elevator arrives at the penthouse, signified by the digital letters PH, and I follow Brie into the entry.

She points at the far corner. "One camera. Any others?"

"No."

I push her suitcase forward into the foyer, stopping at the round entry table. Beside the white orchid centerpiece sits my mail—mundane, normal, safe. The orchid trembles as the wheel taps the pedestal.

"Is someone actively monitoring?"

"No." The admission stings. My home, my resources, and I didn't keep her safe in her own apartment. "I'll have that adjusted tomorrow."

"There's no need." She steps close, hand touching my arm, eyes scanning the mail in my hand. Then her lips brush the side of my neck and everything else falls away. "I just wanted to know if anyone is watching."

She traces a path of soft kisses to my earlobe and bites gently.

Blood rushes to my groin—instant, demanding. I'm hard before her teeth release my skin. The world narrows to the place her mouth has been and the places it might go. To the fact that she's *here*, in my space, safe.

She cups my shaft through my trousers—bold, deliberate

—and I nearly groan aloud. My hand finds her hip, tightens, one last flicker of restraint before I give in completely.

I lift her onto the table in one movement.

Orchids tremble as she opens her thighs to me. The air thickens—heat, breath, the taste of anticipation. My hands frame her hips and the city falls to a murmur beyond the glass.

She fumbles with my belt, but I catch her hands. "Not yet."

First, I need to see her. All of her. In my home, in my light, safe.

I tug at her loose jeans and she shifts on the table, shimmying her hips, lifting so I can pull them down her legs. The baggy clothes she wore for disguise—the wig now discarded, the piercings removed—they hid her. I want her revealed.

"This too." I hook my fingers under the hem of her camisole.

She lifts her arms and I pull the fabric over her head, revealing skin I've mapped in darkness but never here, never in daylight filtering through floor-to-ceiling windows. She's bare from the waist up, beautiful, and mine to protect.

"I should probably shower," she says, suddenly self-conscious. "My hair's been in a wig cap for hours."

"I don't care." My gaze drags over her—heat-dazed, possessive. My fingers dig into her thighs as I spread them wider. "Lean back."

She hesitates—exposed, vulnerable on my entry table in afternoon light—but I spread her wider, not waiting. Not when I need this. Need to taste her safety, her trust, her presence in my space.

My tongue drags through her center and the flower

arrangement rocks precariously. I yank her closer to the edge, one hand splayed across her lower belly, the other gripping her thigh. She tastes like salt and citrus and the end of restraint.

Her fingers slide into my hair—hesitant, then sure—tightening as I work her with tongue and fingers, merciless now. She moans, and I take every sound like proof she's here, she's safe, she's mine.

Broken syllables spill from her—maybe *oh my god*, maybe my name, maybe nothing but need—until her thighs tighten around my head and her back arches off the polished wood.

I gentle my movements, kissing my way up her trembling abdomen, between her breasts, to her mouth. She tastes like breathless laughter from another life—a fantasy made real.

The Tower holds.

Not collapse—revelation. For once, destruction gives way to clarity. She's here because she chose safety. Chose me. Chose us.

When we kiss, she tastes like trust and tomorrow. Her hands fumble with my belt again, and this time I let her. She releases me, slicks my crown with her thumb, then strokes with intention that makes my vision blur.

"Adrien." My name is permission and plea.

The table's the perfect height—almost like I planned this. I position myself at her entrance, meet her eyes for confirmation.

She nods, pulls me closer.

The first slow thrust steals both our breath. Home. This is what coming home feels like—her heat surrounding me, her legs wrapping around my hips, her hands gripping my shoulders like I'm the anchor in a storm she didn't know she was weathering.

"Stay," I murmur against her mouth, though whether I'm asking her to stay in my apartment or stay in this moment or stay in my life, I don't know.

"I'm here," she whispers back.

For now, it's enough.

CHAPTER
TWENTY-FOUR

BRIE

I wake to Adrien's phone buzzing and the disorienting luxury of his bedroom. My body recognizes where I am before my mind catches up—the weight of expensive sheets, his warmth beside me, that particular scent of his cologne lingering on the pillows. After years of waking alone or on assignment, this feels uncomfortably close to something I want to get used to. The blackout curtains make it impossible to tell what time it is, and for a moment I just lie there resting.

Adrien groans. "Sorry. I thought I put it on silent."

For a brief second, I block out the distant vibration and relax into the comfort of the cocoon, the sense of safety, and Adrien's long, sinewy body stretched beside mine. But all too soon, I glimpse the time—and realize we massively overslept—which I never do.

"It's okay. I need to get up." I press a kiss to his shoulder before sliding out of bed.

The simple domesticity of it catches me off guard. When did we morph into a real couple? Because that's what this is, isn't it? We don't have an end date. When the project ends, there's no reason we can't still see each other, is there?

"What time is it?"

"It's after eight. I never sleep this late."

On my way to the bathroom I see him lift the phone and set it back down.

"Who is it?" I wouldn't normally ask, but his expression isn't merely dismissive; there's something else there and given all that's happened…

"My sister. I'll call her back from the office. Get your shower. I'll get us coffee."

I pause in the bathroom doorway and ask, "Are you still planning to let Eddie go today?"

"Yes." He's in his boxers, barefoot, but the way he's looking at me, with his stance and commanding air, he could lead a press conference. He is not a man who needs a suit.

"I'll go in with you. Before you let him go, your security team should be briefed."

"I'm aware. Macon, the head of security, should be in by ten."

In under thirty minutes, we've both showered and dressed. His housekeeper, Maria, is in the kitchen when I enter seeking a refill of the French-pressed coffee.

"Good morning," she says, greeting me from beside the stove. "What would you like for breakfast?"

Is this how he wakes all the time? The casual luxury of it makes me hyperaware of the chasm between our worlds. On the yacht, I could pretend we were both visitors to that floating palace. But here, watching Maria move through his kitchen with practiced ease, I'm reminded that Adrien doesn't just visit this life—he lives it. Meanwhile, my apartment back home has a coffee maker I bought at Target and a fridge that's empty more often than not.

"Just coffee's fine, thanks."

My phone vibrates, and Hudson's name flashes. I lift the phone and say to Adrien, "Work," stepping into the living room to answer. "Hi, Hudson."

"You're with d'Avricourt?"

"Yes," I answer and behind me I hear Adrien instruct Maria, "She'll have the same egg-white omelet I'm having. With fruit."

That's exactly what I would have requested—how did he know? The answer settles warm in my chest: he's been paying attention. Not just to threats and security concerns, but to me. The real me. It's such a small thing, knowing my breakfast preference, but it feels enormous. Because it feels less like fleeting attraction and lust.

I brush away the thought and focus on the call with Hudson.

"I'm going to join Adrien as he makes personnel changes."

"He's letting Eddie go?"

"That's the plan."

"We'll monitor reactions. I've got Jake and Noah scheduled for perimeter support, but should I have them meet you inside?"

"No, but if things go sideways, you can send them in."

"Will do."

"Has he surfaced?"

"Negative on CCTV and inside The Sanctuary." Hudson's tone has an edge that means he's juggling multiple variables. I know the feeling. "He might be avoiding the place entirely."

Interesting. If he's a no-show, then we won't learn much, other than he likely has no plans of returning.

"Does this mean Adrien's looping in his security team?"

"Affirmative." We tapped the staff work phones, but given any complicit party likely communicates on a personal device, that's a partial view of staff reactions.

"I'll have Quinn pull in backup to monitor."

"Copy. Are you back in NC?"

"No. I'm pursuing information on Moira Kelly. I'll touch base later."

When the call ends, Adrien and I eat breakfast, then head out for the day. Given the plans ahead, it all feels remarkably normal.

We stop by his office first, which is across the street from The Sanctuary. Only when we enter, an assistant greets him at the elevator.

"Mr. d'Avricourt, your sister is here."

"In the building?"

"Yes, sir. She arrived five minutes ago. I just made her a coffee. She told me she'd wait until you got in and not to bother you, that you weren't picking up your phone."

His assistant is a young man with a shaved head and a suit jacket with sleeves that fall almost to his knuckles, but below his sleeve hem, his fingers rub each other in one of the oddest nervous tics I've ever seen.

I follow behind Adrien, watching as his assistant trails by his side, so on edge I wonder if Adrien is prone to snapping at assistants.

Adrien lengthens his strides and slows only once he's in sight of his sister. Margot d'Avricourt looks exactly like her photos but moves with more energy, more presence. She's poised, like the photos, but in person, there's a liveliness to her that film doesn't catch. Her dark hair is pulled back, and as I step closer, I'm struck by the unnatural color of her eyes, yellow like a tiger. The longer I study them, I become convinced that they're color contacts.

She turns those eyes on me, ignoring her brother when he greets her with, "Margot. What are you doing here?"

"Who is this?" She pushes up from the sofa, eyeing me like I'm a curious bauble. She's protective of Adrien—I can see it in how she positions herself, how her attention sharpens when she looks at me. I respect that, even if it makes this conversation more complicated.

"This is Brie Anderson."

Margot's mouth opens and whatever she's about to say, Adrien stops it with, "She's my girlfriend. Be nice."

"I'm always nice." She waves her hand dismissively, but my distinct impression is he cut her off from saying something that would have been anything but nice.

"It's nice to meet you," I say, inserting myself between the siblings.

"Anderson…that name's not familiar," Margot pauses, studying not only my face, but also my outfit. "What happened to…" her eyes narrow, and I can practically see her trying to figure out if I'm the woman from Monaco with a different name, or if her brother has already dismissed that woman and moved on.

"Brie, would you mind giving my sister and me a minute?"

"Of course," I say. "I'm going to go down to the basement. Meet me there?"

"Why don't you head to the security office? Macon is waiting. I won't be five minutes behind you."

"Security. This sounds serious. Do you work in security, Ms. Anderson?" Margot asks.

Before I can answer, Adrien's hand falls to my lower back to usher me out of his office. His touch shouldn't affect me in front of his sister, shouldn't register at all when we're about to fire a potential threat. But my body doesn't care about professional boundaries anymore. It remembers last night, this morning—all of our stolen moments.

"Forgive my sister. She's naturally nosy. I'll be with you in a few minutes. Aaron?" His assistant perks up upon hearing his name. "Will you escort Ms. Anderson to the security floor. Tell Macon that I'll be five minutes late to the meeting, and Ms. Anderson will be joining us."

"Yes, sir," he answers, but the office door closes before sir has left his mouth.

Girlfriend.

The word echoes as Aaron leads me toward security. Adrien didn't say bodyguard. Didn't say consultant. He said *girlfriend*.

My first instinct is to correct it—to restore the lines, the distance. But the part of me that woke up tangled in his arms this morning doesn't. That part lets it stand. Just for now.

We aren't normal. I know that. But the word still lands somewhere warm and unsettling.

Aaron is quiet. Polite. A little too eager to be agreeable. Which makes him useful.

"Does Margot visit often?" I ask, keeping my tone casual.

"She lives in France. I didn't know she was arriving."

That tracks. Adrien hadn't either.

"How long have you worked for Mr. d'Avricourt?"

"I'm a temp. But I've been here about a month."

He rubs his fingers together as we walk—like he's trying

to spark warmth. A possible tell. Or just nerves. I'm in no position to judge. I've spent the entire morning policing my own reactions, pretending I don't remember the way Adrien looked at me over breakfast.

"I schedule meetings with his sister." Aaron adds, as if realizing too late that he's said something notable. "You know—time zones and all."

He schedules meetings with her.

Interesting.

Then again, Margot d'Avricourt isn't just a sister anymore. She's the CEO of a billion-dollar conglomerate. Managing access to her—even for family—probably comes with its own protocol.

As we head toward the security meeting, I can't shake the feeling that we're missing something important. Maybe it's just pre-operation nerves, but Eddie's absence feels less like coincidence and more like preparation.

CHAPTER
TWENTY-FIVE

ADRIEN

"What's her story?" Margot's smile is almost predatory.

My sister is a terror when she smells weakness. She doesn't crave scandal—those require cleanup—but a whiff of embarrassment? That she savors. I once believed it came from wanting Father's approval, but even with the CEO title, she still thrives on mockery. It's how she convinces herself she's superior.

I rest my hands on the chair's back, narrowing my gaze, calculating how to explain Brie without surrendering anything private.

"You're not going to sit?" She crosses a leg and drums her fingers on her knee, nails the same burgundy as her sky-high boots. Even her leisure is a performance.

"I don't have time. As you heard, I have a meeting and I'm already late. What brings you here unannounced?" I'd ask why she isn't staying with me, except that I know my sister and there's little she loves more than a splendid hotel suite and Manhattan has those in abundance.

She exhales. "We have a situation."

Of course we do.

I wait, but she's silent. Lips pursed, but her expression is something more than business.

"Is Father unwell?" If so, why fly here?

"Mother and Father are fine—sun-drunk in Greece." She pauses. "But he's concerned." Her long, thick lashes flutter.

My sister never modeled, but she could have—her perfectly arched dark eyebrows, expertly applied charcoal shadow, and what are undoubtedly high-end augmented lashes are truly stunning. It's probably why she's got a thing for changing the shade of her irises the way some change lipstick color.

Another sigh. Now she's drawing it out unnecessarily, and I don't have the time.

"What is it, Margot? What could I have possibly done that concerns him while on another bloody continent?"

"There's an employee you're considering firing. You can't."

"Excusez-moi?" The French slides out before I can stop it. Warning enough.

"Edward Thorne."

I go still.

"What about him?" But even as I ask, ice forms in my stomach. How does she know? Tommy knows I'm firing an employee, but I never gave him a name.

"Have you heard of The Magpie?"

"Why have you?" My stare hardens. Inside, a cold, steady *Christ almighty.*

"So you do know. Then hear me clearly: stop whatever

investigation you've begun. I made an error sending Alicia Morgan to you."

She unfolds her leg and rises, smoothing out her burgundy leather skirt, circling the room until she stops at the billiard table, as if choosing her next move. "But, in my defense, Morgan is someone we want at our disposal too, and she didn't share her reasons for needing to reach you, or that she planned to pursue a thorough investigation of your little sex club."

"It's not a sex club." The words leave through clenched teeth.

"Spare the outrage, Adrien. We're Magpie clients."

"You buy blackmail?" My voice lowers. "Or is it gossip now?"

She licks her bottom lip then sucks it in to chew on it. It's a look I'm familiar with. She's calculating how to best me—but this is insanity.

"We purchase intelligence—market forecasts, design leaks. That's why d'Avricourt Luxe is always one step ahead. Call it competitive insight; Father calls it tradition. Now, before you get riled, no, we didn't know at the time of your acquisition that your club is an information source for The Magpie. Obviously, they source our information from alternative sources."

I turn to the window. New York gray presses against the glass. I need distance before I say something I'll regret.

"Yes. Father believes in one torchbearer at a time. A ceremony of corruption. And I'm not authorized to share this with you, but I know you better than our father. I recognize your stubborn side and as far as I can tell, this is the only way to convince you to stop what you've started."

Her words replay but I still have questions. "So we're a

client—one among many buying secrets. And The Sanctuary is one of their sources."

"Correct. Father built our house by staying a step ahead. Fashion has always been war disguised as glamour. This shouldn't surprise you."

"And now one client's greed has reached Capitol Hill. You think I can simply ask that storm to stand down?"

"No. Obviously Alicia Morgan also needs to be handled. But that's not why I was sent here."

"You're here to handle me."

"The sexual footage is noise, not currency," she says, studying her nails. "Conversations are what sell. My guess is they were stretched for something of value on this particular guy. Typically it's conversations in your restaurants and meeting rooms—that's what's of value—or that's what I'm told. Now I happen to know that this Thorne guy is making a nice mint feeding The Magpie, so that might be a conversation worth having with him." Done with examining her manicure, she lifts a cue ball from the billiard table and rolls it in her palm. "But you can't fire him. Or if you do, you need to replace him. We risk losing our source of information if you fire him. If you keep him in place, we get a discounted price moving forward. I'm willing to share with you the difference, although I know money isn't a likely motivator. But I'm hoping your love for our father, for our family's legacy, will be sufficient motivation." She drops the ball down onto the felt and it lands with a thud. "For me, your little sister. And what do you really care? It's better for you if this whole incident stays secret."

"The photos used as blackmail to the senator were clearly taken here, on site."

"And the senator won't say anything because to do so

would expose his infidelity. You're safe. Magpie will be careful with what they share."

"It must be lovely, that simple world of yours." KOAN won't just walk away because I ask nicely. If anything, I'll be drawn in. And Brie already is. "What about the extortionist? What's to stop him…or them…from sharing the photos?"

"If the senator meets the demands, no photos are shared."

I run my fingers through my hair as I debate sharing with my delightful sister how many people are a part of this investigation, that this black-ops group doesn't just go away. But she's clever. She's always been clever.

"How many are a part of your investigative team?"

"I don't have all the names." And I sure as hell am not about to tell my sister that Brie's on that team. I wouldn't put it past Moira and this Magpie group to see eliminating them all as a viable solution.

"You run a loose shop, do you?"

"It's not my investigation, Margot, remember? You asked me to take the meeting with Alicia Morgan. And when I did, do you know what I discovered? An entire room in my building I didn't know existed. And I'm going to assume a similar operation exists in all five locations, am I right? And let's see, since Edward Thorne only oversees two locations, that means I've got complicit employees in three other locations to be concerned with."

"All you need to do is look the other way. Let it continue. You've owned it for three years and haven't had any issues."

"Dad's friends with Moira Kelly. Isn't he? I was shown a photograph of her—she's familiar. I've seen her in the past. Seen her in photographs with our father at events. Was she more than an acquaintance?"

It's no secret our parents haven't always been faithful. I believe now they are, but they're also in their eighties.

"That's not something I would ever ask Dad." On that score, I believe her.

"Is this the reason Father was so against me buying The Sanctuary?" He'd actually tried to halt the bank from underwriting my investment.

"Maybe. Again, you'd need to ask him." She rolls the cue ball around then sends it rolling into the side of the table. "I'm here to ask you to stop what you can. Keep this Edward Thorne on."

"Thorne's vanished. He hasn't been seen since yesterday."

"He knows you're onto him. He relayed back to Moira. He'll resurface when cleared. That's what I need to get from you—his clearance. If you still plan on firing him, I suppose I won't blame you. He's been essentially skimming revenues if you want to think about it that way. I can tell them you refuse to keep someone you can't trust on. But you've got to stop your part in any investigation."

"And Magpie will 'handle' Alicia Morgan?" I ask, testing how deep she's in.

Her nod is small, self-satisfied. "Now—this woman. Your mystery lover. Tommy says you're quite taken. Should I get to know her?"

"No." The word comes out too fast.

She hears the crack in it and smiles. "You're protective of her," she says. "Tommy's right. It's not just a fling."

Damn Tommy for telling my sister the woman from Monaco surfaced. "She gave me a false name in Monaco because she planned to ghost me." My sister tilts her head back as she laughs. "I met her by chance in Manhattan."

But even as I speak, cold spreads beneath my skin.

Margot may be satisfied with half-truths, but Magpie won't be. Brie's already a target.

"I think I like her," Margot says sweetly, detonating calm as if she hadn't just confessed duplicity. She draws her handbag closer, as if shielding something fragile, and strides to the sofa. "One more thing. If Moira Kelly is touched—arrested, disappears, anything—a dead man's switch triggers. Hundreds of files, names, scandals. Your club, our brand, the whole bloody pantheon. It all burns."

"What does that mean?"

"Files on hundreds of powerful people across many different industries go public. She's been in business a long time–of course she's prepared for discovery. She checks in every seventy-two hours, or the files go public. Your pride and joy, The Sanctuary, becomes fully exposed. As I understand it, your membership will evaporate. But, like I said, you are only a piece of the collateral damage. d'Avricourt Luxe… We have secrets we're better off not coming to light. If this business came out, we'd face lawsuits, there might be an investigation, it's not a good look and doesn't reflect well on our creators. But our issues are mild compared to other clients. The investigation needs to stop." She clutches her prized, rare $250,000 handbag to her chest. "No one says it outright, but this runs deeper than Magpie. Multiple interests will protect the entity at any cost."

She stops at the door, voice soft as perfume. "Oh—and Adrien? They already know about Brie Anderson. You're not a good liar. Don't be stupid."

With the click of the door, understanding settles like a verdict I'm not yet ready to read aloud.

If I continue to help Brie and the KOAN team, I risk severing myself from my family and doing lasting damage to the d'Avricourt name. If I stop—if I play along—I might save the business, but I'll lose something far more permanent.

Either way, The Sanctuary takes the hit.

Margot didn't come to negotiate. She came to make sure I understood that whatever choice I make next will cost me everything I thought I could protect.

There is no clean exit. Only timing.

Margot believes I'll choose blood over truth. Moira believes I'll choose leverage over conscience. And somewhere between them, Brie is already marked as collateral.

The only question left is how long I can let them believe I'm still playing their game.

CHAPTER
TWENTY-SIX

BRIE

Macon Chen is maybe two inches shorter, but broader through the shoulders—built for power. A worthy adversary.

His strength is obvious, but it's not what gives me pause. It's the way he studies the room, the stillness in his stance, arms loose at his sides, fingers slightly spread. Ready.

His hair is cropped into coarse, tight curls, his skin dark; his eyes give away a mixed heritage—Black, Asian. Useful information, but incomplete. His background is in my briefing materials, and I should have gone deeper.

The way he studies me now tells me he's doing the same math.

Once upon a time, I could meet someone without immediately calculating the best way to incapacitate them. But that was before this life chose me.

"You said Adrien is joining us?" he asks.

We've already exchanged names—and we're alone. It's

before lunch, but I can't help but wonder about his staff. Are they missing in action with Eddie Thorne?

"Adrien said he'd be delayed for about five minutes." Macon doesn't move, his gaze steady. "His sister surprised him with a visit."

"Ah. Margot?" He asks it as if he's trying to remember her name.

"Yes. That's the one."

"Well, have a seat." He gestures to an office chair on wheels that's currently pushed up against a desk. I pull it out and, as I do so, he pulls a different chair and sits. His gaze flicks to the monitors, all currently capturing various doorway entrances and corridors. "I take it if Adrien sent you, he doesn't have a problem with your observing."

"I wouldn't know what I'm looking at anyway," I say, offering a smile. It's a half-truth. I'm not big on pop culture, and while I would likely recognize any politicians or business power players, any celebrities would likely be unrecognizable to me.

"Is that right?" he asks, flicking imaginary lint off his trousers. "What is it you do?"

"I'm a consultant," I answer with a practiced smile. "Corporate risk assessment. Mostly boring compliance stuff, but it pays well." Our plan is to notify Macon that Eddie's employment is terminated and to sit back and watch and learn. "Today was my first time meeting Margot. I think Adrien sent me ahead of him to give him a chance to let his sister know about me."

"And what exactly is he letting her know?"

"Oh. That we're dating," I say, playing the part of proud, new girlfriend, all the while knowing full well if Macon is complicit with Eddie, then there's a good chance he's aware my apartment was broken into and that he knows exactly who I am.

"Ah. I've only met Margot once. She's a firecracker."

"She's protective of her brother."

He shifts his legs and his seat twists with the movement.

"Or at least, that's my take."

"It's probably correct," he says, loosening slightly. "Wouldn't know. I don't spend much time with Adrien."

"Oh?"

"No. I've worked for Eddie for six years. Adrien's pretty hands-off. Works directly with Eddie mostly."

Well, that's about to change.

"Are you from New York?"

"Grew up in Rochester. Went to Syracuse University. Worked in Jersey City for a while. Still live in Hoboken."

"What's that commute like?"

"Take the ferry mostly. It's not bad." He glances at his watch, probably getting anxious with our small talk. I can't say I blame him. "What about you? Where are you from?"

"I'm from all over. My father was a Marine."

"Ah." His grin widens. "Military brat."

"Not so sure about the brat part… My father didn't spoil. But yes. And my mom was a translator for the State Department."

"Nice." My background information relaxes him, which is interesting. Many people I've interacted with over the years would have heard that background and immediately tensed, expecting CIA or NSA. "So what languages do you speak?"

I hesitate, as there's value in keeping cards close to the chest, but if he's complicit, there's a good chance he already knows. I'm not working under a cover name, and even if I were, these people accessed my home with all of my aliases stored away in bags. "I'm fluent in French, Spanish, Arabic, and conversational in Mandarin and Russian."

He whistles his appreciation. "Do you live in France? That's where you met Adrien, right?"

"I live in New York. Upper West Side. But I did meet Adrien when I was abroad."

"And a consultant." He slides his fingers over the corners of his lips, contemplative, and if he didn't immediately think to himself CIA, he does now.

My gaze falls to my wrist. What's taking Adrien so long? Is Margot grilling him about me? Warning him off? The thought shouldn't bother me—this is a job, after all—but it does. It bothers me that his sister might be telling him all the reasons I'm wrong for him. Because she'd be right, wouldn't she?

"I wonder if I should go check on Adrien. Possibly rescue him from his sister."

Macon's gaze flicks to the monitors. "Have you seen him enter the building?"

"No. Movement would have caught my attention." Perhaps I shouldn't have admitted that, but it's the truth. I wasn't studying the monitors, but these grayscale screens are of empty spaces. The presence of any living being would have caught my attention. "You don't watch the restaurants?"

"Dining facilities aren't open yet. But, no, we don't monitor those areas too heavily. We have staff in place to notify us if there's a problem. Really, we sit here looking for issues."

"What constitutes an issue?"

"Oh. You know. Too much alcohol. Or a substance that impairs judgment. Drug deals—not allowed. Angry outbursts. Fights. We jump on those. The goal is to stop trouble before it starts."

"And I guess you also step in to protect any women from being manhandled?" The corridors his screens are set to monitor look like the ones that lead to the suites.

"Always. Adrien's turned this place around. Used to be... Well, let's just say the previous owners had different standards. He's taken things up a notch. My take is he's a good guy. I don't know how long you've been dating him; but figure I'll go ahead and offer you my endorsement."

"Thank you for that." We both smile at each other, and glance at the monitors to cover for a lack of conversational topics.

I could be wrong, but I don't think Macon Chen is involved in anything nefarious. He doesn't seem to be a techie, which is how Eddie has managed to pull off his little side hustle without raising any of Macon's suspicions.

"Yeah, the way this place used to be run—wild times. But d'Avricourt's really cleaned the place up. Clientele's increased. It's been good for business. At least in this location. I know in other countries, laws are different."

I assume he's referencing sex work. "I wouldn't know. I've only been to this location."

"Oh. Well, you'll have to get him to take you to the Paris location. I'm hearing it's undergoing a massive renovation. At least, go when the reno is done."

"I'll keep that in mind."

He flicks his wrist, checking the time.

Where is Adrien?

"I'm going to go find him," I say. "I was joking, but he may really need my help."

I push up from the chair and Macon stands. "Well, if you

track him down, I'll be here another thirty minutes. Then I need to make rounds before things start cooking."

"I'll be back," I say, knowing he needs to tell Macon that Eddie's job has been terminated before the end of his shift. I can't imagine what could be taking him so long.

I'm stepping into the entryway, nodding at a woman dressed in a form-fitting sheath and sky-high heels, when Adrien steps through the door. My body recognizes him before my brain processes his presence—a sudden alertness, a pull in my chest, that annoying flutter.

"Adrien. There you are. I was coming to get you."

"Is Macon waiting?"

"Yeah, he has…"

I stop speaking, noticing he's typing a message. He hits send and holds the door for me. "Come on."

"What—"

"Trust me," he says, and the seriousness in his expression raises every internal alarm. I follow along, doing just as he says.

He steps onto the curb and a black sedan pulls up. He opens the back door and I slide in. He comes around to the far side and gets in. He never speaks to the driver, but the car pulls forward into traffic.

On his phone, he opens the notepad app and types, then shows me the screen.

Play along. Someone could be listening.

My blood chills at the words, but I keep my expression neutral, even lean into him like a girlfriend would.

He deletes the words. I glance at the driver and note his eyes in the rearview. Watching traffic? Or us?

I take Adrien's phone and tap into the app.

Where are we going?

I have my handbag and phone, but it will take Quinn a minute to figure out we aren't coming back for the meeting with Macon. Jake and Noah are on surveillance duty, but they'll stay back in the vicinity of The Sanctuary.

Adrien deletes my words and types.

My place. When there, don't speak or say anything. Can you sweep for bugs?

Holy shit. What happened after I left his office? Did his sister tell him someone's listening to his conversations? I take his phone, delete his words, and the car pulls to a stop in front of his place. He lives ridiculously close to his office and we could have walked, but I'm guessing he ordered a car because that's what would be expected. If he'd walked so we could talk on the street, it might have set off alarm bells. At least, that's my best guess.

On the sidewalk in front of his place, I scan the sidewalk. There's no one around. The nearest pedestrian is at least forty yards away. I pull him to me, brushing my lips over his, then acting like I'm giving him a tight hug, speaking into his ear.

"I don't have the equipment to do a reliable sweep."

He pulls back, looks at me, nods, presses his lips to mine, and takes my hand.

Instead of going to his place, he presses the elevator button for the pool level. When the doors open, we walk past a room of fitness equipment and into a humid room with a long pool.

Chlorine fills the air, sharp and chemical, nothing like his expensive cologne or the salt sea. The humidity makes my clothes cling, and I'm hyperaware of everything—the echo of our footsteps, the lap of water against tile, the way Adrien's jaw is set with determination. He looks like a man preparing for war, and something in my chest tightens because I know that look. I've worn it myself too many times.

"Figured this place is as good as any. They'd never think I'd come here, and no one ever uses the pool this time of day."

There are several thick wooden doors along one side of the wall, with signs related to safety, temperature, and gender. I hold a finger up, signifying quiet, and one by one, clear the sauna, the steam room, and the bathrooms.

"Okay," I say, joining him by the pool's edge. "What's going on?"

"I'm not firing Eddie."

It takes a second for me to comprehend what he's saying. I don't get it.

"Why?"

"I can't. There's too much at stake. We've got to play it a different way."

The relief that floods through me is unprofessional—he's not backing down, he's adapting. His tone is pure determination, and god help me, it makes me want him even more.

CHAPTER
TWENTY-SEVEN

ADRIEN

Normally I'd blame the jitter in my fingers on too much caffeine. But sitting in the leather seats of a hastily chartered jet, watching Brie work on her laptop, the tremor feels like a warning light. Instead of coffee, I crave a nice scotch.

The plan is simple in concept, risky in execution: convince Moira Kelly to cut a new deal directly with me, bypassing Eddie entirely. It's either brilliant or suicidal—I'll know which when I'm face-to-face with the woman who could leave me bankrupt. Something she may want to do once I expose her.

I formulated this plan between my office and the condominium swimming pool, and it had better fucking work. I debated bringing Brie, but ultimately insisted she join me, as I believe she's safer on a jet to Paris than she would be back in New York on her own, even if she camped out in my place. I know little about this Magpie organization, but I know how the wealthy elite operate; they prioritize self-preservation. Without knowing who might be threatened with this investigation, I'm not about to leave Brie behind.

In the hold of the plane, she has three suitcases filled with everything she believes we might possibly need. I packed only one small duffel for a fresh change on the return flight tomorrow, as I don't plan to stay.

The hole in the plan is my father. Five messages unreturned. Mom has assured me he's not avoiding me, that he's out on a catamaran with friends. I'd plan to meet him on the dock, but he's in Greece, and I'm en route to France. My gut tells me if I'm going to carry this off, I need to move fast.

Out the window, clouds mix with blue, and farther out toward earth the blue of the Atlantic stretches to the horizon. The woman sitting across from me, a table between us, offers the superior view. But judging from her taps, she's deep into a messaging exchange with her team.

I overheard enough of her phone conversation to know that she's struggling to convince them I can be trusted. Her boss, Hudson, didn't want her leaving the country with me. But she believes she's keeping me safe. Letting her believe that proved to be an effective method of convincing her to come along.

I stare at my phone, willing it to ring.

My plan falls apart without my father. I moved across the ocean for my independence, and here I am needing him once again. It's annoying as hell.

Under the table her knee finds mine; her blue eyes flick up. I slide my hand to the edge of her leg. The Lycra is warm and taut under my palm. Given we'll land late and there's no chance of any meeting before the end of our day, we're both dressed casually.

Everything depends on this working. Not just the club—though losing my first independent venture would be humiliating enough. It's Brie's safety and the trust of every member who believed The Sanctuary was truly sanctuary. I've spent three years proving I'm more than a trust fund heir. I have no desire to let Eddie's betrayal undo all of that. And I sure as hell won't allow anyone to threaten Brie because of my business.

Finally, my phone lights up with my father's name.
I answer it on speaker so Brie can hear everything.
"Dad."
Brie closes her laptop, her attention set on me.
"Adrien. Where are you?"
"Somewhere over the Atlantic."
"What—Margot is looking for you."
"Why? Because you told her I called?"
Brie's lips curve, reflecting amusement, like she's on my team.

"She said you listened and understood. You're not about to do something reckless, are you?" There's an edge to his tone I haven't heard in quite some time. It's his boardroom, no bullshit tone. That's fine. I no longer answer to my father.

"Dad, I need you to set up a meeting for me with Moira Kelly."
"You've lost your mind."
"No, Dad, I haven't."
"Adrien, this isn't a woman to cross. She doesn't just ruin businesses—she destroys lives."
"Then why have you worked with her for years?"
"Because I was smart enough never to cross her."
"Do you really believe that? Think about it. Who cares if you bought competitive insights? It's not like you were using

the information for insider trading. Corporate espionage happens all the time, and you're in fashion. It's not like you're developing nuclear weapons. And as for me? My clients include some of the wealthiest in the world. If she releases their secrets, are they going to be angry at me, or at her? Me? The man who bought a club three years ago and expanded the enterprise without knowledge of an employee undercutting him? Or the woman who built a business on secrets?"

"Moira is elusive for a reason. You'll never find her."

"That's why I'm calling you. I need you to ask her to meet with me."

Silence extends across the line. Brie reaches across the table and covers my hand with hers.

"You're going to sell us out? Throw everything away?"

"No. Because I have no intention of allowing my employee to undercut me. After all, would you allow that? You have a personal relationship with her, do you not?"

"Why do you believe that?"

"Margot told me. She said she's a family friend."

"Intéressant. Why did you leave without Margot?" My father may be in his eighties, but he's not easily duped—never has been.

"Margot has business in New York." At least, I assume she does. She's an efficient CEO. Even if she didn't, she wouldn't fly across an ocean without capitalizing on the trip. "And don't worry, I didn't take the company jet. I left it for her."

The d'Avricourt company plane is far nicer than the private plane I located at the last minute. I would've flown commercial if pressed, but I'm grateful for this plane. It allows me to have this very conversation while in transit.

"Kind of you, given you didn't want anything to do with our company."

Yes, that's a sore point.

"Dad, arrange the meeting. I'm asking as your son."

"You're just looking to cut a deal?"

"That's all." My gaze cuts to Brie, and my gut twists. I'll have to beg for forgiveness from my father later.

"You won't harm her?"

"I'm not a brute."

"She is a friend. We have history."

If I'm right about his history, then I understand what he's saying.

"Dad, come on. I'm your son. You know me. I don't want to hurt her. I only wish to talk with her."

"Ah, yes. My son. A man who willingly walked away from his heritage."

"Because the company is Margot's passion. It's not mine."

"And now…what? You want to enter the game of secrets?"

It's a tough sell. I was born into money; and therefore, I've never been starved for it. "I don't like being screwed over by a man who professed loyalty. I could've let him go three years ago when I acquired the business, but I gave him a chance—and he squandered that chance. I can never trust him. I'm not keeping him in my employment. Margot said that's what's required of me. I won't do it. I refuse. Let me meet Moira. I want a different arrangement."

"She's in Paris."

I don't mention that KOAN already tracked her to Paris. "Then that's where I'll go."

"I'll call her and send you the details."

"Thank you." I look directly into Brie's eyes and smile.

Finding Moira would be challenging and time consuming, but Dad is making this easy. My plan is going to work. "And Dad, I love you."

"Christ, Adrien. You sound like you're saying goodbye."

"Just...take care of Mom. And keep your eyes open."

"Don't make me regret this son."

The call ends, and for a long second, I inhale deeply, fending off the guilt of playing my father. Brie places both of her hands over mine. Without my saying a word, she understands. I'll help track her extortionist. And Eddie will be fired. But there are risks. Even if the meeting with Moira goes well, there will likely be consequences.

"You're doing the right thing." She says it because she knows I need to hear it.

With an exhale, I drink her in. She's lovely, beautiful, but I've known plenty of beautiful women. What I've never had is this—someone who ignores notoriety. Intelligence, independence, integrity; she's far more than a pretty face. Trite but true. I'm falling for her—or, I suppose, I fell for her our first weekend together. I want her in my life, by my side, long after this episode is behind us.

"Are you having second thoughts about walking into the lion's den?" she asks, studying my expression with intent.

"It's better than letting the lion come hunting in my territory." I lift her hands and interlace our fingers. "Besides, I'll have backup."

"One former CIA operative against an international intelligence broker?"

"The best former CIA operative." The smile I give her is more confident than I feel. "And I'm counting on my charm."

Her laugh is soft, thin with worry. "Your charm won't stop a bullet."

"Maybe not," I say, squeezing her fingers. "But I'm not walking away."

CHAPTER
TWENTY-EIGHT

BRIE

The suite smells faintly of bergamot and fresh linen, like calm made tangible—a cocooned hush settling around us, the faint creak of polished floorboards beneath my boots. I set my overnight bag beside the door, unsure whether to exhale or keep the armor on.

Paris hums through the windows. Distant horns, a scatter of laughter, a song from somewhere down the street. The atmosphere feels different here, lighter, though my mind hasn't caught up with my body's arrival.

Adrien stands at the window, shirt unbuttoned at the throat, sleeves rolled, the city lights cutting sharp angles across him. He hasn't said much since we landed. Silence suits him when he's calculating outcomes, but tonight it feels like distance. I think he's still carrying the weight of that phone call, the gravity of what waits for us tomorrow.

I remove the gun I packed—something I could easily do as we flew on a private plane—and place it on the console table.

The metallic click fractures the quiet—an indecent sound in a room built for intimacy and candlelight. He glances over his shoulder but says nothing. The lamp beside him gilds the planes of his face in warm gold, softening everything that makes him appear untouchable.

"Are we really doing this your way?"

"It's a solid plan."

"If your father follows through… what happens to Eddie?"

He exhales through his nose, a small, tired laugh. "He loses his job. No matter what, he's out. And my father will follow through. He always does. Eventually—but not necessarily in the way you expect." There's no hint of reservation. He's set. Determined.

I smile, faint. "That sounds familiar."

He turns fully then, leaning against the window frame, sleeves rolled to his forearms. "That's a polite way of saying I'm impossible."

"I didn't say that."

His mouth curves. "You were thinking it."

He picks up the bottle of wine that room service left—something French and elegant, naturally—and uncorks it with the ease of someone raised around ritual. "Would you like a glass?"

I nod, crossing to him. Our fingers brush as he hands it to me, and something uncoils between us.

"To Paris," he says softly. "And to surviving what comes next." Our glasses touch with the soft chime of inevitability. His knuckles graze mine, the clink of crystal between us almost obscene in its intimacy.

The corner of my mouth lifts. "I'll drink to that."

The wine is cool and dark, grounding. The reminder of

what waits for us tomorrow turns the wine dry on my tongue.

He watches as I sip, eyes mapping my face as if committing it to memory. I've been watched before, but never like this—never by someone who seems to see what's beneath the polish.

"What are you thinking?" he asks.

"That you're hard to read."

"Good. That makes two of us."

He sets his glass aside and steps closer, close enough that his warmth seeps into me. "You don't have to keep pretending you're fine," he says quietly.

"I'm not pretending." My voice catches on the half-truth.

He brushes a strand of hair from my temple, his thumb skimming the edge of my jaw. The touch isn't practiced—it's hesitant, searching. His skin is warm, a whisper of callus that feels disarmingly human for a man who wears wealth like a second suit.

Every muscle in me wants to step back—to keep control—but my pulse betrays me, leaning into the heat I've been pretending not to feel.

"It's not all on your shoulders, you know. If you're worried, share. Let me carry the weight, too."

"That's not how I work."

"I know." His breath grazes my cheek. "But maybe it's time to evolve."

His thumb traces my lower lip; silence thickens between us.

His mouth finds mine, tentative at first—as if seeking permission rather than conquest—then deepens, slow and certain, until the world dissolves into the taste of red wine and breath and something dangerously close to hope. I press closer, feeling the steady beat of his heart through his shirt.

He pulls back just enough to meet my eyes. "Will I always crave you? Always need you?"

I open my mouth to tell him that no, time changes all, but he stops me from speaking with a brush of his lips. "I hate how much the answer is yes."

"Nothing is forever, Adrien."

"Then don't promise me forever," he says quietly. "Just... stay."

I don't answer him. I take his hand and pull him toward the bed.

His hands find my hips, drawing me against him, and I feel myself giving in—not because I've lost control, but because I want this... I want tonight.

The glass clinks faintly as I set it down, the sound impossibly loud in the hush between us.

He traces his fingers down my spine, unhurried, reverent. We should be planning. Reviewing contingencies. Preparing for what happens after we expose Magpie. Instead, we're here—in a Paris hotel room pretending we have time.

Every movement feels like discovery. Every breath like confession. Every touch a truth neither of us can take back.

When his mouth finds mine again, the kiss deepens until thought dissolves into sensation and tomorrow becomes a problem for people who aren't us.

His breathing turns ragged. Beneath my palms, his heart drums staccato.

"God, Brie." He breathes between kisses, his fingers finding the hem of my fitted t-shirt, pulling it over my head. "I want you all the time. Every moment. Everywhere."

"That's not quite possible." I press my lips to his throat

as I take my turn with his shirt buttons—the casual linen he wore for the flight, rumpled now. "Let's settle for now."

His hand slips between my legs, palming me through the thin lycra of my leggings. The friction makes me gasp.

I mirror his action, palming his hard length through his trousers, earning a groan and a soft nip on my earlobe.

I move to his belt and fumble—too many thoughts competing for attention, too much awareness that tomorrow everything changes. When I lean back to see the buckle properly, I'm caught by his dark, hungry gaze.

The moment his pants hit the floor, he steps out of them and crowds me backward. My calves hit the bed and suddenly I'm falling—caught, controlled—and he's over me, pressing me into the plush duvet.

"Don't call it settling." His voice is rough, possessive.

His lips cover mine and his tongue invades as his hand slides up to cradle my neck, his thigh pressing between my legs, his erection digging into my hip through the stretch of his boxer briefs.

"You're a fucking dream," he groans.

I finger his hair, holding him so I can see his eyes. I've been called many things—asset, operative, honey trap—but a dream doesn't sit well. "Dreams end. Fantasies lose their luster."

His hips rock forward, his muscled thigh pressing harder against my core through the lycra. His hair is tousled, undone, his breath shallow, but god, the way he's looking at me—like we're solid, permanent—it's unnerving.

With every shift of his torso, heat spirals through me. My sports bra and panties, his boxer briefs—thin barriers that somehow make the friction more intense. We're grinding against each other on top of a plush comforter, desperate and frustrated and neither of us willing to slow down enough to properly undress.

He licks and sucks at my neck, his fingers yanking my sports bra up, freeing my breast, teasing my nipple between his fingers.

"Tell me you're mine."

My back arches and I twist from the sensitivity. "I'm yours."

He stills. "What's with the smile?"

"I'm happy." The admission surprises us both.

This time, he smiles—rare, genuine, devastating. My fingers caress his ear as my gaze traces the hair that's flopped over his brow. "You're mine too, you know? It's a reciprocal kind of thing."

"I'm absolutely yours." He chuckles, then his hips resume their rhythm, shifting my thigh up so I'm cradling him. With each thrust his erection drags over my core—just lycra and cotton between us, so thin I feel every ridge, every pulse. "You've ruined me for others."

We kiss like we're not planning to betray his family tomorrow. Like we're not risking everything. Like we have forever.

The pressure builds—his weight, his rhythm, the friction against my clit through thin fabric—until I stiffen, brought to the brink by just this.

He pulls back, watching my face as I come apart beneath him. "Beautiful."

Deft hands glide my sports bra up and I arch to help him remove it. As I relax back into the down comforter, still trembling, he trails kisses down my body—between my breasts, over my ribs, my belly.

He backs up, hooks his fingers in my panties and the lycra leggings together, and slides them down my hips. I lift, helping him maneuver them off, legs together, then up and free. He sends them sailing across the room.

Looking supremely satisfied with himself, he sits back, spreading my legs wide. His thumb traces through my center. "Gorgeous."

He settles between my thighs, running his nose along the inside, inhaling. Then he parts me with his fingers and drags his tongue through me slow enough to make me shake.

I gasp. He grins like he's won something. And then he maps me with his mouth. Licking and sucking until I can't stay still.

I bite my lip to keep from saying his name too loudly behind hotel walls, some last thread of discipline that dissolves when his tongue circles my clit and his fingers curl inside.

I'm twisting beneath him, dripping, eyes squeezed shut as stars explode behind my eyelids in a whitewash of light.

When I open my eyes, he's looking up at me—pleased, awed, possessive. He presses his face into my inner thigh, then pushes up the bed, quickly ridding himself of his briefs.

I reach for him—his length hard and proud against his abdomen, skin flushed, thick and veined. My fingers wrap around him and he hisses.

I bend forward, intending to return the favor, but he pushes me back gently. "Next time. Right now I need—"

He spreads my legs, positions himself at my entrance. His crown swipes through my wetness, back and forth, teasing us both until I'm ready to beg. Then he pushes inside—just his tip—and pauses there, straining with control.

"Adrien." I'm falling so fast, so hard. Does he feel it?

He wraps his arms around me, braces his knees, and with a shuddering groan, fully seats himself. The stretch, the fullness—I want all of him, and here he is.

"Fuck, you are heaven."

He lifts my wrists, pinning my hands above my head, and his mouth drops to mine. I taste myself on his tongue—salt and intimacy—as his hips find their rhythm.

The sharp sound of skin meeting skin fills the suite. Tomorrow drowns beneath it. Every withdrawal leaves me wanting. Every thrust rubs my oversensitized clit. Every hard, hammering stroke sends my blood singing.

He's not gentle. Not careful. Not the controlled strategist. Just a man who risks everything and needs this—needs me—like oxygen.

As I let go—back arching, crying out against his mouth—his thrusts grow erratic. His muscles tremble. His mouth devours mine, claiming, until his hips jolt and he groans my name and throbs inside me, pulsing his release.

His head falls to the cradle of my shoulder, forehead damp, and his hold on my wrists loosens. Breaking free, I wrap my arms around him, holding tight. Holding on.

Later, we're entwined beneath the bedding. The city's hum slips to a heartbeat beneath the pale spill of dawn light through gauzy curtains. I lie with my head on his shoulder, the rhythm of his breathing steady against my ear.

"Tomorrow," he murmurs, eyes half-closed.

"Tomorrow," I echo.

Tomorrow feels distant, an enemy with a clock I refuse to watch.

He turns his face toward mine and presses a kiss to my forehead, a quiet benediction.

The steady rhythm of his breathing lulls me backward in time—to another dawn, another bed, another impossible goodbye, and a memory of lying perfectly still, listening to the night sounds filtering through thick glass. Intimacy often does this to me—fractures time.

Somewhere in the marina, a halyard clanged against a mast. A gull squawked. The air smelled of salt and polished teak, the faint sweetness of whatever soap he used still clinging to my skin. Normal sounds of a world outside percolated while I remained suspended in this impossible bubble of a weekend that should never have happened.

I'd thrown my phone away in a Monaco alley thirty-six hours ago. Along with it went any ability for my handler to track my location or contact me. By now, Matthews would already have flagged me as compromised. In our world, silence is betrayal.

The mission had been routine until it wasn't. Every contingency accounted for—except him.

Adrien shifted beside me, his arm tightening around my waist in sleep. Even unconscious, his body curved protectively around mine, as if he could shield me from the world waiting beyond this safe harbor. His skin radiated a slow, human heat against the linen sheets. Moonlight washed across his face, softening him until he looked almost boyish—the cynical lines around his eyes smoothed away, his mouth relaxed, unguarded. The sight ached like a bruise.

I should have extracted myself shortly after evading the Russian. Should have activated emergency protocols, requested immediate exfiltration. Instead, I stayed—and in doing so, compromised my career.

The worst part was that I couldn't even regret it. Lying there, I felt alive in a way I hadn't in years—proof that some part of me still existed beneath the aliases, beneath the armor of competence and command.

But time off wasn't compatible with the life I'd chosen.

I slipped from the bed with practiced silence, my bare feet making no sound on the polished deck. Cool air kissed my skin, smelling faintly of salt and last night's champagne. Sophie's dress hung in the closet, pristine now—someone had steamed out the wrinkles from when he'd torn it off me that first morning. Even his staff took care of me here. I pulled it on, the fabric whispering as it slid over my shoulders, cool where his warmth had been.

With each movement, I killed her.

The art curator who played piano in the early morning hours, who came apart in his arms, who whispered childhood stories in the dark and believed them herself. Each breath rebuilt the operative—the woman who knew how to disappear, how to leave no trace except the kind that scarred.

My shoes were on the upper deck where we'd first kissed. I climbed the narrow stairs quiet as a ghost, muscle memory guiding me through the yacht's layout. The night air was cooler up here, sharp with sea spray and diesel and something metallic that reminded me of the blood in my veins.

From the upper deck, I could see the lights of Monaco's harbor spreading like scattered diamonds. Somewhere in that maze of streets and luxury hotels, my old life waited—a handler to contact, reports to file, questions to answer. I could already hear Matthews' voice, sharp with controlled anger: You compromised an active operation for a civilian relationship. Do you understand the security implications?

But standing there in the moonlight, watching Adrien sleep through the open cabin windows, I understood something else entirely. I understood why people left this work. Why they chose complicated, messy, unpredictable human connections over the clean lines of duty and protocol.

I understood, too, why my parents had never called when they were working. Not because they didn't care—because they did.

Because they knew what the job costs. Because they'd made the same bargain, and they'd raised us to believe the price was worth it.

But what if we'd all been wrong?

My fingers found the railing, gripping the cold metal as I fought against the pull of possibility. The chill sank into my palms, grounding me, reminding me what was real. Two days ago, the answer would have been clear. Now it felt like standing on a fault line.

A sound from below made me freeze—the soft creak of a floorboard. Adrien was awake.

"Sophie?" His voice carried through the cabin, rough with sleep, threaded with confusion.

My hand tightened on the railing until my knuckles ached. If I answered, I'd never leave.

I closed my eyes, memorizing how my false name sounded like the truth in his mouth. By tomorrow, Sophie Dubois would cease to exist, just another identity dissolved back into the ether of classified files and forgotten operations. But for this moment, she was real.

The marina was quiet at this hour, most boats dark and still. I could slip away now, vanish into the night the way I'd been trained to do. By sunrise, I'd be nothing more than another dream Adrien would eventually convince himself had been too perfect to be real.

Or I could stay.

Love and duty balanced like a blade on my tongue. One cut either way, and I'd bleed for it.

The decision crystallized with brutal clarity. I had to leave, and there could be no goodbye. I couldn't trust myself not to waver if he asked me to stay, or to give him some way of finding me, some way of keeping in touch.

I knew what was expected of me: clean exits, no emotional entanglements, no loose ends that could compromise future operations. The woman who'd shared stories about her family and played piano onboard a yacht in the pre-dawn light was a side of me that I couldn't allow to exist. She was the kind of vulnerability that got people killed in my line of work.

My bare feet made no sound on the plank connecting the ship to the marina, though each step felt like walking through quicksand, my body fighting what my training demanded.

On the dock, I paused only long enough to slip on my heels. The click of expensive leather against weathered wood echoed too loudly in the pre-dawn quiet.

Behind me, I heard a door slam open, footsteps on the deck. His voice, louder now, edged with something that might have been panic: "Sophie! Sophie, where are you?"

I ran. Actually ran, like an amateur, like someone with something to lose. Designer heels clicking against wet dock, dress riding up my thighs, lungs burning with something that wasn't just exertion— running from the only man who'd ever made me want to stay.

I didn't look back. Couldn't. Because I knew that if I saw the yacht one more time—saw the porthole that looked into the cabin where we'd made love until we were both breathless and undone—I might lose my nerve entirely.

By the time the sun heated Monaco's harbor, I was gone. By the time I reached the airport, Sophie Dubois was filed away and forgotten, just another alias in an intelligence career.

I made my choice when I deboarded the yacht. The same choice I always made. But for the first time in my career, as the aircraft lifted into the sky, I wondered if I'd made a mistake.

His lips graze my shoulder, and I come back to Paris, to the man beside me, to the fact that the day could take everything. I curl closer anyway—choosing him in the only way that matters: while I still can.

CHAPTER
TWENTY-NINE

BRIE

"This is a kill box, Brie. Everything about this reads trap." Hudson's voice threads through my earpiece like static over wire—too calm, too precise—the kind of tone men use when the math already says loss.

I force a light smile as Adrien glances back at me from the café counter where he's ordering croissants and lattes. Morning light fractures through the window, gilding the air around him—civilian softness disguising a man bred for control.

"Quinn pulled the plans for the Montmartre. No clean approach—she'll see you coming. There's a dozen entry points." Too many doors. Too many unknowns waiting behind them.

Every entrance is an exit. I'd expect nothing less from a woman who's spent decades perfecting disappearance.

"The property was once tied to the Hermès family," I murmur. Old money clings to those walls like perfume that never washes out. "She's rented it—and she's connected enough to do it with almost no notice. She'll want discretion."

"If you're implying she won't fire inside, you're forgetting suppressors," Hudson says. "She can do what she wants and move bodies through the alley. We don't have coverage in place. Push to this afternoon and I can layer support."

"What resources?" The question is from a place of curiosity, as I'm still fleshing out this new group I've joined.

"Our backer can tap a global black-ops outfit."

"Which?"

"Arrow Tactical."

"We can't wait. She'll be suspicious."

"Understood." His disapproval rings clear. "You're carrying, right?"

My hand ghosts over the tote strap, reassurance by reflex. "Debating. If they sweep bags, it sends the wrong signal." One wrong weight on my hip and the meeting shifts from conversation to cautionary tale.

"Not a question. Given your background, she'll expect it."

It's a myth that CIA always carries. Often we don't—collection beats confrontation. Like this. I don't argue with my boss, but my gut outranks the briefing when I'm the one in the room.

I keep scanning the sidewalk through the café window. Paris hums outside—bicycles clicking over cobblestone, a woman laughing in a language that always sounds like seduction.

"Brie?"

"Understood."

"Comms?"

"Pointless—she'll jam them. I'll record."

"She won't say anything incriminating." He's right of course. She'll be careful with her words. "Can he hear you right now?"

My eyes meet Adrien's across the small cafe. He looks frustrated with the speed of service, but there's probably a reason this little café didn't have a line during what should be the morning rush.

"No."

"His plan to take over Eddie's role. Is that a ruse, or does he plan to continue sourcing content for Magpie?"

"Do we care?" It's a question I've asked myself, and I'm curious to hear my boss's take.

"If she's willing to expose the parties extorting the senator, then no. At least, that's the boss's take."

The boss. Our silent financial backer.

"And yours?"

"I'd like to gain more intel before coming to that conclusion."

"The stated plan is to end his role as a source." My gut check is Adrien has zero intention of exposing his membership, but my experience is that many fall to opportunity's siren song.

Adrien arrives at the table with our lattes in to-go cups, his eyes narrowing with the question he doesn't voice. I give him a soft smile I want to believe. The truth is thinner.

His father's message landed with a location—23 Avenue Junot, Pavillon D—and a thirty-minute window. A pulse of coordinates disguised as civility. I didn't need Hudson to tell me we just let Moira choose every advantage.

After I end the call, Adrien asks, "Your boss?"

I nod in the affirmative and break apart a piece of croissant. Hardly the breakfast of champions, but my body hasn't adjusted to the time change, and the request to meet at nine in the morning is unexpected.

I tucked the subcompact in the tote's side pocket. If someone checks the bag, they'll find it. I'm not carrying anything on my body.

If she wishes to eliminate us, we could make the task quite simple for Moira. But if she's friends with his father, if they go way back as photographs indicate, then it's unlikely she'd kill her friend's son. Unlikely, but not impossible.

"What's wrong?" Adrien's fingers lightly brush my shoulder, then he caresses my cheek as he stands beside me, choosing not to sit.

I inhale deeply, clearing the fog and settling the uncertainty. "Nothing. Let's do this. We're about a five-minute walk away." He studies me like he knows I'm lying. Maybe he does. Maybe he loves that I still can.

The black iron gate lifts out of cobblestone like a secret kept too long. It groans as it opens, old metal confessing everything it's seen. Ivy climbs the pillars; dappled light freckles the path. Even the air smells restrained—wet stone, moss, and wealth.

The townhouse-turned-five-star inn is a whispered Paris secret, and Quinn flagged that it can be booked outright. She believes Moira has it through the weekend.

Is it chance that we arrived when she has it reserved? Or is she that connected?

We'll likely never know, and it's not particularly relevant.

I scan the skyline and the old stone wall, covered in a mix of healthy and dead ivy, searching for eyes. Footsteps on stone blend with birdsong, as the scent of earth mixes with car exhaust. A man in black trousers, tuxedo coat, wingtips, and white gloves approaches.

"He needs a top hat, doesn't he?" I murmur. Adrien's mouth twitches; tension breaks for a heartbeat before knitting again.

As the middle-aged man grows closer, I study his profile, searching for weapons. I don't see one, but he could easily have one tucked away. The gate creaks. "Please, come in," he says, and my gaze lifts to the camera perched on the pillar. He doesn't ask our names. Someone's watching and already knows.

The man locks the gate behind us while we stand patiently to the side. "Follow me," he says, taking the lead along the path and never once glancing over his shoulder.

We pass small white iron café tables and chairs with red cushion seats, the colors standing out among the winter garden over evergreens and step through glass doors into a hallway. The absence of others is eerie, if only because I'm positive others are watching, even if it's only through a lens. Silence here isn't emptiness—it's curated, the hush of money buying invisibility.

Adrien remains close to my side, his hand often brushing my lower back, protective in his closeness. Each touch a Morse code of reassurance I pretend not to need.

I appreciate the sensation, but I'm also fully aware that if we find ourselves in a situation that requires hand-to-hand combat, I'm the one with Krav Maga training, and I will not allow him to use his body as a shield.

The tuxedoed man leads us through a series of salons before arriving at a book-lined room. A long brown leather sofa sits on one wall, and a high back velvet armchair in the corner. In the chair sits an older woman with sparkling blue eyes, platinum blonde hair cut in a blunt, sharp-angled bob. Her long black skirt nearly reaches the ground, and black leather shoes with rounded toes peek beneath the hem. The periwinkle sweater with a boatneck softens her appearance, and it's difficult to align this person with a woman rumored to have built an organization others fear. The room smells faintly of spritzed perfume and old paper—refinement masking rot.

She doesn't rise as we enter. Power measured not in movement but in the certainty she doesn't have to.

One door behind us stands open; a hidden panel in the bookcase is cracked; a third door at the back is closed. If I were placing a team, I'd put one behind each of the latter two.

"May I get anything for you?" the tuxedoed man asks the room.

"We're fine, Charles. Thank you," Moira Kelly answers. "You may close the door behind you. We won't be long."

To us, she says, "Please, sit." Her gesturing palm is a small invitation that doesn't reach her eyes. Those eyes could catalog sins faster than any database. Now I see what connected looks like: a woman whose stillness makes the air obey.

Her gaze lingers a beat too long on my tote. She waits until Adrien and I are seated to begin.

"I don't normally take meetings. But your father and I... I'll make an exception for him. As a favor." She crosses one leg over the other, then rests one palm over her knee, and the other palm over the hand, posture erect, shoulders back, eyes sharp and astute. "I suspect this will be a waste of your time, but I sensed you wouldn't accept me at my word unless we met in person."

"What did my father tell you?" Adrien asks.

"It's not so much what your father said, but what I've learned about you over the years. You see, Adrien, I'm in the business of knowledge. I've watched you grow from afar." She smiles. "I have observed you since your toddler days."

"Then you already know why I'm here."

"Why don't you tell me why you're here. I won't ask you to explain Ms. Anderson's presence. I know why she's here. She's your security." Her gaze travels to the cracked door. "I'm not alone either. I don't know what you've heard, but I'm also not a monster. You're safe. I have no plans to harm you."

"I don't believe my father would set up this meeting if he believed you would harm his only living son."

Her lips press together, thoughtful. "And your reason for coming all this way?'

"You've been profiting from my business."

"So I have." Now, she smiles. "People are most honest when they feel beautiful and desired." Her voice strokes the word *desired* like silk over skin, and for a second I understand how she built a business out of closeted confession. "Your facilities create an environment where people feel beautiful, desired, and safe. But, your locations are one of many sources I possess."

"Yes. That's what I came to talk to you about."

"I monetize information." She pauses, studying us both. "Though I suspect you already know that."

"We know Eddie's been selling to you," I say carefully.

"Eddie sells to many people." Her tone is neutral, giving nothing away. "What exactly brings you to Paris?"

Adrien leans forward. "Senator Crawford is being blackmailed with footage from my club."

"Senators receive threats regularly. Why should this concern me?"

"Because," I interject, "the footage came from your operation."

Moira's expression doesn't change. "You seem certain of that."

"We found the server room," Adrien says.

"Servers exist in many buildings." She picks up a crystal paperweight from the side table, turning it in the light. "Tell me, what do you want from this meeting?"

"We want the buyer on Crawford," I say.

"Rivers have tributaries," she answers, setting the crystal down. The crystal flashes light across her face, a halo or a warning depending on how you read it.

Adrien's jaw ticks. "So Eddie has other buyers."

"Water finds its own level." A dry smile. "Your employee is entrepreneurial."

"Then you won't object to my replacing him," Adrien says.

"That depends on what you replace." A glance at him, then at me. "Access is a currency. So is discretion."

"My clientele values privacy," he answers.

"Privacy is a luxury." She stands and crosses to the window. Sunlight webs through the lace curtains, sketching gold across her hair like a saint painted by a cynic. "Information is a necessity. Do you know the difference?"

Adrien's silence says he does, but he won't grant her the satisfaction of admitting it.

Through the window, sunlight plays across leaves. In this

salon, one could be mistaken for believing we're in the countryside rather than the middle of Paris.

"If I understand you correctly, you wish to work with me directly, eliminating Eddie from your operation." Her gaze cuts to me. "And you want more information about the Crawford business."

Her hands clasp daintily below her waist. "I can accept your deal, Adrien, as Eddie violated his agreement with me when he began selling information to others. He has no loyalty to me; therefore, I have none to him. But Ms. Anderson, I'm afraid I can't provide you with the information you need."

"Moira," Adrien says, "That's a condition of our agreement. A condition of my loyalty."

"I said can't, not won't."

"Then who can?" Adrien demands.

Moira turns from the window, her expression calculating. "There are...complications with your senator's situation."

"What kind of complications?" I ask.

"The kind that involves former associates who've forgotten the value of discretion."

"Give us a name," Adrien says.

"Names have consequences." She returns to her chair, settling back with the air of someone who holds all the cards. "Particularly when those names belong to people in sensitive positions."

"How sensitive?" I probe.

"The kind that requires security clearances." Her smile is thin. "The kind that sits in very important meetings."

Adrien and I exchange glances. She's talking about someone in government.

"White House?" I ask directly.

"Such a specific guess." Moira's eyebrows raise slightly. "What makes you think that?"

"The target is a senator. The leverage is sexual blackmail. It screams political operation."

"Or it screams someone who understands political pressure points." Moira's still not giving us a direct answer. "Someone trained in...psychological operations, perhaps."

I feel the pieces clicking. "Former CIA."

"Former many things." Finally, a hint of confirmation. "Elena always was ambitious." The name lands like a dropped blade. A faint hum in my ears—recognition or dread, I can't tell which. "She's a former CIA psychological operations expert, although I don't believe you crossed paths with her. Elena Vasquez." She pointedly looks at me, and I don't respond, because the name is familiar.

Wait. In a flash, it comes to me. "She's the White House Deputy Chief of Staff."

"She was mine before she was theirs," Moira says. Possession, not nostalgia, coats the words. "When she stepped inside the White House, she decided she preferred independence. Some buyers still think they're dealing with me. I'm not fond of the confusion—or her carelessness."

"Are you saying the President of the United States is behind the blackmailing of the senator?" Adrien asks, sounding like he doesn't believe one word.

"No, not at all. I would be shocked to learn he's aware. When Elena struck out on her own, she wasn't searching for yet another boss. I also expect that none of her clients know she's the source. She's operating in the dark." And somewhere in that dark, I can feel the edges of my old life reaching for me. "I've heard some say they thought they were still buying from Magpie. And that's one reason I'm willing to help you Adrien. Eddie contacted me, let me know what's going on—because he works with both Elena and I, and he was concerned you were onto him, and it could fall back on me. When your father called, I was curious what your take would be. I'm glad you're looking for a partnership. And I have no reason to protect Elena. She's untrustworthy. She takes risks. She's cocky. That's not in the interest of my clients."

"How do you want us to proceed?" I ask. She didn't agree to meet us without an angle.

"To uncover your extortionist, you'll need to ask Elena. She doesn't take blind pitches," Moira says. "She'll answer me. I'll tell her there's a change of guard and she should hear you out." We've just been drafted into someone else's chess game, and Moira's the only one who can see the whole board. "She's arrogant enough to believe I've forgiven her. She may not move until she needs you—press too hard and she spooks."

She tilts her head, considering. "If I suggest you hold proof that brushes her operation, she'll prioritize you. My work centers on corporate secrets and the occasional messy estate. She's breaking U.S. laws. I'll imply a deal with you prevents exposure from a larger investigation. She'll want to protect herself. At the very least, she'll want to assess you."

Adrien responds, "I appreciate your assistance."

"Now, once you meet with her, what information she gives you, or how you draw it out of her, that's on you. It's quite possible she may fear the client more than exposure. It just depends on the client."

"It's an interesting business you've built," Adrien says.

"It's the fountain of youth, better than any lotion or oil." She smiles. "Love what you do. But I suspect you already share that notion." Adrien's smile is small, controlled, but the muscle in his jaw betrays him—the d'Avricourt mask slipping for half a breath. "After all, you walked away from your birthright. I approve more than your father does."

"I didn't walk away," he says evenly. "The Sanctuary serves d'Avricourt. Understanding the client is the point."

"You sound like him," she says, checking her watch. "Do we have a deal?"

"Are there more Eddie Thorne's?" His tone is cool, but I can feel the quiet fury under it—protective, possessive, dangerously human.

Moira's lips curve on the ends, her only reaction to his question. "He only has access to two locations." Her smile sharpens, thin as piano wire. Deals like this always draw blood; the question is whose.

"I'll need names," he says. "I'll verify. If you tell me the truth, if I don't uncover an unnamed entity, then we have a deal."

CHAPTER
THIRTY

ADRIEN

Hours later, we're on a private plane, returning home. I'd have given anything to keep Brie in Paris for the weekend, but too much still hangs over us. Duty came knocking early. She's busy with her team, and my mood doesn't match the success we had today.

It's not lost on me that what began as a ploy has become a true opportunity. I could continue the business Eddie Thorne started. I could pick up where he left off—decide which secrets are worth selling, which sins deserve daylight. The thought sits in my gut like good whiskey gone bad—warm, but burning all the same. Tempting, like opportunities tend to be, but the costs are too high.

Moira believes I'm pledging allegiance. What I'm actually buying is time. First, we need to follow the trail to Vasquez. I owe that to Brie and to the senator. Second, I need Moira to provide her other sources within The Sanctuary. And of course, I'll hire KOAN to validate anything she shares. She might have a history with my father, but I don't have a history with her.

The Gulfstream's cabin hums with quiet luxury as we level off over the Atlantic. Muted amber light glazes the cabin walls; the air smells faintly of leather, eucalyptus, and Brie's perfume clinging to my cuffs. She's claimed the conference area, her laptop open, phone pressed to her ear as she coordinates with her team. I've retreated to the back of the cabin, nursing a scotch and staring out at clouds that mirror my mood—gray and turbulent.

Moira arranged the meeting with Elena, passing details through a burn-after-reading system that feels ripped from a spy novel—appropriate, considering what my life has become.

"We've been reviewing the planned meet location," Brie says, ending her call and joining me on the leather sofa. "Very public, very safe for her."

"And very observable," I add, thinking of Gramercy Tavern, a place I've been but don't frequent. It's not monitored in the traditional sense—but it's visible. Too many witnesses for anyone to act rashly. "That's the point. She feels secure there."

Brie curls into the corner of the sofa, studying my face. "You've been quiet since we left Paris."

I take another sip of scotch, letting the burn distract from the knot in my chest. "Just processing."

"Want to talk about it?"

The question hangs between us like the thirty-thousand feet of air beneath the plane.

"I keep thinking about what Moira said." I set down the glass, turning to face her fully. "The truth is, Brie, I do understand my clientele. I've built my entire business around understanding what powerful people want, what they crave, the image they wish to project, what they'll pay for."

"It's not the same thing as exploiting them."

"No. But it puts me closer to the edge than I ever wanted to be." I can feel the moral line blur even as I push forward. "I created an environment where people are free to act without fear of exposure. I would most definitely never monetize indiscretions or base needs. Or so I thought? But isn't that exactly what I'm doing by offering safe spaces?"

Brie's hand finds mine, her fingers intertwining in a gesture that's becoming as natural as breathing. Skin to skin, it feels like confession granted absolution. "There's a difference between providing safe spaces and violating trust."

"It's a fine line—one that's easy to blur. Because sitting in that room with Moira, listening to her explain how she operates... It didn't sound foreign. It sounded familiar." I lean back against the headrest, closing my eyes. "My father built the family conglomerate by staying one step ahead of everyone. Learning that he did it by buying stolen competitive designs changes everything I believed about our family's success. About my own moral inheritance. Margot willingly continues the tradition. I easily could have become them. That's the part that unnerves me."

"Maybe you're exactly who you choose to be."

I open my eyes to find her watching me with an intensity that clenches my chest. "And who do you think I choose to be?"

"Someone who walked away from guaranteed success for independence. Someone who's risking everything to protect people he's never met from blackmail schemes." Her thumb traces across my knuckles. "Someone who spent months searching for a woman who might not have existed."

Turbulence jolts us, and she shifts closer, bringing with her that scent—strength wrapped in softness—a presence I found impossible to forget.

"What happens after this is over?" I ask quietly.

Will she disappear again? It's possible. Probable, even. She'll likely move—someone proved her apartment isn't safe. She's trained to elude pursuit. If she doesn't want me to find her, I won't. The thought makes my chest tight.

"What do you want to happen?"

"I want to wake up with you in the morning." The words come easier than I expected. "I want to argue with you about art for that empty wall in your apartment—or any wall in any place you choose to live. I want to take you to Paris properly." I pause, gathering courage. "I want you to meet my parents as the woman I'm falling in love with, after they've forgiven me. I want time together without fearing I'll wake and you'll be gone."

For a moment I wonder if I've said too much, pushed too hard. Then she's moving—shifting until she's straddling my lap, hands framing my face, and relief floods through me.

"I want all of that too," she whispers against my lips. "But are you sure? Because my work won't change. There will be other cases, other days where I may need to carry a weapon—"

"Then I'll learn to live with worry." I cup her face, thumbs brushing her cheekbones. The idea of her in danger makes me want to lock her away somewhere safe, but I know better. She'd never forgive me, and I'd lose what makes her extraordinary. "Because the alternative—saying goodbye to you, living without you—is worse."

Her lips meet mine—this kiss tastes like promises and possibilities, like the beginning of something that could actually last. Her hands work at my shirt buttons, and my gaze flits past her tousled blonde hair to the closed cockpit door.

There have been times—more than I'd care to admit—when I wouldn't have given a damn if a flight attendant walked in mid-tryst. Discretion was their job, not mine. But this isn't one of those times. This isn't casual or careless. This is Brie, and she deserves privacy. Intention. Reverence.

I catch her hand, stopping her fingers but holding tight. "Come with me."

I grab my scotch from the side table and lead her to the private suite at the plane's rear. The door clicks shut behind us—solid, secure, ours. I set the drink on the nightstand and shrug out of my shirt, letting it fall carelessly.

With a tug on the hem of the top, she understands, and raises her arms, letting me lift the cashmere off, over her head. Her travel sweater set gives easily under my hands, the cashmere sliding away to reveal lace and skin—an ensemble that destroys composure. One simple push on the waistband, and the matching bottoms fall to her ankles, leaving my beauty in slips of the finest lace.

My fingers glide along her soft skin—the curve of her waist, the swell of her breast, her nipple taut beneath the delicate tapestry. I lean in, sucking and licking the sensitive skin of her throat, tasting the faint sweetness of her perfume mixed with something uniquely her.

The cabin tilts slightly with turbulence or maybe just the rhythm of my breathing. She backs up until her legs hit the bed and sits, immediately focused on my belt buckle with that intensity she brings to everything.

When she finally gets it undone—along with the snap and zipper—her triumphant smile nearly undoes me. My trousers fall to my ankles and I kick them aside while she reaches for my briefs.

She removes them with practiced efficiency, wraps her elegant fingers around my erection, and licks. The sight alone—Brie on her knees on my private plane, blonde hair falling forward, those crystal blue eyes looking up at me—could fuel fantasies for years.

I close my eyes, luxuriating in the heat of her mouth, the tight grip, the way she takes me deeper. It's exquisite. Perfect.

But that's not what I want right now.

I pull back gently, tipping her chin up to meet my eyes. I press my thumb over her wet, swollen lips—gorgeous, ruined, mine—and urge her back onto the bed.

She spreads out on the satin coverlet, long blonde hair scattered around her, crystal blue eyes heavy-lidded with desire. She's breathtaking—a daydream made flesh, better than any fantasy I've entertained.

Mine. Finally, properly mine.

I trail kisses up her body, taking my time with her stomach, her ribs, until I reach her breasts. I reach behind her to unsnap her bra—the clasp gives easily—and pull the lace away.

Bare before me, she's perfect. I lavish attention on her breasts, tongue circling one nipple while my fingers work the other, and she arches into me with a soft gasp.

Then I reach for my scotch, fishing out a solid square ice cube. I hold it above her breast, letting one cold drop fall, watching her flinch and smile. Then I press the ice directly to her nipple.

She gasps—her back arching sharply off the bed.

I circle the ice slowly, watching her nipple tighten further, watching goosebumps race across her skin. When I replace the ice with my mouth—hot after cold—she moans my name.

The contrast makes her writhe. Cold shock, then the faint burn of expensive scotch still clinging to the cube, then the heat of my mouth sucking away the chill. She tastes like Macallan 25 and promises I'm desperate to keep.

Beneath me, her hips buck, seeking friction against my thigh. She mewls and twists, shameless in her need.

"You like that?" I ask, though I can see the answer written across her flushed skin.

Her tongue slips over her lower lip as she nods. That small gesture—so unconscious, so sensual—wrecks me. It feels like surrender, like trust, like the first crack in my own carefully maintained composure.

I sit back on my heels, grip her panties, and slide them down—over her hips, past her thighs, knees, calves. I toss them aside without looking where they land.

Then I reach for my highball glass. I fish out the ice cube, hold it between my fingers where she can see it, and with my other hand, I tip the glass forward.

Expensive scotch drizzles down her stomach—amber liquid trailing between her breasts, over her ribs, pooling in her navel, then continuing south to glisten at her core.

"I've been wondering," I tell her, my voice rougher than intended, "what you'd taste like with scotch." I set the glass aside and lean down, dragging my tongue through the trail I've created. "Fuck, Brie. This is exactly what I've been wanting."

The taste of her mixed with fifty-year-old single malt is obscene. Profane. Perfect.

I nip at her hip bone, suck at the sensitive skin of her

inner thigh, then finally—finally—I lavish her with my tongue.

She's already wet, but the scotch adds a sweet burn, a slick glide that makes her gasp. I work her with my mouth—licking, sucking, learning the sounds she makes when I hit the right spot. My fingers join my tongue, curling inside her while I seal my lips over her clit.

The ice cube in my other hand is melting, so I drag it along her inner thigh—the shock of cold against overheated skin makes her jump. I trace it closer, closer, until it's pressed right where my tongue was. She cries out, thighs trying to close, but I hold her open.

"Too much?" I pull back to look at her face—flushed, desperate, gorgeous.

"No. God, no. Don't stop."

I alternate: ice, then my hot tongue. Cold, then heat. Sensation she can't predict, can't control. Her hands fist in my hair, thighs trembling against my shoulders.

"Yes, yes, right there—"

I feel the moment she breaks—muscles clenching around my fingers, back arching off the satin, my name torn from her throat. I work her through it, gentling as she comes down, until she's boneless and panting.

When I finally pull back, I set what's left of the drink aside. Her eyes are still closed, chest heaving.

"I think next time we'll try a good cab. Or maybe champagne."

"Hmm," is all she manages.

"Are you not keen on that idea?" I tease, arms straining to hold myself over her.

"I kind of like the ice." Her eyes flutter open, meeting mine with a satisfied, lazy smile that makes me want to start all over again.

I chuckle and she lifts to kiss me, tasting herself on my lips. Her legs wrap around my thighs, pulling me closer, asking for more.

And Jesus, she's so wet, so ready. I position myself at her entrance—no barriers, no protection, just trust and choice—and push inside slowly.

The sensation steals my breath. Tight. Hot. Home.

"Brie." Her name is prayer and possession.

I start moving, finding a rhythm that has her gasping, her nails digging into my shoulders. At thirty-five thousand feet, disconnected from the world and its problems, we create our own gravity.

Making love at this altitude feels like claiming something—each other, this moment, the future we're choosing despite all the uncertainties waiting on the ground. For the first time in my life, altitude feels like absolution rather than escape.

I shift the angle, driving deeper, and she cries out. Her internal muscles clench around me and I'm close, so close. "Come with me," I growl against her ear. "Come with me, Brie."

She shatters—back arching, my name on her lips—and I follow seconds after, pulsing deep inside her, giving her everything I have.

Afterwards, Brie traces lazy patterns on my chest. Beneath us is satin, over us a cashmere throw, and the only sound is the constant hum of the engines. The rhythm of turbines syncs with her heartbeat against my ribs. It's a heaven I never want to leave.

Outside, the Atlantic stretches endless and dark, the

horizon invisible. For the first time in days—I stop thinking about the next move, the next challenge, the next revelation.

"For what it's worth," she says quietly, "I don't think you'll become another Eddie Thorne."

I press a kiss to her temple, brushing blonde strands from her face. "How can you be so sure?"

"Eddie sold secrets for profit. You'd do it to protect people—to control what gets weaponized. That's not the same thing."

Maybe she's right. Maybe the difference between Eddie and me isn't whether we both profit from secrets, but why we do it and how far we're willing to go. The thought should comfort me, but as the plane carries us toward whatever confrontation awaits with Elena Vasquez, I'm unsettled. I already know what kind of man I am. What I don't know is what it will cost me to keep being him.

"I also don't think your father—or sister—are like Moira. They purchased information. Competitive insights. Illegal? I'm guessing French would say yes, but it's not deadly, it's not the same."

"Perhaps." The trouble is, if my father would stoop to working with the Moira Kellys of the world, what else would he do? What will my sister do? "It's hard to say what I'd do when pressed."

Her finger traces the outline of my lip in lieu of a response. But then she says, "I'd trust you to choose what's right."

She's placing a lot of trust in me. And the only positive I see is… "Does that mean you're planning on sticking around?"

"No more disappearing acts. I promise—I'm not running. Not from this, not from you."

That's good. "I needed to hear that."

It's the truth, and I feel more settled and at ease about our relationship, that is. But I'm not sure I share her trust in myself. I struck out on my own to give my sister the family throne, to find my independence, not because I thought I was better than either of them. Hell, I chose a path many would call questionable.

As I hold her in the quiet luxury of our temporary heaven, I realize the question isn't whether I can walk a moral line. The question is whether I can become the man she believes I am. The Star card, not the Tower—hope over ruin. The man who deserves the faith she's placing in me.

Whatever Elena Vasquez reveals, whatever fallout that comes, I won't face it alone. That knowledge would have terrified a younger me, a man who craved control. But now, it feels like the first solid ground I've stood on in years.

CHAPTER
THIRTY-ONE

BRIE

Jake and I sit in the surveillance van parked half a block from Gramercy Tavern. Despite its sophisticated interior, the space feels cramped. Banks of monitors line one wall, showing feeds from cameras Quinn's running remotely from the KOAN ops hub. The audio equipment hums quietly, pulling in conversations from the wire Adrien's wearing—a nearly invisible device threaded through his shirt collar.

"Target approaching from the south," Noah's voice crackles through my earpiece. He's positioned as a jogger in Gramercy Park, giving him clear sight lines to the restaurant's main entrance. Jake sits beside me, eyes fixed on the screens, his finger tapping the comms console. This is the third assignment I've worked with Jake. He flew in last night to assist today.

I lean forward, adjusting the audio levels as Elena Vasquez comes into view on monitor three. She moves with the fluid confidence of someone who's never doubted her place in the world—elegant gray coat, designer handbag, silver hair perfectly styled despite the October wind. Two men flank her at a discreet distance, clearly security aiming to blend in.

"She brought backup," I murmur into my comm unit.

"Copy that," Hudson's voice responds from command, monitoring from KOAN's mobile relay a few blocks out. "Quinn, are you picking up any electronic interference?"

"Negative," she replies through the comm—her voice faint, piped in from the ops hub's digital feed. "If they're jamming, it's passive."

Through the restaurant's front windows, I watch Elena enter and speak briefly with the hostess. Adrien sits at a corner table, visible through the large windows facing the street—exactly where we want him for optimal surveillance coverage.

The audio crackles to life as Elena approaches his table.

"Mr. d'Avricourt." Her voice carries a slight Boston accent, blended with New York speed.

"Ms. Vasquez. Thank you for agreeing to meet."

"Of course. Please, sit."

I close my eyes, listening to the subtle sounds of chairs moving, the clink of water glasses. Elena's voice again, warmer now, the tone of someone settling into familiar territory.

"I understand you're looking to replace an employee."

"Word travels fast in certain circles." Adrien's response is measured, professional. We rehearsed this—keep her talking, get her comfortable, then gradually probe for information about her buyers.

"In my business, information is currency. Your...former associate...was quite valuable to my organization. I assume you'd prefer to maintain the relationship rather than see it dissolve entirely."

My fingers tighten around the audio controls. She's talking about Eddie like a business asset, which he essentially was. The casual way she discusses human intelligence sources makes my skin crawl—it's everything I hated about the darker side of the CIA.

"That depends entirely on the terms," Adrien says. "And on understanding exactly what kind of business relationship this would be."

"Straightforward consulting. I have clients who value certain types of information—market trends, regulatory insights, personal details that affect business decisions. Your establishment provides a unique vantage point for observing the intersection of power and...vulnerability."

Through the restaurant window, I watch Elena gesture subtly with her hands, her body language open and confident. She believes she's in control of this conversation.

"And the recent unpleasantness with the senator?" Adrien asks.

Elena's laugh carries clearly through the audio feed. "Senator Crawford represents exactly the kind of challenge my clients appreciate. A man with principles who can be...encouraged...to see reason through proper motivation."

"Is that common? Using personal indiscretions to influence legislative votes?"

"Mr. d'Avricourt, you'd be amazed how often personal failings prove useful in political negotiations. Though I must say, sexual impropriety is becoming less effective these days. People are so much more forgiving of human nature than they used to be."

One of Elena's security team moves closer to the restaurant window, speaking into what appears to be a phone but is probably a communication device. Through the monitors, I watch him scan the street methodically. He pauses mid-scan, eyes catching on the reflection from our windshield.

"He's clocking us," I whisper.

"Confirm visual?" Hudson asks.

"Tall guy, dark coat—north-facing window reflection. He's narrowing in."

The security man continues his scan, then speaks again into his device. On the audio feed, Elena's voice shifts subtly —still pleasant, but with an edge of alertness.

"I'm curious, Mr. d'Avricourt. This conversation feels somewhat...official. Are we being recorded?"

Shit. She knows.

Adrien's response comes smoothly, as we practiced. "In my business, discretion is everything. I wouldn't risk that lightly."

"Of course not." But Elena's tone has cooled considerably. "Still, I find myself wondering if you're the only interested party in this conversation."

Through the window, I watch her reach into her handbag —a motion that might be innocent, but still tightens my focus. Her security detail has already shifted, one moving toward the restaurant's side exit, the other holding position on the street.

"There's no need for concern," Adrien says. "I'm simply trying to understand the scope of your operation. How extensive is your network? How many sources like Eddie do you maintain? How often do you plan on calling upon me?"

"Mr. d'Avricourt." Elena's voice carries warning now. "I think you're underestimating the delicacy of what you're proposing. The kind of information I broker comes with significant risks. Dead man's switches. Safeguards. Insurance policies that protect everyone involved."

"Including yourself."

"Especially myself." I can hear the smile in her voice, but it's sharp like a blade. "You see, I've built something quite remarkable over the years. A network that touches the highest levels of government, business, international relations. If anything were to happen to me—arrest, accident, unexpected disappearance—certain files would automatically be released. Files that would destroy careers, topple governments, collapse markets."

"That's quite a claim."

"It's not a claim; it's a guarantee. Ask your senator friend about the scope of my reach. His little indiscretion is barely worthy of a footnote compared to what I know about his colleagues."

Through the audio, I hear the scrape of a chair. Elena is standing.

"I think this meeting has run its course," she says. "You're clearly not serious about a business relationship. And I suspect you have friends listening who are far too interested in my affairs."

This is falling apart. Elena's about to walk, and we'll lose our only direct connection to whoever's targeting Crawford and others. I make a decision that goes against every protocol Hudson established.

"Jake, I'm going in."

Hudson's voice flares in my ear—from command, tinny with distance. "Negative, Brie. Hold."

"She's walking—give me sixty seconds. I can salvage."

Jake's jaw tightens but he doesn't stop me. "You've got eyes," he murmurs.

I'm already moving, stripping off my earpiece and adjusting my appearance quickly—loose hair, different posture, the persona of someone who belongs in this upscale restaurant environment. Jake gives me a silent thumbs up and zeroes in on the monitors.

"Brie, do not compromise position." Hudson's voice follows me, but I'm already out of the van. Cold air sharpens my breath as I cross the street. The traffic slows at the intersection and the bite of exhaust mixes with roasted chestnuts from the corner cart.

The restaurant's interior buzzes with lunchtime conversation and the clink of silverware against china. It's the subtle hum of Manhattan power dining in a hallowed room with Kushner's *Cornucopia*, a colorful piece that feeds the energy.

I spot Adrien and Elena immediately—he's calm composure in a charcoal suit, she's poise sharpened to diamond precision, already half-turned to leave while he remains seated, measured, performing patience.

I approach with the confident stride of someone who belongs here, someone who has every right to interrupt.

"Darling, I'm so sorry I'm late." I lean down to kiss Adrien's cheek, selling the performance while positioning myself to face Elena directly. "Traffic was absolutely brutal."

Elena's eyes narrow as she assesses this new variable. Her gaze travels from my face to my posture to the way I positioned myself—searching for tells that would identify my true purpose.

"Ms. Vasquez, isn't it?" I extend my hand with a warm smile. "I'm Brie. Adrien mentioned you might be able to help with our little problem."

"Your little problem?"

"The competition." I settle into the chair across from her,

occupying space deliberately, giving her a choice: reclaim dominance or appear uncertain. She sits.

"You know how it is in tech. Everyone's always trying to steal designs, poach talent, undercut pricing. Adrien tells me you have a gift for acquiring the kind of information that keeps businesses ahead of their rivals." I keep my tone conspiratorial, the kind of admiration women trade when they both know the cost of playing in men's worlds.

Elena is sitting, but her posture remains guarded—shoulders poised, fingers resting on the rim of her glass like a pianist ready to strike a chord. "And what makes you think I'd be interested in tech industry espionage?"

"Because you're already doing it." I lean forward conspiratorially. "You branched out. The depositions from antitrust cases provide invaluable insights. Your old boss wasn't interested in expanding, but you recognized value and opportunity."

The recognition flickers across Elena's features—surprise, then calculation, then grudging respect.

"You've done your homework."

"I always do. By the way, your team's right, and I was the one listening in—because we need to trust you're the right partner. The question is whether you're interested in expanding the relationship. Adrien's ventures here in New York provide unique opportunities for information gathering. The kind of intimate access that most consultants only dream of."

"Who do you represent?"

"KOAN. But you already know this, right? You're the one who hired someone to research me." Breaking into my home, research, it's all the same in the intelligence field. Her gaze flicks between me and Adrien.

"And what exactly are you proposing?"

This is the moment. Elena's engaged again, her business instincts overriding her caution. I can work with that.

"A partnership. Not just passive information gathering, but active intelligence operations. The kind of sophisticated work that your current network has proven so successful at." I pause, letting my voice drop slightly. "The kind that influences and shapes legislation."

"You think you understand my business?"

"I think I understand ambition. And I think you've built something impressive—a network that can reach into the highest levels of power and extract exactly the information your clients need. But I also think you're selling yourself short."

"How so?" Elena's smile is catlike, conniving. She's enjoying this.

"Because you're still thinking small. Individuals, isolated influence operations, one-off intelligence sales. What if instead of reacting to what powerful people do in private, you could shape what they do in public?" Her eyes sharpen; she likes the word *shape*. It's creative, not criminal—exactly how she justifies herself.

Elena leans back in her chair, studying me with new interest. "That is my business, but I'm interested in your interpretation. Continue."

"You have access to the private moments, the vulnerable confessions, the intimate details of some of the most powerful people in the world. Right now, you're using that information defensively—protecting clients, applying pressure after they've already taken positions. But what if you could use it proactively?"

"You're suggesting I become a puppet master."

"I'm suggesting you become what you already are, but more efficiently. Instead of waiting for clients to come to you with problems, you anticipate their needs. Instead of reacting to legislative votes, you shape them before they happen. Instead of selling information after the fact, you create the conditions that generate the information in the first place."

Elena's eyes have taken on a gleam that tells me I've hit the right nerve. This is a woman who's built her career on understanding human psychology, on knowing exactly what buttons to push. I'm using her own methods against her.

"You think very strategically Ms. Anderson. Exactly what I would expect from a fellow CIA graduate."

The statement lands like a test. She's watching for a flinch. I give her none—just the stillness I learned to weaponize.

"I think like someone who understands that in any business, information is power. And power unused is power wasted."

"And what would you want in return for this...partnership?"

"Transparency. Not about your methods—I understand the need for operational security. But my client is ultimately Senator Crawford. In this instance."

A waiter passes, pouring Pellegrino; bubbles hiss between us like static from a blown wire. Surveillance, luxury, desire —all sharing a tablecloth.

Around us, the restaurant continues its normal rhythm, other diners absorbed in their own conversations, unaware they're witnessing a negotiation that could reshape how information flows through the corridors of power.

"That's the only piece of information we need. And of course, a better sense of our needs moving forward."

"You know," Elena says finally, "I may have underestimated both of you."

"Most people do," Adrien says quietly—his voice low, the sound a vibration against my skin more than something I hear.

"The senator—Crawford—his situation really is quite routine. Sexual indiscretions are so pedestrian these days. But the client who commissioned that particular piece of leverage... now they represent the kind of forward-thinking approach you're describing."

"Meaning?"

"Meaning they didn't wait for the senator to make a decision they disagreed with. They identified him as a potential obstacle to certain defense contracting decisions and acquired leverage preemptively. Very efficient."

My pulse quickens. This is it—the intel we need.

"That sounds like exactly the kind of strategic thinking that could benefit everyone involved," I say carefully.

"Perhaps." Elena reaches for her handbag, a subtle movement that fires warning signals. "But such relationships require absolute trust. The kind of trust that doesn't include surveillance equipment and backup teams."

She's known since her security spotted our van. But she's still talking, which means she's either confident she can control the situation or she has an exit strategy we haven't anticipated. It's not like we're feds. We can't detain her. Not legally. She too has done her research.

"Elena," I let my voice shift—lower, slower, the cadence of truth wrapped in velvet. The tone I use when persuasion is my only weapon. "You've grown something remarkable. A network that reaches into the most powerful institutions in the world. But networks are fragile things. They depend on trust, on mutual benefit, on the belief that everyone involved has more to gain by cooperating than from betrayal."

"Your point?"

"My point is that true power isn't the threat to destroy. It's the certainty that no one wants you destroyed. That they need you to thrive."

Elena's laugh is genuine, appreciative. "Very good. You really do understand the game."

"I understand that you're not going to trigger a dead man's switch because it would destroy everything you've built. Your clients, your sources, your entire operation—all of it would be exposed. You'd go from being the most powerful woman in the intelligence brokerage world—an invisible queenmaker—to a fugitive with nowhere to hide."

"And you're gambling that I value my business more than my freedom."

"I'm observing that someone who's spent decades building a web doesn't trash it over one conversation in a restaurant."

The silence stretches between us, tense with calculation. Elena's fingers still rest on her handbag, but her posture has shifted—less defensive, more evaluative.

"What do you really want?" she asks finally.

"The same thing you want," I reply. "To be on the winning side when all of this shakes out."

Outside, a siren wails faintly, rising then fading. Elena studies me in silence, calculating. In this city, attention is currency—and I've just spent mine.

CHAPTER
THIRTY-TWO

ADRIEN

Elena sits back in her chair, a smile playing at the corners of her mouth that reminds me of a chess master who's just observed her opponent's fatal mistake.

"Let me see if I understand this correctly," she says, her Boston accent surfacing prominently, a sign she's dropped the silk of civility. "You're coming to me asking to join my team, while simultaneously asking me to purchase information. Information that could never trace back to me, of course." Her fingers drum against the white tablecloth. "If I give you this name—tell you who commissioned the Crawford operation—what exactly do I get in return?" Her tone is pleasant, but the question carries the weight of a loaded weapon. "Moira indicated I'd want to meet with you to tamp down an investigation, but that's not sounding like what this is."

Around our table, the restaurant continues its lunch service—the gentle clink of silverware, muted conversations, the soft jazz that makes Gramercy Tavern feel genteel compared to the Manhattan chaos outside. Everything hinges on the next few minutes.

"What do you want?" I ask, redirecting the question, maintaining the composure my father would call negotiation posture, though this feels more like absolution bartered in real time.

Elena's eyes light with the kind of satisfaction that comes from being asked exactly the right question. "First rights to information. You can't sell anything about anyone without offering me the right of first refusal."

It's not an unexpected request. "Agreed."

"That includes Moira."

"Noted."

"And payment for the information you've requested. In the spirit of partnership, I'll charge a reduced rate—two million dollars."

The number lands like the pop of a cork—quiet, final, indulgent.

The price doesn't surprise me. High-caliber intelligence, delivered with the guarantee of anonymity and the promise of ongoing partnership, is worth every penny. I can easily imagine my father parting with a similar sum. "Done. And future arrangements?"

"Rates vary depending on the project value. I'll share thirty percent of my fee with you."

Thirty percent. For access that underwrites her entire empire. It's insulting—and deliberate.

"Fifty," I counter. I'm sure she had a variety of payment arrangements with her other sources, but given I don't actually plan on carrying on with her, and she's agreed to hand over the information we need, I can play hardball here. There's no need to come across as naïve.

Her laugh—low, rich, the sound of temptation cloaked as praise—drags against my restraint. "You do understand this business better than I thought. But thirty is standard for passive sources."

"I'm not a passive source. I'm providing active partnership, ongoing access, and significant risk exposure. Fifty percent."

"Forty is as high as I'll go." Elena reaches into her handbag and withdraws what appears to be a small tablet. "In exchange, I'll adjust the first right of first refusal clause—limit it to information pertaining to a list of companies and individuals I can update at any time."

The negotiation feels surreal—an elegant fever dream. Around us, servers glide, pouring Chablis while we price treachery by the percentage point. But this is the world I've entered, and to protect the people I care about, I shall master its rules.

"Agreed," I say. "I can wire the money immediately if you prefer."

Elena raises an eyebrow, then slides her phone across the table to me. "The account information is in the notes app."

I glance at the screen, memorizing the routing numbers, then pull out my own phone to open my banking app. Two million dollars. I've spent more on art acquisitions, but never for information that could unmake the illusion of integrity my surname was built on.

The transfer completes within seconds—one of the advantages of maintaining accounts with institutions that cater to clients who need to move large sums quickly and discreetly.

Elena's phone chimes almost immediately. She glances at

the screen and nods. "Meridian Defense Systems. Jonathan Pierce." The name hits the air like a drop of ink in water, spreading fast and dark.

The name means nothing to me, but I see Brie's reaction immediately—a slight straightening of her posture, a knowing expression. That quiet precision of hers—the shift from warmth to focus—still catches me off guard, even now.

"The Kansas-based defense contractor," Brie says quietly. "He's one of Crawford's biggest donors."

Elena nods approvingly. "Very good. Though sometimes even donors need additional leverage."

The casual way she describes auctioning democracy makes my stomach turn. We're not talking about corporate espionage anymore—we're talking about the systematic corruption of democratic institutions.

Elena looks between Brie and me, her expression hardening. "I don't like doing business this way. Surveillance, recording equipment, backup teams lurking in vans. You're not my only source of information, and frankly, I worry you're more trouble than you're worth."

She stands, smoothing her gray coat with practiced elegance. "If you ever try anything like this again, it's over. I'll cut you out completely. I'll also expose you." The word expose lands differently when spoken by a woman who trades in secrets; it hits like an intimate threat. "If you don't believe me, just know I've been working with Thorne for years. I possess plenty that traces right back to The Sanctuary. And those leaks will never come back to me."

I stand and offer my hand. She takes it. Her grip is firm, confident—the handshake of someone who's just secured a profitable new arrangement.

"I'll be in touch to discuss arrangements for our ongoing

partnership. I'll send someone to your New York office." Her gaze moves between Brie and me. "I trust this concludes our business satisfactorily for all parties."

She extends her hand to Brie. "A pleasure doing business with you both," Elena says. "I believe this partnership will prove mutually beneficial."

With that, she turns and walks toward the restaurant's entrance, her two security men materializing from their positions on the street to fall into step behind her. The whole operation dissolves as smoothly as it began—professional, efficient, leaving no trace except the knowledge burning in my mind—and the metallic aftertaste of a bargain struck in daylight.

Jonathan Pierce. Meridian Defense Systems. A defense contractor buying legislative votes through sexual blackmail and whatever else Elena has dredged up on anyone they target.

"Well," Brie says quietly, watching Elena's retreating figure disappear into the Manhattan crowd. "That was almost anticlimactic."

"You expected her to try to kill us?"

"I expected something. Elena Vasquez doesn't strike me as someone who leaves loose ends. But maybe Moira was right. She's overly confident and lacks caution." Brie's eyes scan the restaurant, still alert despite the seemingly successful conclusion. "Maybe she really does see this as a business opportunity. If she's competitive, maybe she believes she landed an advantage over Moira."

I signal for the check, suddenly eager to leave this place where I've just entered into partnership with someone who brokers in human misery. "At the moment, she doesn't benefit from harming us. You've got the name. What are your next steps?"

Brie's phone buzzes, and she glances at the screen, then out the window at the street. "They want a debrief once we're clear."

As we leave Gramercy Tavern, stepping out into the crisp October afternoon, I can't shake the feeling that we've just set something in motion that will be impossible to control. Elena Vasquez struck me as many things—brilliant, ruthless, utterly professional—but not someone who forgives being outmaneuvered.

We may have gotten what we wanted, but I suspect we're making an enemy who's far more lethal than we realize. Once the feds come knocking at Jonathan Pierce's door, and eventually Elena's door, she'll seek vengeance—and she's connected in all the right places. CIA, DOJ, FBI, NSA, the White House.

It's an undeniable risk, but a worthy one. Moira sent the names of her contacts at my Paris and Shanghai locations and claims those are her only sources. Now that we've met with Elena, I'll focus on getting my house in order. Firing the guilty and securing the premises.

"Jonathan Pierce better be worth two million dollars," I murmur as we walk toward the waiting car that will take us back to my home, a precautionary step should anyone plan to follow us. Millions for a culprit—though what I've really bought is a line of dominoes waiting to fall.

"He will be," Brie says with certainty. "Elena just handed us the key to unraveling an entire network of legislative corruption. The FBI will be very interested in Mr. Pierce's creative lobbying techniques, not to mention her involvement."

I hope she's right.

But as our car pulls away from the restaurant, I catch a glimpse of Elena in the side mirror—standing on the corner, phone pressed to her ear, watching our departure with the focused intensity of a cobra.

Two million dollars well spent, perhaps. But the true cost is yet to be determined.

CHAPTER
THIRTY-THREE

BRIE

The KOAN debrief takes place the next day in a nondescript Midtown office building, the kind of anonymous space that could house anything from accounting firms to import businesses. Hudson leads us through the aftermath with military precision—what went right, what went wrong, and what Elena's next moves might be once she's cornered.

He's not happy I went against his directive, but Quinn's calm "she saved the op" undercuts his reprimand—I owe her for taking the blast radius on that call. Hudson's scowl at her voice over the speaker tells me she'll take heat for defending me.

"Pierce is currently being questioned," Hudson reports, scrolling his tablet. "FBI with Kansas authorities. Picked him up at his office two hours ago."

Pierce's arrest will send ripples through Crawford's donor network. The senator's coordinating with Alicia Morgan to manage potential fallout.

"What about Elena?" I ask. One scenario we worried over is that we wouldn't get to the right people for an investigation, or that someone in her network would bury it.

"She's gone. By the time federal agents reached her last known address, the apartment had been cleaned out. Furniture still there, but closets mostly cleared. Running theory is she got word that feds were going to pick up Pierce, and she acted."

"She's choosing to flee, not lawyer up," Noah says, head tilted, thoughtful.

I'm not entirely surprised. Elena Vasquez struck me as someone with an exit strategy.

"So we won," I say, though the words feel hollow. "Crawford's safe. If any of his business comes out in deposition or court, I'm sure Alicia has a plan. Pierce is in custody and even if he walks, a court case is in his future and any threats he's made are substantially weakened, and Elena's operation is blown."

"No announcement yet, but rumor is she's out as deputy chief of staff. But..." He pauses. "Vasquez is still out there, with resources. If she'd stayed, the money would bleed into defense. On the lam, she may take a different tack."

"Revenge?" I ask. Fine hairs lift; the chill beads under my skin.

"If I were her, I'd take a step back and assess the damage," Quinn says. "The good news is, all evidence has been passed on to the authorities—in duplicate. I wouldn't be surprised if Pierce talks to cut himself a deal. If you're wondering if she's going to go after d'Avricourt, I don't see the point. She won't gain anything other than adding to the list of charges against her."

Hudson looks at the phone that's placed on the table, the source of Quinn's voice. It's odd that he keeps her down in North Carolina most of the time, but maybe she doesn't like to travel. I've never asked.

"I tend to agree with Quinn. The risk level is low, but it's not non-existent. d'Avricourt's residence is secure, correct?"

"Yes," I nod, but honestly, if Elena were to go after him, I'd envision a setup that feels disconnected from her; a mugging gone wrong in an alley, or a stray bullet that could be blamed on gangs. "What about Alicia Morgan?"

"Her primary residence is in Georgetown," Noah answers. "I can check it out. Do an assessment, but she's known as the fixer. I'd expect this isn't the first time she's been in a risky situation."

"True," Hudson agrees. "And it would be odd for anyone to hold anything against her. She was acting on behalf of a client. But doing an assessment on her home is a good idea. If anything does happen, we'll be faster with recommendations."

"Sure thing," Noah says.

The meeting continues for another hour, covering security protocols and ongoing monitoring, but I find my attention drifting. We've accomplished what we set out to do, yet something feels unfinished. Elena fleeing doesn't sit right. She's what? Early sixties. Would she really disappear to a non-extradition territory never to be heard from again? Didn't Moira say she's too ambitious?

By the time I return to Adrien's penthouse, evening shadows are lengthening across Manhattan. The city lights twinkle beyond the floor-to-ceiling windows, beautiful and distant, like stars in an alien sky.

We arrived within minutes of each other—me from my meeting in midtown, him coming from his nearby office. When I arrived, he'd been waiting in the lobby, likely tracking my approach on his phone. He brushed a kiss across my cheek and we silently ascended to his home. We pass wordlessly through the foyer of his penthouse and the gleaming center table with orchids and a new, stunning fall floral arrangement.

My gaze lingers on the polished walnut table and memory hits—him kneeling, mouth and hands, heat flooding back so fast it leaves me oddly hollow after, missing the urgency and hating this despondent echo. We won. I shouldn't feel like this. But I do, and I can tell Adrien feels the same.

I follow him through the penthouse to the wine alcove off the great room. He quickly selects a bottle and sets about uncorking it.

"Busy day?" I ask, knowing he's likely been insanely busy.

"Eddie isn't someone I can trust, but he did a lot. I'll need a replacement—fast. And now I have two more on staff to terminate, although thankfully they weren't managing directors."

"No?"

"One bartender in Paris, and the other managed the housekeeping staff in Shanghai."

"You believe Moira?"

"Thinking it's odd they're lower on the org chart?" he asks, filling two crystal goblets with a healthy measure. "You're probably right. I'm going to need to visit those locations. I actually talked to your boss this afternoon."

"Is that right?"

"He's going to help me do an assessment of all five properties. He has additional resources to tap." He passes me a glass and lightly clinks his against mine, then takes a long swig, like he's finally exhaled. "Also called on Alicia."

"We talked about her in our meeting today."

"And?"

"Just doing a security assessment on her home; in case there's fallout."

"Smart."

"Why'd you go to see her?" I ask, curious, but I have a good idea.

"Asked her to prepare communications to the membership that explains we've been compromised."

"You think Elena's going to leak material?"

"She'll do what she can to attack The Sanctuary. I feel confident about that. But it'll be known she's the one dripping scandals so the fallout should be limited to those she doesn't care if she offends. She'll aim to do enough to hurt me without making her situation more precarious."

"That's probably a good assessment. So Alicia's drafting communications?"

"They go out tomorrow. I wanted them to go out tonight, but she convinced me to wait until I can be in the office and reachable. She's also sending in her staff to assist with triage. We'll do New York-based members tomorrow. Depending on how they react, I'll either do one-on-one meetings or have a membership meeting. She thinks that most inquiries will come from those whose marriages might be impacted, and the business segment won't immediately connect the risk. Since I've identified the leak and stopped it, she's predicting minimal backlash. And she says it's good that I'm addressing the leaks. That will be important for rebuilding trust."

"You weren't counting on that source of income anyway," I say, although if I'm honest, a part of me recognizes there's something there that could be leveraged. Perhaps I've spent too much of my career valuing intelligence, but it's an undeniable truth that a place where the wealthy gather offers valuable insights—at least for those who listen and watch closely.

"True," he says, swirling his wine, the light catching the crystal. "I didn't expect Elena to walk away so cleanly. No pressure. No attempt to bury it." He glances at me. "That tells me she's confident—or calculating. Possibly both."

"Maybe she has backup operations we don't know about," I say, giving the idea consideration. "Or maybe she's taking stock. Laying low while she plans." That was Quinn's theory. "It all happened fast. I'd imagine she's as angry at Moira for setting up the meeting with you as she is at you. And me. And KOAN, for that matter. KOAN isn't a well-known entity. She's probably researching it. Figuring out what she's up against. If self-assessment is a strength, she might be recognizing the role she played. She trusted too easily, all because she assumed greed was universal."

We settle onto the sofa, and for the first time in days, I allow myself to relax slightly. The immediate threat is over. Pierce is in custody, Elena is on the run, and KOAN has the information they need to unravel the broader conspiracy. The wine soothes the agitated nerves.

Agitated because... Why? But I know the reason. Typically, I finish a project and move on. Repercussions always follow a project, but I'm not usually close to those involved. Now I am. And I'm uneasy about what's going to unfold. If not this week, next week, a month from now. Someone like Elena Vasquez could choose to play the long game. The White House hasn't made any announcements. Even Pierce's detainment hasn't hit the news wire.

"What happens now?" Adrien asks. "With us, I mean."

We've already said I'm not going to walk away and I returned to his place tonight. I exhale, shifting slightly on the sofa to fully face him. "I don't know. I've never mixed personal and professional like this before."

"And?"

"And I find myself missing those walls I used to build." He silently assesses. He'll read this all wrong if I don't explain. "I'm not feeling like celebrating right now. We won. We succeeded. And yet, I'm..." *How to explain?* "I care about you. I'm worried about you." I hesitate, then say it—plain, unguarded. "I love you. And that's new for me. It makes everything feel higher risk."

He stills. His arm doesn't slide away this time—it tightens.

"Brie," he says quietly. "I love you too."

The simplicity of it hits harder than any declaration. No certainty. No promises. Just truth.

We sit there for a moment, letting it settle.

"Before, we didn't get into what our day-to-day lives looked like. This case brought us back together, but it gave us both insights into our...businesses."

"A look behind the image." He sounds doleful, dejected even.

"Our real selves. And I think we're both still evolving. Still figuring out who we are. The question is whether we can build something genuine while we figure it all out."

"I believe we can," he says, reaching for my hand. He toys with my fingers.

"Me too," I say, breathing in deeply and becoming aware that this talk has me feeling lighter.

"You're going to stay here for a while, right? I mean, we know it was Elena who sent someone to your place." I narrow my eyes, well aware he packed everything he could jam into my suitcases when he brought me here. It feels like we're moving too quickly for caution, but I'm also aware that I'd rather be with him until we've got a handle on Elena's whereabouts and plans.

"Brie. Please. I'll sleep better and "

"I'm fine staying here. As long as you recognize I'm not giving up my home. I own that apartment, by the way." It's a pittance to someone like him, but it's my biggest investment.

"Completely understand," he says, lips curving on the ends. Victorious is the word that comes to mind.

"Besides," I take a sip, "I suppose I can get used to living in a place where the flowers in the foyer are replaced daily."

"They aren't replaced daily," he says, scoffing as if I'm being ludicrous.

"Oh. Excuse me. Seasonally." He tilts his head, questioning. "That gorgeous white orchid arrangement that I'm going to guess cost thousands is being replaced by that equally stunning fall display. But that's one that has to be replaced weekly, I'd imagine—black dahlias don't keep." I don't actually care about the flowers; I'm just teasing him and reveling in the subject change. "What do you do? Ask the florist from The Sanctuary to deliver flowers weekly to your home too?"

"What are you talking about?" He looks genuinely stumped.

"You walked right by them..." I gesture in the direction of the foyer.

He looks down the hall, possibly seeing the flowers for

the first time, and pushes up. He strides to the flowers, which have been set in front of the orchids. Perhaps Maria was going to ask him where to put the arrangement. It is huge. More of something you'd see in a hotel lobby than in a home.

He pulls out his phone and dictates a message.

ADRIEN
Where'd the flowers come from?

MARIA
A business associate. I messaged you earlier today asking where you wanted me to place them.

I'm reading the messages as he says, "An associate?"

We look at each other, and my stomach balls into a pit of dread. Adrien moves to the flowers, and I call out, "Wait. If Elena sent something..."

But he's already at the entry table, looking at the elaborate arrangement. Dahlias, lilies, asters, and sunflowers fill a vase of maroons punctuated with golden yellows, accompanied by a small, wrapped box tied with silver ribbon. The card reads: *Congratulations on your successful negotiation. –E*

It's from Elena, but did she send it before or after the DOJ authorized picking up Pierce?

"Don't touch anything," I say sharply, phone in hand,

wine glass left on the table. "Hudson, we need bomb tech at Adrien's penthouse. A gift from Elena."

The next few minutes blur together—evacuation protocols for the entire condominium tower, emergency responders flooding the building, residents being moved to safety while specialists examine Elena's gift. Adrien and I wait in the lobby, watching through his hallway monitoring system as figures in protective suits carefully dismantle whatever Elena left for us.

"Sophisticated device," the bomb tech reports over radio. "Pressure sensitive, motion activated. Would have taken out half the floor."

I think about Maria placing them carefully on the entry table. If the device had been slightly more sensitive, if Elena had chosen a different trigger mechanism, if Maria had decided to transfer the flowers...

"She was sending a message." But what is the message? The goal? "She could have killed us anytime she wanted. This was about showing us she could reach us anywhere. And she's not particularly worried about our deaths tracking to her."

"Nor is she worried about collateral damage."

She's out for vengeance. Elena Vasquez doesn't just know where we both live—she knows who matters to Adrien, who he'd move to protect, who could be used as leverage against him in the future. Fortunately, she doesn't have the same intel on me. It's a benefit to maintaining walls, the reason behind the CIA's protocol. Hence, Adrien has more to lose, and she's probably far more interested in hurting him than someone doing a job.

My phone buzzes with a news alert: *BREAKING: Exclusive photos and video leaked from Manhattan's most exclusive private club.*

The images are already spreading across social media—interior shots of The Sanctuary, footage of unidentifiable members in compromising positions, financial records showing payments to offshore accounts. Everything Elena promised to protect in exchange for partnership, now being systematically released to destroy Adrien's business and reputation.

"How long before this reaches the major networks?" Adrien asks.

I check my phone, scrolling through the rapidly spreading story. "It's already trending. Podcasts and small pubs will be on it immediately. Larger outlets will attempt to verify. It looks like what's playing out on social media is much more of a guessing game of who is in the photos. At least you're not a public company."

He lifts his phone to his ear, presumably calling Alicia.

I watch the bomb disposal team carefully carrying their equipment out of the building, while Adrien paces the corner of the lobby, phone tight to his ear.

The Sanctuary—three years of work, a billion-dollar investment, Adrien's first independent success—crumbling in real time as Elena Vasquez demonstrates exactly what happens to people who cross her.

When he joins me again, I say, "I'm sorry. This is my fault. I pushed to find the blackmailer and–"

"If you hadn't pushed, Pierce would still be extorting votes and Elena would still be operating freely. You did the right thing." He stretches his neck to one side and kneads the area, as if he's moved on and a tight shoulder muscle is now his biggest worry. "We did the right thing."

"Even if it costs you everything?"

"Some things are worth any cost," he says, pulling me into his side. "You're one of those things."

Outside the lobby windows, Manhattan continues its eternal rhythm—traffic flowing through streets like blood through arteries, lights flickering on in windows as people settle into their nighttime routines, the great machine of the city grinding forward regardless of individual triumphs or disasters.

Residents in the tower cluster in pockets around the lobby, waiting to be allowed back up to their homes. Some went across the street to Starbucks. Firetrucks are lined up on the street outside, the red lights flashing but the sirens silent.

"You realize she's a terrorist. She was willing to kill innocent people to make a point."

"True," he says, his hold on me tightening. "After they're done here, we're to meet Alicia at her place in Manhattan. She's offered for us to stay there tonight."

"Do you want to do that?"

"No. The floor and building will be secure. But I do need to go to her place. She's handling member communications at the moment, but I need to meet with her. You'll go with me, right?"

"Of course," I say.

What I don't say is I wouldn't allow him to go out on his own. This kind of enemy requires a different approach entirely. And as I watch the news alerts multiply on my phone, each one documenting another piece of what goes on in his private club, I realize that this war is just beginning. She wanted fireworks on top of public humiliation. Well, she's spun him into a PR crisis, but my gut tells me she won't consider it done until her fireworks explode.

Adrien leans down, his breath warm against my ear. "You know what's good about this?"

"People didn't die?" It's hard to derive any other *good* angle.

"It's a mess, but I'm not facing it alone. You're with me."

And he's right. I am. And for the first time, I have someone by my side too, at least, someone other than colleagues and a mission statement.

CHAPTER
THIRTY-FOUR

ADRIEN

"Exactly what was leaked? I need to know."

The man on the phone isn't worried about corporate secrets; for that matter, none of the calls I've received today have been concerns regarding business matters. Everyone calling me is worried about exposure of their private proclivities. This particular man is in his early seventies and married almost fifty years ago, before prenuptial agreements were commonplace. He hasn't said it, but I'm sure he's concerned his wife will walk with half of everything. Although at his age, the arithmetic is odd; even halved, his fortune will outlive him by decades.

"I'm being straight up with you. I don't know. I discovered the leak and have stopped it. All five locations will be closed while I do a thorough review to safeguard members' privacy."

"Going forward, you mean. Whatever has happened in the past may very well fuck us."

That's one way of putting it. Brie enters my office quietly, her eyes soft with concern.

"If it helps, I don't believe there's any reason information about you will be leaked. From what I can tell, the person who is leaking the images, so far, is taking care to ensure no one in the photos is identifiable."

"Or the videos."

"Yes."

"You realize some of us have identifiable tattoos, birthmarks, or scars."

"Do you really believe your wife is going to be trawling illegally uploaded porn online?"

Brie's lips purse, likely refraining from laughing, but I've had it. Hours of fielding member calls, and yes, my response is unprofessional, but I'm scraped raw. I can't guarantee a video won't leak of him.

"How many years back are the leaks?"

"As my letter said, so far nothing over one year old has been released." From what I can tell, the more personal rooms weren't breached until Elena split from Magpie, but I'm not sharing that level of insight. Could discovery expose more if the DOJ prosecutes Elena Vasquez? Yes. Is that in my control? No.

I feel like reaching out to the owner of Ashley Madison, the site that married couples use to cheat, to commiserate. When the site was hacked, I imagine he went through much the same thing.

All that said, I do feel for the couples who weren't cheating on anyone and rightfully fear they'll be exposed in a public forum. It's not something I would want to happen, and in truth, I've used the rooms here, participated in more than one event. Hell, I might find myself with a sex tape of my own. If Elena possesses such a tape, I'm certain she'd be willing to share it widely without blurring my face. Given she attempted to kill me, humiliation feels beneath her—but not off the menu.

"This is a nightmare," the man growls. The call ends and I lower the headset.

Typically, I'd take calls on speaker to avoid having a phone pressed to my ear, but given the delicate nature of my conversations, I've been avoiding the speakerphone. As I exhale, leaning back in my chair, I close my eyes, throat burning from constant use, tongue sanded with too many apologies, and a budding desire to avoid any more conversations for the rest of the day.

"You hanging in there?" Brie asks.

The red light on my desk phone lights up. I hold a hand out for her, gesturing for her to come to me.

"I'm done for the day. Messages can wait."

It's after eight in the evening and I've lost the ability to remain professional. It's a sign I need to stop and pick it back up tomorrow. Alicia has a team working on this with me, answering questions with pre-approved answers, but my clients include a list of prominent, wealthy individuals who aren't satisfied unless they speak to the owner.

And then my cell rings. It's Tommy. Normally I'd call him back later, but while on the phone with members, both my father and sister called my cell. I hold up a finger, letting Brie know I'm going to take the call.

"Tommy," I say in a tone that implies I'm exhausted and likely not alone.

"You've pissed off Margot."

"What'd she say?"

Brie comes to my side of the desk and rests on the edge, watching.

"Said you blew a contact. Well, she called it a valuable relationship. Was so pissed she switched to French and you know my French sucks. What'd you do?"

"Saved her from herself." I reach for Brie's hand and rub my thumb along the end of her nail absent-mindedly. "Maybe. Did she say anything else? Anything you understood?"

"She's on her way to Greece. Sounded business-related."

And it would be. "Well, let me go."

"You gonna call her?"

"No."

"I don't understand you two."

"Right back at you."

I end the call with Tommy, and press my father's name. "I probably should've called him earlier. Let me get this over. It won't take long," I tell Brie.

She sees the screen in my hand. She knows. She crosses her arms over her middle, tentative.

This time there's no talking father down. "You lied to me."

In the background I hear my mother's sharp warning, "Christian!"

"Nothing's going to happen to Moira." I inhale deeply, drawing on calm. "She wasn't even involved. She passed me a name."

"Yeah. Then why did she cut us off?"

Fuck.

"I'll reach out."

"Yeah? How're you going to do that? You used me to find her." He breathes through the phone and it's not hard to visualize him...skin flushed with barely controlled anger. "You. Used. Me. Your father."

There's no real defense here. I could counterattack. Tell him he's not the creative genius, or even the business virtuoso I grew up believing in.

"I apologize." I leave it at that. My mother always said an apology with a but isn't an apology, it's an excuse.

"You're so fucking stubborn." He curses under his breath. I can't decipher it all but he's definitely not speaking English —maybe a blended mix of French and Italian obscenities.

"Christian!" Mom's shout is so loud it sounds like she's standing over him.

"I can't do this," he mutters. "Let me calm down."

And with that, the call ends.

I hold the edge of the phone to my lips and look up to Brie, those blue eyes filled with concern.

"You okay?"

"I will be. There's a good chance I'm officially cut out of his will, but my mother rules the house."

"You're his son."

"I am. Underneath all that anger, he still loves me."

"And you love him."

I nod.

"Love doesn't require perfection."

"No, but it does require work." I'll have to reach out to Margot tomorrow. Given I handed her the keys to the family business–literally–I expect her to come around. With luck, the worst of her concerns–the d'Avricourt name getting dragged through the papers–won't happen. "Have you heard anything about a French government investigation?"

Brie chews on the corner of her lip. "No. So far all the interest is on Elena Vasquez."

"And she's been targeting me."

"I don't think she'd go after Magpie. Moira may lead it, but our sources claim it's an organization, meaning a group."

My head tilts back and I eye the ceiling, envisioning the heavens above. "With luck, all my sister's worst worries won't come to pass."

"I'd say that's likely." She gives me a soft smile—because that's all she can give. There are so many entities involved now, what happens is out of our control. "Hudson and Jake left for the day. Macon was closing up when I left. It's just us."

The club is closed to members for an undetermined period as I sort through the exposure.

She slides onto my lap and I inhale deeply, breathing in her subtle floral scent—not a single note I can name, just the particular alchemy of her skin and the products she uses. I know this because I rummaged through the cosmetics she unpacked in my bathroom to sate my curiosity, to learn if she'd changed perfumes, but the scent will forever bring memories of comfort, of heaven, of Brie.

"Have many withdrawn membership?"

"I'm not sure. I sent the staff home today, remember? Numbers will undoubtedly decline, but it won't mean the end. I'll rebuild, and I'll do it the right way." I lift a wave of golden strands from her shoulder and twist them around a finger, forging a ringlet. "How was your day?"

"Busy. Probably not as busy as yours."

"It's not a competition."

She grins. I like seeing her smile. She lightens the weight of the day, tilts the balance back toward bearable.

"We're going room by room. Given so much is wireless these days, it takes time, but you should be safely up and running next week. Your employees…We still maintain Eddie didn't work alone."

"Right."

"But we are working on recommended security protocols. After all, you're not the only business that has to worry about employees selling client data. Credit card companies, brokerages, insurance companies—you're not the first to grapple with this issue."

"I'm more worried about Elena's next step. Any luck on tracking her down?"

"No."

"Well, I've got us a room at the Peninsula. I had Tommy's assistant reserve it so it will be more time consuming to trace the hotel reservation."

"We could just stay in Alicia's place. She gave us a standing invitation."

I shake my head slowly. "Elena knows about our connection to Alicia Morgan. It doesn't feel safe to me."

"Well, I believe in trusting one's instinct. You ready to go?"

As she asks, a single mechanical beep sounds. Brie stiffens, then pushes up as if alarmed.

"What? What is it?"

She's already at the door, peering into the waiting area and my receptionist's desk. "That's the alarm we installed. A door opened." She holds a finger up. "Stay there."

Like hell.

Within seconds, I'm beside her, listening.

And I hear it. A soft foot fall.

Then another.

Brie pushes me back into the office, shutting the door.

She taps the light switch twice—lowering the light to half-dim.

"Do you have a gun?" she whisper-shouts.

"No." I give her a look that says I was raised with different tools—contracts and cameras, not handguns. "Why would I?"

She huffs and I recognize it for what it is—frustration. She's not armed either.

But as I think that, I realize I'm wrong. She's opened her handbag, a simple leather clutch, and she lifts a small handgun with a pearl-inlaid handle.

"It's small, but it's powerful. You stay here."

"Absolutely not."

A shadow crosses the threshold below the door.

There's a knock.

Brie and I look to each other and she guides me to the side, near the billiard table.

"Yes?" she calls out.

The latch clicks, and the door unlocks.

Brie spreads her legs into a strong stance, arms raised, gun pointing.

Eddie Thorne steps into the room.

The man looks like hell—bloodshot eyes with dark circles beneath them, wrinkled clothes, facial growth unruly, and a handgun that's significantly larger than Brie's pointed directly at us.

His hand shakes slightly, a notable difference from Brie, whose hands are rock solid.

"Eddie," I say, as friendly as I can muster, aiming to calm the situation.

"I don't want to shoot you," Eddie says by way of greeting.

"Good to know," I offer. "I'd be more likely to believe that if you lowered your gun."

"I need to know… What's going on?"

Ah, the question of the hour. So many people with a need to know. "What exactly are you asking Eddie?"

I step to the side of Brie and she crosses in front of me once again. I have half a mind to yank her behind me, but on account of the guns in the room, I grind my teeth and stay still, knowing that if I step closer, Brie will likely repeat her move and the end result is moving her closer and closer to the end of Eddie's barrel.

"Are the cops coming for me?" He looks past Brie, his dark eyes pleading, a man defeated. "That's all I need to know. I've been monitoring news coverage. There's nothing. Can I go home? Or is someone coming to my door?"

"That's what you're afraid of?" This day has been eye-opening for me. Not one client question about business interests, and now Eddie's greatest worry isn't his job, or how he betrayed me and countless others, but whether he's facing time in the slammer.

"I can't imagine anyone will attempt to prosecute you, but I don't have an in at the DOJ," I say, hedging—KOAN has ties, but I'm not offering him a pipeline.

"You're more valuable to the authorities as a source," Brie says, her tone dry and entirely unsympathetic. "If you shoot either of us, that changes."

He blinks, like he's processing the truth of her statement. The slight tremors in his hand are reminiscent of a drug user, as are the blown pupils.

Christ, is he high?

"If you lower your gun, I'll lower mine," Brie says, her voice calm and commanding.

Eddie lets the muzzle dip and releases it from one of his two hands to rub his forehead, damp with sweat. "This is such a fucking nightmare," he grumbles.

"You're not the first to say that to me today."

He glances up, eyes pleading. "I never meant for all of this to happen. The other group, they don't work like this."

"You mean Magpie?"

He flinches, then nods. "Elena…she runs a different game." The whites of his eyes give him a wild appearance. "I didn't mean this," he says, glancing down at the gun. "She sent someone to my house. She wants me dead."

I scratch at my jaw. Brie has lowered her gun, but she's still standing forward, no doubt so she can lunge between us if needed.

"She tried to kill us too," I admit, aiming to ensure Eddie doesn't see us as the threat. Eddie is a bomb, and I want to defuse it.

He nods solemnly, and somehow I don't think this is news to him. But then again, he said he's been monitoring the news and the bomb located in my condominium tower has been all over the local news, probably national as well.

"But you…you didn't turn me into the cops?"

"Your name has been mentioned. But they're far more interested in the people who used the information you sold for extortion."

"Eddie," Brie begins, "If you're scared, have you considered witness protection? I'd bet we can get that set up for you."

"And my family?" he asks.

She nods.

"You trust them? They're good at their—" He stops, backing up. "No. Elena is the government. I'm not trusting them to keep me safe. But at least I know anyone coming after me isn't legit."

"At this stage in the investigation, other than an FBI agent knocking on your door, no, I don't think anyone else would be a legitimate investigator," Brie answers.

"I'm going to lay low then."

"I can get you protection," Brie says, trying again.

"No. Sorry. Don't trust it. You two better be careful. It's not just Elena. She's connected. There are names that aren't going to want to be exposed. And those names are going to back her up." He steps back. "And Adrien, I am sorry. This whole thing was small scale before you bought in. Business shit that didn't really matter. It's all just snowballed."

"I understand." There's not much more to say.

He looks down at his hand with the gun and it's like he can't quite believe he's holding it. He's not a gunman—just a man in free fall.

"Be careful, Eddie. Get some sleep." I have half a mind to tell him to lay off the drugs, but I'm not risking confrontation, not when he has a gun and Brie is in the room.

"You two be careful. Don't underestimate her. And ya know, Elena always said the best defense is making your enemies look like the real criminals. If I were you, I'd check what lies she's been spreading."

He turns to leave, and a thought hits me. "Wait. Do you know where she is? Where she might be?"

"You going to go after her?"

"Yes," Brie confirms. "We don't know where to look."

"She has connections. Could be anywhere. But if I were to guess, she's at a beach house. It's not in her name. Used to be Magpie's and somehow she got it in the divorce, if you want to call it that. I handled some of the transfer of ownership. It's owned by a trust. Her name's not on the deed. If you get on my computer, find the folder labeled MPV Trust... I kept a copy of what I had notarized for her. Address is on the paperwork."

As Eddie disappears into the shadows of the hallway, his words echo in my mind. What lies has Elena already set in motion—and how quickly will they metastasize? And is she done with bombs or only beginning?

CHAPTER
THIRTY-FIVE

BRIE

The beach house sits like a fortress against the gray Atlantic horizon, its modern glass and steel structure incongruous among the weathered cedar cottages that dot this stretch of the Long Island coastline. Even in October's fading light, I can see why Elena chose this place—isolated, defensible, with clear sight lines in every direction.

"Two vehicles in the drive," I murmur into my comm unit, adjusting the tactical vest beneath my jacket. "Looks like a black SUV and what might be a sedan."

Hudson's voice crackles through my earpiece. "FBI is in position on the perimeter road. Her security team surrendered their guns. Claim no one else is with her. You've got fifteen minutes before they move in. Let's see if you can get her to talk."

Fifteen minutes. That's not a lot of time for a productive confrontation, and I'm skeptical it will amount to anything.

Elena Vasquez is unlikely to give up information freely, and she's already proven she's willing to kill.

Adrien shifts beside me in the passenger seat, his jaw tight with tension. We were told to hold until the perimeter units made contact with her team—if there was going to be a gunfight, it wouldn't be ours. This is good news. It's not entirely unexpected that her hired security team would step aside for the FBI, but it could've gone either way. Now, we're up.

"You sure about this approach?" He's understandably concerned, but he's an important part of this plan, and I need him alert but confident.

"She's cornered and desperate. She's also a former intelligence operative who understands the value of information over violence." I check my sidearm one final time. "Plus, she's not going to want to fight murder charges. If that bomb had succeeded, she would have counted on it never tracing to her. All we have to do is tell her the FBI is outside her door, and she won't shoot."

What I don't repeat is that Elena's profile suggests she'll want to gloat first—to explain how she's outmaneuvered us even as everything crumbles around her. That psychological need might be our only advantage. That and our quick response time. We pulled this together within twenty-four hours of learning her location. Chances are any plan she's developed isn't fully loaded.

If the FBI brings her in, she'll lawyer up. And worse, she's got ins with the FBI, definitely with the DOJ. I'm not sure I trust them to bring their A game.

The house's security lights flick on as we approach the front door, motion sensors tracking our movement. Through the floor-to-ceiling windows, I can see into a sparsely furnished great room with a view from the glass front door straight through the back of the house to the ocean. Elena Vasquez stands with her back to us, phone pressed to her ear, gesturing animatedly at whoever is on the other end.

"She's got to know we're here," Adrien observes. "Assuming her guards haven't informed her, almost all security systems offer a view of the driveway."

"Remember, if she's aware of the FBI's presence, this will be quick. If she's unaware, we play to her ego."

I press the doorbell, the sound echoing through the house like a funeral chime. Elena turns slowly, her silver hair perfectly styled despite her predicament, her posture still radiating the confidence of someone accustomed to being the smartest person in any room.

She ends her call and walks to the door, opening it without any hesitation.

"Officer Anderson. Mr. d'Avricourt." Her voice carries that familiar slight accent, refined by decades of careful cultivation. "I expected a phone call, not an in-person visit. But I must say, as I've learned more about you, I'm not surprised you found me."

I'm no longer a CIA officer, but I don't gain anything by correcting her. Perhaps she's a believer in 'once CIA, always CIA'. "May we come in?"

Elena steps aside with exaggerated courtesy. "By all means. Though I should warn you, we don't have long before this conversation becomes academic."

The interior of the house is as stark as its exterior—expensive furniture arranged with clinical precision, no personal touches beyond a laptop open on the glass coffee table and stacks of file folders scattered across every surface.

Evidence of a woman trying to save herself through paperwork and connections.

"Busy evening?" I gesture toward the laptop.

"Productive evening." Elena moves to pour herself a glass of wine from an open bottle of what looks like a very expensive Burgundy. She doesn't offer us any. "I've spent the last several hours providing federal prosecutors with a comprehensive account of how Adrien d'Avricourt conspired with Jonathan Pierce to manipulate Senate defense appropriations."

The words hit exactly as intended. I feel Adrien stiffen beside me, but I keep my expression neutral. This is the gambit Eddie warned us about.

"That's an interesting story," I say. "What evidence supports it?"

Elena's smile is razor-sharp. "Please don't act like you've come here in ignorance. You're well aware of the evidence." She's speaking to us like she believes we're being recorded—and a team is listening in, so she's correct. "Phone records showing multiple calls between d'Avricourt and Pierce in the weeks before key votes. Financial records indicating suspicious transfers between d'Avricourt Luxe subsidiaries and Pierce's consulting firm. Testimony from a concerned federal employee—me—who discovered the conspiracy and felt compelled to report it."

"Fabricated evidence," I say, but I have to admit, I admire her twist.

"Prove it." Elena takes a sip of wine, savoring both the vintage and our predicament. "Even if you could—which you can't, because there's evidence—the investigation alone will destroy Adrien's business and possibly his family's too. His reputation with the banks, with the public. All of it gone while prosecutors sort through the complexities."

"And you claim innocence?" Adrien speaks for the first time since entering, a carefully controlled stillness to his frame.

"I am the whistleblower who exposed governmental corruption at great personal cost. A patriot who sacrificed her career to protect democracy." The grin on her face strikes me as demented. Elena moves to the window, gazing out at the dark ocean. "Any charges against me—which I'd like to remind you, right now there are none—will disappear. If my position in the administration is revoked, I'll relocate. Rebuild. If I lose my spot within the government, the sacrifice will be worth it to know that I stopped an extortionist from forcing votes from senators."

The audacity is breathtaking—and exactly what I expected from someone with Elena's psychological profile. Unfortunately, I don't see an in to negotiate or to draw out anything truthful.

If glares could kill, Adrien's deadly stare would end her. I'm certain if he wasn't hyperaware of the feds listening in he'd strangle the woman. His jaw clenches; the breath he takes is controlled, expensive whiskey turned to ice.

"There's just one problem with your plan," I say.

"Oh?" Her cheeks are rosy, although it's not clear if that's from joyful exuberance at winning or if she's been drinking all evening.

"You're too late."

Elena turns from the window, and for the first time, I see uncertainty flicker. "Meaning?"

"The men you hired for perimeter security? They're currently having a very reasonable conversation with federal agents about the benefits of cooperation over obstruction of justice. Turns out they're not particularly loyal to someone who can't guarantee their paychecks. Or maybe it's just that there are limits to loyalty and prison is their line."

The rosy color fades.

"This house is surrounded, Elena. FBI tactical teams, local law enforcement, and Coast Guard offshore. There's no exit strategy. No one's going to buy what you fabricated. Pierce talked. That much you know. The bomb? It didn't take the FBI long at all to trace the delivery to you."

"You're bluffing."

I am lying about the bomb. We're still working on tracing the source, but I know she's responsible.

"Really? Then why didn't your security stop us? Meet us in your driveway?"

I pull out my phone, showing her the text I received five minutes ago.

> Perimeter secure. All subjects in custody.
> Green light.

Elena stares at the message, her composure finally cracking. "You have no idea what you've done."

"Enlighten me."

This is where she'll ask for lawyers.

She drains her glass, then strides to refill it.

Adrien and I exchange a glance. Any minute now the FBI will likely approach.

With her back to us, she says, "Pierce was small-time. A pathetic little man who thought he could buy influence with Champagne and empty promises." Elena's voice takes on a manic edge, and with a full glass of whatever she's drinking, she twists to face us. "You think he was the only one buying?

You have no idea how deep this goes. Defense contractors, pharmaceutical companies, foreign intelligence services—no one wants this to come out."

"Names, Elena. Give me names and this ends differently for you."

Elena laughs, but there's no humor in it. "Right. You probably expected me to ask for lawyers, right? No one's going to leave me in a cell."

If she thinks she's going to walk scot-free, her ego is bigger than her profile suggested.

"The network doesn't die with me—it just finds new leadership. There are people who won't let this investigation destroy decades of carefully cultivated assets. Those men out there? The ones presumably listening who have surrounded us? Their bosses don't want the truth coming out."

She reaches for her purse, a Fendi bag sitting on the glass table beside the laptop. My hand moves instinctively to my weapon as she withdraws a small, nickel-plated pistol.

"Elena." I draw her name out, tracking her line of sight to Adrien. "No one will get you off murder charges."

"You think I'm afraid of prison?" She grips the gun with both hands, but instead of pointing it at us, she points it under her chin.

My stomach freefalls.

"I spent my career in shadows, controlling the power players, shaping history from behind the scenes. I won't spend my final years in a cage."

"Elena, you've planned your court case. You've already laid the groundwork." She hasn't. We'll blow through her fabricated evidence, but she's egotistical enough, she might buy my pitch.

Elena's eyes meet mine, and I see not fear but calculation.

"Tell Alicia Morgan she knows too much. Tell her the network remembers its friends—and its enemies. Oh, and your little company. KOAN, you call it." Out the window a flash of the SWAT team approaching catches my eye—hers too. "They're being watched. The Moores... Tell them they're making enemies."

FBI agents, guns raised, approach the front door.

We all clock them.

Elena's grip steadies, resolute.

Before I can respond, before I can lunge forward or find words to stop her, she pulls the trigger.

The sound echoes through the glass house like thunder, and then there is only silence and the glimmer of moonlight over the water beyond. Blood splatters on the cream sofa and floor. Her lifeless corpse crumbles. The Burgundy topples, dark silk spreading across the rug, a stain that looks almost elegant until it doesn't.

Ten minutes later, as federal agents process the scene and EMTs confirm what we already know, I stand beside Adrien on the deck, both of us staring out at the dark Atlantic.

"It's over," he says, but his voice carries no relief.

"No," I reply, thinking of Elena's final warning, of the names she didn't give us, of the network she claimed would outlive her. "I don't think it is."

She knew that Caroline Moore funds KOAN–that's not easily accessible information. And it seems we've pissed off some people who don't want a group like KOAN to exist.

My phone buzzes with an incoming call. Hudson's name appears on the screen.

"You heard everything?"

"Yes. You good?"

"I'm good." I look at Adrien, who has his arm around me,

but his attention is directed to the swarm of FBI agents.

"Noah did a security assessment for Alicia Morgan, right?"

"Yes. Completed two days ago."

"She needs security."

"So I heard. Update relayed. She's aware. So is the boss. You and Adrien headed back to the city?"

Adrien's standing beside me, and he hears the question. He mouths the words, "Up to you."

"Yes. When we're cleared here, we'll head back to his place."

"Sounds good. Regardless of what she said, you should be safe. No one's going to do anything that risks leading a federal investigation to their door. We'll regroup tomorrow."

CHAPTER
THIRTY-SIX

ADRIEN

Two Weeks Later

The Hamptons house sits like a quiet benediction against the steel-gray Atlantic, its weathered shingles and wraparound porch offering exactly what I'd hoped for—silence, space, and Brie. After two relentless weeks, this borrowed sanctuary feels like breathing again.

I watch her from the kitchen window as she stands on the deck, coffee mug cupped in both hands, golden strands whipping around her face in the salt breeze. Even in jeans and an oversized sweater, she maintains that ballerina-straight posture—the one that never quite relaxes, even when she's supposedly at ease.

My phone buzzes on the counter. Margot's name flashes across the screen for the third time this morning. I let it go to voicemail again.

"Avoiding someone?" Brie asks as she slides back through the French doors, bringing the scent of ocean air and the faint warmth of sunshine with her.

My father and I have more or less put this behind us. At least, last week he called to confirm my size hadn't changed as he said he was holiday shopping with mom. The conversation was short, slightly tense, and complete bull. Mom made him call. Less than two weeks—better than the two months required for him to have a cordial conversation after I told him I wanted Margot to take the reins.

"Call her," Brie urges, not with the brash emotion the women in my family leverage, but in that way she possesses, a blend of soft and firm.

I pick up the phone. She answers on the second ring.

"Margot," I say.

"I can't believe I had to hunt you down." It's true. I avoided her calls.

"I'm on the line now." I lean back against the counter. "Go ahead. Say what you need to say."

"And what exactly do you think I need to say?" Yes, she's still pissed.

"You hate me. I get it."

"I don't hate you. You don't get it. Jesus, Adrien, you risked everything."

"There was a bigger picture at play."

"Bigger? Than the d'Avricourt brand?"

"Yes." I meet Brie's gaze and she takes a step back...and is she smiling?

"You are unbelievable," Margot snaps—and then her voice shifts, pitched into a cruel imitation. "'Take the lead, Margot. It's all you, Margot.' And then you sabotage—"

"I did no such thing. And might I remind you that

nothing has happened? All the fallout has happened stateside."

"You burnt our source. We'll never get competitive insights again!"

"Stolen. That's what you mean, right?"

"Don't go getting judgmental. Everyone does it."

"Well, they can't all buy from the same source. Go find another source. Or, better yet, hire the best creative and…I don't know…be fucking unique."

"Obviously, that's the goal."

She's exasperated but so am I. Her breath comes across the line like heavy static. "You could have told me your plan."

"I didn't believe we'd see eye to eye." Actually, I know my sister. She would've done everything in her power to stop me.

"You chose to be righteous instead of loyal—and that's not something I can forgive."

"I knew you'd never forgive me—and I decided I could live with that."

"You're infuriating."

I am. I know.

"If we were in the same room right now…" she lets it hang.

"You'd what?"

"I don't know. Something that would get me in trouble with mom."

Well, yes, that I can see.

"It's so annoying. She always takes your side. Always."

"She's the reason you've been calling."

"She wouldn't let it rest."

Interesting. Through all of this, she hasn't said a word to me about reaching out to my father or sister. I suppose she did take my side, but then again, I've only spoken to her once, briefly to check in. My hours have been insane. "I suppose she loves me best."

"You fucker," Margot says, but there's no anger, no bite.

Silence fills the line and Brie sinks into a chair.

"I heard your membership took a hit," Margot says finally. "What are you going to do?"

"Work through it."

"Is that really what you want to do with your life?" She means life as a club owner.

It's probably not my life's end goal but I'm not about to quit. Nor am I ready to share the finer details with Margot.

"I'll let you know when I figure that out."

"Don't bother," she says quietly.

She's interrupted by someone in the background, and we bid adieu.

"That went well," Brie says, rising from her seat.

She doesn't move closer. Doesn't step away either. Just watches me, waiting for what comes next.

We've been in this strange limbo between lovers and colleagues, between the crisis that brought us together and straddling the future. The intense, long hours left little time to sleep, much less talk.

"Want to take a walk?" I gesture toward the deck. "It's brisk, but the beach is secluded, owners only."

She nods, and twenty minutes later we're strolling along the water's edge, jeans rolled to our calves despite the cold front's chill. The wind has an edge to it that promises winter, and the cold bite against our skin is invigorating.

"So," she says, stepping around a cluster of seaweed, "have you decided what you're going to do about The Sanctuary?"

"I'm keeping it."

She stops walking. "Really?"

"It'll take a hit this year. Run at a loss. But I still believe there's value in what it was meant to provide—a place for people to connect, to escape, to be themselves without judgment or risk of exposure." I pick up a smooth stone and skip it across the water. Three bounces.

"And your original plan? Using it to understand your customers better?"

"That remains." The words come easier now that I've said them aloud. "Observing fashion trends and gaining consumer insights. I'll dedicate a couple of years to rebuilding it properly. Then I'll take what I've learned and build something new."

"Like what?"

"Men's fashion, maybe. Or something completely different. The luxury market is evolving—people want authenticity now, not just status symbols. I want to learn about fashion sustainability. It's an evolving trend with promise. It could be the future." I glance at her, noting the way she's listening with unflinching attention. "What about you? What are your plans?"

"For now, I'm staying with KOAN." She kicks at the sand, sending up a small spray. "The fact that someone sees us as enough of a threat to come after us proves there's a need for what we do."

"Do you know the Moores?" I ask, remembering Elena's final warning.

"Caroline Moore founded KOAN. Her husband, Dorian, isn't involved, at least not to my knowledge." She pauses, considering. "I don't know her well, but Sydney does. You haven't met Syd yet, but you will. She's one of my colleagues.

She left the CIA for the same reason I did—lost faith in the leadership. For now, I'm confident I'm working for good people, and in my field, that matters."

Good people. It's such a simple phrase, but coming from Brie, it carries weight. She's spent her career reading people, understanding motivations, identifying threats. If she trusts Caroline Moore, that means something.

"Will you stay in Manhattan?"

"For now. Noah relocated to DC temporarily to coordinate protective detail for Alicia—as a precaution. I'll remain in New York, but I could be pulled if needed." She stops to examine a shell, then straightens, meeting my eyes. "For now, I'll be working with Quinn and Sydney researching ties to the network. As you know, Eddie caved—he's in witness protection with his family–but I'm coordinating a meeting to question him further. With him feeling safer, he might be more open about the information he sold."

"Looking for more prosecutions?"

"Not necessarily. Information is valuable."

I nod. "That's my father's point of view too."

We walk in comfortable silence for a few minutes, the rhythmic crash of waves filling the space between us. There's something I want to share with her, something that's been nagging at me.

"I had a tarot reading last week in Paris," I say, immediately feeling foolish for bringing it up. I stopped in on a brief break while overseeing the renovation and handling personnel issues, just needing to clear my head.

Brie turns to me with raised eyebrows. "You believe in that?"

"Not believe, exactly. It's more...entertainment. But Celeste, this woman I found, she's been remarkably accurate over the years. There's something about the patterns, the psychology of it." I run my hand through my hair, a habit that's become more pronounced since meeting Brie again. "I'd love to take you to Paris sometime; let you experience a reading with her."

"What kind of reading would you expect if we went together?"

I stop walking and turn to face her fully. The wind whips her hair across her face, and she pushes it back with one hand, looking at me with an expression I can't quite read.

"She'd probably say something about a union being in our future," I say, my voice dropping to something more serious.

Brie's lips curve in a small smile. "Would she now?"

"I believe that's exactly what she'll say." I step closer, close enough to see the dark rim around her stunning blue irises.

The words carry on the wind, mixing with the salt air and the distant cry of gulls. This isn't a business setting or the controlled environment of a fashion show. This is real—raw and honest and terrifying in the way that only genuine vulnerability can be.

Brie studies my face for a long moment, and I can practically see her processing—analyzing risks, outcomes, and probabilities. Then her posture loosens by a breath, and the woman I fell for on holiday returns.

"That's quite a reading," she says softly.

"I'm a businessman. The reading might be financially secured. I'm not one to leave long-term strategy at risk."

She laughs, and the carefree sound scatters across the waves. "And what does your long-term strategy look like, Adrien d'Avricourt?"

I reach for her hand, threading our fingers together

despite the chill. "Well, let's see. The strategy stems from goals. I aim to rebuild The Sanctuary into something worthy of its name. Learn what real luxury means—not just surface beauty, but authentic connection. I want to create something meaningful. And on a personal level..." I pause, meeting her eyes. "I want the same."

"Long-term...lots of variables to account for."

"The best plans are flexible." I bring her hand to my lips, pressing a warm kiss to her skin. "Besides, I have an excellent consultant now."

Her smile widens, and for a moment, the careful distance she maintains dissolves completely. This is the woman who found me in a bar and escaped with me, who disappeared from my life and left me searching across Europe, who walked back into my world and tore down the scaffolding around my illusions.

"I suppose I could be convinced to take on a long-term assignment," she says.

"Good," I murmur, pulling her closer as the wind picks up around us. "Because wherever you go, I plan to follow."

As we stand there on the empty beach, waves rolling endlessly toward shore, I think about Celeste's cards and the patterns she reads in their ancient symbols. But looking at Brie—really seeing her, not as Sophie from Monaco or as an intelligence professional, but as herself, complete and real and choosing to be here with me—I don't need mystical guidance to know what the future holds.

Some unions don't require prediction. They require courage, commitment, and the willingness to build something genuine in a world full of beautiful facades.

For the first time in years, I'm done selling fantasies. I'm ready to build a life—one we choose and keep.

EPILOGUE

BRIE

Six Months Later

The yacht rocks gently beneath my feet, the Mediterranean stretching endless and blue beyond the rail. I'm standing exactly where I stood three and a half years ago, champagne flute forgotten in my hand, watching Monaco's lights twinkle as dusk settles over the harbor.

Except this time, I'm not Sophie Dubois with a fake identity and an exit strategy. I'm just Brie. And I'm not alone.

"You're thinking too hard." Adrien's voice comes from behind me, warm and familiar. His arms slide around my waist, pulling me back against his chest. "I can practically hear the gears turning."

"I was just thinking about the last time we were here." I lean into him, letting his warmth chase away the evening chill. "How different everything is now."

"Better or worse?"

I turn in his arms to face him. He's traded his usual suit for linen pants and a button-down with the sleeves rolled to his forearms—relaxed in a way he never was when we first reconnected.

"Infinitely better," I say. "Though I do miss the thrill of a fling."

He laughs, the sound rolling through his chest and into mine. "And I rather miss thinking you were an art consultant instead of a former CIA operative who could probably kill me seventeen different ways with a corkscrew."

"Eighteen, actually. I learned a new technique last month."

"Of course you did." His lips brush my temple. "Should I be concerned that Hudson approved this vacation?"

"He practically insisted. Said I needed a holiday after the Foster case." I grimace. That investigation had taken three months and involved more surveillance footage than I care to remember. "Though I suspect he wanted everyone to take a break so he and Quinn could have some time to regroup."

"Have the two of them come out in the open?"

"Not yet, but it's only a matter of time."

We stand there for a moment, swaying with the yacht's slow rhythm. The crew is somewhere below deck, giving us privacy as the sun sinks lower. The boat belongs to one of Adrien's friends—a tech entrepreneur who owes him a favor and was more than happy to loan out his vessel for a week.

"I got a call from Margot today," Adrien says, his tone shifting to something more serious. "She and Tommy are having dinner in Paris next week."

I pull back slightly to look at him. "Another *accidental* meeting?"

"Third one this month." He shakes his head, smiling. "I give them six months before one of them admits what's happening."

"Your sister and your best friend. Are you okay with that?"

"Are you kidding? I'm delighted. Tommy deserves someone who'll actually challenge him. And Margot needs someone grounded." He pauses. "Though I'm not looking forward to getting pulled into their disagreements."

"Think they'll be worse than ours?"

"My love, we rarely disagree. Those two…"

"Rarely? How long ago did we not see eye to eye on the need for The Sanctuary's new security system?"

"That was a discussion. And your point of view was correct, as you love to remind me."

"I was *quite* right about it." I grin up at him. "Just like I was right about hiring Macon as your director of operations."

"You do realize that *I* hired Macon, not you."

"After I strongly suggested it."

"Is that what we're calling it?" But he's still smiling, his thumb tracing lazy circles on my hip.

The past six months have been a delicate dance of negotiation—figuring out where my work ends and our relationship begins, learning to trust each other with the messy, complicated parts of our lives. It's not always easy. There were nights when I came home from surveillance operations too wired to sleep, and days when Adrien's family or business pulled him away for weeks at a time.

But we made it work. We're still making it work.

"I saw the tarot cards," I say quietly.

His expression shifts, something vulnerable flickering across his face. "Hmm."

"You left them on the nightstand. I wasn't snooping, I just…" I touch his jaw. "The Fool, the Lovers, and the World. That's quite a reading."

"I went to see Celeste last week. While you were finishing the Foster case." He looks almost embarrassed. "I know it's superstitious, but—"

"But you wanted to know what the cards said about us."

"About our future, yes." He captures my hand, pressing a kiss to my palm. "The Fool for new beginnings, the Lovers for partnership and union, and the World for completion and achievement. Celeste said it's the strongest positive reading she's ever given me."

My throat tightens, mainly because I hadn't been sure what they meant, or why he was holding onto them. "And what do you think it means?"

"I think it means I should stop being afraid of what I want." He releases my hand and reaches into his pocket, pulling out a small velvet box. "I think it means I should stop overanalyzing every possible outcome and just ask you."

My heart stutters. "Adrien—"

"I know this isn't a well-staged proposal. No rose petals, no string quartet, no photographers for the society pages. Margot will scold me." He opens the box, revealing a ring that catches the fading sunlight—a sapphire surrounded by diamonds, elegant and understated. "But this is where it started for us. Where I met a woman who made me want to be more than what everyone expected. Where I found something real in a world full of beautiful facades."

I can't speak. Can't do anything but stare as the shoreline lights blur in my peripheral vision.

"Brie Anderson, former CIA operative, periodic pain in my ass, love of my life—will you marry me?"

The laugh that escapes me is half-sob, half-genuine amusement. "You really know how to sweep a girl off her feet."

"Is that a yes?"

I grab his collar and pull him down to kiss me—hard and sure and full of every emotion I'm terrible at expressing with words. When we finally break apart, I'm breathless, and his eyes hold that heated promise that says we won't be making it to dinner anytime soon.

"Yes," I whisper. "Obviously yes."

He slides the ring onto my finger—it fits perfectly, of course, because he's Adrien, and he's probably had my ring size since the third week we reconnected—and then kisses me again, slower this time, reverent.

He exhales a shaky laugh, still holding me. "You know what Celeste told me when I left her studio?"

"What?"

"She said to stop chasing what's already mine—and to fill the empty space."

I blink. "Meaning?"

He reaches into the pocket of his linen pants and pulls out a folded photograph—a vibrant abstract by Adam Ball, color and light exploding across the frame. "This. It's finished. He shipped it to your building in New York this morning."

It takes me a second to find my voice. "You commissioned a piece from Adam Ball? For me?"

"For that wall in your apartment that's been empty since before we met. You once said you couldn't find anything that felt like you." He brushes a strand of hair from my cheek. "I wanted you to have something that does. Something that reminds you where this all began."

Emotion catches in my throat, unexpected and sharp. "You remembered that?"

"I remember everything." His smile softens. "And before you argue—yes, I know you love that apartment, and no, I'm not asking you to give it up. But maybe consider renting it out…or turning it into an office. Because as much as I admire your independence, I'd like you to live with me full-time."

I huff a laugh. "You mean move in permanently, not just fill a drawer or two at your place?"

"Exactly that. Move in officially. Keep your space, your view of the park, whatever you need—but come home to me. Your fiancé. And one day, at the date of your choosing, your husband."

There's no manipulation in what he's saying, just hope. Completely justifiable, and the thought of taking this next step together feels right.

"I'll think about it," I say, mostly to make him grin. It works—his mouth curves, slow and sure.

"Good," he murmurs, kissing me again. "I love you."

"Is that so?"

"It is. You're the most lovely person I know."

I feign a frown.

"And I mean lovely in all the important ways." His palm flattens against my chest, warming the skin. "In here, my love."

"You're irresistible. I never stood a chance."

"Of life without me?" He grins. "No, you didn't."

We stand there on the deck as night fully settles over the sea, the warm weight of the ring on my finger still unfamiliar but somehow exactly right. Tomorrow we'll call our families and deal with the inevitable chaos of announcing our engagement. Eventually we'll head back to New York—to our complicated jobs and the beautiful, messy life we're building.

But for now, we're just two people anchored offshore, choosing each other again and again, building something genuine in a world that too often settles for surface beauty.

Some unions don't require tarot cards or mystical predictions. They require courage, commitment, and the willingness to be seen—really seen—by another person.

As he laces his fingers through mine, I squeeze once, deliberate.

"I love you," I say, like a promise I intend to keep.

And as Adrien leads me below deck, his hand warm and certain in mine, I know I wouldn't trade this reality for any fantasy the world could offer.

Not even close.

BONUS EPILOGUE

ADRIEN

One Year Later

The drive into Paris feels different. Maybe because I'm seeing the city through her eyes—the glass reflections of the Seine, the slow swirl of headlights around Place Vendôme, the promise of tonight waiting in the coming hour.

The Sanctuary glows against the skyline, a cathedral of light and shadow. Last week was the grand re-opening, and we greeted investors and members. Tonight isn't about ownership or appearances—it's about what I've wanted since the moment I asked her to marry me.

I've reserved the evening for the woman beside me, the woman who reigns over my thoughts, for the steady awareness of her body in my orbit, and the certainty that I'm already undone long before we step inside. When the car slows outside of The Sanctuary, she narrows her knowing eyes. "You've planned something."

BONUS EPILOGUE

"Opening night was chaotic. Performative. Tonight is for you."

"For us," she corrects with a tilt of her soft, plush lips.

As I come around the car, waving off Jacques, letting him know I'll open my wife's door, I scan the entrance, the steady flames housed in the gas lamps, and give a curt nod to the man waiting to let us in.

Tonight, it's only us. Perks of ownership.

When I open her door, her smile curves as I offer my hand. "My lady."

We enter The Sanctuary with her hand in mine, and I lead her straight to the elevator.

The city sprawls beneath us, lights glittering on the water as the glass elevator stops. She's quiet. There are no questions, but perhaps she too shares the undercurrent of anticipation.

The doors open to silence.

Amber light pools in alcoves, the music reduced to a low pulse you feel more than hear. No members thread through the corridors. There's no carefully orchestrated temptation. Just a corridor of suites, emptied of everyone but us.

She pauses, alert as ever, taking it all in.

"Strange," she says. "How different it feels without the members."

I move beside her. "That's the point."

She glances at me, one eyebrow lifting. "Closing the entire club? Staffing it for just us two. That's excessive even for you."

"I'm aware." I catch her hand, turning her toward me. "But I wanted you to see it this way. Not as my wife under scrutiny." I pause. "As my wife. In a space that belongs to us."

BONUS EPILOGUE

Her fingers tighten around mine. "Then show me what that means."

At the door to the private suite, I stop.

She meets my eyes, and there's a question there—not about permission, but about intention.

"Say the word and we walk away," I tell her. "Nothing about this matters unless it's what you want."

"I know." Her hand lifts to my chest. "But I want to see it. Not just the renovation—I've had a tour. I want the experience you've planned."

I open the door.

She takes in the room, her expression softening. "You remembered everything."

"I remember you," I say simply.

I trace the line of her neck with my thumb, feeling her pulse against my skin.

Her fingers trail over a small refrigerated drawer—discreet, elegant—and when she opens it, she finds what I requested: champagne truffles, fresh berries, and a silver bowl of ice.

"Not your typical hotel amenities," she murmurs.

"The Sanctuary doesn't do typical."

I've been thinking about this for weeks—planning every detail, imagining her response. The way she'd look in this light. The sounds she'd make. How it would feel to have her here, in a space that belongs to both of us now.

Outside, the bells of Notre-Dame chime the hour, faint but clear through the open window. The city feels suspended in time, as if Paris itself is holding its breath.

"This room isn't like the others in New York."

"No. The Paris location offers a wider array of suites."

"Ah." She drags a finger across the marble top of a dresser. "Is this your favorite?"

"I wouldn't yet know."

Her lips curve into a tease. "Don't play innocent."

"Me? Never." There are no mirrors, but I'm quite certain I've failed at controlling my smirk.

"Tommy did once share that in your heyday you didn't make wide use of the rooms."

"I wasn't ready for anything that stayed," I say.

"Why?"

"Because back then it was about convenience, perhaps even control, not desire. At least, nothing more than fleeting lust." I move toward her.

She turns to face me fully. "And now?"

"Now I want more, I choose more." I reach for her, slowly. "There's no part of me that misses those days. You believe that, right? That's not why I brought you here."

Her hands find my shoulders, pulling me closer.

I stop close enough to feel the warmth of her, the question hanging between us. When she tilts her head up, I finally close the distance. Her breath stutters against my mouth, and that small sound undoes whatever control I thought I possessed.

My hands find the zipper at her back. The silk whispers as I drag it down slowly, feeling her shiver beneath my palms. When the dress pools at her feet, she steps out of it gracefully, and I step back—just for a moment—to look at her.

Black lace. Barely there. Her skin glows in the amber light, and I'm struck by how different this feels from those early days—the nights when I'd bring someone here for novelty, for distraction. This isn't distraction. This is devotion.

BONUS EPILOGUE

"Adrien." My name is a question and a demand.

I shrug out of my jacket, then work my shirt buttons, letting her watch. Her gaze tracks every movement—hungry, appreciative—and the heat in her eyes makes my pulse kick harder. When the shirt falls away, I reach for my belt.

She steps forward, her hands covering mine. "Let me."

Her fingers work the buckle with practiced ease, then the button, the zipper. My trousers fall and I step out of them, standing before her in just my briefs, already straining against the fabric.

She palms me through the thin material and I hiss. Her touch—confident, knowing exactly what I need—nearly undoes me.

When she reaches for the waistband of my briefs, I catch her hands. "Not yet."

"No?" Challenge in her voice, that confidence I've always loved.

"I told you I wanted to show you this room." I kiss her—hard enough to taste her lipstick, feel the edge of her teeth. "Let me."

No performance. No witnesses. Just the two of us, learning each other again in a space built for play.

Before I guide her to the chaise, I press her back against the floor-to-ceiling windows. Paris glitters below us—distant, infinite, beautiful. But not as beautiful as her.

"Here first," I murmur, dropping to my knees. "Take in the city while I worship you."

She gasps as I kneel before her, spreading her legs, shifting the scrap of lace to the side. She's stunning in the night light, one hand lifted to the glass behind her. The vulnerability of the position—standing, exposed, nothing but glass between her and Paris—makes my breath quicken.

BONUS EPILOGUE

I start without ceremony, my mouth finding her already wet center. She tastes the same—salt and heat and home—but standing like this, she's different. More vocal. Less controlled. Her palms slide against the glass, leaving handprints that will fog and fade.

"Adrien—I can't—my legs—"

"You can," I murmur against her flesh, holding her thighs steady. "Hold on for me."

I work her with tongue and fingers until she's trembling, gasping my name, and when her knees finally buckle, I catch her weight and guide her to the chaise.

"Now," I say, settling her against the leather. "Let me show you what I planned."

I cross to the console, retrieving the silver bowl of ice water and the cognac. When I return and kneel between her legs again, her breathing has already changed—faster, shallower, anticipating.

I dip my fingers into the ice water, then trace a cold line from her collarbone down between her breasts. She gasps, arching up, and I follow the path with my mouth, warming every inch I've chilled.

"Adrien—"

"Patience, mon cœur."

Ice against her inner thigh, then the heat of my tongue. A frozen berry pressed to her nipple until she's squirming. I sip the cognac, tip the glass and let it drip onto her stomach in amber drops before licking it clean.

Her hands reach for me, but I press them back gently. "Not yet. I'm not finished."

I trail the ice lower, circling her clit with the cold, then replace it with my hot tongue. The contrast makes her cry out—not quiet, not restrained. Her hands fist in my hair as I work her with my mouth, holding an ice chip between my lips, letting it melt against her most sensitive flesh.

"Adrien, please—I can't—"

"Yes, you can." I add my fingers, curling inside her. "Come for me, love."

She does—beautifully, without restraint—her back bowing off the chaise, my name breaking into pieces on her lips. Her thighs tremble against my shoulders as she pulses around my fingers.

She's still trembling, oversensitized, when I rise. I cross to the warming drawer and retrieve massage oil—almond and vanilla, warmed to body temperature.

"Turn over for me," I murmur.

She looks at me, dazed, but obeys—shifting to lie on her stomach along the chaise, cheek pressed to the leather.

I pour the warmed oil into my palms and work it into her shoulders, down her spine, over the curve of her ass. Not a full massage—just touch, worship, heating her skin further. When I spread her legs from behind and trail my oiled hands up her inner thighs, her breathing changes.

"Adrien—"

"I know what you need."

I rid myself of my briefs finally, position myself behind her as she's still on her stomach, and grip her hips. The oil makes her skin slick, and when I press the head of my cock against her entrance from behind, we both groan.

"Yes," she breathes. "God, yes."

I push inside slowly—this angle impossibly tight, impossibly deep. She's so wet from everything I've done to her, and the slide is perfect. When I'm fully seated, I have to pause, have to breathe, or I'll lose control too soon.

"Brie—" Her name is prayer and promise.

BONUS EPILOGUE

I start moving, finding a rhythm that has her gasping into the leather. My hands grip her hips, pulling her back to meet each thrust, and the sounds filling the room are obscene—skin against skin, her breathless cries, my own ragged breathing.

"More," she demands, and I oblige—harder, deeper.

But I want to see her face.

I pull out—ignoring her sound of protest—and turn her over. Back on the chaise, legs spread, flushed and beautiful and mine.

"I need to see you," I tell her, positioning myself between her thighs again. "Need to watch you come apart."

I push back inside and her legs wrap around my hips immediately, pulling me deeper. This angle is different—intimate, facing each other, her eyes locked on mine as I move.

The chaise is the perfect height, the leather giving just enough beneath us. Paris glitters beyond the windows but I barely see it. There's only this: her body beneath mine, the wet slide of our joining, the way she says my name like a prayer.

"Harder."

I acquiesce, giving her my all while angling my hips to hit that spot that makes her see stars.

She tightens around me, close again—impossibly, after everything. I drop my head to her throat. "You're so beautiful like this," I murmur. "Taking me. Taking everything I give you."

She feels perfect. Hot and tight. Mine. Always mine.

"Don't stop." Her nails dig into my shoulders. "Please don't stop."

I don't. I withdraw almost completely, then drive back in —hard enough that she gasps, her back arching. I set a punishing rhythm, one she matches perfectly, her hips rising to meet every thrust. My hand slides between us to circle her clit. "That's it. Let me feel you."

She comes—violently, beautifully—her internal muscles clenching around me in waves, her nails scoring my back hard enough to leave marks I'll feel tomorrow. The sensation of her coming apart pulls me over the edge.

I thrust deep—once, twice more—then still, burying myself as far as I can go. My orgasm tears through me, pulsing into her in hot waves while she trembles beneath me.

"Brie—" Her name is all I can manage.

For a fleeting second, it's complete surrender—not the careful control I've cultivated, but raw, honest need. This is what the suite was always meant to hold. Not transient pleasure, but this: earned intimacy. Chosen love. Real desire stripped of everything else.

I bury my face in her throat, and for a moment the world narrows to her heartbeat, her scent, and the warmth of her skin.

After, we don't move. She's still beneath me, our bodies slick with sweat and satisfaction, her legs still wrapped around my hips. I can feel her heartbeat against my chest—fast, then gradually slowing to match mine.

Her hands gentle in my hair, fingernails scraping lightly against my scalp. I lift my head to look at her, and her eyes are soft, satisfied, utterly content.

"Well," she says, slightly breathless. "That's one way to christen the space."

I laugh—surprised by it, by the ease of it. "Not what you expected?"

"Better." Her hand cups my face. "Because it wasn't about the room at all."

BONUS EPILOGUE

When I lower my head and kiss her, it's not the way I used to—desperate, claiming, needing to prove something. It's slow. Reverent. The kind of kiss that says *I see you. I know you. I choose you.*

Eventually, I shift just enough to reach for the warmed towels, careful not to break the spell. I clean her slowly, reverently, the way I've learned to do everything with her—without hurry, without assumption. She sighs as I brush damp strands from her forehead, her body pliant now, open in a way that still catches me off guard, so unlike the woman who moves through weekdays armored and alert.

When we finally move to the bed, it's not with urgency but with ease. She curls into my side, her head fitting beneath my chin as if it's always known the shape of me. I draw the sheets up around us, the city still glowing beyond the glass, distant and unimportant.

Her fingers trace idle patterns on my chest. Not seductive or demanding. Just present.

"This feels different," she murmurs.

"It is," I say. And for once, I don't feel the need to explain myself further.

She shifts slightly, propping herself up on one elbow to look at me. Her eyes are soft, unguarded in a way they rarely are. "Do you ever think about our future?"

I don't hesitate. "All the time."

A small smile curves her lips. "Not tomorrow. Or next year. Just… later."

I run my thumb along her shoulder, following the slow rise and fall of her breath and her thoughts. "I think our children will be dangerous," I say mildly. "Observant. Stubborn. Far too clever for their own good."

She laughs quietly, the sound warm against my skin. "They'll have your intensity."

"And your instincts," I counter. "And our daughters, your beauty, which worries me far more."

"Plural?"

"At least two." We've talked about this. She wants sons, I want daughters, but they do say to be careful what you wish for.

She settles back against me, thoughtful. "We haven't yet been married a year."

"I'm well aware. There's no rush."

"One day. I don't know when," she says. "Or where."

Where is a fair question. My father would love for us to make France our permanent residence, but my priorities have shifted. My highest priority is Brie's happiness.

"But I'm thinking about it more and more. I want you to know that."

I brush my lips across her temple, appreciation and love for what she's just said. "I just like knowing it's possible."

Her hand stills on my chest, fingers splaying as if she's anchoring herself there. "Me too."

"Sometimes I dream of a baby girl, well, not a baby, a toddler. Blonde, blue eyes, a mini-you, toddling on the shore. I like to think she's our baby girl, my little Brie…telling me that one day she'll be here with us."

She lifts up, smiling. "Really? You've had that dream?"

"More than once," I admit, and she presses a kiss over my heart before settling back down against me.

We fall quiet again, the kind of quiet that doesn't demand filling. Outside, Paris continues its endless motion—bridges lit, cars tracing lines of gold across the water. In here, everything is unhurried.

BONUS EPILOGUE

Her breathing deepens as sleep edges closer. I hold her there, the weight of her trust, her love, our dreams more profound than anything I've ever owned.

This is what I've been chasing all along—not the illusion of beauty that can be bottled and sold.

It's this.

The quiet between two heartbeats, the simple truth of a shared future left deliberately unwritten.

The world will always worship what glitters.

But me?

I've learned that what is truly lovely, endures.

AFTERWORD

Behind The Sanctuary's velvet curtains, the elite are being watched. Their most private moments cataloged—desires documented, assigned blackmail value, prepared for weaponization.

This is lust in the twenty-first century—ammunition.

The ancients warned that unchecked desire could topple cities. They weren't wrong. They just didn't foresee how efficiently modern power would learn to exploit it.

For decades, intelligence services understood what moralists only claimed: human desire creates vulnerability. The Soviets famously deployed their "Red Sparrows"—operatives trained to seduce targets, gather kompromat, extract secrets pillow talk reveals. Sometimes they wanted information. Sometimes just photographs. Always, they wanted leverage.

The sin is no longer desire itself. It is the decision to treat vulnerability as opportunity.

Sex outside marriage no longer ruins careers—but illicit activities captured on hidden cameras still can. The moral framework shifts, but the weapon remains the same: inti-

AFTERWORD

mate moments transformed into leverage, human connection converted to currency, authentic want repackaged as ammunition against the wanting.

When Adrien d'Avricourt discovered his exclusive Manhattan club was being used for systematic blackmail, he found himself at the center of an operation as old as espionage itself. The Sanctuary's hidden servers held terabytes of surveillance footage—club members in compromising positions, private conversations captured and cataloged for extraction. Defense contracts. Merger plans. Political leverage. All weaponized by those who understood that captured desire becomes power.

Brie Anderson knew this calculus professionally. Years of CIA training taught her both sides—how to use attraction as tactical advantage, and how to recognize when it was being used against her. She'd seen honeypot operations, kompromat files, pillow talk transcripts entered as evidence. She understood that in the intelligence world, vulnerability is treated as inventory.

When she walked into a meeting about extortion, she expected to find the usual blackmail mechanics—surveillance, leverage, exploitation. What she didn't expect was to rediscover the man she'd met three years earlier in Monaco. The weekend that felt different. The connection that seemed authentic in a world of performed intimacy.

The complication: Adrien d'Avricourt now owned the very club being used to weaponize human desire against the powerful. His business ventures had always walked the line—luxury experiences that sold fantasy, managed attraction, commodified beauty. But The Sanctuary's surveillance system crossed from commerce into espionage, from service into weaponization.

AFTERWORD

The conspiracy they uncovered reached beyond one exclusive club. It was an intelligence operation that used human sexuality as collection mechanism—gathering secrets while targets believed themselves engaged in consensual pleasure, building blackmail portfolios while the surveilled performed intimacy in supposedly private spaces.

The blackmailers didn't create lust. They weaponized it.

Only the Lovely explores this modern sin from every angle—and at the center, two people trying to reclaim authentic connection in a world determined to exploit it.

Adrien learned that selling fantasy isn't the same as weaponizing intimacy—that there's a line between providing luxury experiences and enabling systematic blackmail. Brie discovered that understanding lust professionally doesn't protect you when you experience it authentically. Both confronted the reality that in an age of hidden cameras and kompromat files, choosing vulnerable connection becomes an act of resistance.

Because here's what the extortionists forget: you can capture bodies on surveillance footage, but you can't weaponize what people freely choose. Authentic desire—shared between equals, chosen without coercion, grounded in trust—refuses to become ammunition.

The conspiracy tried to turn human vulnerability into power. Adrien and Brie chose to make it into connection instead.

The courage isn't in suppressing desire. It's in refusing to let it be weaponized—by choosing authentic connection despite the risks, by maintaining human dignity in spaces designed for exploitation, by loving openly in a world that profits from shame.

Moscow may still hold kompromat over officials' heads.

AFTERWORD

Intelligence services may still run honeypot operations. Hidden cameras may still record supposedly private moments. The surveillance will continue, because human desire will always create vulnerability, and there will always be those who see opportunity in others' exposure.

But there will also always be people who choose connection anyway. Who refuse to let the weaponizers win. Who reclaim intimacy from those who would exploit it.

Welcome back to the world where ancient tactics wear modern technology, where human desire remains the most reliable intelligence vulnerability, and where love—chosen openly, built on trust—becomes the ultimate act of defiance.

After all, the things worth keeping are the ones that can't be weaponized.

The world may always see lust as opportunity.

But what is truly lovely resists.

GRATITUDE

Many years ago, when I was starting out in advertising, a beautiful, glamorous woman with shoulder-length silky gray hair took me under her wing. I was a lowly associate account executive and she repped media sales—The Village Voice among other publications. Carol Oppenheimer lived a bi-coastal life, splitting her year between LA and New York, with an adorable apartment that granted her access to Gramercy Park. She took me to lunch at the best places—Gramercy Tavern and beyond—making me feel seen. I lost touch with Carol, but she inspired me in countless ways, and she continues to be a muse. This one's for you, Carol, wherever you are.

Mr. Jolie loved this story from the first draft. His enthusiasm (and his willingness to read multiple versions) means more than he knows.

Karen Cimms, your editorial eye catches what I miss—the questions you ask sharpen every scene, every character beat. Thank you for making me a better writer with each book.

Regina, your patience and perseverance through multiple cover iterations paid off. The final version captures exactly what this novel needed. Thank you for seeing it through.

To my beta readers—Your questions caught plot holes I didn't see and your enthusiasm reminded me why I write these stories. This book is stronger because of you.

To my Isabel Jolie ARC readers—Your reviews and word-of-mouth support have built this series one reader at a time. I'm grateful for every post, every recommendation, every kind word you share.

And to my readers—whether you've been here since *Only the Wicked* or you're just discovering the Sinful State series, thank you. Your trust in my storytelling is a gift I never take for granted.

ALSO BY ISABEL JOLIE

Sinful State Series

Only the Wicked (Rhodes and Sydney)

Only the Devil (Jake and Daisy)

Only the Lovely - (Brie and Adrien) Releasing February 26, 2026

Only the Lucky - (Noah and Alicia) Releasing May 21, 2026

Only the Hunter - (Gabriel and Evie) Releasing 3Q, 2026

Only the Fury - (Hudson and Quinn) Releasing 4Q, 2026

Arrow Tactical Security Series

Better to See You (Wolf and Alexandria)

Sure of One (Jack and Ava)

Cloak of Red (Sophia and Fisher)

Stolen Beauty (Knox and Sage)

Savage Beauty (Max and Sloane)

Sinful Beauty (Tristan and Lucia)

Gilded Saint (Sam and Willow)

Scarlet Angel (Nick and Scarlet)

Blind Prophet (Dorian and Caroline)

The Twisted Vines Series

Crushed (Erik and Vivi)

Breathe (Kairi and David)

Savor (Trevor and Stella)

Haven Island Series

Rogue Wave (Tate and Luna)

Adrift (Gabe and Poppy)

First Light (Logan and Cali)

The West Side Series

Blurred Lines (Jackson and Anna)

Trust Me (Sam Duke and Olivia)

Finding Delilah (Delilah and Mason)

Forgetting Him (Jason and Maggie)

Chasing Frost (Chase and Sadie)

Misplaced Mistletoe (Ashton aka Dr. Bobby and Nora)

Standalone Romances

How to Survive a Holiday Fling (Oliver Duke and Kate)

Always Sunny (Ian Duke and Sandra)

The Romantics (Harrison and Zuri)

ABOUT THE AUTHOR

Heart-pounding romance. Unforgettable heroes. Sizzling happily-ever-afters—with a side of suspense that'll keep you up way past bedtime. These are the books I love to read and write.

I dreamed of being a writer as a kid but took the "safe" route: journalism degree, advertising career, MBA, corporate gigs at Chase and Universal Studios. Then in 2020, I said screw it and published my first book. Twenty-five books later, I'm living the dream.

I'm also a mom to two teenage daughters who are perpetually mortified by my career choices. My husband's an entrepreneur whose latest product is Nampons (yes, it rhymes with tampons and yes, it's for nosebleeds). Between my spicy romance and his biz… we've cornered the market on parental embarrassment.

My books feature tough characters facing tougher choices, compelling suspense, and storylines that'll make you think. But no matter how dark things get, my people always choose love.

Sign-up for my newsletter to keep up-to-date on new releases, promotions and giveaways. (**Pro-tip** - There's a free book on my home page…just scroll down after arriving at my site.)

Shop and save on ebooks and signed paperbacks when buying direct from me at www.isabeljoliebooks.com

Copyright © 2026 by Isabel Jolie.

All rights reserved.

Editor: Karen Cimms

Cover Design: Regina Wamba

No part of this publication may be reproduced, stored, or transmitted in any form or by any means, electronic, mechanical, photocopying, recording, scanning, or otherwise without written permission from the publisher. It is illegal to copy this book, post it to a website, or distribute it by any other means without permission.

This novel is entirely a work of fiction. The names, characters, and incidents portrayed in it are the work of the author's imagination. Any resemblance to actual persons, living or dead, events or localities is entirely coincidental.

Isabel Jolie asserts the moral right to be identified as the author of this work.

Isabel Jolie has no responsibility for the persistence or accuracy of URLs for external or third-party Internet Websites referred to in this publication and does not guarantee that any content on such Websites is, or will remain, accurate or appropriate.

Designations used by companies to distinguish their products are often claimed as trademarks. All brand names and product names used in this book and on its cover are trade names, service marks, trademarks, and registered trademarks of their respective owners. The publishers and the book are not associated with any product or vendor mentioned in this book. None of the companies referenced within the book have endorsed the book.

❦ Formatted with Vellum

www.ingramcontent.com/pod-product-compliance
Lightning Source LLC
LaVergne TN
LVHW040038080526
838202LV00045B/3383